Praise for The Fate Factor

"Pure magic from start to finish. The Fate Factor is an ode to all the different ways that love shapes the course of our lives."
-Kristyn J. Miller, author of *Given Our History*

Praise for *Wish Lists & Road Trips*

"All the stars and more for this stunning, emotional romance."
-NYT Bestselling author, Helena Hunting

"A steamy, sweet, rummy bear fueled comedy of errors."
-NYT Bestselling author Abby Jimenez

"A pitch perfect story. I couldn't put it down."
-KJ Micciche, author of *The Book Proposal*

Other titles by Lauren H. Mae

Wish Lists & Road Trips

The Summer Nights Series:
The Catch
The Rules
The Exception

THE *Fate* FACTOR

Lauren H. Mae

For Suna
Friends are soulmates too.

Author's Note

Hello, and welcome to Portland, Maine... or my fictionalized version of it. As a Portlander, I hope the depictions of the city come close to capturing the magic that exists on the waterfront here. I hope you can feel the salt in your lungs and the twist in your ankle from the ancient cobblestones. But also as a Portlander, I have to confess there are a few things I took liberty with for this story.

1. You absolutely can not see a house in Willard Beach from any fire escape on the peninsula.

2. You should definitely not swim off of the rocky beaches near Spring Point Ledge at night (even if a beautiful man tells you it's safe)

3. As successful as Jamie Bishop is, he would still be hard-pressed to be able to afford to live alone in the apartment I described.

But this, friends, is why fiction is better than reality. Enjoy!

Prologue

Noel

I COME FROM A family of dreamers. My father left my mother and me when I was eleven months old to go on tour with his band Northern Boots. They played an eclectic mix of rock-country, and the way Mom tells it, he was destined for stardom. We haven't heard from or of him since, so it's likely it didn't pan out.

Mom couldn't bring herself to fault him, though, despite leaving her to raise me alone at twenty years old. She loved him too much. And her dream was that someday, someone or something would love her that way too. She chased it with everything she had. We chased it.

When I was ten, I missed a week of fourth grade so we could go to North Carolina to visit an airman Mom met at a bar while he was on leave. She had to quit her job to take the time, but the possibility of this man being her destiny was worth the financial risk. Of course it was; she was a dream chaser, a free spirit unconfined by things like practicality, responsibility.

And when the airman turned out to be less of a catch in the light of day, Mom pretended it had been a girls' trip from the beginning. Something for me and her. She hid her disappointment behind sunglasses and beach selfies, and I smiled from the back seat with the map, and a stomach ache that started when I was eight and hadn't quit.

I watched her pretend she was happy and free, instead of disappointed and tired, and it was like looking at an abstract painting and watching it shift. That's the moment I knew: Dreams and nightmares are made of the exact same stuff. The only thing that separates them is how much of yourself you're willing to lose in the chase.

Needless to say, I didn't inherit the dreaming gene. Every reckless adventurer needs a foil, a sidekick, a supporting character who keeps their ambitions from overtaking common sense, or their habit of dream-chasing from getting the lights turned off or the car repossessed. Someone had to keep their feet on the ground between the two of us, and it was me.

The thing about the roles we slot into as kids, though, is that they tend to follow you into adulthood. Which is why, even though I'm enjoying the late-summer party currently going on around me, I can't help but scan the crowd intermittently, keeping an eye out for someone who might need to swap their beer for water or find a safe ride home.

I'm on the roof of a brick multi-unit in downtown Portland, Maine, just across the bridge from the sleepy neighborhood of Willard Beach where my Nana lives, and where I spent my summers as a kid. I still do, actually, but only for a week or two rather than June through August. Instead of dream-chasing like Mom, Nana reads books and paints. She's a devout Catholic, except when she's a little bit pagan.

When I was a kid, she would read my tea leaves and tarot cards at night. Telling my future like a fairytale bedtime story

I didn't really believe, but found charming nonetheless. Her house was quiet and predictable, if not a little silly with all of the talk of magic, and it's still my favorite place in the world.

Tonight, I left Nana on the couch with a book and a cup of tea and let my best friend Kate coax me here. We're lounging on faded, second-hand patio furniture that belongs to one of Kate's coworkers. White string lights sway above us in a salty breeze, and no doubt someone somewhere is shaking their fist at the volume of the music.

"You're not doing it right!" Kate slaps her hand on my thigh, offended that I would get the details of the game we're playing wrong. "It won't work with beer."

I throw my head back and groan. "You have no way of knowing that. The last time we did this we weren't old enough to drink."

Kate grew up down the street from Nana. When I met her, she was wild with golden red hair and boobs before her time, and I was careful. Perpetually nervous. The only thing we had in common was that we were two pre-teen girls in close proximity, but sometimes the place and time you meet someone makes all the difference.

"It doesn't matter," she says. "It has to be the same way Nana does it."

Kate's dating a new guy this summer, and he chuckles into his beer. Colin's a med student on track for emergency medicine, and so far I've deduced that he's quietly brilliant. Which is why I'm mortified that she has insisted I introduce him to my grandmother's witchcraft tonight.

Clearly she's never heard of saving your weird family shit until you get to know someone a little. Kate's in her final year at Maine Law, though, so for the most part I avoid arguing with her.

I lift the knockoff Yankee Candle, simply labeled "Beach

Dreams" (not exactly the fancy white pillar candles Nana keeps in her velvet lockbox, but Kate apparently doesn't mind that concession)and borrow a lighter from a guy smoking a joint behind me to light the wick.

"Alcohol might make the wax float weird or something," Kate explains to Colin who remains skeptical. He should be because we're totally playing him right now. Like the tarot cards and the gemstones Nana wears to influence her energy, this whole thing is a silly game.

Granted, she did once predict that my high school boyfriend would break up with me and start dating his Spanish study partner. Shocking all of us, Nana nailed it almost down to the day. Though, to be fair, it was the day after the home-coming dance I couldn't go to because I needed my shift at the restaurant I waitressed at to deal with the car repo thing.

I dump the beer from my cup into a nearby potted plant and make a gimme motion. "Colin. Your Poland Spring."

"Fine," he says, handing me the bottle by his feet. "But in case it's important, you should know it's just tap. I refilled the bottle."

"What the fuck, babe." Kate smacks his bicep playfully. "Noel, tell him that causes cancer!"

"She would know," I say. "She's been off phthalates since middle school."

She points a finger at me. "Because I was ahead of my time. You would not believe the lawsuits that have come out of that shit."

"Says the girl huffing candles." Colin pinches her side.

"It's soy!" Kate shrieks, dodging his attack.

I laugh alongside them, my abs aching from it, and when I turn to brush a strand of windblown hair off of my face, my eyes catch on a man's. And it's as if they just get... stuck there.

He's seated precariously on the perimeter wall of this roof, three stories up, which is dangerous enough to notice, but he also has the kind of face that I might want to remember for later when I pick up my pencil and sketchbook before bed. That heavy brow and incredibly straight, almost sharp nose, full lips that rest in a lazy smile—they're practically begging to be drawn.

My gaze falls lower to his biceps where black tattooed leaves poke out of his short sleeves, and something incredibly unfamiliar flares inside me. A quick pulse of unbridled want. I have to swallow it down like a lump in my throat.

He raises an eyebrow from beneath a backwards baseball cap as if to say *having a good time over there?*

And because I've been drinking and apparently possessed by the spirit of someone much braver than me, I respond with a prissy little pursed-lip smile and shrug that says *wouldn't you like to know?*

Then I check the rest of him out because Beer Bravery is a very real thing. He's taller than average, long legs dangling carelessly from his reckless wall seat, and his right forearm is covered in more ink. Not a full sleeve, but a flock of birds spread over the soft skin on the inside, silhouette style. Branches twist between them, thick and thorny.

Everything about this man screams wild, unsteady, not for me. And yet, there's also something striking about him. Something I can't look away from.

It's his eyes, I decide as mine slide back to his face. They're deep-set and the color of whiskey. Moody, if I'm being poetic about it, which I'm just buzzed enough to do. It's his eyes and the way they don't fit the rest of his vibe—cool, confident, comfortable here. Basically everything I'm not.

As if conjured by that thought, a tall blonde in cut-off jean shorts appears at his side, draping an arm over his shoulder. I jerk my gaze away, motioning for Kate to scoot down so I can slide in front of Colin.

"Okay, pay attention," I say, with a flick of my head to shake that off. I pour Colin's water into the cup, swirling it like a spooky sommelier. "You have to get your mind right."

"We're doomed then. My mind hasn't been right since I started clinicals."

Kate pouts. "Aw, babe. In, like, ten years you'll be a hot-shot ER doctor with a mountain of debt. Think positive."

"We don't know that yet. Let's see what Noel's prediction is. Maybe I quit school and play guitar for tips in Monument Square."

I snort, tipping the candle over the cup and letting the wax drip—One. Two. Three—just like Nana does it. It spreads into the shape of a blob that vaguely resembles a dog with a few extra lumps, before hardening on the surface of the water.

Colin sniffs. "Looks like the last scan I read. Fingers crossed it's benign."

"Shhh. I'm working." I press my fingertips to my temples, biting hard on my lip to keep a straight face for this performance. The nostalgia Kate and I have for Nana's weirdness demands I give it my all.

After a moment of humming and rubbing my temples, I push out my bottom lip in an exaggerated Sad Face. "Looks like med school's a bust. Luckily your musical talent is discovered, and you live a long life playing Ed Sheeran covers at weddings and proms. Oh, and you lose your hair really early." I wince. "Sorry."

Colin laughs like the good sport he is. "I was just starting to like you, Noel."

"My turn." Kate hoists herself onto Colin's lap, and he gives a loud oof despite her being generally twiggish.

Plucking the solid wax from the surface, I chuck it over my shoulder, and tip the candle a second time. Kate's wax forms on top of the water and I scrunch my nose. "It says your future husband will leave you over your misguided crush on Channing Tatum and you'll spend your old age alone writing Magic Mike fanfic."

She fake gasps, then snort-laughs. "I'll negotiate the house in the divorce, right?"

"Obviously."

Colin groans and they lock eyes, grinning at each other. It's like watching a ship go down, slowly and inevitably. I've seen this before—Kate with her claws in someone. Kate sees, she wants, she takes. All the years I've known her, I've never stopped wondering what that must be like. Probably like jumping from a cliff with cement blocks for feet.

"Is there a fee?"

I look up to find the guy from before standing beside my shoulder, grinning at me. The rest of the party may as well have poofed out of existence. All I can see is him.

"A fee for what?" I manage, more than a little mesmerized.

"For the fortune telling."

Those moody brown eyes lock onto mine, and now that he's closer, I notice they're slightly asymmetrical. His right eyelid is heavier, hooded where the left one isn't. It's something only a person who's been taught to draw faces would notice—a perfect imperfection—and my fingers subconsciously mime the pencil stroke I would use to sketch it.

"Oh. Um... yes, actually." My drink has been lost to the game, so I point to the makeshift bar tucked into the corner of the rooftop. "A shot gets you one reading."

His grin widens, flashing a straight white smile, and my belly dunks like a duck into water.

"What's your poison?"

"Uh..." I blurt out the first bottle I spot on the bar: "Jäger."

Oh, God. My stomach preemptively turns at the horrible

decision I've just made, but I'm not the type of person who has a drink order at the ready. Especially not a shot.

"Your hangover," he says, shaking his head and laughing. "I'll be right back."

Kate's jaw hinges open as the stranger steps away. "Do you know him?"

I shake my head.

"Hottie."

Colin makes a noise in the back of his throat like a snort and my cheeks burn, feeling called out in the worst way. Like I've let some secret slip that could make me look foolish.

"He's here with someone," I reply. It's silly, the deep disappointment when I say it out loud. It's not like I was going to do anything about it even if he wasn't.

He returns with my shot, and I down it quickly, hoping the burn will dull this weird tingly feeling in my blood.

"What's your name?" I ask him as he takes the seat across from me.

"Jamie Bishop."

"Okay, Jamie. I'm Noel. Remember, you have to be open to it." I wiggle my fingers over the candle, making the flame jump. "You know, let the spirits in."

He nods, eyes suddenly serious.

"Is there anything specific you want to know about?" I ask like I'm not just going to make up something ridiculous for the sake of the game.

"No. Just, ah, whatever in general." Long, comma-shaped dimples carve into his cheeks when he gives me as lightly-nervous smile. I get the feeling he might actually believe in this, which is kind of cute.

I twist my long hair over one shoulder and lean forward, grasping the jar near the bottom to keep from burning my fingers while playing psychic. Slowly, I raise it just over the cup of water and let it hover.

Kate has moved to my couch to let Jamie sit across from me and I hear her snicker.

"Are you ready to see your future?" I ask in a creepy, mystical voice.

Jamie's Adam's apple bobs and he nods once.

I tip the candle, watching the wax pool at the edge, then drip over the side, but the Jäger must hit me at the exact same time because my head rushes, stars appearing behind my eyelids. I blink them back.

"Everything okay?" he asks.

"Fine." I cast my eyes back to the water. The wax is still shifting shapes oddly.

Why hasn't it formed yet? There must have been some beer left in the cup. Kate's right. It's messing with the buoyancy or whatever.

I clear my throat to tell him it's not working but then it's as if someone grabs my chin to redirect my attention away from this table. Here, it says. Listen.

But I don't hear it, I feel it. Like a nagging hunch stirring in the back of my brain.

"Are you worried about money?"

I immediately regret asking it. First, it's an incredibly rude question, and second, I have no idea why I'm even entertaining the idea that I might know something about him. We're playing a game.

Jamie sits up straighter, cocking an eyebrow.

"I think you're supposed to turn down a job," I blurt.

What the hell? It's like someone has injected information straight into my brain, translating what's barely a gut feeling and spitting it out as words.

Jamie blinks at me, his full lower lip slowly separating from his top until he's slack-jawed.

"Do you know what that means?" It's clear from his face and the way he's gone mute that he does. My pulse takes off in a sprint.

Kate is looking at me now, concern all over her face. It's the right reaction. I'm acting unhinged, giving this man career advice based on whispers in my drunken brain.

That has to be what's happening. It's the Jäger. What is it they say? Beer before liquor, never been sicker. Maybe there's more to that than just the likelihood of vomiting. Maybe it makes you say crazy things to people you should have just walked away from.

"You know what? This was a bad idea," I say, reaching for the candle to blow it out. Whatever I've tapped into, I want it gone.

"Wait." Jamie wraps his fingers around my wrist, and before I can extinguish the flame, a picture flashes so vividly in my head that for a moment I think I've been dreaming this whole time and I'm just now waking up.

It's the blonde he's here with, sprawled out in something scant and lacy and definitely not meant for my eyes.

I pull in a startled breath and my nostrils fill with the scent of perfume and sex. It's so strong, my cheeks burn in second-hand embarrassment.

Jamie's fingers still circle my wrist and I yank it back, gaping at him. My instant reaction is to warn him to keep his brain PG while we're doing this, but what the hell does that mean? That's not even how this works.

I mean, it doesn't work, because it's a game, but the game is to seethe future, not read someone's horny thoughts.

God, I hope Nana couldn't read my teenage mind all of the times she did this with me and Kate.

I'm deep in that mortifying thought when a wave of emotion hits me square in the chest. But it's not a vague inkling like before. This time my heart feels like it's cracking down the middle. I have no idea what I'm feeling but it's so strong, tears come to my eyes.

And then I see it, playing somewhere in my brain like a movie I didn't buy a ticket for. The blonde again, her head tipped back in pleasure, and there's a new problem. It's very clearly not Jamie she's under.

What the hell is happening?

I crush my palms into my eyes, trying to rub away the sight, but it doesn't work. It's there every time I blink, and I don't know how to make it stop. "Shit."

"Noel," Kate says at the same time Jamie asks, "What is it?"

Colin sits up straighter, and I pretend to scratch my forehead, discreetly pointing over Jamie's shoulder with my pinky. "Um, the woman you're here with. She's your girlfriend?"

Jamie turns to look at her and the wariness on his face flashes briefly to the kind of smile any woman would be happy to have pointed at her. My stomach descends another floor. "That's Becca." He lowers his voice. "I'm thinking about proposing. Thought maybe you could tell me how it's going to go."

Oh. Guess I misread the flirty eye thing from before. Foolish, Noel.

That's the least of my problems, though, considering what I just saw. This game isn't fun anymore. Nana's supposed fortune-telling was basic and vague. If you wanted to believe, you could find away. This is really freaking detailed, and I have no idea where it's coming from.

What I do know is I don't want any part of it.

My hands are shaking, stomach sour. Jamie can tell I'm stalling, and whatever hopeful awe he had quickly slides off his face. "Shit," he mutters.

"I think we should stop." I get to my feet and so does Jamie.

Colin stands too, saying something to Kate, and tension ratchets in my chest. The last thing I want is to be the reason for a scene. My mother makes scenes. I avoid them.

It's obvious Jamie doesn't share that inclination, though. He doesn't even bother to lower his voice. "Noel, wait. Just... tell me."

Oh, damn it. I want to ignore it, tell him I haven't seen anything at all because I'd like to believe that myself, but I can't. Not knowing what I know about the unfairness of a thing like this. The way love can absolutely ruin a person when it implodes.

"She's um... Becca, she's um." God, how do I explain this? "I'm sorry. I think maybe there's something she's not telling you." I shove my thumbnail between my teeth. "I'm sorry."

"Holy shit." He pushes a hand beneath his hat, rubbing his head.

I need to get out of here. This is too much. I reach for my coat.

"Noel," he says, rounding the table so we're face to face. "Hold on, just... Please."

I stop, my heart in my throat. Maybe I shouldn't have told him. What if I'm wrong because this is insane?

But I also know I'm not wrong. Like I've never known anything else.

"I thought this was a joke," he whispers.

"It was."

He glances at Becca, then back to me, eyes desperate. "Are you sure?"

I've already said enough. It's time for me to go, but he's blocking my exit. I put my hand on his elbow to slide past him and nearly whimper when I realize my mistake. I've touched him again and the stars are back behind my eyelids. Then a new picture.

It's Jamie this time, shirtless against a bright white sheet like you find in a hotel. He's lying on his stomach, eyes fluttering open, looking thoroughly bedded.

Why the hell are all of these visions X-rated?

I freeze, pressing my eyes with my palms, but it's no use. The picture before was like a flash, a still snapshot, but this one lingers, and I can't make it stop. I feel myself sway as it pans around the room like a movie camera. I'm there and here at the same time.

My brain snags on the cut of his hair. It's longer than it is now—short on the sides, wild on top. A wavy piece has flopped onto his forehead.

When he tipped his cap up a few minutes ago, I saw that his hair was practically buzzed. A wiffle cut, as Nana would call it.

There's a tattoo on his back, scrolling words mostly covered by the sheet. It's a block of black text over his left shoulder blade, the letters too small, and in a handwritten style script too hard to read from this ethereal vantage. I'm desperately trying to make it out when Jamie rolls over—dream Jamie, not this one—and I see a woman there, on the other side of the bed. He pushes his face into her neck. He's smiling, happy.

Finally, some good news. Apparently, there's a happy ending to top this whole thing off. If there's a point to all of this, it has to be that. Nana never ended a reading with bad news.

The woman's face is obscured by a mess of dark hair, but I catch the bright pink splotches on her chest. Sex spots. It's a joke between Kate and me. We both get them, to our utter mortification. I could have done without that detail, but it just affirms that this must be a good thing. Clearly, he gets over Becca.

His hand moves beneath the sheet, and it feels intrusive to keep watching, voyeuristic, but I'm curious now and besides, I don't know if I have a choice.

The room is cozy—a blue quilt at the foot of the bed, a fireplace, a snowy mountain in the window. I find myself wanting to stay. Like a good dream you cling to when your alarm goes off. It doesn't feel urgent anymore, blinking it away.

Dream Jamie brushes the woman's hair from her face. She scrunches her nose, small and freckled and...

Pierced.

My breath catches.

My fingers fly to the tiny diamond stud in my nostril. The one I got when I was nineteen and toying with a rebellion that never took off.

It can't be. It's definitely not.

"Noel?" Kate's voice is beside me. My skin heats with awareness that I don't want to acknowledge just yet.

They're so similar...

The woman rolls over and smiles back at him and—

—the cup of water slips from my hand, splashing onto the floor, soaking my jeans. I suck in a hard gasp, choking on nothing. "That's my face!"

Kate squeezes my shoulder. "What are you talking about, babe?"

What the hell is going on? Am I having a sex dream about a stranger while awake? Am I awake? I smack at my cheeks like an absolute lunatic.

Jamie's face has lost all color, but instead of running in the opposite direction the way he probably should, his fingers tighten around my elbow. "What did you see? Was it bad?"

No, dude. It looks like it was really good. That's the problem.

This isn't real. None of this is real. I have no rational explanation for this.

Unless...

I turn to Kate. "I think someone put something in my drink."

It has to be some sort of hallucination.

Colin is eyeing Jamie with murder in his eyes. People's heads swivel toward us.

"What the hell are you talking about?" Jamie hisses. "I got it from the bar ten feet away. You watched me!"

I don't know what to say because I did watch him. I'm grasping at straws and now I've just accused him of a crime. I need to go.

"Did you see something else?" he begs.

I shake my head vigorously, bile burning the back of my throat. "I didn't see anything."

"Well, something has you freaked."

That's putting it mildly. I'm shaking, fear climbing up my throat. I slip out of his grip and grab my jacket from the back of the couch, shrugging it on.

"Noel," Jamie says, but Colin steps between us, arms crossed.

"The game's over, man."

Jamie heeds the warning and doesn't come any closer, but his expression pierces my soul. I'm stuck between this weird sense of responsibility and the urge to get the hell out of here. I don't even know this guy. I don't owe him anything. And This. Isn't. Real.

Still...

Overcome by human empathy for the shitty thing I've just witnessed, I push past Colin and reach for Jamie's face, squeezing his cheeks in my hands. "Listen to me. I'm sorry, but your girlfriend over there, she's sleeping with someone else. I don't know who it is. Blond hair, tan? It wasn't you, either way. And like I said, don't take the job. You're waiting on cash. You'll get it. That's... all I saw."

There's no way in hell I'm telling him the rest. If he wants to believe in this, fine, but I'm out. As far as I'm concerned, this is the first and last night Jamie Bishop and I are acquainted, cosmically or otherwise.

One

Two Years Later

Noel

Violet: Let's take today's meeting out of the office, yeah?

I power down my laptop and shoot her a quick **Sounds good!** in reply. Not that she was expecting me to counter. Vi, my boss, likes to phrase her questions in a way that makes you feel like you've already agreed. She does it with her edits too. *Green would be a bolder choice, yes? The font's a little understated for this client, wouldn't you agree?*

It's quirky in a pretentious way but I like it. I like that the answer that will please her is served up on a silver platter. Knowing how to please Violet has earned me a coveted permalance designer position at Brickstone Graphics. Last year, she even submitted one of my projects—a branding overhaul for a non-profit counseling center—for a feature in *Design Strides Magazine*. "Noel Kasey possesses a keen eye for the emotion of color," they'd said.

Ironic, a little voice whispers in my ear as I kick off my leggings and pull a dress over my head, *since you can't feel much of anything at all these days.*

Vi sends me the name of a coffee shop downtown that I can walk to, and I confirm with a thumbs up emoji. This meeting was a last-minute calendar request, and I have no idea what she wants to discuss. I shove both my laptop and drawing pad into a messenger bag, and lock the door behind me, happy for the sun that hits my face immediately.

I'm a little desperate for human interaction if I'm honest. My condo has been obnoxiously silent since Mom left. This latest idea of hers—heading cross country to tour the West Coast in a converted Sienna with a man she met online—is her most chaotic to date. Being roommate-less is great for remote work, even more so when the work takes me into the evening because I can't seem to find inspiration. But it's not so great for the other hours, when the hollowness of empty rooms reminds me a little too much of myself at the moment.

The place Vi picked is small enough that when I walk in, she hears the bell over the door, turning from her spot at the counter. She waves before accepting two mugs from the barista, hers with a string hanging from the side, mine with a dollop of whipped cream melting on top.

"Sit, sit," she says, tilting her chin toward one of a handful of mismatched tables where I recognize her coat on the back of a chair.

I make myself comfortable, stealing a glance at her while she finishes paying. Stilettos, palazzo pants wider than a four-lane freeway and the color of fresh pomegranate seeds. She's choosing a chocolate croissant while wearing a stark white blouse because she is fearless.

I tug self-consciously at the hem of my floral skater skirt. I don't see Vi in person all that often, but every time I do, I find myself intimidated all over again. Where I'm watercolors and script font, Violet Divine is jewel tones and slab serif. She's hard where I'm inherently soft. The modern, artsy Brickstone office in downtown South Norwalk, Connecticut is designed to invoke a seascape—aqua textiles and white couches—and I've always pictured Vi as an iron anchor in the center of it.

Vi finishes with the barista and joins me, handing me my mug of gourmet hot chocolate. "Thank you." I dip my head in a nod.

She waves this off and takes the seat across from me, her face as neutral as the architecture firm's logo I was working on when I got her text.

It's odd, I realize—the lack of expression. I hadn't thought to be nervous about this mid-day meeting until right now.

Vi sets her tea down after one sip, folding her hands in her lap. "Noel," she says. "Are you happy with your work?"

I freeze, the chocolate burning my tongue before I remember to swallow. I can't tell if she's asking me if I'm fulfilled by it or happy with it in the sense that maybe it could be better. "If there's something I could improve on..."

"It's not your skill," she says with a short shake of her head, and the pitiful smile that follows smacks me with the realization that, *oh*, I've been summoned to the principal's office.

"It's just that lately, I feel there's a distinct lack of emotion in your designs," she continues. "They're a bit matte. No shine. No shimmer. I don't have to tell you that art is... Well, it's inherently emotional."

"Of course." I nod confidently, but I'm swallowing too much to pull it off.

Vi taps a nail on the side of her mug. "How are you feeling after your grandmother's death?"

Matte, I think. *Unemotional.* But I have the good sense not to say that out loud after having just been accused of it in a way that sounded a lot like: *You're losing whatever value you bring me*. Instead, I smile and give her a cheery, "I'm doing fine. Everything is fine."

Her brows draw together, and I get the immediate sense I've given the wrong answer. I picture a surgeon studying an X-ray, exclaiming, 'By God, there's no heart in this rib cage!'

My stomach drops so fast I'm woozy from it. If Vi can see this little... *problem* I'm having, well, it's worse than I thought.

It's been happening a lot lately, the feeling of looking at a blank page where some emotion should appear. The overwhelming urge to slap my cheeks to see if I'm awake or merely in the midst of a lucid dream. The truth is I made it through Nana's funeral without shedding a tear, zipping around like a robot, fixing flower arrangements, making tea and mini sandwiches for the guests. Comforting Mom. When it was over, I slept for twelve hours and woke up feeling like it had been twelve years.

Thinking back on it is like catching the low hum of a siren in the distance. A warning of things to come. That's when Kate started calling more. Watching me with an expression not unlike the one Vi's wearing now whenever we'd Facetime. Asking me if I was absolutely *sure* I didn't need her to come stay with me for a while.

Of course I'd never put her out that way. But also, I wasn't sure I wanted her close enough to see how off kilter I was. It's much easier to sugar coat from three hours away.

Now this blankness I've been battling is affecting my job.

My mind immediately begins its monthly tally of all the bills Mom left me with when she took off, and a hundred lines of worry start to knot together in my belly.

Vi sets her teacup down and leans back in her chair. It makes an embarrassing squeak, but she's far too sure of herself to notice. "Ned Majors is leaving," she says. "He's moving to New York January one to work for *The Times*."

"Oh. That's great for him." Ned's the only graphic designer on staff at Brickstone and very deserving of a gig like that. We all have a favorite medium, and Ned's in love with graphics the way I'm in love with paint. The other three designers, including me, are varying degrees of freelance, which means I make my own hours, but I also buy my own health insurance.

Vi cocks her head, studying me. "I want to give you his job, Noel," she says. "But I'm not entirely sure you want it."

"I do," I blurt, but I can hear how it sounds, hollow and reactionary.

Vi's asking me a question that amounts to: Do you want to be able to pay your mortgage? Feed yourself? Of course I want it. *Sound like you want it, Noel.*

I force my smile bigger. "I definitely do."

The span of time before Violet speaks again is the full gestation period for the anxiety forming in my chest.

Finally, she folds her hands on the table and says, "I want you to take some time off."

"I... what?" Is she offering me a job or firing me? "Whatever is wrong with me, Vi... my designs, I'll fix it."

"This is not a punishment, Noel. It's a gift. To you and the artist I know you are. And an investment in the designer I know you'll be for me once you work out whatever has you blocked."

My stomach sinks at that word, the acknowledgment that this is, indeed, a professional problem. An artist who's blocked is like a pianist with broken fingers. Useless. She's saying I used to be someone who deserved this promotion. Now I'm not.

My fingers curl into the skirt of my dress. Every one of them has permanent wrinkles in the same spot from this habit. "How long?"

"I won't be assigning you new work until the end of the

year."

She must notice the way all of my muscles seize because she holds a hand up. "*But* I'm asking Marj to process your final payment for all of your current jobs in advance to cover the time. Three months. You'll come back and tell me if this is what you want."

"I don't need a break to figure it out." But her patient smile tells me she's made up her mind, and I blow out a resigned sigh. "Okay. Of course. If that's what you think."

"I do." She squeezes my wrist, then stands to leave. "Keep the hands working, Noel. Your heart will catch up."

"So she offered you a job, then rescinded it, then gave you vacation time as a consolation prize?" Kate kicks off her heels and tosses her keys. They land in a clatter somewhere I can't see.

I Facetimed her as soon as I left Vi, and she answered on her way home for a quick change from pantyhose and a pencil skirt to 'something sparkly and much shorter.'

She recently started a fancy job working for an environmental PAC in Portland, and though she's not required to dress like a senator-in-training, she says it doesn't hurt. I look down at the leggings and fuzzy socks that I changed back into immediately upon closing my front door, and decide our respective outfits are a poetic vignette of our opposing lives. Kate, a vibrant, social twenty-something. Me, a woman deeply in touch with her inner house mouse.

"The job's not off the table," I say, rubbing at my temples. "It's just on pause. And I don't get vacation time."

Kate props the phone on the counter and pours some gin

into a glass of ice, then splashes some tonic in. "Are you pissed about it? I'd be pissed about it."

"Not really."

"Well, are you excited about the job?" The camera wobbles as she takes her cocktail to her bedroom and props it on her dresser. She unzips her skirt, not bothering to step off camera before letting it fall.

I drop my gaze to the quilt on my lap. "I'm not really that either, and I think that was her point. I should be excited, motivated. This could be life-changing, but when I left the meeting, the prevailing emotion was just... exhaustion."

"Exhaustion is to be expected, Noel. I think you should give yourself a little grace here. You've been through a lot between Nana and your mom these past few months."

She has a point, but it's the numbness riding alongside the exhaustion that worries me. I feel like a painting left out in the sun. All my colors are faded. It's scary, wondering if this is just a symptom of burnout like Google suggests or something worse. Something more permanent.

"Unfortunately grace won't pay my mortgage. Mom hasn't paid me rent since she left."

She's been gone since the funeral, and I'm like a ship captain's wife, pacing my condo waiting for her return, wondering how much damage there will be. Will this be a financial tragedy or an emotional one? Early signs point to both.

I lean back against the couch and Nana's calico cat, Pixie, absently bats at my hair, catching a strand on her claw. I scoop her up and set her in my lap, scratching her head. "Vi's been a great boss but she's not running a charity. If I can't figure out what's wrong with me, I could end up worse than I started. I have to fix it, Kate. I have to fix me."

Kate sits on her bed, still in her nylons and bra. "Okay," she says, swirling her gin. "I have an idea, and I want you to hear me out. I read this story on *Vox* the other day where this journalist was feeling disconnected and directionless after her kids moved out—"

I laugh, but my pulse skitters like a nervous mouse. "I'm an empty-nester before thirty?"

"I mean, kind of! You've been taking care of Nana for the last two years. Your mom's been living in your spare bedroom even longer, and now, suddenly... " She stops short of saying it out loud: *You're completely and utterly alone.*

"Anyway, maybe that's the problem. This woman, she decided to up and take a sort of sabbatical to see what lit a fire under her. She hiked mountains and explored cities by herself. Meditated."

"This sounds very much like a thing I would not do."

"Exactly."

"*Kate.*"

"*Noel.*"

I let out the sigh of all sighs and drop my face into my hands. "So, what? Should I call my mother to see if I can join her and her new man in the desert? Hashtag Van Life."

"Nope," Kate says. "We're still letting that shit storm simmer. Look, I'm not suggesting you scour Tinder for a travel buddy, but getting out of your empty condo is a start. And you happen to have a place to go." She sips her cocktail while the suggestion hangs in the air, cooling my blood.

"I can't."

"Why not?"

"Because it's—"

"Yours? Come on, Noel. You haven't been back since you moved her out and turned her cottage into an AirBnb."

She says this without judgment, but with a commiserating disgust. She knows I hate it too, this necessary evil. After her stroke two years ago, I was forced to move Nana to a nursing facility here in Connecticut to better manage her care. It broke my heart to tell her she had to leave the cottage. Then last July, when she passed, she left the house to me officially.

Unfortunately, it's an inconvenient truth that our generation can't afford coastal property, even if it's the last thing you have to remember someone by.

Renting it out from May to September pays for the upkeep, but turns out my beloved childhood refuge is a huge tax burden. I canceled all of my streaming subscriptions, switched to non-organic vegetables, and lowered my 401k contribution, but I still have to check my online banking app before I buy name brand tampons. And it means Mom not paying her share of the bills here is nearly impossible to absorb long term.

What Kate doesn't know, though, is that sometimes, when I get the rent deposit that lets me hold onto it for another month, I wonder if the ensuing nausea is my punishment for keeping the thing I have no business keeping. Holding on to two homes is the epitome of impractical. It's the one indulgence I've ever granted myself. My one irresponsible decision.

But even though I won't get rid of it, I haven't been able to bring myself to actually go back there. Not if Nana's not there. I've been holding on to it tightly with one hand and pushing it away with the other.

Now, I look out the window of this condo that I bought for the off-street parking, out to the oak trees that line the curb. The tips of their leaves are starting to yellow, a stiff breeze taunting them. Tragically, I picture snow piling up outside while I sit in my pajamas, staring at a blank page on *InDesign*. It covers the windows until no one even knows I'm in here, desperately trying to squeeze inspiration from nothingness. As uncomfortable as going to Nana's alone makes me, even I can admit this alternate plan is not stellar.

I shove my thumbnail between my teeth, chewing. "A sabbatical."

Kate sits up straighter. "Or call it a retreat. Isn't that what artists do? Vi gave you to the end of the year to figure your shit out, so you do it here. If you want to feel something, you're going to have to open the gates a little, babe. No matter what comes next, you have to move to get there, right? So start with a baby step, something you already love. Come smell the salt water, watch the sunset, eat rich food, have amazing sex. That's how you get a little life back into your art. Into you."

I chuckle. "Who exactly am I having sex with on my solo vacation, Katherine?"

"Who knows? Who *cares*?"

A laugh squeaks out of me, and *there*, I think. Right there. That was a little, bitty blip of an emotion. Maybe it's a sign or maybe I'm due for some random nerve to fire accidentally, but I latch on to it with both hands. "Okay," I tell her. "It's worth a try."

Two

Noel

NANA'S HOUSE, IT TURNS out, looks a lot different with August already in the rearview. I stand on the porch, the breeze from the deserted beach across the street toying with the ends of my hair, and take it in. The two-story Craftsman cottage sits on a dead end, in a tidy row of identical buildings separated by tufts of dune grass. When I was a kid, I would spot the red flower pots lining the porch steps from the car window as we approached, and relief and excitement would buzz in my veins like I'd been plugged into an outlet.

Now I picture the frayed end of a chewed-through cord as I shimmy Nana's little brass key into the lock. Shoving the door open with my suitcase, I set Pixie's carrier just inside and turn to load each arm with a bag before crossing the threshold. The pale wood floors groan and creak with my steps, and I can't tell if they're crying for the way they were abandoned or cheering the return of a familiar face in the sea of strangers who have been traipsing around with their swimsuits and weekend bags.

The first surprise is that it looks the same somehow, even with the heart of it missing. The cottage is a big open square with shiplap walls, slip-covered furniture, copper fixtures—shabby chic before it was cool. The living room is separated from the kitchen by a breakfast bar with peel and stick tile. A worn, white couch still anchors the space in front of the fireplace where I'd draw at night.

But the small things are noticeably gone. The basket of yarn beneath the end table, the out-of-season holiday napkins she'd buy in bulk at Christmas Tree Shop. Her jungle-like houseplant collection. This could be any old rental house in Maine now.

Which is probably for the best. It's bound to be easier this way. I didn't come here to bunk with ghosts.

Pixie yowls through her little air holes, and I crouch down to release her. She darts out of her carrier, disappearing into the sunflower-yellow kitchen where her food bowls used to sit, and flops down into a dust speckled sunbeam. I wonder if she realizes she's home, if her cat brain remembers it at all. She's grown so much since she was last here.

It hits me that she's the only one. Nana only got older and sicker once she left this place.

And I've stayed exactly the same.

After a quick trip into town for groceries, I make myself dinner and wash and dry my single plate. The habits of this house suggest curling up in front of the fireplace with my sketchbook, but I shake away the idea, terrified I'll find that familiar blankness still staring back at me. If it's not going to work, if

I've come here for nothing, I'd rather find out after a good night's sleep.

Instead, I send Mom a text before bed. California is three hours behind Maine, so it's possible I'll catch her at a roadside diner or a gas station with cell service.

Noel: I'm staying at Nana's for a while. Call or text so I know you're alive.

I delete the last word because it sounds kind of bitchy and replace it with "**doing okay.**"

That same silly hope flickers when I hit Send. The one that comes each time I reach out, lasting until the excuse of our time difference ticks away and it's clear another day will pass without a response. I've always been cautious about expecting too much from my mother, about asking for disappointment instead of just waiting for it to come on its own. So I didn't expect her to have some weird maternal instinct that there's something wrong with me and want to answer my calls. But I did let myself hope.

It's barely nine, but an embarrassing yawn springs from the depths of my chest. I dropped my stuff in the mudroom when I got here, seeing as I have nothing but time to unpack, and I head there now to grab the bag that holds my pajamas and toiletries. I locate it in the pile, sling it over my shoulder, and freeze, suddenly unsure which way to turn.

The bedroom door to my right—Nana's door—is closed, and I feel like a monster when I'm relieved by it.

The loft space where I always stay has odd-shaped windows and slanted ceilings that, even at five-three, I bump my head on. It's wide open to the living room via a slatted half wall. I'm an adult and alone here now. I should probably take the master bedroom with real walls and a closet.

My eyes flick to the door again. Nana isn't even the last person to sleep in there. Guests have been using it all summer.

To them, though, it's just another quilt-covered bed. A picture window that faces the water across the street, reminding them why this was the perfect spot for their vacation. It probably still smells like Oil of Olay hand cream and incense, but they wouldn't know why.

I will, though, and I can't do it. I drag my bag up the staircase to the loft, and throw myself at the lumpy double bed at the top like it's my long lost lover. The metal frame takes up most of the painted wood floor, and squeaks obnoxiously every time I move, but it will do. It always has.

Pixie's claws tap on the hardwood stairs. She does a little butt shake and pounces up onto the bed, flopping down beside me, purr box rattling. As I stroke her head, I think about Nana's spells and rituals, and wonder with the tiniest suspension of disbelief whether she would have had one that would fix whatever is wrong with me these days. A cosmic paintbrush that could put some color back in.

I'm here, which is a start, but if I'm truly hoping this three hour drive north will help me find whatever I need to uncork my inspiration, I'm going to need a little more guidance on what comes next.

I'm not sure who I think I'm speaking to when I start talking—Her? God? The universe?—but I say it anyway. "Whatever it is I'm supposed to be searching for, please don't make it too hard to find."

The only trouble with that, I think as I drift off to sleep, is I'm not sure I'd recognize it if I saw it.

Three

Jamie

I F HEAVEN HAD AN address on earth, it would be in this city, in this repurposed warehouse, at my bar. I push the brim of my hat up and wipe the sweat off of my forehead, grinning like an idiot. Happy hour ended over an hour ago and the crowd hasn't let up. I'm in the back room, switching the hoses on a keg of Pale Ale as the cover band launches into a Rolling Stones song. I can't help but bang out a little drum solo on the keg.

A year ago, when I opened the doors to Fortune Brewery, I was lucky to sell twenty pints a day. Tonight, I've tapped a keg in the middle of a rush and I'm ecstatic over the inconvenience.

I wipe my hands on my jeans and push back out into the main bar, scoping out the line four deep with hipsters and college kids starting the weekend early. There was a longer-than-I-care-to-admit stretch of years when I spent Thursday through Sunday partying on this same strip of bars.

But *this* bar, and the beer we serve, belongs to me. It's still a little surreal.

I'm working so hard, my T-shirt is stuck to my back when I notice a couple of guys elbowing their way to the front. I recognize one of them from school and have to bite back a groan. I prefer the nights when none of my customers remember me as a sixteen-year-old fuck-up with a barely passing GPA and a first name familiarity with the local cops, but Portland's not big enough to hide from your past.

"Jameson Bishop," he shouts, giving the kid in front of him an *I know the owner* wink as he cuts the line. He's drunk, but since he got that buzz buying my beer, I can't really complain. The two of them sidle up to the bar.

"Call me Jamie," I say to his friend. I pour a pint for a guy with a buzz cut and a styled mustache, then reach over the bar for a quick handshake.

"Man's named after a whiskey and finds himself brewing beer," he says.

"And I find myself doing quite well, thanks." I know he doesn't mean anything by it, but having dodged a few jabs about my profession from my family, I never let a comment like that slide. Plus, I'm feeling cocky tonight.

I gesture to the line of eight taps—five more than when I opened—and lift my chin to him. "What can I get you?"

"Gimme that orange one."

I turn to his friend.

"What do you suggest?"

I shrug like I'm not chomping at the bit to show off my newest recipe. "We're launching the autumn ale tomorrow night. Dark. Spicy. I could let you have an early taste."

He gives me finger guns, and I pop open a bottle from the reserve fridge and pour it into a glass so I can keep the label under wraps until the party.

The guy takes a sip and his mouth curves upward. "Boy knows his stuff."

I bristle a little at "boy." I can't help but hear one of my former stepfathers who always referred to me as "Laura's boy" instead of using my name. As if I were a piece of furniture she brought along to the marriage, one that he had to concede to but would've preferred I'd been lost in the move.

I turn another glass under the tap, drawing the perfect amount of head, and slide "that orange one" across the bar.

"This is fantastic, Jamie. Really."

My face pulls into one of those goofy smiles I get when people like my beer. I have a small team of brewers on staff and most of my beers are collaborations, but this one in particular is all my creation. It's nutmeg he's tasting and to say I took a chance combining it with the other flavors would be an understatement. Clearly it worked, and the praise is like a shot of endorphins.

"Jamie!" Em bursts through the door from the back room, her forehead damp beneath the plastic snapback of a backwards Bruins hat. She's been busting ass beside me all night. "Get the hell out of here."

I look at the digital clock on the register and, *shit*, I need to be across town and suited up in thirty minutes. The hockey league I play in on Thursday nights is my one night away from this place. I think it's Em's favorite night because in the two years she's worked for me, first on the brewery floor, now at the taproom, she never lets me leave late. She also never lets an order get missed or a shift go uncovered. That she doesn't have the official manager title is solely due to the fact that I keep forgetting to order her new business cards.

I glance at the line again. "You sure you can handle it?"

"You sure you meant to say that out loud?"

I laugh, tossing my towel on the bar, and quickly cash myself out. "Give the band a refill when they break."

Em salutes me, then in case I thought she was going to take an order, flips her hand around to give me the finger.

The rink we play at is over the bridge and into the suburbs. It's half an hour from downtown but most of the guys are married now with huge houses and manicured lawns out here, so I'm the only one who has a commute.

I drop my bag on the bench and lace up my skates, watching Trev and Derek do a few laps around the rink to warm up. Greg falls into the seat beside me, stretching his tricep across his chest. "You bring your A game tonight, Bishop? I'm not losing to a goddamn accountant and a high school music teacher again."

I laugh at the trash talk. Most of us have known each other since we played pee-wee so it's all in good fun. We're competitive, but no one is under the illusion that we're not a handful of years out from being an official old man league.

"If I remember correctly, it was your boneheaded penalty that gave us the power play."

He pretends to scratch the side of his face with his middle finger. "Kelsey coming to watch?"

I squint at him, surprised Greg even knows about her. Even if he got the details wrong. "It's Kelly, and no."

"Because she's busy or because you didn't invite her?"

"Both," I say, snapping my helmet on. "It's not like that."

Yesterday I sent Kelly a text to see if she's planning to show up for the launch tomorrow—a pretty big night for my career—and she has yet to reply. *That's* what it's like.

"Where's this coming from?"

"The guys were chatting about you and her the other day at the pool."

I tilt my head. "You were talking about me at your kids' swim lessons?"

"I said the new instructor seemed nice and maybe we should slip her your number."

"Oh, so you were trying to set me up at your kids' swim lessons. That's so much less weird."

Greg shrugs, showing zero remorse for the overstep. When we all hit thirty, they started doing shit like this—dropping random comments about their wives' friends and how single they were. Asking pointed questions to draw attention to some flaw in whoever I'm casually seeing at the time.

I'm aware that Kelly could be a little more supportive, but she's a good time and a great distraction—exactly what I'm looking for while I'm building my empire. Basically, it's hockey on Thursdays and Kelly on Saturdays that keeps me from burning out with the number of hours I'm putting in. But, fuck it, I'm young and healthy. I can work myself to death now and reap the rewards later.

Besides, I tried the whole *Love me forever?* thing with Becca, and the answer was *Kinda busy sleeping with someone else, thanks*. I may not have been the best student in school, but that's the kind of lesson you learn hard and you learn once.

"Don't get your hopes up." I shift on the bench, my stomach suddenly tight. "And send me a picture of the swim instructor."

Greg slaps me on the shoulder with a chuckle, like he's giving up. "You never change, Jamie."

We hit the ice five minutes late because of all the bullshitting, and after a solid hour of play, Derek calls a water break. Chase is breathing heavily as he slumps against the glass and squeezes water through his goalie mask.

"You guys coming tomorrow night?" I ask, panting just as

hard.

Greg's face pulls into a smile. "Course we are. We're fucking proud of you, bro."

I accept the compliment even as a little voice reminds me that, though I work damn hard, not all the credit for my success is mine to take. Do I go around telling people that my biggest business break came from a psychic at a party? No. But anyone who knows me knows I'm not exactly a business mastermind, and the name says it all: Fortune. Luck.

Derek slaps me on the back. "Looking forward to it. Hoping it will be a little classier than the parties you used to throw."

I shake my head because I know where this is going.

Trev leans on his stick, making a face. "You don't think he's planning on celebrating this business milestone by drinking a bottle of Fireball and sleeping in his car?"

Derek points his water bottle at Trev. "That's the after party."

Maybe it's the *you never change* comment from Greg, but an age-old insecurity tightens my jaw. We all know I stayed in my dumbass phase a lot longer than these guys, but sometimes I wonder if they've even noticed that I'm out of it now. Or trying like hell to be.

I pretend to fix the snap on my helmet. "You three reminisce like a bunch of old men."

Derek makes a show of stretching his quads. "I take a hundred-fifty milligrams of ginkgo biloba every day to be able to remember all of that shit, so I'm gonna bring it up when the moment calls."

I laugh. "You can remember it all because you finally stopped getting high every weekend." He also traded cans of Natty Ice for a vintage wine cellar in his basement and his beater Altima for the latest Audi A6.

He shoves me with his gloved hand. "Can still drink you

under the table."

"It's sad how badly you wish that were true."

Chase taps his stick on the ice. "Are we playing or you guys wanna grab a box of wine and make a scrapbook?"

I shake my head and take off to center ice. I'm keyed up for tomorrow and I need at least one more period of crushing cardio if I'm going to get a decent amount of sleep tonight.

I'm thinking about the band and the number of kegs I've stocked. Whether this event will help me beat my record for sales from the last product launch—a number I need to hit if I'm going to keep digging my heels in on the argument my brother Wes and I are currently embroiled in.

And maybe a little about the fact that my friends were all talking about my love life at the community center like they were planning an intervention.

My attention is hovering somewhere outside of the game the entire time. I'm definitely not thinking about keeping my head up and leaning into the hit when Greg checks me from the left with two-hundred-forty pounds of gear and dad bod—perfectly legally this time.

The red boards come at me quick and violent, and my skates disappear from beneath me. The last thing I remember thinking before I eat ice is whatever's broken better be fixed by tomorrow night or I'm royally screwed.

In hindsight, I probably shouldn't have attempted to drive myself home. Headlights from an oncoming car flash across my face and my head pounds at a decibel I've never felt before. I groan, replaying the moment I heard the crack that I knew immediately was bone—right before everything went black. We don't hold back, and I've taken a few hits before, but this one rang my bell as my old coach would say.

When I came to, Trev was kneeling over me, holding up two fingers and asking me if I could see them. Of course I could fucking see them, it was my ribs that felt like they'd turned into serrated knives, sawing each time I took a breath. I was also pretty sure I wasn't going to be skating or walking on my left knee for a while.

I'd iced up and taped it as best I could, then let Greg pack my gear as an apology before assuring them all I could make it home. In the back of my rattled brain, I thought that if I didn't go to the hospital, I'd somehow magically be able to work tomorrow. Maybe I'd be a little sore. Nothing I couldn't handle.

That hope is dimming.

Four minutes into the half-hour drive, my vision started to double when I turned to switch lanes, and now, a mile from the highway ramp I need to take, I'm genuinely concerned that I'm going to puke in my own lap.

I ease my car to the edge of the road and dig around my gym bag unsuccessfully for my phone. I can't bring myself to take a full breath because of the pain in my side. It hurts so bad, my forehead is starting to sweat.

Letting my head fall to the steering wheel, I mumble a request for my car's Bluetooth to call Kelly. She hasn't returned my text from before, but she usually answers my late night calls.

Her voicemail picks up, though, so I guess it's not late enough.

"You've reached Kel. Leave a message or don't."

The shrill beep is an arrow through my brain, and I clap my hands over my ears like a little kid in a thunderstorm.

Fuck.

The rest of the guys are still on the ice so they won't be answering their phones, and I can't pull Em away from the bar on a busy Thursday night. I wouldn't call Wes if I were stranded at sea and he had a boat.

Some neuron in my brain that's still working remembers the story Trev told tonight, the one about the bottle of Fireball. He got it wrong, though. I didn't sleep in my car.

An idea starts to emerge from the fog. It's been a few years since I've been stuck across the bridge, unable to drive myself home, but it's definitely not the first time. Back then it was because we'd partied too hard on the beach and our blood-alcohol level was too high to get back to the city. Luckily for us then, and for me now, we had a place to crash when we needed it.

I pass the on-ramp and head toward the water instead. I'm maybe three minutes from my stepdad's rental property at Willard Beach. He owns a few of them right on the water, and I have a key so I can check on them for him when he needs me to. My family still thinks of me as a glorified bartender, so he assumes I've got the time.

His low opinion of me is about to save my ass, though.

I turn down the access road and it's as dark as midnight. Almost every house down here is seasonal and the season's over, which is how I know Bob's place'll be empty. It has linens and hot water. Everything I need to sleep this off.

Yeah, I'm still clinging to that pipe dream.

The fog along the water is thicker than the brain fog I'm battling, but after a mile or so of squinting at dark house after dark house, I pull into the crushed oyster shell driveway and drag myself and my gym bag out of the car. At least I have some extra clothes that I can sleep in, since this T-shirt looks like a prop from a horror movie. The gash on my forehead from my face hitting the ice bled like a mother.

I make it to the front porch before a wave of nausea sweeps through me and I have to lean over the edge and gag a few times. Nothing comes up, thankfully since the flower pots lining the stairs look new, but I still wipe the back of my hand over my mouth.

This scene is too familiar for comfort—the stumbling across the gravel driveway, the slow climb up the porch steps, holding the railing in a death grip. The way my head spins. I hate the way it instantly brings me back to a version of myself that I've been trying to shake for years.

There's no helping it, though. My grown-up life is about seven miles too far away, and my minutes spent upright are ticking down.

I stare at the front door and try to judge how many steps I am from a mattress. Filling my lungs is still epically painful, so I'm surviving on shallow pants of air. My knee is screaming at me to stop trying to use it.

Fuck it. The couch will be fine.

I find the key on my ring and lean against the wall while I attempt to push it into the lock. It slides in, but the damn thing won't turn. My fingers are sweaty because I'm still fighting to not throw up, and when I pull it out to try again, the key slips out of my hand, barely missing falling through the slats of the porch.

It might as well have. It looks like it's a million miles away lying there beside my sneaker. Without thinking, I slam my palm into the door in frustration, and blinding pain shoots through my ribs. I stumble backward until I hit the railing and slide down to the floor to get the weight off of my knee. As soon as I feel the floorboards beneath me, my body taps out. My vision flickers like an incoming power outage and all of my muscles go lax. I take a shallow breath that hurts like nothing else, and the world goes black.

Four

Noel

A DISTURBING THUD YANKS me from my sleep. Sitting up sharply, I clock my surroundings in the dim light from my nightlight—my blue suitcase lying open on the dresser, my glass of water on the bedside table—and let out a shaky breath. It must have been a bad dream. I've always slept like the dead here, with the ocean air and Nana's cozy quilts, but this isn't a normal trip.

Something scrapes along the wood outside the cottage, and I freeze.

I'm not dreaming now, and I definitely heard that. So did Pixie. Her ears are pinned back, tail puffed.

I look at the clock. Only just past eleven, but with the rest of the street put away for the season, it's pitch black outside.

Hands shaking, I swing my bare feet to the floor and creep toward the window. A light breeze rustles through the dying beach roses, not nearly hard enough to cause the noise I heard. To the left, a silver sports car is parked haphazardly in the driveway, like someone killed the engine the minute all four tires were off the road.

No normal visitor would park like that, and since it's the middle of the night and I don't know anyone in Maine besides Kate, there's no such thing as a normal visitor in this scenario.

My chest goes clammy, sweat springing up even in the mild, indoor temperature.

It can't hurt you if you don't let it, Noel.

Though, externally my mantra loses some of its power. I'm small boned, and gravitate toward therapeutic exercise like walking and yoga versus the strength-building kind. If whoever is out there lurking wants to hurt me, no amount of self-hype can keep it from happening.

This was a terrible idea, sleeping here alone in the off-season. I'm just asking to end up on a true crime documentary. I don't know why I *ever* listen to Kate.

I grab one of my high heeled pumps out of my suitcase and hold it over my head as I slink down the narrow staircase in a cotton cami and a pair of sleep shorts. I wish I'd grabbed a sweatshirt or something. If I'm going to die, I'd rather it not be with my nipples pointed at my murderer.

I slow at the landing, pushing to the balls of my bare feet, listening. *Nothing.*

Maybe it was just a friendly raccoon or a lost seagull. Though that last thump sounded at least two hundred pounds heavier than a bird.

Channeling a whole lot of fake courage, I lunge for the front door, ripping it open with one hand, weapon in the other, and see... nothing.

My breath rushes out, a puff of mist in the chilly night air. But when I turn to go back inside, something catches in my peripheral vision, and I turn back into a statue. A sneaker. That was definitely not there before. Heart in my throat, I peek my head out a little farther despite my body screaming at me to go back inside. The sneaker is untied, seemingly on purpose, and it's attached to a bare leg—hairy and definitely male—sticking out of athletic shorts. I have to crane my neck a little more to see his torso and the white T-shirt that's covered in some sort of…

Oh my God, that's blood. There's blood on that guy's shirt!

At my banshee-like shrieking, the man on my porch startles upright, then clutches an arm around his middle and makes a sound like a wounded animal before crumpling back to the floor.

"*Fuuuuck.*" His voice is like air whistling over sandpaper as he brings his knees to his chest.

"I have a weapon," I shout. It's a stretch but given he's already bleeding, I might be able to take him.

He coughs, then whimpers again. "What?"

"I have a weapon and I'm not afraid to use it." I picture myself actually attempting to subdue this man with a shoe and I realize I am absolutely afraid to use it. He doesn't need to know that, though.

He glances at me through slits, then rolls to his side and seems to go back to sleep. "Just kill me if you're going to. I'm in too much pain to care."

What in the holy hell is happening here? Did this guy get into an accident and crawl all the way to my porch? Does he owe someone money? I can safely say that out of all the nights I've spent in this house, this is the first time I've found a bloodied man at the door!

Moonlight shines on his body—curled in the fetal position, labored breathing—and I creep closer. Rationally I don't think he's in any condition to hurt me. There's no way he's faking the pain on his face, unless he's hiding an Academy Award in the gym bag at his feet.

I loosen my grip on the shoe and attempt to speak without shaking. "Why are you here?"

"Needed to pass out." He makes a face like he's trying not to puke. "This was the closest place."

"My porch was the closest place?" I look up and down the empty, dark road. "To what?"

"There shouldn't be guests here this late in September," he grumbles.

"I'm not a guest. What the hell are you doing on my porch?"

"Bob's porch."

"Who is Bob? This is my Nana's house." I have no idea what he's talking about, it's pain induced nonsense. My hackles settle a little since this is clearly a huge misunderstanding and he *really* doesn't look good. I reach out and pat his shoulder like I'm greeting an unfamiliar dog. He's hot to the touch and his T-shirt is damp with sweat.

He turns his head and squints through one eye at the number beside the door. "Shit." Then he laughs and it's borderline hysterical. It makes me think he really needs to get this head wound checked. "Wrong house."

"No kidding. Look, are you lost? Can I call someone for you?"

"I'm not lost—" He winces but manages to point a finger behind him. "I'm just supposed to be next door."

Well, that's just great. If he can't walk by himself, he'll be sleeping where he is. There's no way I can drag him across the driveway.

He stares at the porch ceiling for a few slow breaths before blinking his gaze toward me. When our eyes meet, his mouth falls open like *he's* the one startled. "Holy fuck."

"What?" I shriek. I'm on a hair trigger.

"I'm dead, aren't I?"

I shake my head and consider yelling: "You're going to be

if you try anything" but that would be an idle threat. I'm quite sure that unfurled to his full height, he's over six feet, and definitely looks strong enough to disable my shoe-weapon if he wants to. "You're not dead," I tell him. "Why would you even say that?"

He blows out a shaky breath. "Because you're the angel."

Angel? Is he hitting on me or just really out of it?

"I'm not an angel, and you're not dead." Still clutching my shoe, I kneel down beside him, trying to figure out an angle I might be able to lift him from. But before I can decide whether I'm actually willing to touch him to get him off my porch, he whispers something that sounds strangely like, "Noel."

Blood rushes, pounding in my ears. *Did he just... ?*

I scramble backward, inadvertently trapping myself against the porch railing, and my pulse goes haywire. "How do you know my name?"

The man's bruised cheek lifts, deep dimples cutting through his stubble. "I can't believe I found you again."

That smile.

It hits me like, well like whatever hit him, and my stomach flips. I *know* this man. The dark blanket of scruff on his face is new, and his eye is swollen and purple, but it's him—the comma dimples, the cream soda eyes, the way they crinkle at the corners.

Oh God. He's even wearing the same hat. How did I not notice that? I mean, besides the fact that half of the guys in this city are wearing that hat right now—the blue one with the red B. But I recognize the frayed brim on his, a rogue splash of something that looks like paint on the side. It had looked old even then.

Then being the night I've been trying to forget about for two years.

"It's Jamie," he says. "Jamie Bishop." He tries to lift a hand to his chest but he can't make it. It flops down by his side.

"What is *happening*?"

"Hockey," he says, clearly misunderstanding the information I need from him. "I think my ribs are broken. Don't you remember me?"

"No. Nope. No." I want no part of this reunion. For God's sake, when I said I wanted to feel something, I didn't mean abject terror.

He keeps going, though, oblivious to my internal spiral. "From the party that night. On the roof—"

"Uh, you're bleeding from the head," I say, cutting him off. "Maybe try not to talk so much."

At that, he presses his fingers to his forehead, inspecting a gash that seems to have opened back up. His eyes go comically wide, then roll backward.

"Woah. Jeez." I barely catch his head, lowering it into my lap. "What the hell is this? Are you stalking me?"

"Are you stalking *me*?" he asks.

"Of course not. I'm on sabbatical!"

He looks like he's going to question that but quickly clamps his mouth shut. After a thick swallow, he says, "I think I need to go to the hospital."

"Um, yeah. I think you do."

"Could you please call me an Uber... or an ambulance?" His head flops to the side and he makes the most pathetic sound.

I sigh, regretting immensely what I'm about to do. "I have a car."

The ER is a slog of hurry up and wait, which gives me plenty of time to continue my spiral into madness. They put Jamie in a curtained area but there's little privacy. He's sitting up on the bed, an ice pack strapped to his bare torso which, incidentally, is as well-defined as I remember from The Dream.

That's what I've taken to calling it, the thing that happened between me and Jamie that night. Whatever I saw at that party was some weird lucid dream brought on by an ill-advised shot of Jäger, *not* a glimpse into the future.

The drunken dream theory is something I can explain—sort of—and for two years, I haven't been able to bring myself to consider any alternative.

Until Jamie's pain meds started to kick in and his questions had intensified. *Where have you been all this time? How can you not remember me? Did you know I was going to show up tonight?*

I've been dodging them as best I can in between nurse visits, but I want to throw that last one back in his face. If I had known Jamie Bishop was going to pass out on my porch, I surely wouldn't have taken Kate's suggestion to come here.

I'm not a psychic or fortune teller or whatever he thinks. That night was one bizarre moment in time, and it's *not* something I'm looking to repeat.

Of course, having that argument means admitting I remember him, which is a non-starter, so instead I've been gaslighting him by reminding him he's concussed and not thinking clearly.

I might have convinced myself if not for the fact that, sitting this close to him, I have to admit there's some things I can't explain. At the top of the list of my problems: he looks exactly like he did in the dream.

When we arrived, a nurse secured a bandage to the cut on his forehead, and the wrap made his hair stick up like an anime character. It's because of the haircut. The same as I saw that night: short on the sides, sexy floppy thing on top.

Haircuts I can rationalize. A coincidence. Current trends and all that. But then the same nurse had taken a pair of surgical scissors to his bloody T-shirt, and when the fabric fell away, I saw them—the freckles across his chest and stomach. I knew they'd be there. Then there's his belly button. An outie. I saw that too. In the dream.

I googled what percentage of the population has an outie belly button, and it's ten. Ten measly percent. There's no way I could have guessed this. I can't explain that away no matter how hard I try, and oh, am I trying.

The curtain swings open, and a new nurse steps in.

"Good evening," she says. "Oh, that looks painful."

Jamie gives her an *aw shucks* look and pink paints her round cheeks. She checks the oxygen monitor on his finger just as his phone buzzes in his lap.

He lunges for it without thinking, whimpering in pain as he connects the call. "Kelly," he rasps. "Hey. Listen, babe—" *babe?* "—I took a pretty hard hit at hockey and I'm at the ER. Can you come get me?"

Whatever he hears on the other end of this call is not what he expected because his ears flush red and he flicks a glance at me. I pretend to read the juice box they gave him on hour one.

"Uh, no... I can't come over... My knee's fucked and I have three broken—" He runs a hand over his face, sighing the rest of his sentence. "—ribs. I'm not even sure how I'm going to work tomorr—"

A shriek rings from the phone and he winces.

The nurse clucks her tongue and shakes her head in my direction like *can you believe this woman*, but as much as I'm inclined to agree, I don't feel like joining in.

I do, however, mentally add a check to the **Different** column. Jamie is currently sleeping with someone named Kelly.

Not the girl from that night—Becca, I think her name was—or you know, *me*.

"Look, do you think you could pick me up? I can't drive." His jaw twitches and his voice drops an octave. I don't have to know him in some other dimension to know he's pissed. "Seriously? Just drop me off and you can go back—Okay... yeah... thanks for nothing, Kel." He ends the call with a growl, tossing the phone on the bed.

So, cool development: an hour into this reunion and I'm bearing witness to yet another break up for Jamie. I'm trying my hardest not to read into that.

The nurse turns to go, and I contemplate clinging to her scrubs and begging her to stay and act as a full-time buffer for this awkward situation I've found myself in. She doesn't register my mental anguish, though, and I'm left alone with Jamie who looks like he would maybe punch something if he could lift his arm.

"You know, Noel. I'm starting to rethink the whole guardian angel thing."

I'm desperate to know why he keeps referring to me this way, but I tug at a piece of string on the flannel pajama pants I threw on, pretending to watch the television in the corner.

"This is so fucked up." He waves a hand between my chair and his bed, and despite the bandages and smell of antiseptic, I blush at the sight of his firm chest, the shadow of abs every time he moves. "You obviously know who I am."

Blinking away from all *that*, I meet his annoyed gaze. We'll get to that part, but first I need more information. "How long has your family owned the house next to my grandmother's cottage?"

"Bob's not my family," he says. "He's my mother's husband, and he's owned it longer than I've known him, which is the last eleven years."

"Do you crash there a lot?" And what I really mean by that is: *Did we sleep next door to each other before I played that party game with you? Maybe even that night?*

If so, it's possible I saw him once before in passing and that's why my brain chose to cast him in the dream. An entirely rational piece of evidence.

"Not anymore," he says rather vaguely. He gestures for the juice and I hold it up while he sips. "Bob usually calls me to close it up for him, though. That's why I have a key."

"You work for him then?"

Something snarky passes over his face. "I can see why you might think that, but no. I own my own business. The brewery. You really don't know this?"

I scrunch my nose. "How would I?"

"I don't know." He lifts a weak hand to his temple then lets it fall. "I was never clear on how it worked."

Oh, jeez. He thinks I read his entire life in that candle wax. Or that I can pop in and out of his head on a whim. "It definitely doesn't work like *that*," I say, and his swollen cheek twitches into a smug smile.

"I knew you were lying about remembering me."

My body deflates. I don't want to argue with him. Although, I could certainly point out that our growing irritation with each other is going in the **Different** column too. It looked like we were getting along quite well in the dream.

I'm still not willing to tell him that part, though—the me and him naked part—so I turn back to the TV, my thumbnail ragged now from my teeth.

I should go. He's a grown man, he can handle the rest of this visit himself. But I just witnessed someone he referred to as "babe" abandon him when he needed help and it put a bad taste in my mouth. And maybe I *could* learn a little bit more about him, now that he's here and basically captive. For better or worse, I lost that chance when I bolted the night we met.

I'm not looking to relive that experience, but it's not like I haven't wondered about him from time to time, in between long bouts of extreme denial. If ever the wondering might edge out the denying, it would be when I'm back and inexplicably sitting in the Emergency Room with him.

I shift on my plastic chair. "That night," I say, and my heart riots in warning. "Um... How *did* it work?"

Jamie shifts too, pain rippling across his face as he turns toward me. "You told me I'd get the money," he says. "And I did. It's how I opened my brewery."

Goosebumps trickle down my arms. Okay, maybe I don't want to know more, because this sounds bat shit. "It's a coincidence," I hedge. "I'm sure it would have worked out even if I didn't tell you that."

"No, Noel. It wouldn't have." He's suddenly dead serious. "I'd been looking for investors for a while, had a few good leads, but bills were due, and nothing was panning out. My stepdad's buddy had a job opening. I was pretty much resigned to it the night I met you."

"The job I told you not to take?"

"Same one. I needed a steady paycheck because I was... well, I'm sure you remember."

I'm thinking of proposing. "Right." I swallow.

"It wasn't a bad gig, managing a bar on the pier in Old Orchard. It was probably better than I deserved at the time. Nepotism at best, but giving up the dream sorta broke my heart. Then you told me to wait, that the money would come. I canceled the interview the next day. Two weeks after that, my neighbor at the time knocked on my door completely out of the blue. I used to bring him six packs from my home brew set up, and it turned out he was sitting on a big settlement for some accident years ago. He offered to invest. I got to open my place. Just like you said I would."

I pull back, searching his face for a sign that he's joking. There's no way he diverted his entire livelihood based on a chance meeting with a stranger. A potentially unstable stranger. "What would have happened if you didn't get the money?" I ask, though I'm not sure I can handle the answer.

"Considering I was barely making rent at the time?" He shrugs. "I would have been broke, possibly homeless. Probably ruined my credit. Most likely, I'd have ended up couch surfing and pouring someone else's beer instead of mine."

Oh my God.

"Jamie! I can't believe you told him no, just like that, because of what I saw. What if I was a lunatic?"

"I knew you weren't."

"You had no way of knowing that. You don't make major life decisions on a freaking candle." I feel like I've just missed getting hit by a bus, despite this having happened two years ago. If I'd been wrong, it would have messed up everything for him. How could he have taken such a huge risk, and how can he be so casual about it now?

He blows out a breath. "Well, there was the other thing."

I meet his eyes and the whole thing is still raw and right there. His girlfriend. That look he'd given her before I threw a psychic bomb into their relationship. I remember the way the light drained from his face that night, and the indignation coursing through me softens. "It was true, then?"

"Oh, yeah." He laughs quietly and kneads at the back of his neck like the entire experience has settled in that one spot. "I couldn't just ignore the other piece of advice you gave me when that one was so spot on."

"I'm sorry," I whisper, because what else am I going to say? I broke horrible news about someone who he wanted to be his wife. This was miles away from Nana's sweet little fortune telling game. The worst thing she ever predicted for me was a disappointing loss in the annual art contest in eighth grade. I never even entered, and I always thought her readings were pretend anyway, so no harm done. But that night on the roof, I played what I thought was a game and ended up messing with someone's whole life.

Jamie tips his head to his shoulder in a half-hearted shrug. "It was supposed to happen, right? Everything you told me came true, Noel. The good and the bad. It's incredible."

"Mr. Bishop?" The tie-dye nurse returns pushing an empty wheelchair. "Time to get fitted for some crutches."

Jamie drops his head into his hands and groans.

Being in a car with Jamie Bishop is one of the more awkward experiences of my life. After another hour, he's finally discharged with a list of instructions and, based on his glassy eyes, a high dose of painkillers.

On the way in, he was in too much pain to do much more than slump in his seat and whimper whenever I hit a bump, but this time, we're entirely more aware of each other. My Jetta is so small, our arms keep brushing, sending me cowering into my door panel, and his new crutches had to be propped on the console between us to fit.

He's wearing his hoodie with nothing underneath but that nasty bruise wrapped around his side, and it's impossible not to think of him in the dream, his bare chest beneath soft white sheets. His hair mussed, cheeks pink from sleep or sex. The ink on his bicep flexing as his hand moved beneath the—

I jab at the AC, suddenly boiling from the inside out.

Luckily, it's only a few blocks before Jamie motions for me

to pull into a gravel parking lot. I put the car in park and peer at the dark windows of what looks to be a bar.

"Thanks for the ride," he mumbles, reaching for the door handle without a glance.

"Jamie, wait." Even if I don't care to see him again, it doesn't sit right, this tension. I press my fingers to my temples, then drop them when I realize I look like I'm trying to summon something. *Jeez*.

"Look, ah, that night, on the roof? It's just that nothing like that has ever happened to me before. It was a fluke. A glitch in the Matrix. I don't know what it was, but you have to understand it was *terrifying*." Goosebumps pop up on my arms just thinking of it.

"So was you passing out on my porch in the middle of the night, by the way." I smile playfully in an attempt to thaw this ice. His quiet chuckle is a win.

"I guess I can see that."

"Anyway, I freaked out, okay? It was a normal human reaction to something so... not normal. That's why I lied about not knowing you and I'm sorry. Really."

He leans back against the headrest, finally sparing me a glance. "I just assumed you were used to it. The psychic visions or whatever. I thought maybe you were a witch."

He smirks and I shoot him a look, but I deserve that soft jab. "Definitely not."

Jamie's quiet for a beat, those moody brown eyes I remember from the party swimming with contemplation. And narcotics. "So you're saying... I mean if that was the only time, then... It's only ever happened with me?"

I nod once in response, and his eyes widen before he schools his expression and nods back. "Wow."

"Yeah. Wow." I wrap my arms around myself. "We were totally screwing around that night, joking. For the last two years, I've convinced myself it was a dream."

"Or that I spiked your drink."

I wince. "*Yeaah*, I guess since I'm apologizing..."

"Hey, you brought me to the hospital instead of letting me bleed out on your porch. Let's call it even."

"That's dramatic. You would have gone into a coma from the concussion before you bled out."

"Comforting." He gives me a bashful smile that's somehow familiar to me even though I don't think I've seen it yet, and a shiver snakes through my shoulders.

"This is my taproom," he says, gesturing out the window. "I have an apartment upstairs."

Oh. I'm unprepared to find myself face to face with the brick and mortar version of my brain blip. My heart is in my throat as I peer through the windshield for a better look. It's a two-story converted industrial building, navy blue brick. Long picnic tables and Edison lights sit outside in a parking lot beer garden. It's very Portland cool. The type of place I would hang out if I lived here.

Then I see the sign—Fortune Brewing—and my arms break out in gooseflesh. Somehow, I know it's a nod to me. The fortune teller he thinks I am. And why wouldn't he?

I'm going to need a minute to wrap my head around this. Alone. Elsewhere.

Or maybe I won't. Maybe when he climbs out of this car, we can just chalk the whole thing up to a weird story and go back to being complete strangers. "Okay, well if you're all set getting in... "

"Wait." Jamie touches my wrist and I practically jump through the sunroof.

"Sorry," he says, pulling back.

"It's okay. It's just, I don't know when it might... We probably shouldn't touch."

"Right."

There's no psychic flash when I meet his eyes, though. Instead, I'm surprised by a sort of desperation on his face that would be clear to anyone, no sixth sense needed. "Come back tomorrow night."

"What?" *No.*

"To the bar. It's sort of a big night and I want you to see it."

I glance at his hand wrapped around his ribs. "You're working?"

"I don't think so." His shoulders sag like I've reminded him of an assignment that he forgot to do. "I was supposed to, obviously, but we'll have time to talk now."

I'm shaking my head before he even finishes. I *am* sorry I was rude to him, but this isn't something I want to play with. Jamie's charming, sure, and there's obviously something weird between us, but I don't have a good handle on whether it's a good weird or a bad weird. I definitely shouldn't go out of my way to hunt it down. "It's not a good idea," I tell him.

"Why not? It's Friday night. Beer is on the house, of course."

"You don't have to do that."

"Does that mean you'll come?"

"Jamie..."

"Please, Noel," he says. "I just want you to see it."

I pull my lip between my teeth. He looks defeated and desperate the same way he did on that roof. And just like that night, a soft spot for him appears. "Okay. I'll try."

"Come at seven," he says. "If you like music, that's when the band starts."

He winks at me and then he's gone.

Five

K ATE ARRIVES FIRST THING in the morning, a flurry of squeals and nearly-dropped take-out coffee cups. She took today off of work so we could spend the day catching up, and I didn't realize how much I needed to see her until she was standing in front of me.

"I can't believe you're here!" she says, bounce-hugging me on the porch. She breaks the hug, pushing my shoulders out. "You look like a fucking supermodel."

I snort. I'm still in the pajamas I wore to bring Jamie to the hospital since I spent the last few hours staring at the ceiling until sun-up, wondering if there was maybe a book somewhere on how to handle running into the guy you slept with in a psychic vision. "Why do lies and cuss words come so easily to you?"

She shrugs. "Three years of law school. But I'm serious.

Your hair is so long and I'm loving the color."

I run a hand through it, pulling at a tangle. It's past my shoulders now and an unintentional ombre. The top three-quarters, or maybe a year of growth, is back to my natural near-black, having had zero time to get the warm highlights touched up. I wonder if Jamie would have recognized me so easily if I'd still had them.

I don't have time to catch up on my balayage right now, though. Important cosmic questions need answering.

I pull Kate through the wooden screen door, letting it bang with a *thwack* behind us. "Look at this place." She kicks off her shoes on the mat in the kitchen and spins around the cottage. "It's exactly the same."

"Some of it," I say, digging through the kitchen drawers. Pixie makes herself known with a stretch and strut, and Kate picks her up. "The property management company put a gingham-lined basket of lobster-shaped soaps in the bathroom."

Nana never had a cohesive design for this place, but she was fervently anti-kitsch.

"Gross," Kate says plainly, making me laugh even though internally I'm on a ledge, tipping forward with every second I spend not talking this out.

This has always been Kate's superpower, pulling me back from a spiral. Whenever I felt myself getting nervous about something as a kid, meeting someone new or straying too far from the safety circle I'd built myself, she'd remind me that my biggest leap was probably a tiny step for most people.

And just like that, the whole thing would snap into perspective.

I need a little of that right now—perspective—because I'm starting to feel like an unwitting character in a movie.

I find the lighter I was looking for in a drawer, and start

flinging open cabinets. Nana's turquoise stone bowl sits on the top shelf, and I pause, torn between wanting to make sure I do this little ritual right, and the anxiety I feel about holding that bowl in particular. Like the white pillar candles Nana insisted on, the ones tucked in the top of her bedroom closet, she only ever used this bowl to catch the wax. I've already decided I'm not going into her room to get the candles, so in the name of quality control, I stretch to my toes to pull the bowl down. I should use at least one of her props.

"So tell me how you spent your first night back," Kate says unaware of my existential angst. She lifts a jar candle from the island to sniff it, and I snatch it from her. I line it up on the island with the lighter and the bowl, now filled with water, and shove my thumbnail between my teeth.

Kate watches me warily. "What the hell is going on?"

"I need to try something."

"Okaaay."

"Something... *weird* happened last night."

"Oh my God." Her eyebrows jump to her hair. "Did Nana, like, visit you?"

"Really, that's where your head goes? Ghosts?" Though, it's pretty bold of me to scoff at the supernatural considering what I'm about to do.

She shrugs. "She was always so mystical. If anyone could come back, it would be her."

I nod in agreement because Kate always finds a way to bring me around to her side of ridiculousness. Though, I didn't need her help to get to this place, did I? The place where I'm about to reenact that night on the roof in hopes of... well, I don't know what I'm hoping for. The possibility of being assaulted by another hallucination is less than comforting, but if I can make it happen with someone other than Jamie, that removes one complication.

Discovering some latent psychic ability is one thing. But a cosmic link to a stranger, especially one that ends the way my vision on the roof did, is more than I have the capacity for at the moment.

Lighting the candle, I wave my hand over the wick a few times to get a good flame. Kate has seen this enough times that understanding clicks on her face. She sets Pixie down and reaches across the island to press her palm to my forehead. "Babe, are you okay?"

"I'm fine." *I'm not.* "But I need to put an end to something right now."

"With Nana's candle thing?"

"Yes. Just let me!"

She holds her hands up at the pitch in my voice. "Fine. If we're doing this, lottery numbers would be great."

Ignoring that, I lift the candle while the wax turns liquid. I've seen Nana do this a hundred times, on this very kitchen island, but I've only done it myself as a joke. I don't know the finer details of the ritual. For good measure, I grab Kate's wrist the way Jamie grabbed mine that night. I'm desperate to find the key to this thing and Nana's not around to ask. Is it the candle? The candle and the touching? The candle and touching *him?*

The wax is pooling, so I take a deep breath and slowly tip it into the water. The moments before it congeals feel like eternity, but when it finally takes form, I realize I don't have any idea what I'm looking for. That night with Jamie, it wasn't the wax at all. The pictures just... formed in my head. But right now, the only thing knocking around in my brain is a nagging question regarding my sanity.

Defeated, I shove the bowl away, water sloshing over the edge, and drop my face into my hands.

"Are you going to tell me what's going on?" Kate grabs a dish towel and mops the mess I've made.

"I ran into Jamie last night. Jamie *Bishop*."

She makes a face, then it dawns on her. "*Wait*. Roof Guy?" She slaps her thigh. "Holy shit, the one whose future you told?"

"I didn't tell his future," I snap, then bite down on my lip again so hard I taste copper. My standard response to this has recently taken on an air of mistruth, if not become an outright lie. After last night, it seems as though I really did tell his freaking future.

Kate pushes herself to the edge of the stool she's perched on. "How the hell did you run into Jamie Bishop? I texted you at eight and you said you were going to bed."

"You're never going to believe this." Actually she will and I know exactly what she's going to say. Kate spent a good six months after that party insisting that the universe was telling me something and that I should "ignore it at my own peril."

I tell her the whole ridiculous story—finding Jamie bloody and concussed on my porch, how I thought I was going to be murdered. About the long night at the ER where a couple hours into the reunion, another relationship of his ended abruptly.

I tell her that his family owns the house next door, and based on the timeline he gave me, we most definitely had some overlapping nights here. When I'm finished, she stares at me, jaw unhinged.

I flap my hands, blowing some much needed air on my face. "Say something!"

"I can't believe it worked that quickly," she breathes.

"What? What worked?"

"Oh, come *on*, Noel! You come here on a retreat to figure out what's going to snap you out of this emotional rut, and *boom* the universe drops the hot guy who starred in your post-coital psychic vision on your literal doorstep."

I scrunch my face at the word post-coital. "The retreat thing was your idea," I tell her. "I'm only mildly participating."

"Liar! This is exactly why you came here. Open the gates. Find something you love. Does any of this ring a bell?"

"I was thinking more like how much I love walking along the cobblestones downtown or smelling the salt water when I wake up. The seagulls."

Kate groans. "No one loves seagulls, you dork."

"I do!"

"Oh, really?" She throws the wet dish towel at my head. "Is it their beady eyes? The way they eat trash?"

I toss it back harder. "It's the way they shit on my car." I trail off into a laugh and Kate joins, but I know it's only a stay of execution. She won't drop this.

"Ugh. Even if I wanted to believe this is meant to be, who am I for the universe to intervene in my love life? Why not just let me struggle on Tinder like everyone else?"

"Maybe not everyone else asks."

I pull back, eyes wide. "I did *not* ask for this."

"No, but you played with the candle that night knowing how much Nana believed in it."

"I poured wax into a Solo cup as a *joke*. That's hardly a plea for supernatural intervention." Though, my guilty conscience reminds me that I did know this was never a joke to Nana. Her predictions were always frivolous and light—a kiss from a boy (Kate), the winning goal in a soccer tournament (me), but even though the consequences may have been frivolous, her belief in it wasn't. She was all in.

My brain flashes with the little plea I sent up to the sky last night before falling asleep: *Don't let it be too hard to find*.

No. No, no, *no*. Am I here to try to wrestle some feeling back into my life? Sure. But the cosmos guiding Jamie to collapse on my doorstep because we're supposed to fall in love? *That's* ridiculous.

"It's a small city. A coincidence," I tell her and myself. "And for the hundredth time, we have no idea if it was a vision."

Except the belly button thing, and the haircut, his thriving small business that he straight up told me he only has because of that night... My heart takes off in a sprint.

"Whatever it was," Kate says, "it was you and him *naked.*"

"I can't stand you. Truly." I twirl a lock of hair around my finger and tug.

Kate knows me well enough to see this for what it is. A stress response. A nervous tic. This whole thing is so far beyond my comfort zone that I'm led to believe just those few hours with *Jamie Freaking Bishop* could count as a life-altering experience. Check the box and head home.

"Okay," Kate says. "Start back. Did you flip the fuck out? Because that's how I imagine you handling this."

I scoff self-righteously and lie through my teeth. "Of course not. But mostly because I didn't recognize him at first. He was pretty beat up and it was dark. But then he said my name and he called me *the angel.*"

She snorts. "Smooth."

"He said it more than once, this guardian angel thing. That night was a big deal for him." In a different way than it was a big deal for me. "He named his business after me. Or... the incident. His whole life changed that night, Kate."

"He told you that?"

"Yes! And I googled him, obviously." I pulled out my phone as soon as I dropped him at the bar—*Jamie Bishop, Portland, Maine*, click—and my screen filled with his face, unbruised, just as handsome. In addition to his personal Instagram—checkered with candids of him on the beach, dressed up downtown, on a mountain somewhere bundled in cold weather gear—and the brewery's account with staged photos of pint glasses and taps, I'd also found a plethora of articles and interviews.

He's quite successful it seems, turning a small microbrewing operation into a mid-scale craft beer business and a popular local taproom in the Old Port district. There were pictures of Jamie behind a row of taps, his arms crossed over his chest, hat backwards, and a huge grin on his face. Others of him in a dress shirt being interviewed for a piece on the future of craft beer. Article after article about the new kid on the brewery scene had appeared in my search, but the headline that stuck out the most read: **In a city that boasts beer juggernauts like Shipyard and Gritty's, local man Jamie Bishop is somehow keeping up and keeping on.**

"Holy shit," Kate says again like she's forgotten the rest of her vocabulary.

"I know."

"All of this time, you've been pretending that vision was some side effect of the alcohol and he's been building his whole life around it."

"I wasn't pretending." Except last night on the porch when I lied about remembering him. "It never happened again. Not once. What was I supposed to think?"

"That the universe is trying to set you up with a smoking hot, super successful guy, and you should probably say thank you!" Kate makes a sound like I am truly dense.

"A smoking hot, super successful lunatic! Kate, the man took a party game and made a huge financial decision based on it. He's…" I wave a hand, searching for the right word. "*Reckless*! You know who would do something like that? My mother."

"That's not untrue, but it is irrelevant. We're not talking about your mother here."

"We might as well be. That kind of impulsiveness ruled my entire childhood. There's no way *I'm* fated to a guy like this."

"The universe works in mysterious ways. What about him? Did he leave that cheating girlfriend?"

"I guess so. He seemed to be dating someone else, but she, ah, couldn't come to the hospital, so I stayed." Longer than I needed to if I'm being honest. But I'm not.

Kate throws her head back. "God, aren't you the least bit curious, Noel? If not for the sheer hotness factor here? I mean you made out well if it's true."

Leave it to Kate to focus on the fact that Jamie is good looking. Beautiful, actually, with that careless hair and the dimples of a damn cherub... but that's beside the point.

"There are a lot of handsome men out there who don't cosmically belong to me, and we've already established that this one is bonkers."

"Welp." Kate folds her hands under her chin. "I hate to break it to you, babe, but you said it yourself: this city is like the size of a high school. You can't expect to avoid him indefinitely. Something wants the two of you in the same space."

Well, that's foreboding.

I let my body slump forward, dramatically resting my cheek on the cool countertop. "Why is it that you don't think I've completely lost my mind? This whole time, you never questioned this."

She pulls one of the takeout coffees she brought from the tray and pushes the other toward me. "I was there that night, Noel. There's no way all of us were imagining that, drunk or not. And besides, if this thing *is* some kind of mental breakdown..." she shrugs. "I still kind of want to see how it plays out."

Six

Jamie

I F THERE WERE ANY justice in this world, I'd be waking up this morning feeling like a kid on Christmas. I've been looking forward to launching this new beer for weeks—the biggest night of my career since I opened. I should be high on an upcoming night of hustling behind the bar, working until my muscles give out.

But instead, when my eyes blink open to the wedge of sunlight cast over my pillow, all I feel is the kind of pain that leaves you wishing you could just crawl out of your own skin and into a hole to die.

Considering the conversation I'm about to have with Wes? That doesn't sound so bad.

By the time I got to the hospital, I knew I was going to be out of commission for more than a minute and that there was no getting around this conversation. I waited until

I knew he'd be asleep, then texted him to confess that I'd fucked up—something that's pretty high on my list of shit I hate doing. He replied with an urgent calendar invite for way-too-early o'clock. You'd think my own stepbrother would know better than to expect me to be coherent before ten.

But Wes is also the head of operations for Fortune Brewing—I manage the product and the people, he manages all the other shit that turns that into money—and I've just made his job a lot harder.

I force myself to sit up with a groan, swallowing against the pain. My concussed brain desperately tries to come up with lies to tell Wes and then myself—*a few more hours of sleep and I'll be able to work through it. Maybe if I just take extra breaks*—but then I reach for my water bottle rolling around on the floor beside the couch where I passed out and real tears spring to my eyes at the sharp stab in my side. Fuck this hurts.

The pain brings flashes of the hospital slinking back to me, mostly fond memories of Vicodin, but also Noel sitting in the chair beside me for hours while I was drugged, and X-rayed, and set up with the damn crutches now leaning against my kitchen island.

I can't believe I found her again after all this time.

I can't believe I bled all over her porch.

She's still untouchably gorgeous even under fluorescent hospital lights, fresh out of the sleep I stole from her. I've wondered over the last two years if maybe I'd built that part up in my head, how striking she is, but she's just like I remember. An angel. A prophet. A hot witch with dark hair, bizarrely beautiful gold eyes, and a tiny diamond stud in her nose.

Her face has been a recurring daydream for the past two years, and now she tells me I'm the only one she's ever had a freaking psychic vision about? Well, let's just say the basest part of my brain lit up like a Christmas tree despite the blinding pain.

The jingle of keys rips me out of that thought, and my front door swings open, then the overhead light flips on. I throw an arm over my eyes to block it, and maybe to take five extra seconds of peace before I'm greeted with the look that's inevitably on Wes's face right now.

"You awake?" he asks. Sitting up again feels unachievable, so I wave over the back of the couch.

He rounds the corner, and his eyes go wide at my bare chest. My entire right side's a deep purple. "Wow. That's ugly as fuck."

"Thanks." I'm slightly surprised that he's taken the time to assess me before launching into business, but it can only mean I look worse than I thought.

"We need a plan," Wes says, tugging at the legs of his slacks before sitting in the chair across from me.

My head throbs, and I press my palms into my eyes. I can already tell he's Crisis Wes right now. Not my favorite Wes.

"I asked Em to take over managing for the launch tonight," I tell him. I texted her as I was limping into my apartment after Noel dropped me off. "She can handle it."

And I'll handle the hit to my pride from being forced to watch on the sidelines.

"What about the rest of your shifts? Running the taproom on a skeleton crew was the only reason we were able to open it, but it's about to royally fuck us."

I hate that he has a point. I was the one who pushed for the taproom when Wes wanted to focus on retail distribution. It was the first time we disagreed. My first time taking lead on a decision. Selling direct to customers is how I get to flex the few muscles that I bring to this venture—my people skills, my likable (pre-black eye) face, and my beer. That and jamming every brew fest and beer event I can find into my schedule.

I'm damn lucky this didn't happen in July, but to be fair, I'm barely in my thirties. I'm supposed to be invincible. No one plans to be unable to work when they're my age.

Or maybe some people do. I'm sort of a late arrival to this adult world.

I rub my fists into my eyes to ease my blurry vision. "Maybe we could swap jobs," I say. "You can pour pints and I can sit behind the desk for a while."

"If you could read a spreadsheet, I'd consider it."

I grind my teeth, glaring at him. That was a low blow.

Wes glares right back and I know exactly what he's thinking. "This doesn't change anything," I say, beating him to it.

"Jamie, this type of thing is exactly why you should be considering this offer. One accident and everything we've worked for is in jeopardy. You're going to be laid up for weeks. You can't work behind the bar, you can't do your 'charming people into sales' thing. It feels like a sign."

A sardonic laugh springs out of my mouth. "That's rich coming from you."

Wes has made it very clear he doesn't believe in signs or fate. Or more specifically, the supernatural occurrence that brought me everything I have. He doesn't even like when I mention it.

Two weeks ago, Wes took a meeting with NEBev, a large-scale beer producer in the tri-state area. They want to buy my brand, make it just another line in their craft portfolio, and they gave me until the end of the year to decide. I'd work for them. Wes too. But NEBev would own the majority share and all the control. My family already thinks of me as a glorified bartender, and at that point, I would be. My beer wouldn't be mine, and neither would the marketing decisions, so they could paint me and my company however they want. It was a knee-jerk no from me, until the number they put up made my eyes bug out. It was enough that Wes hasn't dropped it.

NEBev calling the shots for my brand feels a lot like ceding my own destiny to someone who couldn't give a flying fuck about me or what I've built. I know I don't want that—to be the stepkid of some huge corporation. It's the rest of it I'm not so confident on. Like whether I have any business challenging Wes's professional advice on this.

His comment about the spreadsheets was fucked up but true. Saying I struggle with numbers would be an understatement. My brain literally doesn't comprehend them.

Growing up, it was a much bigger issue. I didn't know why math class felt like a foreign language, or why I couldn't write my fives and sevens the right way, or outline an essay correctly in English class. All I knew then was I was confused a lot, couldn't get my brain to play ball, and hiding that was a top priority.

When I was diagnosed in college with ADHD and dyscalculia, the doctor provided the why, but not the how. As in how to keep digits from swapping places when I try to do simple math in my head, or how to read the sales reports Wes sends me in Excel—my personal hellscape.

My beer is top notch and I kick ass at convincing people to drink it, but I literally have no idea how the business end of my business works. Wes knows this better than anyone.

Worry starts to make its way through the pain in my head and I dig my palms into my eyes. It's not easy to pull rank while shirtless and curled into the fetal position, but I try. "Like it or not, it's my call, and I need more time."

Me being sidelined is a temporary problem—*albeit a huge one*—and I'm not going to make a permanent decision because of it. Not yet. I still have three months.

"Fine." Wes stands, dismissing me. "I'll see you downstairs

in a few hours."

I give him a left-handed salute, since my right side is immo-bile, and Wes heads toward the door, not exactly slamming it, but giving it a little extra shove as he leaves me alone with a sinking feeling and a headache from hell. And a little hope that Noel has shown up again at the exact right time.

Looking around the bustle of my bar tonight is bittersweet. The crowd is already swollen past normal Friday night num-bers. The entertainment is setting up in the corner and people are filling in around the bar. The night is going off without a hitch. And without me.

"You're not supposed to be down here, Jamie," Em shouts over the crowd. She doesn't look at me, just continues pouring my beers while she gives me shit.

"I'm not behind the bar."

Em hands off her order, then comes to stand in front of me. "But you *are* taking a seat from a paying customer. And annoying me."

I take out my wallet and throw down a twenty. "There," I tell her. "That's at least another hour's rent for this stool in my own bar."

"Don't get snippy with me," she says, not surprising me when she pockets my cash. "I know you're in pain, but that pout on your face is bringing down the whole room. People come here for the dimples, Pretty Boy. Give 'em what they want or get out."

"I can't take being upstairs alone anymore, Em. I have five streaming subscriptions and I think I've reached the end of them all."

She taps her temple. "You're concussed, asshole. You're supposed to be bored, and you're not supposed to be watching TV."

"That's why I came down here!"

"Yeah, well sitting on a bar stool the day after a hit like that is prime idiot guy shit."

She has an unfortunate point, but there's no way I'm sleeping through this night. I'll play the good patient tomorrow. And besides, I have a very good reason why I need to be here right now. "What time is it?" I ask.

Em looks at the clock behind her. The vintage analog one that I have trouble reading even without a concussion. "Seven-oh-six. Three minutes since you last asked."

She's not coming. I don't know why I'm holding out hope. Noel was pretty clear that I'm not her favorite memory.

The guitar player tests his mic, and I turn over my shoulder to pretend like I'm supervising something. Anything. We had awesome success all summer with live entertainment in the tiny courtyard I sectioned out of the parking lot, so when the nights turned colder, Em and I decided to remove one of the long wooden tables from the front corner to make room for a stool and an amp.

Bonus: I swiped the table and brought it upstairs to my apartment so I could finally have a place to eat meals that wasn't my couch. I spend all of my time in the brew house or behind this bar, so my loft is a little barren. I'm acutely aware of it now that I'm going to be confined there for a while. I can already feel my skin start to itch from the impending solitude.

But before I have a chance to sulk about the turn my life has taken, the front door opens, and Noel walks in, looking as beautiful and magical as she did last night. Maybe my luck's about to turn around.

Seven

Noel

A GROUP OF GUYS in flannel shirts hold the door open for me as I step tentatively into Jamie's bar. Alone. Kate declined my invitation-slash-pleading to come along. "Sorry, Noel," she said, "I'm not crashing your first date with Mr. Destiny. That's seriously messed up."

I'd snapped that it wasn't a date even though I knew she'd said it only to irritate me.

"Why are you so nervous, then?" she taunted.

I don't know, Kate. Maybe I'm afraid of having some sort of psychotic break in public.

It was the other thing she said, though, about not being able to avoid it, that I couldn't get out of my head. I replayed it over and over until it morphed into Nana's voice. I could almost see her puttering around the kitchen, dish towel tossed over her shoulder, doling out cosmic advice in a sing-songy voice: *Something wants the two of you together.*

I decided facing Jamie Bishop was easier than facing that

memory-slash-hallucination. Though now that I'm here, I'm not so sure because wow. Here it is. The manifestation of what happened that night.

I rub my hands over my arms and look around. The bar is all cement and wood with rippled antique glass windows and a spray of round tables and black metal chairs across the floor. The walls are painted navy blue with a colorful logo that takes up one whole side. A wreath of pinecone shaped flowers, pale green and white, with a block font, gold F in the center.

An impressive wooden bar stretches along the entire back wall, and I head toward it. Even the taps are colorful and interesting, like a mini art display.

The bartender stops in front of me, hands on her hips. She shares my unimpressive height but her short, purply-black hair and lip ring tell me she doesn't let it hold her back. "What can I get for you?"

A banner above the bar announces that there's a new fall ale being launched, and I assume that's what Jamie meant when he said it was a big night for him. I know from my due diligence internet stalking that he's maintained the head brewer position despite the astronomical growth of his brand over the last two years, which means he's kind of the head beer chef. Brewing is a more creative process than I realized, and I wonder if his recipes are as personal to him as my art is to me.

"I'll have the fall ale," I tell her.

While the bartender pours my beer, I fidget with a little pop-up tent on top of the bar that says a portion of tonight's proceeds will go to a local children's learning center. A smile I haven't agreed to bubbles up. I guess I have to give Jamie points for philanthropy.

She slides the glass of dark beer across the bar, her gaze lifting over my shoulder just as a warm body steps into the air behind me.

"Put it on the house, Em."

A shiver wiggles down my spine at Jamie's deep, honeyed voice. Slowly, I turn around, somehow unprepared to see him again despite getting myself dressed and into a car to do just that. With a flush of heat to my cheeks, I'm reminded what Jamie looks like when he's not in a hospital bed. And let's be honest, he looked pretty darn good there too.

Tonight, though? Even the butterfly bandage on his brow and the purple beneath his eye can't dull how handsome he is. His hair is perfectly mussed, wavy pieces sticking up every which way like the surface of a lake on a windy day.

Those dimples carve in deep, and it takes everything I have not to turn tail and run for the door. If the universe knew me at all, it would accept that I am far too awkward to handle a man with this kind of presence.

"You came," he says.

"I said I would."

"I know." He laughs. "I guess I'm still not sure you're real."

Ha! I know the feeling.

He opens his arms as if to hug me hello, but I dodge it by lifting my pint glass in a dorky cheers motion. My body feels like it's bracing for impact just being in his space. If these visions *are* real, I still have no idea how they work. What triggers them. I do know that I don't want it to catch me without any warning. Hence why I'm acting as if Jamie's a metal pole in an electrical storm.

He nods over his shoulder. "Let's sit."

I follow his slow trek across the room. He's only using one of his crutches tonight which means he's either feeling better or being negligent in his recovery. First impressions tell me it could be either.

Jamie lowers himself onto one side of an empty booth, the

only free one in the place, and I sit across from him, hands folded in my lap. I look like I'm at a job interview, tucked tidily into myself while he man-spreads across the entire bench. I'm a kitten staring at a tiger.

"So what do you think?" His mouth edges up on one side—hesitant, hopeful. He's looking for my blessing, a grade on what he's accomplished with the information I gave him. My God, this is weird.

I spin my gaze around the room again, taking in the energy. It practically has its own pulse. "This is... impressive." I'm not exaggerating. Portland doesn't lack for eateries and watering holes. But with the crowd here tonight and the articles I read, this looks like making it. I take a sip of my ale and it's really freaking good, so I'm sure that helps.

"The internet told me you were successful," I say. "But you know what they say about believing everything you hear."

He grins at that. "You looked me up."

"I wanted to make sure you weren't a burglar since you know where I live."

"Good thing I took 'burglar' out of my LinkedIn profile," he says, tapping his temple.

I roll my eyes. "Please. Everyone lies on LinkedIn."

He laughs, eyes sparkling. "Why wouldn't I have burgled you last night if I were a burglar?"

"You could barely stand last night. But you could come back."

"Right. Can never be too careful." He tips his water glass to safety before sipping. The gulp I take of my beer is bigger.

"Seriously, though. Congratulations, Jamie. This is amazing."

"It all started with you." The look he's giving me is positively reverent, and it makes me squirm. "I looked for you after that night, you know. Not in like a creepy way, but I asked around.

It was like you just disappeared."

Oh. Here I'd been praying to forget the name Jamie Bishop, and he'd been out looking for me? I wonder what would have happened if he'd gotten in touch with me before now. If he'd run into Kate and she'd given him my number. I probably would have blocked him.

"I guess I kind of did disappear," I admit. "I've spent every summer here with my grandmother since I was a kid, but the last couple of years I, ah, haven't been able to make it."

It's not a lie, but it's a spin, and the smile I hang on my face to pull it off feels like it's made of plaster. Fragile and hollow inside.

"Oh, shit." He groans, running a hand down his face. "Was your grandmother there when I passed out on your porch?"

He looks so adorably mortified, and I wish I could laugh, but instead I'm back to spiraling over the blankness I feel when I say, "No. She passed away in July."

I've said it like a robot, and there's a flicker of curiosity in his expression. "I'm sorry, Noel."

"Thank you." I clear my throat. "I'm here on sabbatical, actually."

"That's right. You said that on the porch. Is it like an *Eat, Pray, Love* type thing?"

I fake a pout even though I'm inclined to laugh at myself. "Don't make fun of me."

"I promise I'm not." He lays his hand over his heart and the gesture wiggles something open in me. I'm talking to a man who built a whole life around a psychic vision. I guess I shouldn't have expected him to judge me for a silly Find My Feelings mission.

"It's more of a work thing." I bite my lip at another white lie. It's a pretty big me thing too, being broken this way. "Anyway, I'm here until the end of the year."

His eyebrows jump, which looks painful with that cut. "What do you do?"

"I'm an artist. Graphic designer. I can work from anywhere, but my boss actually gave me some time off." I leave out the part where it wasn't my choice.

"What a coincidence." He waves a hand over his midsection. "My boss gave me some time off too."

I chuckle into my beer.

"Well, it sounds like an adventure," he says, still grinning at me with something like fascination.

But my face falls at that word. I've hated it since I was a kid, when Mom used adventure synonymously with recklessness. It's a perfectly-timed reminder that this man has that same recklessness written all over him. I've thought so since that very first night when he smiled at me from the edge of a roof. I feel like I'm on that edge now, teetering into dangerous territory.

Chasing magic can't be without consequences. He called me an angel, but he could be an actual demon for all I know. The kind that tricks you with their sexy jawline and soft eyes until you're taking your clothes off in their apartment-slash-sex dungeon.

Oh my God, Noel. He drives a Honda and lives above a bar. He's not a demon.

I'm losing my mind, but I knew that when I agreed to come tonight.

"Look, this place is great, Jamie. I'm just not sure why I'm here."

"Right." I watch his Adam's apple bob with a thick swallow. Jamie's face is like a slideshow of boyish expressions—the *aw shucks* grin he gave the nurse, the playful smile he beamed at me that night on the roof—and if I had to label the one I'm looking at now, it would be guilty mischief. "The truth is I was, um, kind of hoping you might do it again."

"Do what again?" I'm genuinely curious because he obviously doesn't mean *read* him. I was pretty clear on my stance on that.

Jamie leans back, wrapping an arm around his ribs, and my gaze betrays me by tracing the line of his bicep, the ink poking out of his T-shirt sleeve the same way it did that night. "Look, ah, it's just that your timing is sort of impeccable. Some things are up in the air here with my business. This might sound crazy, I mean, I guess this whole thing is crazy, but the last time I had a big decision to make, you appeared. And now I have another one and here you are again."

He shakes his head as though he's utterly bewitched by this coincidence. I'm not. "That's why you invited me here, then? You want something."

"Well, when you put it like that... " He chuckles, running a hand through his hair. "I just wanted you to see it, Noel. To see this thing that came out of whatever happened that night. And yeah, I'm kind of at a crossroad and I guess I was hoping you might be able to help me get my sure thing back. Can you blame me?"

I'm already shaking my head. "All I told you was that the money would come to you. You had to have trusted your own judgment for a hundred decisions after that."

"Sure, but I mean, confidence breeds success, right? Two years ago, I was deciding whether to go all in, or abandon this dream all together. What you told me was a pretty clear yes. Why would the universe give me a sign like that just to point me in the wrong direction? It kinda felt like I couldn't lose at that point."

"Then you don't need me. You can't lose."

His shoulders fall. "This time is different."

"Why?"

"Because this is either the moment I prove myself or the moment they all find out I've never known what the hell I was doing."

For a blip of insanity, the desperation in his voice almost stalls my exit.

Almost.

Swallowing, I remind myself this is all conjecture, hopes and wishes. I'm sorry he feels this way, but he has no idea if I can help him and we definitely don't have enough data to be sure it won't hurt. "I'm not your guardian angel, Jamie, and I didn't come here to be your personal fortune teller." *Why the hell did I come here?*

"Okay, maybe not," he says. "But there's something here, right? You said this has never happened before or since, so it has to mean something." He leans across the table, pinning me with a serious stare. The first crack in his *que sera sera* vibe. "Don't you want to know what it is?"

Aren't you the least bit curious?

Goosebumps prickle up and down my arms. I try to rub them away but it's no use. "I told you that night was terrifying."

"I know, but you also told me you don't have much control over it either way, so what's the harm? We'll be friends, spend some time together. If it works, great. If not... well, no pressure."

No pressure. Right. He's asking me to summon some vague breadcrumb from the universe after he already admitted he made a huge life decision based on the last one. A huge decision that seems to have worked out well and now he's looking for an encore. That's the definition of pressure.

Sure, I'm sitting in his bar that he supposedly only has because of me, and I once had a vivid, alcohol-induced daydream where I imagined what he might look like naked with startling accuracy. But I'm not going to read him again. I have no reason to believe I even can. It was a terrifying experience that happened to be a cosmic boon for him. He won that encounter and he needs to drop it for both of our sakes.

"Thanks but no thanks, Jamie. I'm going to pass on being your human Magic 8 Ball." I grab my purse and push out of the booth, pausing to gulp the last of my beer because it's really good and I need to settle this buzzing nervousness in my chest. "I appreciate the drink," I say, smacking my lips with finality. "See you around."

"Noel." He moves to stand, probably to follow me like he did last time, but lucky for me, he's a little slower, what with being in the ER last night. *Reckless.*

I make it all the way to the front door, sweet escape just inches away, but when I push against the metal bar, someone grabs it at the same time from the outside and I nearly stumble forward.

"Sorry," yet another man in a flannel shirt says, stepping to the side, but it's the wrong side and I still can't get by. We do this weird little shuffle dance which gives Jamie enough time to catch up.

Jamie reaches above my head, holding the door, and I'm suddenly caught in a forcefield of body heat and salty cologne. The man on the other side takes my freeze-frame as an invitation to go first, and once he's done an awkward slide past us, Jamie pivots so he's standing in front of me, body squared.

"Noel, please just wait."

"I'm sorry. No. I can't." I duck under his arm, but it's a tight fit. Carelessly, *stupidly*, I press a hand to his chest as I slide by. And that's when it happens.

It hits me hard enough to make my head snap back, a picture. Him. Me. A lot closer than we are now.

Instinctively I clap my hands over my eyes, but that only plunges me deeper. Behind my lids, I see the two of us. On the porch at Nana's. I'm on Jamie's lap on her old wicker loveseat, my knees bracketing his thighs. It's raining outside, a summer rain, hot and sticky. The strap of my dress falls off of my shoulder, and his T-shirt is soaked through like we've been caught in it.

I trace the outline of the logo with my index finger. It's a vintage Peak's Island Summerfest shirt. I tell him I used to go there with Nana. There's a hole in the shoulder seam and I push my finger through it. His skin is hot. Damp. And then we're kissing.

He's laughing against my mouth, then he calls me baby.

I hate that term of endearment.

I absolutely do not hate it when he says it.

"Come on, baby," he says, his eyes sparkling with mischief and a sweet familiarity I find jarring. I don't know this man, but here, I do. Here, when he slides his hands beneath my thighs, excitement flits through my veins. *Want.* It's a feeling I haven't experienced in so long, and I wish I could gather it up and bring it back here to the dimension my actual body is in.

I lock my fingers behind his neck, and he stands with my legs around his waist and...

Like a fist closing, the vision squeezes around the edges, shrinking to a pinprick of light, and it's over.

I look up at Jamie, *real* Jamie, and my eyes roll back before...

"Shit."

Eight

Jamie

"**S**HIT." NOEL'S LEGS GIVE out and she tumbles forward into my chest. I drop my crutch and catch her, crashing painfully against the door frame as I absorb her weight. "Noel? Hey. Can you hear me?"

I've got her in a bear hug, trying to keep her feet under her, but she's pressed against my bruised ribs, making it really hard to breathe.

One of our regulars who happens to be nearby watches me try to maneuver her and rushes over to grab her other elbow, helping her stand. "Is she okay?"

"Can you get her some water?" I jut my chin toward the bar, and he hustles off. Noel's eyes are open now, blinking wildly at me. "Are you alright?"

"I'm fine." She moves to touch her face. When she realizes I still have a hold of her arm, she jerks away so quickly, she almost falls again. "Don't touch me, *please*."

"Okay." I hold my hands up and step back. I did just keep

her from cracking her head on the floor, but I'll try not to take that personally. "I won't touch you. Will you please sit down?"

The customer appears again with a glass and hands it to her while I pick my crutch up off the floor. Not an easy task. I give him the *all set* head nod and turn to Noel.

"There's not even a candle," she says, pressing the condensation from the cool glass on her pulse point.

I don't know if it's the lingering concussion or how distracting that bead of water left on her neck is, but it takes me a moment to catch up. When I do, my eyes jerk to hers. Holy shit. I think it happened again.

I try to keep my face from reflecting the fact that I'm ecstatic about this development because she is definitely not. "What did you see?"

She shakes her head. "No."

"No?"

"It had nothing to do with you."

I'd be disappointed if she wasn't such a bad liar. "You said it only happened with me."

"I know what I said!"

"Okay. Okay. Jeez." I pull out a chair and step back, hoping that will entice her to sit. The guitar player is overly loud and she's still rubbing at her temples.

"Don't ask me," she says, taking the seat.

I make a zipper motion with my fingers to my lips. But I do take the seat across from her. Three women slide past our table, headed toward the bar, and she scoots her chair in. Our knees brush, and she jerks away again. Her pink cheeks have gone ghostly white, and I gesture to the water instead of trying to hand it to her.

Thankfully, she takes it. Once she's swallowed a long sip she says, "I don't like this."

She looks up at me, gorgeous gold eyes rimmed in water,

shoulders curled in, and there's a twist of regret in my stomach for asking her this—solutions to my business problems at the expense of her terror. I do believe it scares the hell out of her, rightfully. But it doesn't seem either of us have much control over it and desperation is nipping at me. I can't take Wes on by myself on a good day and now I'm not only bucking his advice, I'm doing it from the sidelines. I feel like the waterboy trying to call plays.

"I know you don't." My fingers flex with the urge to touch her, to protect her, maybe, from the part that scares her, but that's clearly the last thing she wants.

"I don't even know what it means."

"We'll figure it out together." I push to the edge of my seat. "But you might have to tell me what you saw if you want me to help with that."

"Not yet," she says firmly.

I nod and stack my hands in my lap, trying to look as harmless as possible. I think it works because some of the fear slides off of her expression. "I won't do the candle thing again."

"Okay." I'm disappointed but I get it.

She chews her lip. "It doesn't seem like I need to anyway."

"Right."

"We'll just be friends, like you said. If it happens, it happens."

I realize I'm still staring at her teeth dug into that bottom lip and I stifle a quick pulse of regret that I've framed it that way—*friends*.

This is more important than my attraction to her, though. I can't turn down this offer from NEBev just to fall on my face, and she's the only one who can tell me if that's what's destined to happen if I dig my heels in. "Great," I say. "Perfect. I'm a good friend. You'll see."

From the gust of her sigh, I don't think she believes me.

Nine

I DRIVE TO KATE's twelve hours after leaving Fortune, half for an excuse to leave the cottage, and half because I need to talk this out. I'm filled with anxious regret. Did I really agree to be friends with Jamie Bishop, the man who causes my brain to short circuit whenever he enters my personal bubble?

I suppose, looking back, the word burst from my mouth as a sort of shield. Friends. A line. A boundary in this seemingly boundless thing.

I have to admit he was also making a bit of sense at the time. I can't control it, obviously, and I'm left with a lot of huge questions that I can't really answer without him, but I still feel like I've unbuckled my seatbelt at the top of a rollercoaster.

Kate opens the door in yoga pants and fuzzy slippers, eyeing me with giddy suspicion the way I used to when she'd show up at Nana's for breakfast in the same clothes I left her in downtown the night before.

"This is not a good thing." I shove past her, waving to Colin over my head as I flop down on her couch. "I wasn't even playing with the candle!"

"What did you see?" The only details I've provided so far was an all-caps text that said: "IT HAPPENED AGAIN."

"It was me and him." I lower my voice to confess this next part. "We were like, full on making out on Nana's porch."

Blood rushes my cheeks, and Kate barks a laugh. "You two are so horny in these things."

"Will you please be serious?"

"I am being serious." She sits across from me. "How many times does the universe have to tell you you're destined to bang him before you just do it?"

"I don't even know him!"

She shrugs. "Sure you do. He's the guy you banged in a psychic vision."

I shiver. "Oh my God."

Colin comes shuffling in from the kitchen in a tee and flannel pajama pants, his blond hair flopped over his forehead. I'm hit with a brief flash of surprise at how domestic this is, like I blinked and missed their relationship shifting into permanence.

Kate's still thinking out loud. "What if Jamie's your soulmate? This could be your epic love story."

"Wow. Straight from a vivid dream and some pretty dimples to soulmate?" I laugh but it comes out like I'm being held hostage. My brilliant "dream" excuse has burst into flames, and now the visions have happened twice. This thing is obviously real, but falling into bed with someone and falling in love with them are two different things.

"What Jamie wants has nothing to do with soulmates or epic love stories," I tell Kate. Unfortunately he's after something a little more complicated than making out with me.

"What's that mean?"

"Apparently, he has a whole new business problem and I've shown up just in time to give him another psychic tip."

Kate's eyebrows arch upward, and I know what she's thinking: Timing. Fate. All the magical things. Just like Nana would.

What I'm thinking is: Lunacy. Instability. How unhinged a person would have to be to make decisions this way. I've had enough of that kind of caution-to-the-wind approach to life. It has never suited me.

But then I remember how vivid the vision was last night. How the feeling I've been searching for reached all the way through the time-space continuum just to hit me in a place that's been so empty for so long.

And it was terrifying.

I drop my chin to my chest and breathe through a swelling panic. This is too much. I was willing to try this whole sabbatical idea to find some inspiration, to get unblocked, even if it meant putting myself back at Nana's house. But now I've been shoved hard by something Kate wants to call fate and I'm tumbling. "This isn't the baby step I was hoping to take, Kate."

Colin, who up until now has been silently taking this in while nursing his coffee, turns to me. "Why not?"

"Why not what?"

He pushes his glasses up his nose bridge. "Why isn't this a baby step? I mean, if it's... magic, it seems like a pretty safe bet."

"In what world is playing with the supernatural the 'safe' choice, Colin?"

"Come on, anyone who's seen a movie with a time loop or a magic fountain knows these things always have a lesson. And if this guy is really your destiny, or whatever, then that means you're his too. Why would it want to hurt either of you?"

I scrunch my nose. "You're comparing my actual life to a

movie starring Jason Bateman?"

He grins. "Couldn't find a *Scientific Journal* article on this one." When I don't laugh, he leans forward and squeezes my knee. "What I'm saying is, if you decide to take a leap for once, Noel, all signs point to the universe catching you."

I let that settle in—this theory, or gamble, really, and the fact that it's coming from Colin. What might that look like? Magic intervening to teach me something.

Magic I learned from Nana.

I rub at my chest where it suddenly feels tight. "You think this is for my own good?"

"Just... maybe don't assume it's not."

I tip my head to the painted tin ceiling in Kate's apartment until the tears I feel coming dry. "Are doctors even allowed to believe in magic?"

"All science was magic until we understood it."

God, I can't decide which part is more outlandish: that I'm actually seeing the future or that these visions are trying to help me.

I lean back into the couch cushions, blowing out a gust of air. "I feel like it should take more than a five second hallucination to go down this whole soulmate road."

"Two," Colin says around his coffee mug.

I raise an eyebrow.

"Two five-second hallucinations."

Kate grins evilly. "Both horny."

By the time I leave Kate's, I need to walk. Think. Downtown is just stretching its arms to the morning. Late-season tourists exit their hotels with sunglasses and maps, shop owners are putting out their folding signs. I take a left on a whim, heading away from my car and down toward the waterfront.

Kate has always been as true a friend as anyone could wish for, but she's made of fire and brimstone, and she doesn't know any other kind of love than tough. She's been bulldozing my safety walls for two decades, and I've built up a sort of tolerance to it. But Colin is gentle and rational with the exceedingly calm bedside manner of someone used to dealing with traumatic wounds, and he chose a language that spoke directly to my nervous heart. The potential built-in guarantee of it all.

It's like what Jamie said about the universe not pointing him in the wrong direction with his business. *It kind of felt like I couldn't lose.*

So maybe I can apply some of that logic to my own situation. Maybe the universe *is* giving me an assist here. Or maybe I am losing my goddamn mind. I suppose I owe it to myself to decipher which one it is.

I've been round and round this in my head with no great breakthrough, and I've also tapped my advice from the gallery. There's one other person who has a vested interest in figuring this out. The *only* one who can actually help me sort through any of it.

We'll figure it out together. That's what he said.

I pull out my phone and stare at the number Jamie gave me last night. Then I bite my lip and type. *Here goes nothing.*

Noel: Do you have plans today?

Ten

Jamie

MY PHONE BUZZES AGAINST my face, startling me from a dreamless, pain-induced sleep. That's what I get for scrolling in bed last night against concussion protocol.

I reach for it, squinting at the bright light of the screen, then try to remember if the doctor said concussions can cause hallucinations because the last thing I expected was to see Noel's name.

I rub the sleep out of my eyes and text her back.

Jamie: No plans. Kind of sidelined at the moment.

Noel: I'm downtown. Do you want to start being friends today?

Hell yes, I do. I roll out of bed, my first two steps an exaggerated limp before I adjust to the pain in my knee. I know I said I would play the good patient today, but I'm not missing a chance to see her.

I text her back on my way to the bathroom.

Jamie: Have you eaten breakfast? If you pick me up,

I can come back with you and get my car out of your driveway.

Noel: Be there in ten.

She agrees much more quickly than I anticipated, and a jolt of panic has me moving faster than I should. I haven't shaved in two days—lifting my right arm is unbearably painful—and I'm growing a full neck beard.

I glance at my closet while I brush my teeth lefty. I managed to put on real clothes last night for the launch, but it was exhausting and I had to take a few breaks. I don't have time for that today. I probably shouldn't show up looking like a mess, though.

I settle on my nicest pair of black joggers and a green Fortune tee I've been told looks good with my eyes. Skipping the product, I pull my hat on my head, shove my feet in sneakers, and make it downstairs to the front door just in time. Noel's walking into the parking lot, her hair in a ponytail tied with a ribbon and a blue dress swinging around her knees.

I'm stopped short at the sight of her through the glass. Sundresses are my kryptonite on a regular day. Noel in a sundress makes me want to put my fist in my mouth and bite. Her skin is sun-kissed, and her sandals are the kind that lace up around her ankle and tie in a bow. I picture pulling the knot loose, then doing the same with the ribbon in her hair. Unwrapping her like a fucking present. And then I picture punching myself in the face because this is not appropriate or helpful.

Get it together, Bishop. This is basically a business meeting.

The fact that Noel is beautiful is not a new revelation for me, but I've been trying to ignore it for several reasons. One, this is too important for distraction. If it takes a hundred reminders that I need Noel's help more than I need to let my mind wander into *what if* territory, I'll do it a hundred and one.

And two, Noel's incredibly sweet. Kind. Cute as hell. And I speak fluent pick-up line. It's never going to happen.

Noel's the kind of woman you fall for, and even if mixing business with pleasure wasn't a terrible idea in and of itself, mixing *affection* with pleasure is an even worse one. Her reading on the roof showed me that too.

She puts a hand above her eyes to block the sun, and I push out to meet her. "Hi, friend."

This gets me a little smile, and okay. This is good. She seems way less stressed about being around me than she did last night. "My car is a few blocks away," she says. "We can grab it after we eat?"

"Great. I know a good place, unless you had somewhere in mind."

"Anywhere is good." When she turns, her skirt flares around her thighs and I have to look to the sky for strength. If only getting it together was a little easier for me.

I take Noel to my favorite greasy diner on Commercial Street. It's a closet-sized nook nestled between a fish market and a marine supplies store, but it's New England famous.

A couple of weeks ago it would have been impossible to get in here on a Saturday morning, let alone have a choice of where to sit, but after Labor Day rolls around, the townies get our favorite spots back.

The waitress appears at the host stand in a T-shirt that's a little too neon for my lingering concussion. "Hi, Fran."

"Jamie Bishop." She gives me a look like she wants to roll up a newspaper and smack me on the head with it. "How's your mother?"

I grin. "Beaming with pride, last I saw her."

"Hmph." Fran's worked here since the Stone Age, and she has a long memory that includes the late nights my buddies and I came in for two A.M. bacon and eggs. We weren't always well behaved.

Noel, on the other hand, in her pretty dress and ponytail, looks like a good girl whose reputation I'm about to tarnish. The look on Fran's face says she's thinking the same thing, despite it being the better part of a decade since I've made trouble for her.

Don't worry, I want to tell her. *I'm not planning on touching this one.*

"Sit wherever you want," she says, glaring at me over Noel's head.

Noel flashes those big eyes at me, and I gesture to a booth, following behind and gingerly sliding in across from her the same way we sat last night. Hopefully this time I can keep her a little longer. Hopefully this time she doesn't pass out.

"How are you feeling?" she asks when she catches me wince as my back hits the wooden booth, and I'm back to thinking about her in flannel pjs, waiting with me at the ER even though she could have easily ditched me at the door. *Sweet. Kind. Beautiful.*

I blow a breath through my teeth. "I'm not sure what's worse, the pain or the boredom. I actually googled if I could still play hockey with broken ribs but it was a pretty clear no."

She snorts. "That's ridiculous."

"Thank you for your sympathy. It feels really genuine." My mouth is curved into a teasing smile, but Noel's cheeks still turn the most adorable shade of pink.

"Sorry," she says. "I just meant... nevermind."

I didn't mean to embarrass her, but I don't hate getting

a reaction out of her either. It's better than the fear or the general distaste from before. Besides, if she knew how long it had been since someone was concerned about my pain, she wouldn't be embarrassed. I would.

"Anyway," I say, nudging her knee under the table. "How are *you* feeling?"

"I'm not the one with the fractured sixth and seventh ribs and sprained knee."

"Fair." I chuckle again. "But I meant, ah, about this whole... thing. You scared the hell out of me at the bar when you fainted."

She winces. "Right. I'm sorry about that."

"Don't be! That's not what I meant. It's just... is it always like that? Were you dizzy, or...?"

"I think I was just shocked. It's not always like anything. It was only my second time, remember?"

"Right." That Christmas tree in my brain lights up again. Only twice. Both with me. "You know, I never properly thanked you for taking me to the hospital. And staying."

She waves this off. "I'm sure you did."

"I didn't," I say, dipping my chin to catch her eye. "It was really kind of you. So is this."

Noel tilts her head, and in the most subtle of shifts, she's holding *my* gaze now. Studying me in a way that makes me feel a little uncomfortable and excited at the same time.

Then she abruptly looks away. "So what's the deal with the woman who left you hanging that night?"

The smile tumbles from my face and I groan. "I was pretending you didn't hear that conversation."

"We were in a space the size of a postage stamp. Everyone heard that conversation."

"Right." I clear my throat. "Well, don't worry. It was only my ego that got bruised."

"She's not your girlfriend, then?" she asks, picking at the corner of her napkin with her thumbnail. Shredding it, actually.

"Definitely not. What about you?"

"What about me?"

"Your boyfriend must have been jealous that you spent the whole night standing vigil by my bedside."

She rolls her eyes and sweeps her hair away from her face, cheeks pink again. I'm developing an addiction to that color. "I don't have a boyfriend," she says, and Fran, bless her, appears before I can reply with anything stupid.

"Specials are on the board," she says, slapping menus on the table. "Coffee?"

Noel orders something French vanilla flavored, and I ask for a can of Java Jolt. Hopefully Fran heard me since she was already turning away.

Noel pretends to gag. "Java energy drink? Why not just drink coffee?"

"It's locally made. My friend Em used to work for them, and I got hooked on it."

"The bartender from last night."

I nod. "We went to college together. When I opened Fortune, I poached her from them. Besides, I don't like hot beverages."

Noel blinks at me dramatically and it's like her face comes alive with this little bit of snark. "As in, all hot beverages?"

"All."

"Hot cocoa?"

I shake my head.

"Hot toddy?"

"No one likes those."

"I do!" She clutches her heart. "My Nana made them every Christmas."

I laugh. Between this and the way she's sitting all prim and proper in this torn pleather booth, I'm beginning to think Noel might be a little old lady wearing a gorgeous twenty-something disguise.

Although, the Christmas part sounds nice. I'm always intrigued by other people's family dynamics. Traditions and such that lasted longer than a year or two until you moved in with another family and started all over. But hot toddies are pretty disgusting. "I'd rather have a cold beer," I say.

She visibly shivers. "What about hot soup?"

"Soup isn't a beverage."

"It's a hot liquid, what's the difference?"

I flash her a quick grin. "The same as the difference between drinking milk and eating cereal?"

She fights a smile, conceding the point with a few beats of silence, then shouts, "Warm apple cider!"

My shoulders shake with silent laughter. "You're not going to suddenly come up with a new beverage that has somehow escaped me for thirty years."

Fran brings our drinks, and I order my regular: Southwest omelet with home fries and fruit. Noel doesn't even look at the menu before ordering pancakes with whipped cream.

"Is that how old you are?" she asks me when we're alone again.

"I'm thirty-one. I figured the first year doesn't count because you only eat mush."

"And drink milk. Warm."

"What about you?" I ask, grinning.

She takes a big sip, smacking her lips. "I love warm drinks."

"I meant how old are you?"

"I'm twenty-eight."

I raise an eyebrow. "So that makes you twenty-six when we first met."

"Mmm," she hums around her coffee. "And that makes you the old guy at that party."

I laugh again. "So you spent summers here?"

"Since I was a kid. Nana moved to long term care closer to us two years ago, though. Right after that night on the roof."

"Us?" I glance at her left hand. She's not wearing a ring, and my chest deflates in relief. Which I quickly kick myself for because this is a business meeting with a beautiful woman who can see my future. Not a date.

"Me and my mom." Her smile is tight.

"You live with your mom?"

"She lives with me, actually. In my spare room. Well, currently she lives with her boyfriend in a van."

"A *van?*"

"It's exactly what it sounds like."

I snort. "That's wild."

"Very. Anyway, Nana needed a lot of care management, and she took care of me for so long."

"That's young to take that on. When I was that age, I was living with three other guys in a shitty three-unit on the outskirts of the city, brewing beer in the garage, and spending Thursday through Sunday at the bars."

I'm what my stepdad used to call a late bloomer when it came to getting my shit together. I've been playing catch up ever since, no matter how successful the brewery has become. Sometimes this whole grown up job thing still feels like a disguise or a costume I'm trying on.

Noel raises her cup. "Sounds like career training to me."

"Maybe I was smarter than I thought." I huff a laugh. "So, your parents didn't mind you being gone for months at a time?"

"It was just me and my mom then too, and it was either that or spend the summer in a different camp each week, which she could *not* afford. She relished her own time, anyway."

There's more to that story. I consider asking her about it, but my own childhood was messy enough that I know not to treat other people's dirt like it's my business.

"It was just me and my mom when I was a kid too," I tell her. "Well, us and whatever guy she was married to at the time. Actually, it was mostly just me."

Fran comes back, dropping our food. She shoots me another less-than-fond look, and this time Noel notices. "Not your biggest fan?"

"Fran? She's coming around, I think. Another ten years or so and we'll be vacationing together."

"What did you do to piss her off?"

I squeeze ketchup onto my plate, flashing her a grin. "Let's just say, I've had to grow into this charming personality."

This earns me a laugh, a giggle actually, with her cheeks full of pancake and a dot of whipped cream on her upper lip. I stare at it until she licks it away. Until I can almost taste the sugar on my own tongue.

Friends. You're a goddamn idiot, Bishop.

Eleven

Noel

I FEEL LIKE A top that's been given a good spin by the time Jamie collects his car and is pulling out of my driveway. After breakfast, we took the long way back to my car, walking Commercial Street where the fancy restaurants and the hustle of the working waterfront all mix together in a uniquely New England cocktail.

Colin said science and magic used to be one in the same, and I found myself studying Jamie like a specimen, comparing his dimples and lazy grin to my own sweaty palms and general awkwardness. The way he seemed completely at ease with this supernatural chess game while I had to stop my brain from spinning out on multiple occasions. A mismatch if I've ever seen one.

But as I kick off my shoes and wade back into the silence of Nana's cottage, I have to admit that in between the studying and the spinning, I *had* enjoyed myself. Just like he promised. *I'm a good friend. You'll see.*

I'm not ready to claim friendship, definitely not more, but it would be a lie to say I didn't like the new little bits of Jamie I spent the morning collecting, once I decided to stop being so afraid of him. Like the way he sometimes trails off mid-sentence, an ellipses hanging in the air while his brain catches some other drift. Or the extra pinch in his right eyelid that I'd noticed the night on the roof. I could see it again, now that the swelling around his eye has gone down, and I find it just as charming.

Rationally, though, I know it's possible I've convinced myself that I'm *supposed* to like these things. Our magical history is like a weight added to Jamie's already abundant charm. I've seen myself knowing Jamie intimately, liking *something* about him enough to wake up naked in his bed and make out with him on Nana's porch. Not to mention Kate and Colin have filled my head with thoughts of soulmates and love stories. The jury has been unequivocally tampered with if not completely tainted.

To keep my head on, I'm sorting my current life into boxes, and for the rest of Saturday, I put Jamie in his, fit the lid on top, and shove it away for something more pressing and concrete—my future ability to pay my mortgage.

I unpack my laptop and settle in at the dining room table to work. This sabbatical was meant to help me convince Vi she should give me Ned's job, but I've been here three days and this is the first time I've even checked my email. Before I left Connecticut, I delivered drafts on the two remaining designs that Vi gave me an advance on, and she sent them back with only minor edits. Of course, I'd immediately panicked that I was already in the middle of the interview, that the sparse feedback was a test to see if I'd find a way to evoke the emotion she wants without her having to hold my hand. Now, I find myself fretting over the smallest of decisions until I can't seem to look at my screen without seeing my uncertain future in every blink of the cursor.

Usually when I feel like this, I'll give myself a brain break. Light a candle, put in my earbuds, and set a timer. I sketch until it dings, and nearly always come out of it centered and inspired. But I'm not really into playing with candles right now, and my whole life feels like a big blank piece of paper, so it seems unlikely I'll find the solution in another one.

Being blocked professionally is one thing—scary, stressful. Sure. But being unable to do the thing I love, to tap into what's always made me *me*, is a lot harder to stomach, and I'm afraid that's exactly what I'll find if I swap my mouse for a pencil.

Maybe, I think, practicing that grace Kate told me to give myself, *I just need the weekend to rest.*

Or maybe you're blocked for good and this thing that allows you to feed yourself will never come back.

The thing about searching for emotion, is you can't choose which ones will pop up out of their hiding place first. Sunday morning when I roll out of bed, the floor of the loft is ice on my feet, and I'm hit with the sullen reminder that, just like Nana, the summer is also missing from this year's trip.

Seasons change. It happens every year, and yet, the difference rubs at me for the rest of the morning, like an uncomfortable piece of clothing. If that wasn't bad enough, on my way to the bathroom, I stub a toe on one of those silly gingham-lined baskets from the property management company, set by the door to collect shoes and beach towels, and it's a sucker punch straight to my soul.

I asked for it, the staging service. I paid them to make the cottage into a place people would want to stay the week so that their vacations would keep me from having to sell it. But understanding the practical reasons for something unsavory isn't the same as literally tripping over the consequences of it.

The urge to escape sets in again, that tingling in my limbs and shoulders like my muscles want to burst into a sprint, but I can't seem to find a destination. The forecasted scattered showers have turned into a surprise downpour, which means spending the day at the beach is out, so is heading back downtown.

By noon, the cloud cover has darkened the cottage like a shroud, so I flip on every light in the house, pull up Spotify on my laptop for the company, and send another text to Mom—my third since Friday.

I send one to Kate too, even though I know she's likely driving to her parents' on the Midcoast where they moved after Kate graduated high school. She goes there weekly for Sunday dinner, she and her two brothers, and now Colin. And then I sit, stewing in the silence of the cottage until it feels like fingers pressing on a bruise.

I've never considered myself to be lonely. Introverted, sure, in that way artists tend to be always tuned into the world inside their head instead of the one around them. And I've been a bit of a homebody since I was a kid, not always by choice. It's hard to connect with other kids when you're thinking about rent being due, or what your mom's situationship meant in his morning-after text. My closest companion besides Kate was a seventy-year-old woman.

Now I'm starting to wonder if maybe that feeling of losing my color is just loneliness in disguise. Maybe Kate's empty-nester comparison wasn't so off after all.

I'm in the middle of making myself a peanut butter sand-wich for one when my phone pings with an incoming text. I lunge for it, assuming that Mom is granting me some sign of life. But it's not her.

Jamie: Did you know they did a study on human isolation and the guy who made it the longest only did eight days?

The grin that jumps to my face catches me off guard in the same way as the sucker punch feeling from this morning, just inverted.

I set the butter knife on the counter and type back, a smile pinned between my teeth.

Noel: Is someone feeling sorry for themselves?
Jamie: You have no idea. What are you doing?
Working, I lie.
Jamie: I remember work.
Jamie: And fun.
Jamie: And not being in pain.

I abandon my lunch completely and drop onto Nana's couch, tucking my legs underneath me.

Noel: You could use your crutches. That might help.
Jamie: I would, but there's one problem.
Noel: What?
Jamie: I hate them.

I can so clearly see the look on his face, a seriousness that is entirely feigned, and I giggle out loud alone in this room.

The conversation weaves through the rest of the day, ping-ing each other back and forth in between my much-later lunch and a bit of laundry, then picking up again after I run into town to grab more cat food and a replacement for the shampoo I forgot to pack.

Jamie tells me more about brewing beer, including sending

a picture of him in goggles and rubber boots that I promptly save. I tell him about Vi, how I'd met her at an alumni event smack in the middle of a post-graduation panic, when I was sure getting an MFA had been the most foolish choice. She was like a fisherman tossing me a line. I took graphics in college, and I knew it paid way more than you could ever dream of as a watercolor artist. The relief of that first paycheck outweighed the churning discomfort of abandoning ship.

Around ten past four, Jamie suddenly stops replying. Forty minutes after his last emoji comes through, my heart does a little untied-balloon fizzle, deflating in my chest, and I quickly chastise myself for it.

Until at six, a close-up selfie arrives, his eyes puffy (both, not just the bruised one) and hair *insane*. An oddly right-angled mark frames his good eye.

Jamie: I wasn't ignoring you. Fell asleep on my phone. I'm sorry. I'm on a lot of drugs.

I save that one too, obviously. I'm about to type a goodnight message and justify putting my pajamas on before dinner, but my blood is buzzing with an unfamiliar excitement that seems to have expanded ten-fold the moment I got his company back.

I'm not ready to give it up again—this feeling I haven't named yet.

And it does seem sort of a waste, him caged up by his injury, me practically climbing the walls with my need to escape this place.

Isn't this what we agreed on? Friendship?

Hanging out when we're both bored is a friend thing to do. If it were Kate, I'd already be headed to her apartment.

I shove my thumbnail between my teeth and type with one hand.

Noel: Can I come over?

He replies immediately.

Jamie: I can't imagine the guy who says no to that.

I park in the same gravel lot where I dropped Jamie off days ago after the hospital, and check my phone.

Jamie: My apartment's through the side door. Top of the stairs.

For some reason my mind hears this in his lower-octave voice from the hospital, and a stray flutter that has no business in this careful exploration flushes heat over my skin. Grabbing my things, I scan the side of the building. To the left of the main entrance, cut out of a corner, is a private door. The stairs I find when I open it feels like they were built well before modern building codes, narrow and mountainside-steep.

Jamie must hear me climbing them, because as soon as I lift my fist to knock on the door at the top, it swings open and he's there.

"Hi, friend." He's leaning casually on the door frame, wearing a grin that I feel like warm water poured all the way down to my toes. My God, he's a lot to handle. Exploring the possibility of fate is nerve wracking enough. Exploring it with a man who looks and charms like Jamie Bishop is on a whole other level. This new part of me who's considering the idea of magic wonders if the cosmos knows this about me, and that's why the vision was of Jamie and me in the safety of the afterglow. Like when you recommend a romance novel to your grandmother but make sure it's the fade-to-black kind.

Tonight, he has on a pair of gray joggers and a black zip-up hoodie, low socks that show his ankles. It's a far cry from his crazy, sexy, cool vibe at the bar that first night, and somehow even more intimidating.

The hat is missing too, and a lock of hair (the one I knew about before I knew about it) somersaults onto his forehead as he steps aside to let me in.

He looks down at the grease-stained paper bag I'm holding and arches his bruised eyebrow. "You brought food?"

"Thai food. Do you like?"

He smiles. "I like."

I'm pleased to my core at my choice, but I try to be casual. "I assumed you hadn't eaten yet, and you bought my breakfast. It was my turn."

"Thank you."

Setting the bag on the counter, I spin around, taking in his space. I'm not sure what I expected but I'm instantly impressed. If Nana's cottage is shabby chic, Jamie's place is urban swank. Cavernous lofted ceilings, an open floor plan—I feel cooler just being here. A leather couch anchors and divides the space, set across from a huge TV hung over a gas fireplace.

To the right, three steps lead to a raised level that serves as a bedroom. The far wall sports a row of windows that must have a killer view of the city, but my gaze homes in on a king-size, platform bed, unmade and fitted with wrinkled gray sheets that look softer than a newborn kitten. My mind goes exactly where it's led: Picturing him there. Me there. Us there.

It's not the bed from the vision, though. No headboard. No fireplace at the foot. I didn't think about possibly walking in and seeing that bedroom until right now, and the discovery that it's not here both shocks and disappoints me. Not that I'm here with the intention of sleeping with him, of course. *Of course.* But any clue about where or when that vision was from would be something.

"I'll get some plates," he says, tapping my hip as he passes on my right. I try not to jump at the contact. I want that comfortable company from before. I came here chasing it.

Jamie reaches for the upper cabinet, one hand over his ribs, and a flash of pain ripples through his expression. His cheeks are flushed, dark purple swept under his eyes.

"You're hurting."

"Pretty much everywhere, yeah." He says this like not being in pain is something he should have been better at and it presses somewhere soft inside my chest.

"I'll get this," I say, taking the plates from him and waving toward the living room. "You sit."

I'm slightly surprised when he takes that order with no more than a raised eyebrow, but when I see the way he eases himself onto the couch, I suspect he's been waiting for an excuse to lie down.

"Have you been icing?" I ask, watching him over my shoulder while I unpack food boxes, scooping fried things onto plates.

"Uh..."

"What?"

"It's just that the freezer is so far from the couch." He smiles, though it's significantly dulled by pain, and it's a good thing he's cute because what the hell.

"This is a pretty big injury, Jamie. You need to take it seriously."

He winces. "Yeah, I'm starting to see that."

The reusable ice packs they gave him at the hospital are shoved in the corner on the counter. I fill one with cubes from the dispenser on the fridge door, then twist it into a tight pack and hand it to him, my eyebrows raised expectantly.

He has the good sense to look chastised. "Thank you," he says. "Again."

"You're welcome." I set the plates on the coffee table, but I don't join him on the couch yet. I'm easing into this, being in his space. Also, I want to keep snooping.

Lingering in the living room, I spot some photos in an impressive gallery formation and wander over for a closer look. They're snapshots, stuff you would see on social media—in fact I think I recognize one of them from Fortune's Instagram—but displayed like this, they're a whole vibe. "Were these taken downstairs?"

He nods, taking a bite of a spring roll, before pushing the plate away. "Em took them throughout the first year we were open. She gave them to me last Christmas. You can see more and more customers in each photo, then the band playing when we added live music. It reminds me of those people who have photos done of their kids each year and hang them in a row so you can see the changes."

I smile at Jamie showing off his bar child.

He's in a handful of them and I notice the same effect with his various states of facial hair. From clean-shaven just like when I first met him, to a couple of mountain-man looks, back to this thick stubble thing he has going on now. In the center, there's a photo of him and another guy standing back to back, arms across their chests, grinning. Jamie has one of his sinfully tight-fitting Fortune tees on, and the other guy is in a shirt and tie. It's mid level beard and I try to guess the timeline. Summer, based on the girls in dresses in the background. Two of them are clearly staring at Jamie, their crushes accidentally immortalized. Just like the flutter in the car, the jealous ping in my chest is also a surprise.

"Who's the guy you're posing with?"

"That's my brother Wes. He's my business partner."

"Oh." I look again with new interest. Jamie's complexion is fair, like he might burn easily in the sun. Wes, on the other hand, looks like he has a year-round tan. They both have dark hair, but Jamie's is soft, with a wave so perfect it must have been bestowed on him by an angel at birth. Wes's is sleek and near black, like a vintage cologne ad. He's Armani to Jamie's Abercrombie.

"You two don't look like brothers."

"We're stepbrothers. Well, ex-step. His dad and my mom were married for three years. They divorced when we were seventeen. But we're brothers in the ways that matter."

"What ways are those?"

"We fight like brothers." He laughs to himself, but it's edgy like maybe he's not speaking in generalities but in present tense. "I don't know, growing up together, we just get each other on a different level. For good or bad."

I give him a sympathetic smile, thinking of Mom and how I know exactly what he means about the bad. Sometimes I wish I didn't know the reasons she does the things she does. It would make it a lot easier to be angry instead of sad when she disappoints me. "It's hard to hide from family."

"You can say that again."

Rounding the couch, I take the seat beside him, and he hands me the TV remote. I'm not sure if it's because he thinks I don't want to watch what I think is a rerun of *The Walking Dead* or because he's in too much pain to pay attention anyway. His eyelids are barely at half-mast, and he hasn't touched the food he seemed excited about.

"Aren't the meds helping? When's your next dose?"

"Two hours."

Oof. I glance at the ice pack beside him, then the way his chest rises and falls, controlled like he's being careful with each breath. He's clearly miserable, and I could help if I could muster the courage to touch him.

That element of this connection is still untested, though. Both times it happened, my hands were on him or his on me. But we've also touched without anything happening: In my car after the hospital, when he held the door for me at breakfast and my arm brushed his stomach, momentarily striking me with the fear of God. I'm still as clueless as ever as to how and when these visions will come about.

But he looks so pathetic.

"Come on, sit up." His eyes pop open, and I gesture for him to turn his body away from me. "Let me help you."

He shuffles to the side and I lift the back of his sweatshirt, pressing the ice against his ribs. He groans. Or moans. I'm not sure, but *flutter, flutter, flutter*.

"I'm sorry," I say, my voice suddenly raspy. "Did that hurt?"

"No, it feels good. Thank you."

He curves forward so I can lift his shirt a little higher than I dared to, revealing more freckles on his lower back that match the ones on his stomach. The ones I shouldn't know about.

I quickly refocus on the purple and red streaks like claw marks wrapped around his side. "God, this looks so painful."

"I really appreciate this, Noel. I know you didn't agree to hang out with me to play nurse." He scratches his neck. "I'll be better in no time. I'll take you somewhere fun, okay?"

The guilt in his voice is too much. "It's fine, Jamie. Really. You're actually doing me a favor."

He snorts. "Sure."

"I'm serious." He looks at me over his shoulder, and my cheeks heat like the surface of the sun under his attention. "I... may have invited myself over here because I was trying to avoid something."

He shifts then, and he's suddenly closer. One big shoulder practically nestled against my breastbone. I pray he can't feel my heart pick up speed. "Avoid what?"

I turn him away again and press the ice more firmly against his skin, as if that might contain him. "The house."

"Your grandmother's house? Seems like it would be hard to

avoid when you're staying there."

"It's surprisingly not." I gesture to his living room, my current escape. "And not just now, I mean over the last two years. It used to be my favorite place, and now..." It feels like a pair of pants that don't fit right anymore. Uncomfortable when it used to be like a second skin. "I can't bring myself to stay inside those walls for longer than I have to, which I know is counter-productive to my whole reason for being here."

"I thought you were here for work."

Right. I did sort of make it seem that way. "It's complicated."

"How mysterious."

"Sorry, it's just kind of embarrassing. I work freelance right now, but there's a permanent position up for grabs. My boss said she wants to give it to me, except I have to do some work on myself first. So I came here to do it."

"What kind of work?" he asks, and I immediately wish I hadn't started down this road with him, a virtual stranger. But I also really like the way he's said this, incredulous on my behalf. The way Kate had been. All I've felt about it so far is tired and blank and stressed.

I stare at the back of his neck, chewing on my words. I suppose I've been privy to some pretty intimate details of Jamie's life. And in my vision, I saw myself being far more vulnerable with him than this minor confession.

"I've been having trouble feeling things."

"Like..." He gestures to his temple, teasing the psychic elephant between us, and I manage a laugh.

"No. Like regular things. It's affecting my designs. My job. My Nana passed two months ago, and I haven't cried. It's weird right? I mean, she was eighty, and she hadn't been really *here* for two years. It wasn't exactly tragic, but... it was tragic to me."

As soon as they're out, I wish I could gather the words back.

I might as well have just handed him a note that said: *Psst, careful. This one's a little broken.*

"Noel," he says, turning toward me again. The ice pack falls away from his ribs, and I tut at him, pretending to fuss with fitting it back under his sweatshirt.

"Sorry," I say. "Ugh. That was... too much."

"It wasn't."

I look up and those deep dark eyes are back on mine. There goes that spinning top again. "Come on," I say. "I can't reach." I set my hand to the base of his neck, squeezing slightly to reposition him. The muscles there are like granite, strung tight in the way mine sometimes get in the winter, when my shoulders are forever up near my ears to ward off the cold.

I dig my thumb a little harder, and this time his head flops backward, his hair tickling my chin. "*Fuuuck.* Can you keep doing that?"

"Someone's easy," I joke, but on a real note, I think he might crave this fussing on a cellular level. He's practically purring at my touch, his body going completely lax beneath my fingers. "Did you decide to store every stress you've ever had in this spot right here or did it land there on its own?"

He laughs quietly. "I'm just not used to lying around on this couch all day. I didn't realize how badly I was jacking up the rest of my body."

"Well, you need to stretch more. Maybe on the way to the freezer to get ice."

"Maybe." He shifts his hips so they're square, putting more weight on me. "You know, I get what you mean about loving something but also feeling oppressed by it. I feel that way about this whole city sometimes. Like it knows me as someone I'm not anymore, and I'm trying to get used to the new fit."

"What does it know you as?" I ask quietly.

"I wasn't a well-behaved kid. Teenager." He winces. "Early adult."

"In what way?"

"Nothing that went on my permanent record or anything. I got into trouble at school. And out of school."

I'm quiet, watching my thumb press into his skin. It feels as though this confession of his is pressing back. The guilt in his voice doesn't entirely match my first impressions of Jamie—carefree, a little daredevilish. His confidence has done nothing but shake mine since we met, but something new starts to come into focus behind that cocky, easy-going vibe. A vulnerability he's showing me. I have to swallow against a sudden rush of affection for it.

"And then what?" I ask, softening the stroke of my thumb to a caress of his hairline. Something meant to comfort. "You left your wicked ways behind and grew up to be a successful businessman?"

He waits a long time before deciding on, "Something like that."

I'm warned off of prying any more when he tosses me a grin over his shoulder that feels like a curtain being swung shut.

"Well, then," I say lightly, letting him off this hook he's hung himself on for my benefit. Solely to make me feel understood. "You get why I needed to get out of there tonight."

"Yeah, I do."

"See? Even trade. Now stay still."

He settles his shoulder into the couch cushion, and I press the ice back into place. He's quiet for so long, I think maybe he's finally found enough relief to sleep. But then his scratchy, quiet voice cuts through the easy silence. "Do you want to stay and watch a movie with me?"

"Yeah." I smile at the back of his head. "I do."

Twelve

Jamie

MONDAY MORNING, I'M AT the brewery before the sun even comes up. It's brew day and I've never missed one, broken bones be damned. I check on the beers we have in the cellar, schedule deliveries for the rest of the week—all the things I can accomplish with my ass in a chair.

The guys who work for me have had to pick up a lot of slack since I can't shovel grain or move kegs, and navigating the wet floors on an unstable knee is too risky even for me, so I DoorDash them some coffee and doughnuts as a thank you before I head over to the taproom to meet Wes.

By the time I pull into the parking lot, my entire body is aching, which has the inconvenient side effect of reminding me of Noel's hands on me last night. Her fingers at the back of my neck.

I've forgotten what it feels like to be touched by a woman like that, soft and *tender*. Her pretty laugh chiming beside me while we sat shoulder to shoulder watching *Little Miss*

Sunshine. I could still smell her perfume on my couch this morning.

It's been years since I found myself replaying a night with a woman, and the realization jerks through me like a snap of fingers in front of my face.

I hold open the door with my crutch and struggle my way into the bar, making it halfway through before it slips and hits me in the ass.

Em busts out laughing. "Smooth like butter, Jameson."

I give her the finger and pick the damn things up, limping the rest of the way to the bar without them. I only brought them because Noel told me I should. "Thanks for the help, dick. You laugh at old ladies trying to cross the street too?"

She presses a hand to her chest. "Never. But you looking anything but cool always makes my day a little brighter."

I wink at her. "It's so rare, I can see why."

"Sure, J."

"You're late." Wes emerges from the hall to his office, his expression a portrait of annoyance. I'm not in the habit of letting that bitchy tone slide from him, but I'm too exhausted to scrap with my brother right now. And I am actually almost fifteen minutes late.

"I forgot to set a reminder on my phone," I tell him. A fatal mistake for my chaotic brain. Especially when all of my executive functioning is being used to manage multiple broken bones. "Sorry, man. Pain's messing with my head."

Wes is unmoved. "Here are the numbers for the launch."

He tosses a spreadsheet on the bar in front of me and it lands in a drop of water, the top corner shriveling like my good mood. I wish he wouldn't do this here. He has a fucking office with a door.

At least Em's the only one here as I climb onto a stool and set my crutches against the bar, scooping up the paper. Wes watches me read the columns, sorting the numbers slowly so they don't evaporate into my brain. I know he does this on purpose. He could bullet it for me, give me the info he knows I want, but he keeps control where he can. Always has.

When we were kids, it was trading chores in exchange for him doing my math homework so I wouldn't get benched from hockey. He'd make a point to keep my grade just barely passing. If I'd come home with any higher, he reasoned, no one would buy it. Now that we work together, it's this shit. The little reminders of why I need him.

Focusing on the bolded numbers at the bottom, I note they're all black, every single one, and this part I understand. "Looks like we live to see another day."

Wes leans back on the stool and crosses his arms. "That was never in question. It's how well we want to live that's up for debate."

"I think we have different ideas on what living well means, bro." I fold the paper in half, tucking it in the pocket of my hoodie. I'll go over the lines later when I can focus. "There's something to be said for making a decent living while staying local, true to your roots."

Wes rolls his eyes. "Stay broke for the pride of it all. How noble of you."

"We're hardly broke."

"We could be a lot richer."

"We don't have to make *Forbes* to be successful, Wes. If we can maintain what we have, I'd call it a win."

He huffs. "You would, Jameson."

"What's that mean?"

"It's just telling where you place your bar for success is all."

The throbbing in my head settles behind my eyes, and I press my palms there. There goes all of the relief I got from Noel last night. *Didn't I just say I wasn't going to get into it with him?*

Em clears her throat. She plays the de facto referee between the two of us enough that she can sense we've turned an unpleasant corner. "Speaking of the launch, Jamie. The woman whose drinks you were buying that night—is she the Kelly rebound?"

Shit. If Em was trying to steer Wes and I away from an argument, bringing up Noel was a wrong turn. I haven't told Wes that she's back in town for a reason. He's not going to like my plan to spend time with her in hopes of another tip, and I'm not going to like whatever he chooses to say about it.

"I don't need to rebound from Kelly," I say, hoping that will be the end of it.

Em's smile tells me it's not. "I haven't seen this one before. She's not one of your usual groupies."

I frisbee-toss a cardboard coaster at her. "Her name's Noel. She's an... old friend."

Wes's eyebrows do a slow ascent to his hairline. *Fucking Em.* "I'm assuming this is the Noel I think it is."

"One in the same," I admit. I've smartened up in the last five minutes, though, so I'm not telling either of them that she was at my apartment last night, or that I'm seeing her later today.

"How did you get back in contact with her?" Wes asks.

The hazy, concussed memory of Noel staring down at my broken body comes back to me. The way I was sure I was dead. "Weird coincidence."

Wes huffs a laugh that grates at me. "I suppose you still think she's some magical angel from destiny land because she warned you about Becs."

The careless way he says this hits my stomach like a punch. That's the thing about working with family, everything is personal even when it's not. Like a secret hand signal only we understand, Wes knows bringing up Becca is the quickest way to remind me of my biggest shortcoming—misreading a situation, getting important things really fucking wrong. That's why I can't rest on the courage of my conviction about declining this offer from NEBev. He's reminding me that my conviction has a piss poor track record.

"Wait," Em says, her eyes going wide. "That was the girl from the party? The psychic?"

I give her *drop it* eyes but she either doesn't notice or doesn't care. "All the times I've heard this story and you never mentioned she's freaking gorgeous? No wonder you've been obsessed with her for two years."

"I wasn't obsessed with her," I fire back. *Okay, maybe a little.* Maybe I spent more time thinking about her than made sense, given the briefness of our first meeting, and maybe those thoughts weren't always *business* related. Em's making it sound creepy, though. It's not like I built a shrine to her in my loft, sacrificing shots of Jäger to summon her back. I was just... intrigued. Who wouldn't be in my position? She gave me everything good that I have. It would be impossible not to hold affection for her. That's the extent of it.

Or it used to be. It was a lot easier to remind myself that I know better when she wasn't right in front of me.

For a woman who boldly demanded a shot in exchange for a moment of her time, Noel's adorably awkward—sitting all prim and proper at breakfast, fingers twisting in her skirt. And last night, those apple-round cheeks with their easy blush that's becoming my new favorite game, her bare thigh touching me every time she moved. My daydreams about the girl from the roof and her pretty smile had nothing on the real thing.

I look up to see Em's mouth curl up on one side, slowly like a cartoon villain.

"What?"

"Your face."

"What about my face?"

"You're sleeping with her. Damn, I thought sitting on a bar stool in your condition was a bad idea, but that has to be in the 'no' column in your discharge instructions."

"I am *not* sleeping with her." *What the hell had my face been doing?* I gesture to my crutches to sell my story. Which is completely true and doesn't need much selling. "I'm not really up to dating right now, Em."

She gasps. "Jameson Bishop, think of your fans!"

"Knock it off." I say it casually but it feels like there's a spotlight suddenly shining on me.

"Whatever," Em says. "You always get the cute ones first, Jamie. Maybe that bruise on your face will put us on an even playing field."

"You wish," I shoot back. "And it's not like that."

"Then what is it like, Jamie?" Wes asks. "I mean, you have enough friends to keep you company, so if you're not trying to sleep with her..." His eyes narrow as if he's reading something on my face. "Christ, you want her to do it again, don't you?"

"It has nothing to do with that," I snap, because lying to Wes is easier than winning an argument with him. We don't see eye to eye on a lot, and choosing my battles is pretty key to our working relationship.

The only problem with that is I'm a shit liar, and Wes knows it. "Bull shit," he says. "I know how much you believe all this nonsense. There's no other reason she would be here."

I turn on my stool and grab my crutches. "This really isn't any of your business, Wes."

That was the wrong choice of words. His nostrils flare like a bull. "I think it is my business if it has to do with *this* business. Do you remember what my dad told you when he picked you up from County that night, Jamie?"

I hate when Wes brings up that night like it's some pivotal moment from a TV drama. The screw-up gets scared straight. For the record, Wes was at that party too. It was sheer luck he ditched out before it got busted up. I've never seen anyone so relieved as Wes's dad when he got downtown and found out it was just "Laura's boy" sitting in a cement cell, not his real son.

"I remember that night well," I say. "Thanks."

He continues anyway. "He said if you've always got your head in the clouds, you're bound to step in some shit. It's time to be a grown up, Jamie. We don't make business decisions this way anymore. Not while I'm around." With that, he spins on his heel and takes off for his office.

At least this time there's no confusing things. I've definitely just made things worse.

Thirteen

"IS THIS ONE A date?" Kate asks. "Because this one feels like a date."

I set my phone on the bathroom counter so I can still see her while I gather my hair into a ponytail. Then drop it. Then gather it again. My hands are clumsy. Not exactly shaking, but I wouldn't trust myself with a paint brush at the moment either.

"It's not a date," I say, scooping my hair again.

"Right. I should have known by how casual you're being about it."

"The problem—" I explain around the hair elastic between my teeth, "—is that I would know how to act if it were a date." I drop my hair again, my shoulders sagging. "But advice on hanging out with a guy who hopes you'll give him a psychic business tip, but who also might be your soulmate is surprisingly sparse."

Kate hums. "Did you check Reddit?"

"First."

"Damn, where's Dear Abby when you need her?"

"Dead, I think."

"So where are you going?"

"I have no idea. He wouldn't tell me." Last night when I left Jamie's loft, he'd only said he had somewhere he wanted to take me, and to be ready by noon. I give my outfit one more look in the mirror—a pair of cut-offs and my hand painted Chucks, a vintage Matchbox 20 tee. Also makeup and perfume, but I'll deny it in the interrogation.

"Wow," Kate says.

"What?"

"Nothing, I'm just remembering the time we went to Boston to see *Hamilton* and you made me send a schematic of the parking garage so you could 'plan ahead.'" She makes air quotes and I flip her off.

"I'm taking Colin's advice. Trusting the universe." Which is *so* something that shouldn't come out of my mouth, so of course Kate doesn't buy it.

"Oh my God."

"What?"

"You like him!"

I turn away from the phone so she doesn't see the pink flaring on my cheekbones. I hate being called out. Having to admit something before I'm sure it won't come back around swinging.

I do like him. Which, I suppose shouldn't be *that* surprising given what I've seen in the visions, but I didn't anticipate that it would be this easy. That I'd go from tolerating this arrangement to looking forward to it. After the massage and the movie that followed, both of which I'm conveniently not mentioning, I'd felt newly light despite all of the then-cold Thai food I consumed. I'd left wanting more of it. The company, yes, but specifically his.

And I woke up this morning with these clumsy hands and a distinct slick of sweat at my hairline.

The pressure of Jamie possibly being my destiny is overwhelming. If I like him the way I think I might, I'll have to admit how much of my future is out of my control, which is terrifying. But if it ends up going south now, it will be a sign that there is no fate, and the world is the big ball of chaos I thought it was, which is just a different shade of terrifying. Normal date jitters truly have nothing on this situation Jamie and I find ourselves in.

Or, I suppose, it's only me who finds myself here. My claim on Jamie exists only in the ether at this point. All of this is an exploration that he has no idea he's even participating in, and I have no evidence that what I saw between us is even something he's thinking about. At least not as much as the psychic tip he wants from me.

My shoulders sink and I pull my lip between my teeth. "Please be nice to me," I beg Kate. "This is already so far out of my comfort zone."

"Okay, okay," Kate says in that calming tone she's used since we were kids. "Look, all I'm saying is I'm proud that it didn't instantly occur to you to freak out about this. In fact, one might even call it a sign."

"Cow," Jamie says, pointing out my window as we cruise down a sun-bleached country road. My head swivels just in time to catch a reddish-brown dairy cow standing in a field, and my grin splits. We're in a pickup truck today with Fortune Brewing emblazoned on the side, headed west out of the city. About twenty minutes into the drive, the houses and storefronts started to melt into rolling hills and trees with their tips turning gold. That's when he'd challenged me to this cow-spotting game.

"I think you have them plotted on a map."

He grins, but doesn't deny it. He has on one of his tight-fitting T-shirts that makes his inked biceps look obscene, and the baseball cap I'm beginning to think is his signature sits high on his forehead like he accidentally knocked it askew batting away a mosquito or a swooping seagull and didn't bother to fix it.

Forcing myself not to straighten it is a good distraction from the dark stubble that's been filling in on his jaw since yesterday, the way it changes his face to something a little more in line with the mystery of this whole thing.

Eventually, we turn down a winding dirt driveway. Open fields line either side and Jamie pulls to a stop in front of the single, white sided building occupying a swath of land that rolls as far as I can see.

"What is this place?"

"It's a farm," he says, killing the engine and unbuckling.

I sit up taller, scanning the fields for a duck or sheep or some other cute animal I might get to pet, but it's just hills of green. "What kind of farm?"

"Hops." His grin explodes. I don't really know what hops are, except that they go in beer, but he's clearly happy to be here and my veins start to fizz in secondhand excitement.

Jamie pulls a backpack from behind his seat and climbs out of the truck. He comes around to my side, offering me a hand down. My sneakers hit the gravel, landing toe to toe with his boots. Not the rubber ones from the silly picture he sent, but dark brown work boots, water stains on the toe.

The night at his bar, his hair was styled with product, jeans designer label, and the sneakers he wore to breakfast had been very expensive. This, I think, is a little glimpse into Work Jamie. I'd be hard-pressed to pick a favorite.

"You look like a brewer today," I say, nervously tightening the ribbon in the ponytail I'd finally decided on. A farm might be the only place he could have taken me where I'd be over-dressed.

His cheek hitches up. "What did I look like before?"

A Nike model, I stop myself from saying. "Just, you know, a guy."

"Bishop." A bearded man in a John Deer hat heads our way, hands in the pockets of a pair of brown coveralls. He greets Jamie with a genuine smile and shoulder-slapping handshake.

"Hey, Ronnie. Long time, man."

Ronnie pats his round belly. "Had to lay off the ale for a while. Get my summer bod in shape. Good thing winter's coming, because I'm thirsty."

"I think I can help you out with that," Jamie says, laughing. "This is Noel."

"Well, hello." Ronnie holds a meaty hand out. His eyes roam me curiously as we shake, and I wonder how many of Jamie's friends know about our history.

"Nice to meet you, Ronnie."

"I was going to take a last look before harvest if that's okay," Jamie says with a hand to my lower back.

Ronnie nods. "Of course. Go take a gander at your be-trothed plants."

I wave goodbye to Ronnie, and Jamie leads us around the barn, over a small hill, up to the edge of what looks like a tunnel of foliage, the walls twice as tall as him. The green is so vibrant, I immediately want to try to recreate it with paint. The urge catches me off guard, like a friend I hadn't expected to run into, and I press a palm to my chest, trying to physically keep it from disappearing again.

"This is gorgeous."

Jamie's eyes light at my reaction, as if he'd been hoping for it. "Watch your step," he says, as the ground dips, taking us straight into the mouth of this thing. The plants climb up a simple string grid, where they're led overhead in a canopy. Vines trail from the sky like tendrils of Demeter's hair, and they're dotted with pine cone-like flowers in the same green, odd little things. I recognize them immediately.

"These are in the wreath on your logo and..." I reach for the sleeve of his T-shirt, pulling it up. The same wreath wraps around the thickest part of his bicep, drawn in black. "In your tattoo."

"The tattoo came first," he says, grinning as if he somehow manifested his own destiny by marking himself this way. I can't bring myself to argue with any of these possibilities anymore.

I touch a fingertip to one of the ink strokes, tracing it. I can't help myself. They're lovely. It's done in all black like the birds on his other arm, but with a lighter line. And the detail! Each petal seems to lift right off of his skin. "I didn't know hops plants flowered," I say, looking up to see him watching me, lips slightly parted.

"It's not a typical looking flower," he says, swallowing, "but yeah. They do." Sunlight filters in through the greenery, dappling his face as he reaches for one of the plants above us. Under the leaves and backlit like this, he's almost painfully gorgeous.

"Flowers are kind of my thing," I say, stretching to touch one myself. "Botanicals."

"Yeah?" He drops the backpack and pulls a fleece blanket from inside, watching me for more.

"My Nana used to have these beautiful gardens behind the cottage, mostly native flowers. It's the first thing I learned to sketch. Now they're pretty much all I paint."

She also kept fresh cut flowers in Mason jars all over the house. It was my job to change the water every few days and pluck the spent petals of white peonies and orange lilies. At night I'd sit at the kitchen table with my sketchbook and draw her bouquets by lamp light, teaching myself how to shade and show dimension.

Nana would putter around me, fixing dinner, poking her head over my shoulder. She was an artist too, and she had the ability to spot the most interesting details—a speck of pollen ready to fall, the deep pink vein in a white peony petal—and she'd point at it silently, draw my eye to it.

"Is that what you were working on," Jamie asks, tagging my attention back to the moment. "This weekend?"

I shake my head. "I haven't had much time to paint lately." Six months, to be exact. That was the last time I took out my watercolors.

"I'd like to see them. Your flowers." I drop the pinecone and turn to see him looking down at me earnestly, like it's the honest to God's truth, not just the polite thing to say.

I imagine flipping through my watercolor book with him or showing him my abandoned Etsy shop where I've uploaded some of my designs for stationary and digital downloads. It had a brief spark of success in the early days, but then Nana had her stroke, and I set it aside to take on more work with Vi. It's been my little secret since then. A labor of love that I've been reluctant to take any further in case I get attached. "Yeah," I say. "Maybe."

Jamie sits gingerly on the blanket, and I drop down beside him a little closer than I did on his couch. There's something inherently romantic about this place. I tip my head back and slide my eyes to his profile. "Why'd you want to come here?"

"I had to look at my plants." He says this with feigned

innocence, and I nudge him with my knee.

"Tell me."

"The brewery is my second favorite place. The taproom is my third. This is my first." He nudges me back. "And I thought you might like it."

I smile down at my shoes, relieved he didn't say something like: *I wanted you to wander around in this field and see if you get struck by a vision.*

Not that he couldn't. That's what I signed up for, but... I'm glad he didn't.

I look again at the vibrant green, thinking of the way I might capture it. There's no way he could have known the effect this place would have had on me. But he thought I might like it.

"I love it," I whisper.

"The harvest is tomorrow. All of this will be gone."

"What?" I cry, and he chuckles.

"Everything has its season, flower girl. And next season, we get to drink it."

"Huh." I'm still not sure how these quirky little flowers become beer. "It smells like a pine forest," I say, "... but also fruit salad?"

"Good nose." Reaching behind him, he plucks one of the flowers, pinching it between his finger and thumb before holding it up for me to smell. "It's grapefruit. These hops are what we use for our IPA and our summer blonde. The beer you had the other night, my fall ale, uses a different plant. There's less fruit scent in that one. More spice. Still has the pine."

He takes the flower back and squishes it again. I watch, entranced by the way the delicate nubs roll between the pads of his fingers. "Let me see your hand."

I oblige, holding my arm out, and he presses the two fingers he just held the flower with to the thin skin on my inner wrist.

"Some people use the oils for a natural anxiety reliever,"

he says. "Or they'll put dried plants under their pillow to help them sleep. I've tried it, actually. It works." He lifts my wrist to my nose. "Smell."

My eyes fall closed, and I take a long pull of the fragrant oil. I feel it too, a natural calm hitting my veins. "Do you have trouble sleeping?"

He shrugs. "Sometimes. I have a lot of energy. That's why I don't mind working until two a.m. every night."

"God. I'm tired just thinking about that."

He chuckles, and I think of the mismatch I originally saw in the two of us. Sitting together admiring his flowers, though, it feels more like complimentary colors. A yin and a yang.

"Back in the early nineteenth century," he says, "hops farmers used to have trouble staying awake for a full day of work. That's how they discovered the plant could be used that way."

I laugh delightedly, picturing a field full of grown men, napping in the sun like cats.

Jamie seems to notice he's still holding my wrist, a fact I've been acutely aware of, but instead of letting go, he pulls it to his face, pressing it under his own nose. His lip rests against my wrist bone, stubble scratching. Heat flushes through my body, a whip of it right through my center. I imagine that scratch on other sensitive skin, the heat of his breath, and it's a bit of a jolt that my mind goes there so easily.

Though, I suppose when you've already seen yourself naked with someone.

This is So. Freaking. Weird.

Jamie lets his eyes roll back and pretends to pass out on my shoulder, his fake snore blessedly breaking the tension.

I shrug him off, embarrassing myself with another one of these girlish giggles I can't seem to control.

"How did you learn about all of this stuff?"

"Ronnie and I used to bounce downtown together," he says,

tossing the pinecone flower from hand to hand. "That's how we met."

"Bounce?"

"Like, man the door at the bar. Check IDs."

"You were the muscle?" I cover my laugh with the back of my hand. "With those dimples?"

He scrunches his nose and proves my point. "I'm six-four. I'm very intimidating."

It's not his build—his height is unmissable, and he has thick hockey player thighs, and the sculpted arms of a man used to hauling kegs. Physically, I would trust him to intervene in a bar scuffle. It's more that I can't imagine him having the temperament. It would be like choosing a Golden Retriever puppy for a guard dog.

"You're more adorable than intimidating." I say. "I can't see it."

"Adorable, huh?" He flashes me a grin I've labeled the Jamie Smile. It's three parts sex and one part that boyish mischief from before. I dedicated my childhood to avoiding mischief. I was the mischief police from age nine to nineteen. Why do I like this hint of it on him?

"Don't let it go to your head."

He's laughing as he stretches out his other leg, then lowers himself onto his back, staring up at the canopy, and it's with a burst of courage that I do it too, sinking down until we're shoulder to shoulder, our heads in the grass.

"Adorableness aside," he says. "I wanted to learn the industry, and I had no experience, so I started there. Some nights were pretty slow, and we'd basically get paid to stand there and geek out about beer for a few hours. I got moved to bartending pretty quickly, though. It's where I met most of the people who would give me a chance later when I started brewing my own stuff."

Huh. Most beer guys I've met are nerdier, scientists at heart. Jamie strikes me as a party guy who figured out how to make a living at it.

"That's creative," I say. "And smart."

He turns his head and there's surprise there, like maybe people don't often notice this. Little does he know I'm on a mission to notice everything about him, prop his pieces up and study them in the light of what I know about us: That we might be destined.

Despite the fact that having my brain hijacked is still not something I'm looking forward to, a small part of me starts to hope that I'll be able to give him what he wants. That I'll see something to help him. He's passionate about this. I think it would make me want to root for him even if I wasn't there for the inception of this whole thing. Even if he hadn't asked me to help him with the future of it.

We fall into that same surprisingly comfortable silence as last night, staring up at his flowers. The vines sway softly in the breeze, and I sigh contentedly. A flower farm. How could he possibly have known how much I would love this place?

I wish I could keep one, put it in a jar in the cottage. I don't know how it works, though. Maybe he has to pay for them or something. Maybe each one is important and it's a big ask.

Jamie sees me chewing my lip and grins.

"What?"

"You're looking at that plant like you want to take it to bed."

"I'm not!" My cheeks scream pink.

He holds his finger and thumb an inch apart. "A little."

I glance at his too-handsome-to-look-at face. Then away. Then back. His grin is easy and open, and I'm suddenly braver than I was just before it.

"Can I have one?" I ask. "To paint? I mean if it's not a problem."

That grin births the most beautiful laugh. "Why would it be a problem?"

"I don't know!" I laugh back.

Jamie gets to his feet, reaching up to cup a pinecone flower in his hand, weighing it like he's choosing something precious. He tests another few before deciding on one directly overhead. Once he's plucked it, he chooses a few more, handing me the miniature bouquet. I pull it to my nose, and my eyes fall closed. Affection pools warm and low in my belly, and for the first time in a long time, I feel some of that color coming back.

It's all over my face when we get back to Jamie's truck, that color. He's outside of the barn saying goodbye to Ronnie, and I wait for him in the cab, staring at my reflection in the side mirror. My hair is tangled from the windy ride in, the last of my highlights catching gold in the afternoon light. My cheeks are colored from the sun. The lipstick I put on for this non-date is gone, but my lips are still a bright pink. I feel like an indoor plant that's been set out on the porch for the afternoon. Revived. Vibrant.

I slide my gaze to Jamie. His hat is backward now, shirt stretched across his broad shoulders. *Okay, yeah*, I say to the imaginary Kate in my head. *I like him.*

He turns toward the truck, and I jerk my head forward, pretending to adjust the visor while he climbs in. "Sorry about that."

"It's fine."

"Are you ready?" he asks, pressing the ignition.

I twirl the stems of my flowers between my fingers. "Yes and no. I kind of want to live here, take naps under the plants."

He laughs. "You might rethink that when they're under a foot of snow."

I'll be back in Connecticut when the snow comes. The thought comes like a pin prick to a balloon, and I sink back into my seat.

I remember that bitter feeling I'd get as a kid, whenever August would wind down and my time here would end. Knowing that for the next nine months I'd ache for my favorite place, my favorite parts of myself that seemed to fade out like a bad connection the further away from Nana's I got. I wasn't sure I'd find much of that to cling to here without her, but the idea of *this* trip ending soon suddenly fills me with that same longing.

Not in any small part because of the man beside me. A man who I'd initially been afraid of, then curious about, and now find myself... very fond of.

"Thanks for taking me here, Jamie."

He looks over, eyes soft, and for a moment so quick I almost miss it, they settle on my mouth. That thing I saw between us, I think maybe we're both thinking about it after all.

He sets his hand over mine, squeezing affectionately in response, and there's a flip in my stomach that was a lot easier to ignore yesterday. Yesterday, I was afraid of that touch. Now I find myself imagining what would happen if I didn't let go.

He does let go, though, because *obviously*. He wraps his fingers around the gear shifter, leaving my skin too cool and my brain conjuring the vision of that hand sweeping over my shoulder and down beneath the sheet. Big palms. Clean, short fingernails. Just like I remember.

Except... There's something new. I lean forward for a closer look. It's a crescent moon shaped scar below his knuckles. It's purply-red against his fair skin, and spans the whole back of his hand. Impossible to miss.

"How did you get this scar?" I ask, pointing.

He glances at it as he pulls away from the farm. "Cut it on a broken pint glass."

"When?"

"The day I opened." He gives me a little smile. "Bled everywhere. Made for a rough time behind the bar. Good thing it took me a bit to get this popular."

I tilt my head, look at it again. So he got it after we met on the roof, and at the place he said he wouldn't have if not for that vision. But it wasn't there in the vision of us. I don't pretend to know how telling the future works, but that seems strange to me.

I decide that kind of detail is above my paygrade and cast my eyes out toward the windshield. We pull onto the main road, passing a sugar maple turning yellow, the color slowly seeping into it too.

"Jamie?"

"Hmm?"

I suck in a breath for bravery and remember the safety net of knowing the future. "Do you want to hang out again tomorrow?"

He looks at me with that full smile, and it's like a rogue wave engulfing me. I'm completely sunk. "Yeah," he says. "I do."

Thank you, universe.

Fourteen

Noel

T HE MORNING AFTER THE farm, I wake like a Disney princess—eyes bright, cheeks flushed, snoring cat curled on my belly.

I displace Pixie, despite her best attempts to cling to my tank top, and push open the curtains in the loft. Even the sun seems game to be part of my fairytale morning. I gather my tea cup from the nightstand and pad down the stairs in bare feet to greet the mess I left on the counter last night.

As soon as Jamie dropped me off, I rushed inside and searched the cupboards for one of Nana's Mason jars for my little hops bouquet. Nana went through a purge phase after she was diagnosed with kidney disease, the condition that eventually led to her stroke. She donated boxes and boxes of things, then inexplicably adopted a kitten.

"I don't need stuff," she said, holding Pix like an infant and spoiling her forever. "I need life."

"Sure, Nana," I replied. It was the last day of my visit that year, and I'd been searching closets for her fall coat before I left, only to discover it had apparently not made the cut. "But you might need some of the stuff."

The jars, sadly, must have also not made the cut. So instead, I rummaged through the cabinets until I found a mug that read The Cards Say Coffee with a picture of a tarot deck, and stuck the stems in that. It was unexpectedly perfect, Jamie's odd little flowers in Nana's silly mug.

Now, here they sit surrounded by my pencils and loose leaf sketching paper.

The pinecones had opened up a bit by the time I got them home and into the water. Their huge heads tipping over the side of the cup, like fish jumping out of a pond. I placed them in the center of the breakfast bar, inspecting the petals, looking for the ones that stood out the way Nana taught me.

I'd been so eager to paint the flowers that I quickly changed into pajama pants, threw together a ham and cheese sandwich for dinner, and started sketching in between bites. I did one rendering in charcoal and one in pencil, each from different angles. Then I took my sketchbook to the couch, snuggled up with one of Nana's quilts on my lap, and played around with some other flowers. Blooms I can sketch from memory because I've been going back to them since I was a child. Pansies, peonies, beach roses.

I started sketching when I was eight, and it became a nightly routine all the way through to adulthood. The way some people read before bed, I'd pick a flower and draw it. If I was tired, it would be no more than a doodle, a cartoonish sunflower or a carnation with an oversized head. If I had more energy, I might end up with something that I'd save. Something I could digitize and play around with to make a pattern or a greeting card. Those late night sketches are where most of my inventory came from when I built that Etsy shop.

Last night I was afraid picking up my pencil again would feel the way it has for months, like bleeding a stone, but instead it just flowed out of me. And it lit something deep inside of my chest, a spark I've been trying to make catch. It caught so hard that I stayed up past midnight for the first time in years just drawing for fun. Cultivating a garden of charcoal blooms.

But that's not what I wanted Jamie's flowers for. I wanted them for the color. The unique green that I really want to master, and that's what I plan to do today.

I haven't even unpacked my paints yet. They're sitting in a small plastic tote in the mudroom, beneath a duffle bag stuffed with shoes, and I lug the box into the kitchen, unwrapping the paint pots one by one on the little two-top table. I'll have to find a way to shield them from the morning sun so they don't dry out, but they look like a flock of colorful birds all lined up there, and it makes me deliriously happy.

Next, I pull down another coffee mug and fill it with brushes, then a glass with pencils. I spin around, scanning the cottage for something to store my watercolor paper in where it won't accidentally get creased or have something spilled on it.

There. On the catch-all console near the front door, there's a two-pocket folder left for guests. Local menus, a list of emergency numbers—that sort of thing. I open the single drawer and dump all of the paperwork into it, then refill the folder with my paper. I stack my sketchbook on top of it and fit it at a right angle beside the paint, then stand back with my hands on my hips to survey the space.

It's a rag tag set up and it will be pretty damn inconvenient whenever I need to make a meal, but it's worth it.

I feel loose, even while my cheeks are tight with a mild burn from the sun yesterday.

I feel confused by this thing brewing with Jamie, but in a good way. A curious way.

And when I sit down to paint his weird little hops plants, I feel like it's maybe not an accident that I might be fated to a man with flowers on his skin.

By the time late afternoon hits, I've done two paintings that I'm happy with, and a third remains unfinished for another day. I'm cleaning brushes in the sink when my phone buzzes on the counter behind me. Jamie said he had a work meeting today, but after that he was all mine. I've been waiting like a giddy child for his call.

I quickly dry my hands and scoop it up, my chest buzzing like a jar of lightning bugs tipped over.

"Hey, you."

"Noel!"

The brush slips from my fingers, bouncing into the sink basin. "Mom? Um, hi."

I'm acutely aware of the way the smile I had tucked in my teeth drops. I've been waiting weeks for some sign that she's alive and not buried in the desert somewhere, but the weight of this conversation feels so much heavier on the heels of the first truly happy mood I've had in months. I consider brushing her off, telling her it's not a good time. A voice inside my head that sounds a lot like a cranky toddler reminds me that if she's calling, she's alive.

But I also know *alive* doesn't mean *well*. She was alive on her trip to St. John when she called from the TSA office after being detained for leaving her carry-on bag unattended beneath the seat at the bar. I need to hear for myself. "Where are you?"

"Wait," she says. "I meant to video call."

The request comes in and I accept it. Her smiling face fills the screen and she waves while panning the camera around. It's still midday there, and behind her is a panoramic view of copper-colored mountains.

"Isn't it pretty? We're somewhere north of San Diego."

"Most of the state is north of San Diego."

Mom leans against the side of the van, ignoring my tone. "How are you, sweetheart?"

"I'm fine. Normal as ever." Things are the opposite of normal, actually, but I'm not telling her that.

"Dennis wants to say hi." She turns, her voice muffled. "Wave, honey!"

In the background, her new friend lifts a hand to me while tossing pretzels to a flock of birds. Dennis Hammond: fifty-two-year-old, single white male from Las Vegas. Former Navy man, current hobby survivalist.

He's older than the last one. More broke too.

I wave back, but I'm nervous all over again. "How are things with him?" I ask, keeping my voice low, trying to suss out a look or a tone that will convey something true she doesn't want to admit. I could always read her. That's probably why she wanted to video call. She wants me to see it.

"They're great, honey! I did want to talk to you about something, though." *Finally. She's come to her senses and wants to come home.* I'm already making travel arrangements in my head.

"Sure, what's up?"

"The van is having a bit of engine trouble."

"Oh, do you need help booking a ticket home? Where is the nearest airport to you?" I turn toward my laptop, waking the screen.

"No. No." She laughs. "I'm not coming home. I was hoping maybe you could lend me some cash so we can get it fixed up? We still have so much to do, and the mechanic said we could drive it, but it would be a fifty-fifty chance of either making it to the next stop or getting stranded on a dark desert highway."

She starts twirling, humming the opening line from "Hotel California," always imagining herself as a character in a story. I wonder if she even realizes this one is about a drug-filled delusion.

"What exactly is wrong with the van?" I ask.

"Oh, I don't know. They told me, but it was Greek to me. You wouldn't believe how expensive everything is out here. I thought Connecticut was bad. Anyway, I wouldn't ask if I didn't need it. You know that."

My shoulders sink, though they have no right. I was hoping for a call and I knew it would be for something like this. I've never said no to her, so it's my own fault she feels entitled to it. And really, what kind of daughter would let her mother break down in the desert with Dennis?

"I'll Venmo you," I tell her, wincing on behalf of my bank account.

A strand of her hair blows in front of her sunglasses, and she wipes it away. "Thank you. I can always count on you. My beautiful daughter."

"Right." I swallow hard and turn to dump the water from my brushes down the sink. "So, after you're done in California..."

"Oh, who knows. I'm having the time of my life. It's so different from the East Coast. You should see the sunsets, Noel. The colors. It's magic."

"I've seen a sunset, Mom." I'm being a brat, but it's the word *magic* that pricks at me. I don't like it from her. Not when I'm currently chasing magic of my own. Just like I didn't like it when Jamie called my sabbatical an adventure—it's a reminder of the way I'm teetering on the edge of something I promised not to be.

"Honey, I have to go. Dennis wants to get to this rock and roll museum he read about on Trip Advisor before it closes. Or before the engine on this thing conks out. Talk soon, okay?"

"Wait. Can you give me a time when you'll call, Mom? We need to sort—"

"Of course, yes," she says, just as static appears on the line, distorting the promise. "Have fun at Nana's!"

The video stops and I let out a huff of frustration. What could her end game possibly be at this point? Does she honestly think this is her new life? She doesn't even have a job. She quit it to go on this trip.

I'm still staring at the blank screen when it lights with a text, and the pendulum swing of emotion nearly knocks me off my feet when I see Jamie's picture.

Right. Magic.

Jamie: I have an idea.

I know I'm not getting the details, so I send him an equally vague response.

Noel: ...

Jamie: I'll pick you up in half an hour.

There's a mess of paper and paint all over the kitchen, all over me. That won't work.

Noel: Give me a whole one?

Jamie: Deal.

Fifteen

Jamie

I T's HARD TO TOP **the farm**. That's what I tell myself as Noel and I make our way down an unusually busy Commercial Street, dodging tourists with laminated badges hanging around their necks. She's in front of me, walking single file so we can squeeze through the crowded sidewalk more easily, which means I can't even talk to her. This was not at all what I had in mind when I texted her.

Yesterday in my truck, when she'd asked if I wanted to hang out again, I'd put together a whole plan in my head. I thought we could walk the cobblestones, breathe in the fall ocean air. I figured there'd be a band playing on the deck of at least one of the waterfront restaurants, and I could buy her dinner, give myself the same bullshit "this is practically a business meeting" reminder while looking at her under the string lights and setting sun.

But my plan's been ruined by a cruise ship docked at the pier and a lighthouse tour bus that's stopped in town for lobster rolls. When the hostess at the third place we tried said it would be an hour for a table, she might as well have kicked me. We ended up splitting some poutine and a couple of sodas from the takeout counter of a seafood place.

If it had been a date, it would have been a pretty shitty one, and I'm starting to realize that might be the reason I'm so pissed about it.

Our path clears enough that I can step to her side again, tuck her between me and the buildings that line the water. "So, did you paint my hops?" I ask, shamelessly bringing up yesterday as a reminder that I'm still one for two in the good idea department.

"Mmhmm."

I want to ask her when I can see them, but there's a prickly edge to her tonight, something nervous and stiff. I haven't known her that long but in my job, you get to read people pretty well, and right now, normally sweet and timid Noel is a little pissy.

And I'm irrationally annoyed at the city for not somehow being on better behavior, as if everyone should part around us so I can stand as close to her as I'd hoped when I made this plan.

Another pedestrian decides to pass directly in between us instead of going around, and I feel myself start to approach the edge of my patience.

"Hey, hold up." I catch her elbow and gesture with my head for her to pull over. "This idea kind of sucks," I admit. "I'm sorry."

She blows out a breath in polite agreement. "It's okay."

"Do you want to do something else?"

She glances out at the water. "I am getting kind of cold."

"And kinda annoyed?"

She smiles, maybe the first one I've gotten out of her

tonight. "A little. But not at you."

Well, that's good news, but her confirmation that she's unhappy lands in the center of my chest.

"Me too," I tell her. "Here." I shrug off my hoodie and slide it over her shoulders. She clutches it closed.

"Thank you." This time when she smiles, her face melts into it's normal soft, sweet expression, and it renews my determination to fix this. Downtown was a bad idea, but it's not like I don't know this city like the back of my hand. I should be able to come up with an alternate plan.

"Maybe we should—"

I'm cut off from thinking out loud when, out over the water, the ship horn sounds, warning the passengers not to miss their call time. Noel and I both turn toward it, and just like that, my original idea gets a new setting—sunset, somewhere quieter. Just me and her.

"Can you see these ships from your house, Noel?"

"I think we could see these ships from space."

I remember watching them pull out of the harbor from the beach across from Bob's place, and I run it through my mental GPS, reverse it. "You know, you could probably see your house from here," I tell her. "If we were high enough."

She scrunches her nose. "There's no way."

My grin splits. "Only one way to find out. Come on. I know how we can get high enough."

"Absolutely not."

I laugh. "Come on, Noel. I promise it's safe."

When she aimed that skeptical look at me, I was hit with the compulsion to prove this to her. Not because I want to be right, I know I am, but because I think she'll get a kick out of it.

"Safe or not, it's illegal to climb a fire escape and—" She gestures wildly to the windows. "People will see us!"

"It's a commercial building. Everyone is gone for the night." One arm protecting my ribs, I kick over a couple of pallets that are leaning against the wall. "And it's only, like, misdemeanor illegal."

She gapes at me. "Only misdemeanor? *Only?*"

Biting my lip to keep from laughing again, I push the pallets into place with my foot, then climb up carefully. From here it's an easy reach to the extension ladder on the fire escape, and I pull it down with my left arm, then step back to the ground in front of her. "Ready?"

"This is why Fran doesn't like you, isn't it? This kind of stuff?"

"That's offensive. I've never even looked at Fran's fire escape," I say, but she's turning on her heel. "Wait." I catch her around her waist, laughing. "Come on. Don't you trust me?"

"Not particularly," she says, but she's already given herself away, relaxing against my chest, her arm covering mine where it wraps around her.

"Please?" I whisper it with my lips pressed to her hair, which is a sensation I'm not sure I'll ever get over. The softness of it. The floral scent pressed right into my olfactory system. "I promise it's safe."

Noel bites the tip of her thumb, looking back and forth between me and the iron steps. "Can we really see it?"

"Promise."

She closes her eyes and blows out a slow breath. I see the muscles in her neck and jaw tighten, then slowly go loose. "I am putting so much trust in you right now."

I know she is, and damn if it doesn't puff my chest right up.

"Alright, come on." I maneuver her forward, keeping my hand firmly on her hip for as long as I can. "Up you go."

"I have to go first?"

"This way I'm between you and the ground. Just in case."

Her eyes flare, then narrow when she sees my grin. I'm kidding her, of course. I'd never put her in danger.

I wait while she weighs it, prepared to abort this mission if she really puts her foot down, but eventually she starts climbing. When we get to the first landing, the air is noticeably cooler, tinged with salt. There's still a potent ache in my side when I fill my lungs, but I suck it in anyway. It's a small price to get this kind of oxygen hit.

In front of me, Noel's skirt flutters in the new breeze. "This better be worth it," she mutters. "My hamstrings haven't had this much action in a long while. Oh my God." She stops short, and I bump into her back. "Your knee must be killing you. *Jamie*!"

"It's fine. Better. We're almost there now, anyway. No sense in turning back."

She swallows and keeps going, but her grip on the railing has turned white-knuckled.

"Doing okay?"

"Fine."

"You sure?"

"Yes," she snaps, but she turns to look at me instead of where she's stepping, and her toe catches the next tread. She pitches forward.

"Woah." I grab for the railing with one hand and catch her with the other, pulling her tight against my chest.

"Oh my God. Oh my *God*."

"You're okay," I tell her. *Better than me*. I set my chin on her head and squeeze my eyes shut against the throbbing pain where her elbow caught my side.

"I almost fell to my death."

"You didn't."

"Why do you sound like that, then?" she demands. And yeah, I sound like I can't pull in a full breath because my vision is white with pain. My knee might be on the mend, but my ribs are still sore as hell, and that was a direct hit.

"This was a ridiculous idea. I don't know why I even—"

"Noel. I will concede the point, but I need a second. I'd rather not pass out this high off the ground."

"Oh," she says, looking over her shoulder. "Oh!" She spins toward me and claps a hand over her mouth.

"Fuck," I choke out, gripping the railings on either side of us and letting my head drop.

"Are you okay?"

"Yup." *Nope.* "I will be. Just gotta breathe through it for a second."

She seems to forget she's mad, fussing over me instead. She's two steps above me, and bent over like this, the top of my head is in her cleavage which is, quite frankly, confusing. I discovered that night on her porch that pain doesn't seem to dull my reaction to her, and it's fifty-fifty whether a pair of broken ribs are worth this little bit of concern she's showing me.

"You're a terrible patient," she says quietly. "Your doctor should fire you."

I laugh, then wince, and her fingers leave my forearm, brushing the hair off of my forehead where I've broken a sweat from the exertion of managing this much pain. The gesture is so sweet, so gentle, and my heart is lodged in my throat as I watch all of my laughable lies flutter away into the night air, the ones that involve this being some sort of business-related friendship.

If that were true, I wouldn't have been so irrationally angry about my failed dinner plans tonight. If that were true, I wouldn't be thinking about using what little bit of strength I have right now to kneel down in front of her on these steps and touch her as sweetly as she's touching me.

When she drags her nails lightly through my hair, like a dog wanting its belly scratched, I let my head fall into her palm. Something happens inside my chest that I haven't felt in years. A sensation like falling backwards on a trampoline and riding the momentum back up. It feels so good, and I am so fucking gone.

"Better?" she asks.

"I'll survive." My voice is scraped raw with an embarrassing amount of emotion. "Are *you* okay?" I ask when I've unfolded myself slowly, testing how much air I can pull in without pain.

She gives me the sweetest, guilty smile. "I think maybe I was okay the whole time."

"Maybe." I feel drunk as I reach for her ponytail, stroking my fingers through to the curled ends before giving it a quick, teasing squeeze. It's an indulgent risk, a spread of my cards face up on the table.

But when those big gold eyes meet mine again, wide and a little hazy, just like that, I'm reminded of the high of adrenaline that comes with doing something particularly risky. My blood rushes, and I see it like a flashing neon sign, the same thought that's been in the back of my head since she came back here: Noel and I were never going to be friends.

She swallows, then shivers. Then because she's ever responsible, she takes a deep breath through her nose and lets it out slowly, like a silent agreement that whatever we were both thinking would be better to revisit on solid ground.

"Are we going up or down?" I ask, and she pulls her lip between her teeth, looking over the railing. "It'll be worth it. I promise."

Nodding, she turns around and keeps climbing, steady and slow, but determined.

Don't look at her ass, Bishop. You do not get to look at her ass after that.

We make it to the top landing, and there's a gooseneck ladder there leading to the roof. Noel glances at it, then back at me. "I'm not going up that."

"This is high enough, but you have to come to the railing."

Her back is plastered against the brick wall, arms spread. "My heart is beating out of my chest."

"That's how you know it's worth it. Come on."

Slowly, she points her toe in front of her, then lets her heel drop. When it doesn't spontaneously go through the steel, she shifts her weight and takes a step. The landing is maybe four feet wide, so one and a half more and she'll get the view we came for. I put my hand out, and she eyes it with a teasing smile.

"Why do I feel like you're Peter Pan convincing me to go to Neverland? Oh, God, does that make me Tinkerbell?"

A laugh bursts from my chest making me clutch my side. "I see the resemblance. You've got her nose."

"Her *nose?*"

"It's true. It turns up at the end." I'd noticed it first thing, how cute her nose was—tipped up and freckled. I even had a recurring daydream of her doing the nose twitch like Samantha from *Bewitched* making all of my dreams come true. I drop my eyes to the little stud in her nostril, remembering it from that night, how it had flickered in the candlelight, and how I'd felt guilty for liking it that much.

"Anyway," I say, clearing my throat. "I think that analogy makes you Wendy, but either way, they were both in love with Peter." I bounce my eyebrows.

One eye roll and a few deep breaths later, she takes my

hand. I resist the urge to tug her toward me, instead letting her use me for leverage to do it herself. She finds the courage, putting one foot in front of the other two more times until she's beside me, and I take her hands and set them firmly on the railing. "See, you're fine," I tell her, shifting behind her, locking her in.

"I'm fine."

"Now look." I point across the water to where a small lighthouse blinks at us, and I know she's orienting herself when I feel her nod against my chest. "Look for the fishing shacks." Another nod. "To the right. There's the white church. Behind it, you can see that row of pine trees that abuts your road."

"I see it!"

"Look for the hip roof."

"Which one is mine?"

I have no idea. They're a blur of gray from here. But I give my best guess from memory of how many houses she is from the turn off. "Fifth one in?"

"Yeah," she whispers. "I think that's it."

Her head tips back, resting on my chest, and I feel like I've just been given an award. Despite the nagging ache in my side, I think this was my best idea to date.

Sixteen

Noel

J AMIE PUSHES THE LADDER back in place, and I watch shamelessly as he wipes his hands off on the back of his jeans.

He turns his head and catches me looking. My heart thuds twice in quick succession.

It's been beating erratically since that moment on the stairs, when he stood to his full height, my hand dropping from his hair, and stared at me like if we weren't three stories up and he wasn't nursing multiple injuries, I'd be on my back.

Another shiver runs through me, and I clutch his sweatshirt tighter. "So what's next, James Dean? A bank heist?"

He steps off of the stack of pallets, smirking. "That's a lot of snark coming from such a big smile."

I roll my eyes, but he's right. The agitation that was chugging in my blood after my mother's call has burned off like sea smoke, lost to a sunset that looked like a painting and a man just as beautiful.

He steps to my side, bumping me with his shoulder. "Want

to go for a drive?"

"Sure."

It's a few blocks back to Fortune where he's parked in the back lot. His car is new and spaceship-like. Fancy enough to convey success without flaunting it. Red and blue lights and scrolling messages light up the dash when he plugs in his phone. The cab has captured his scent and infused it into the air, salt and grass, and I breathe it into my lungs. If it's true what they say about pheromones, Jamie's are in full agreement with fate because my legs squeeze together involuntarily.

An Airborne Toxic Event song comes through the speakers, and Jamie steers us out of the city, over the drawbridge. He turns left at the end, heading toward the water, then makes a right, cutting through the community college. "Where are we going?"

"To the beach."

I pull my heels to the edge of my seat. "It's dark out."

"Lucky for us, it's still there even after the sun goes down."

"Funny."

He skips the public lot—though I suppose it would be closed anyway—instead pulling to a stop on a dark stretch of road, beneath a street light that flickers every so often.

Twenty-eight years of muscle memory have me tensing at this dark beach at night, but when he puts the car in park and looks at me with those deep, moody eyes. I'm sucked back into his forcefield. A forcefield that now involves a lot more touching than it did before. Touching that I want more of.

We leave the car on the side of the road, and I take his hand, letting him lead me down a small embankment, through the overgrown dunegrass. The light from the street disappears as soon as we hit the sand, but a harvest moon sits low in the sky, making the water look like it's lit from below. There's not much beach with the tide in, and what's here is black and scattered with broken shells. Jamie kicks one with the toe of his sneaker.

"It's really dark down here," I say, my fingers squeezing his.

"Yeah. It's so the lighthouse doesn't get polluted with extra light."

I look out at the rock jetty that leads to Spring Point Ledge. Surf crashes against it violently. "No one knows where we are."

Jamie pulls to a stop, his head whipping around, eyes wide. "Shit. I'm sorry, I wasn't thinking. Of course you'd be nervous to be here with me—"

I shake my head quickly. "It's not you. I'm just nervous. Usually. As a rule."

He watches me for a minute, then digs his phone out of his pocket. Opening the camera, he twirls me around so my back is pressed to his front and extends his arm to snap a selfie of the two of us, his chin set on my head.

"What are you doing?" I laugh.

He types something over my head, then lowers the screen so I can see.

Jamie: Noel and I are at the boat launch.

"My friend Em," he says. I smile. He texted our picture to her.

She texts back immediately.

Em: I'm taking a piss. Good talk.

I giggle and let my weight relax into him, sighing when his arms wrap around me and squeeze the way they did earlier. "Let's keep going."

"You sure?"

I hold my hand out in reply, and he clasps it tight, leading us to a flat, dry spot. He sits down, and I lower myself beside him. I'll have sand in every crinkle of this skirt, but I don't care.

"Are you feeling better?" I ask.

"Yes. Thank you. Again. I think you saved me from permanent damage the other night on my couch." He tips his ears to his shoulders one by one. "How did you know how to fix my neck like that?"

I shrug knowing I didn't do much besides squeeze muscles I really wanted to touch. "Maybe I knew an exceptionally reckless man in another lifetime."

He laughs and drapes his forearms over his knees. "Do you believe in that? Other lifetimes?"

He's said it casually, but how can a question like that be casual when you're staring out at the ocean with a man who you might be fated to? I mean, if you believe in psychic visions, alternate timelines aren't a big stretch.

"I think one lifetime is enough to handle. If there are others, they'll have to exist without me considering them."

"I don't know," he says. "Sometimes one life seems like a lot. Other times, it feels like one shot at it isn't nearly enough."

"One shot at life?"

"Yeah. Especially when you spend so much of it with an undeveloped brain. Like if we only get ninety or so years on this ride, if we're lucky, we should get to start with the wisdom we need to make the most of it." He shifts his weight, and I move closer, daring to let my legs hang beside his.

"What about you?" he asks. "Maybe it's not a whole other lifetime, but would you change anything?"

I blow out a contemplative breath. The question seems magnified through the lens of things I know that Jamie doesn't, about us and the possibility that these visions are the result of some higher power giving me a chance to fix something I keep screwing up because I'm afraid.

"I had this little business a while back," I tell him. "With my art before Nana got sick. I turned my paintings into paper goods like planners, bookmarks, greeting cards. Invitations were my biggest seller. I even have one design that was licensed for a wallpaper—poppies."

"That's incredible."

I smile. "It was. Sometimes I think in another life, I'd do that."

"Why can't you do that in this life?"

I shrug and stare out at the water. "Savings, 401Ks, health insurance. Lots of reasons. Plus, my mother lives with me, so my finances aren't entirely my decision."

"I thought you said she lived in a van."

"Mmm. For now, she does." Until the engine dies and I run out of money to lend her.

"You shouldn't drop it if it's something you really want to do. When I was starting out, I bought my own insurance. Invested with a private firm. It's doable."

"It's risky."

"So is spending your life making someone else rich."

I shoot him a look, and he holds up a hand in apology. "Sorry. I'm overstepping. It's just a common debate between me and my brother."

"What is?"

"The, ah, business problem I have. It's just kind of a fight between us."

He's suddenly clammed up, his eyes darting away like he didn't mean to take this turn.

But we're here and I want to know what I'm missing in this agreement. I'm suddenly shocked at myself for not asking before, but I was preoccupied with my part. The part Jamie has no idea about. "What are you fighting with your brother about?"

He looks at me for a beat, then back out to the water. "I have an offer on the table to buy my brand," he says. "It's more money than I've ever seen, but it's in exchange for a piece of myself, something I want to keep. Wes thinks I should do it—sell out. I don't want to, so we're... debating."

Nerves start to percolate in my belly. "That's what you want my help with? That's a really big deal, Jamie."

"The last one was a really big deal too." He grins at me but I don't return it. "Look, I wasn't even going to tell you. I don't want it to freak you out."

"Kind of late." When he said he had a decision to make, I hadn't given it much thought, but I can see now that was a misstep.

Though, I suppose he's right. The last decision was a big deal too, but he didn't ask for my help with that one. It was an accident that I even saw what I saw. And the question he did ask, about Becca, well, I don't think he ever considered the answer wouldn't be the one he wanted.

This one, though, is huge and so is the pressure he assured me didn't exist.

He blows out a regretful breath. "It's just that Wes is the businessman, not me. I'm a hometown kid who likes beer. We both know I'm out of my depth."

His jaw goes tight, and I remember what he said at the bar that night. *This is the moment I prove myself or the moment they all find out I've never known what the hell I was doing.* I'm torn between the ratcheting anxiety in my chest, and a softening at that vulnerability.

"Imposter syndrome," I say.

"Huh?"

"It's called imposter syndrome. It means you don't believe you deserve to be in the place you are. Like you think one day everyone is going to find out you're a fraud who got here by some stroke of luck."

He half laughs, half groans.

"What?"

"That's exactly how I got here. A stroke of luck. Magic. Look, I have no idea what would have happened if you didn't tell me about the money, Noel, but I know the decisions that led me where I am weren't born from some shrewd business sense. Your vision told me what to do. I just followed it." He must see the way the blood drains from my face because he sighs. "Look, I'm sorry. I didn't mean to make this whole thing worse for you."

"No," I say, wrapping my arms around my knees. "It's fine." Maybe I should be concerned that Jamie's hoping for too much from this thing, but on the other hand, I trust this, or I wouldn't be here at all. The farm, the inspiration I feel returning, the way we are after such a short time—these are dominos falling into place. I know this better than Jamie, and somehow he's not the one who needs convincing.

"I must have spent hundreds of hours at this beach when I was a teenager," he says, stretching out his long legs.

I tilt my head to see him. "This spot in particular?"

"The cops don't come down here," he says, like a list of ways to evade the local police is something everyone keeps track of.

He laughs at my prissy little, "*Oh.*"

"And you can't see the fire from the road. That was important."

"That sounds disturbingly like 'no one can hear you scream.'"

He grins at my joke. His little mischief spot is unexpectedly romantic, and I stretch my legs out too, letting our knees brush, thinking of that look he gave me on the fire escape.

"Tell me you didn't swim here," I say. It's open ocean where we are. The water is frigid.

"Every summer."

I shake my head. "Ridiculous."

"One might say invigorating."

"Hmm. Well, I wouldn't know. I swam at the state park." It's a cove. The water is glass and probably a good five degrees warmer for its protection.

Jamie snorts, and I swing my eyes to him. "What?"

"Of course you did."

"What does that mean?" I kick his foot, pretending to be offended.

"Nothing, it's just your memories sound very touristy."

I bark a laugh. "Oh, you're *that* kind of townie, huh?"

"I'm just saying." He looks down at me, mischief sparking.

"I wasn't a tourist. I was a... summer resident."

"Same thing." He shrugs in a way that's clearly meant to get under my skin. It works.

"It most certainly is not."

"Prove it." He jumps to his feet. "Swim with me."

"What? In the *water*?"

"Hard to swim in sand."

Before I can argue, he's made quick work of the buttons on his overshirt. He shrugs it off, then, with barely a quick glance over his shoulder, and zero warning for me, he shoves his jeans down over his hips, stepping out of them as he walks.

I nearly swallow my tongue. He's standing there in a T-shirt and a pair of skintight, royal blue boxer briefs. They leave absolutely nothing to the imagination. When he gets in the water, they'll be wet and stuck to those thick, hockey player thighs and... everywhere else. I press a hand to my cheek.

"Someone's going to see you!" I shout after him. Though, I know that's not true.

He smiles over his shoulder like the devil himself. "Let 'em."

Of course, I take that as explicit permission to look at every magnificent inch of him. Wide shoulders, a slight bow to his legs. I remember that from the vision, how much I liked his body, or what I could see of it.

He has another tattoo on the back of his calf that I haven't seen yet—a line of pine trees that wrap around the muscle. His body is like a treasure hunt. There's a scar just below it, jagged and dark.

"Where'd you get that one?" I shout. "On your leg."

"The trees?"

"No, the scar."

He looks down. "Fell through a skylight when my buddies and I were on his parents' roof." When I gasp, he adds, "Not all the way through. Just my leg."

"You're a menace."

"Reformed."

I watch him walk into the frigid water of the Atlantic in October, and I seriously doubt it. I swear this man has changed my DNA, because it sends a thrill through me.

"Are you coming?" he asks.

Am I? This seems incredibly reckless swimming off this rocky beach, pitch dark water, but Jamie's standing there, looking at me with my favorite smile, all that skin beckoning me.

I'm getting to my feet before I even realize what I'm doing, brushing the sand from my thighs and walking toward him with my smile caught in my teeth. I shuck my skirt off as I go, then Jamie's hoodie and my sweater underneath it. When they fall to my feet, Jamie's eyes turn as black as the ocean.

Inside, my heart takes off in a canter, and so do I, running toward the surf. I squeal when my toes touch the water, but I keep going until I reach him. "You're crazy," I say, breathless from the cold water hitting the backs of my knees.

"Let's be crazy together, then." He's staring between us, biting his lip so hard I want to press my thumb there to check for blood.

"Okay." It's just a whisper, but it's enough for him to take the reins. He steps backward, water hitting the bottom of his boxers, darkening them, and when I follow, he smiles, sliding his hands over my shoulders, down to my waist, then back up, the hem of my tank top caught on his thumbs. Cold air hits my stomach, the bottom of my breasts, and my hips tilt toward his, seeking heat. He stops when my tank is up around my rib cage, pausing to let me decide the rest. It's an easy decision. I'm completely under this spell.

I take over, lifting the cotton over my breasts, and freeing my arms. Jamie takes it from me, casting a web of goosebumps over my skin as his eyes trail over me. I've worn a simple black bra. Cotton. But I'm not self-conscious. Fate promised me this man and I'd like to collect now, thankyouverymuch.

Jamie's eyes are hooded, lips slightly parted. He's so serious right now, tension thicker than the black water swirling between us.

I'm serious too when I tell him, "Your turn." And God that grin. It's my final undoing.

I help him roll his T-shirt up, running my fingers over each inch of skin as it's revealed to me. I've seen him shirtless, of course, in the vision and sitting in the hospital bed, but not where I could touch him, press my hand to flat muscles and soft hair.

We come together again, pulling in twin breaths as bare skin meets bare skin. A swell hits my butt cheeks and I gasp.

Jamie only laughs.

"The urge to splash you is very strong right now," I say through my chattering teeth.

He grins at me. "You won't do it. You're too sweet."

"Maybe I'm not as sweet as you think I am," I say, then immediately suck my lip between my teeth.

"If you're offering me a taste, Noel. I'm going to take it."

Woah.

I don't want to misread this because I think I know the future. But I'm also pretty sure I know the future. Even so, my heart goes berserk in my chest, and I remind myself what he said on the fire escape. That's how you know it's worth doing.

"I'm offering it," I say.

Jamie's eyes flare with something new. Some hunger I think may have been on a very short leash until now. He steps closer, and the moment seems to trip over itself like a die being thrown. Where will it land?

He slides his hand into my hair, then his thumb beneath my chin, tipping it toward him. My head falls back in enthusiastic agreement, but he doesn't take my mouth. No, the first time Jamie Bishop's lips touch my body is at my neck. The heat of his breath spills through me, straight down between my legs, and I whimper. He sucks once, dangerously, teeth right at my pulse point, then moves to my collarbone. Then, and this is the one that makes my knees go weak, the softest brush over my cheek.

He pulls back, leaving my mouth empty and my eyes clenched shut. When I finally pry them open, a violent shiver shakes my whole body like some embarrassing dance move I pulled out at the wrong moment, and Jamie tips his head back and laughs at the sky.

"Are we swimming?" he asks.

"Bastard."

"Come on. It'll be warmer once we go further." He lobs our shirts to the sand left-handed, and I follow on tiptoes, legs shaking. "Stay with me." It's a warning, another quick glimpse into a more serious side he keeps tucked away, and I appease it with a quick cross over my heart.

"I promise."

Satisfied, he turns toward the water, catching my hand on

the way. Ice splashes up my thighs but my heart is glowing warm. I let myself be pulled along, let myself look at him in the moonlight. The freckles on his back, the muscles in his shoulders that I felt on his couch the other night.

But then something else catches my attention, like a hook snaring a fish, and my smile slides.

Another tattoo, curling around his shoulder blade. It's beautiful. Blue ink, barely more than a pencil sketch in form but it has amazing detail. The artist in me wants a closer look, but the rest of me slows to a stop, confusion pressing behind my breastbone.

It didn't register at first. I was too caught up in his bare skin, buzzing too brightly at the adventure. Now, my stomach that was just doing little flips and leaps, starts to twist and turn sour.

It's different. The tattoo I saw in the vision of us. It's not there.

Jamie's arm pulls taut when I dig my feet in. He spins toward me. "You gotta stay with me, gorgeous. It's dark."

I stare back in response, words lost to the spinning in my brain. *How could this be? Am I remembering it wrong?*

But I know I'm not. I recognized the wreath on his bicep, the birds on his forearm. Those were the same.

Of course, I'd seen those in person, on the roof that night. But the freckles on his chest and stomach—I only knew of those from the vision, and there they are.

The tattoo is in the same spot—on his right shoulder blade—but it was words before. A quote maybe, or lyrics?

This artwork takes up a lot of real estate. There's no way I could have misremembered it. No matter what I told Jamie, I've thought about that night far too many times to get this huge thing wrong. Which means the vision was wrong.

"Noel. Are you coming?"

God, if he'd just leaned forward in that hospital bed, I would have seen this too.

I blink up to his face, suddenly freezing and way too aware of the dark. "No. Wait," I say. "I want to go back."

I rush back to shore, gathering my discarded clothing as I go. I don't understand what this means. I saw the future. How could I get this wrong?

Or maybe I didn't get it wrong. Maybe it changed. And if this can change, what about the rest of it?

The old me who spent two years debunking this entire thing finally found her first hole in all of this. But the *me* right now, the one who dashed into the ocean at night with a gorgeous man, who was starting to believe in magic and that maybe it was somehow on her side? That me's heart has slid out of her chest and pooled at her feet on this cold sand.

I feel like a tiny toy, batted around by some unknown force for entertainment. Shouldn't you have to agree to these kinds of cosmic interventions? Sign a waiver maybe? At least a mental health screening. God, what if this whole thing is really a mental breakdown after all?

Suddenly I see this entire scene from somewhere outside my body. A dark beach, a man I barely know. My eyes turned to stars.

Fate, a voice whispers. Then another, *Fool.*

Jamie's behind me in an instant. "Noe," he says, shortening my name in a way that feels too intimate now. "What's wrong? What happened?" He pulls me against his bare chest and rubs his hands over the goosebumps on my arms, giving me his warmth. God, he's not even shivering. He's acclimated to this wildness. I never belonged in it.

My teeth knock together violently. The water's too cold. It's too dark. We're not even supposed to be down here.

"I messed it up. That has to be it. Can that be it?"

"What could you have possibly messed up?"

I groan and step out of his grip. "I need to go home."

"What? Now?"

"Sorry, yeah. I'm just suddenly really tired."

Disappointment flashes over his face. "Well, can I see you tomorrow?"

"I don't know. I should probably focus on figuring out my—" I wave a hand near my head. "Mental block or whatever. That's why I'm here, right?"

Jamie watches me for a long moment, eyes bouncing around my face. It's cruel, this flimsy explanation I've given him. But it's hitting me like a punch to the face, how flimsy this was from the start. *Let's be friends and see what happens.*

I reach down to hold my sneaker still, balancing on one foot while I stuff the other inside, sand and all.

"Noel, if I did something..."

"You didn't." My ankle wobbles, and Jamie catches my arm, steadying me. I open my mouth to tell him some version of it's not him, it's me, but the words don't come because I'm distracted by light behind my eyelids.

Then a picture.

It was just a flash this time, not enough to tell what I was looking at, but enough to make my legs feel weak beneath me. "Shoot."

"What's wrong?" Jamie adjusts his grip, holding more of my weight.

"Nothing, I—" My brain starts to swim again. My God, I was practically feeling him up a few minutes ago, and nothing. Now this?

If I've learned anything, it's that fighting it makes it worse. The vision filters in, Jamie and me on a cobblestone street, people mulling around and bass coming from somewhere in the distance. He's wearing a beanie instead of the ball cap, long sleeves that hide his tattoos. It's a side street lit with lamp light, and it shines on his cheeks, red from the cold and under far more scruff than he has now.

He steps closer, pressing me against the wall of a building, an arm propped above my head. Then he leans in. People turn and smirk at the PDA. But I don't care, because the kiss that follows, it's not the kind of kiss that was about to happen back there. That kiss would have had lust behind it if our teasing words and the rough squeeze of his fingers was any indication.

This kiss I'm seeing now, it's tender. Intimate. It's the kind of kiss that feels like a confession.

With the slow contraction of darkness, it's over.

"Noel?" Jamie's voice sounds like it's underwater.

When I open my eyes, I'm leaning into his chest, my chin tipped to him the way it was in the vision, but my lower lip trembles.

God, I forgot how unnerving these things are. Even more reason why I shouldn't be playing with this. Colin said it wouldn't want to hurt me, well, he's never had his head possessed.

I step back, and Jamie just watches, his hands flexing like he's afraid to touch me again. "Please tell me what's wrong," he says, and his voice doesn't crack, but it's not steady either. Everything about this is unsteady.

"I'm just not feeling very adventurous anymore."

The muscles in his face fall, then quickly struggle for a smile. "Right," he says.

"I'm sorry."

Jamie turns to get his clothes. "Don't worry about it, Noe. This wasn't part of the deal. I get it."

You don't, I want to say. *You only know half of it.* But I know better than to say anything else to complicate this moment.

Seventeen

Jamie

A SLICE OF BRIGHT light beams across the television screen, obscuring my view of the movie I'm half watching, half using for company. I've been lying here long enough for the sun to round the top of my building and come at me from the west, which officially marks the end of the third day I've spent stewing on this couch.

I can't stop thinking about the beach and the way it took all of five minutes to go from my mouth at Noel's neck to her dropping my hand and *running* away from me.

If you're offering me a taste, I'm gonna take it.

I groan at the memory. "You're out of your mind, Bishop." I knew I was. But then color had crept up her neck, and I pictured myself tasting her there, biting a little. There was no coming back after that. And she'd said it. *I'm offering.*

Even now, the memory makes the front of my jeans tight and I reach down and adjust myself.

What the hell is wrong with me? Why can't I just accept

a thing is a bad idea and let it be? I've thought about Noel, wanted her, for two years, but talking to her like that, touching her like I did, I'm setting myself up for a big fall.

And yet, if she didn't run away, I would have turned backwards, closed my eyes, and let myself tip.

I forgot how vulnerable this type of thing makes me feel. I haven't cared about whether or not a woman liked me in a long time, not since everything imploded with Becca. The side of me that wants that kind of thing has learned his damn lesson, so I don't know why he insists on popping up again now.

Noel's leaving. I can spend every day with her, be stupid enough to cross my own lines, but at the end of the year, she's gone.

The thought feels like a foot on the center of my chest, and I sit up and rub at it.

I just can't help the feeling that if it weren't for that piece, the rest wouldn't be so insurmountable. There's a certain possessiveness that comes with being the only head Noel's been in. Despite the rules and boundaries I set for myself with women, it's hard to imagine a world where we don't explore that. Kissing her on that beach felt like we were just slotting into our rightful place. Like when you misthread the top of a jar at first, but then you hear that satisfying click when you set it right.

I push off the couch and head to the fridge, popping open an energy drink. Part of me wishes I could go back to when all I wanted out of this thing with Noel was a psychic tip. A favor. But even if I had the ability to rewind, I'd be hard-pressed to find a time when I wasn't into her beyond that, which is why this whole agreement was a stupid move in a long line of stupid moves.

The reports Wes gave me from the launch are still sitting

on the kitchen island, taunting me, and a sigh rips from my chest at the mental work it's going to take for me to decipher them. Half the time I just don't do it. I tell Wes I do, but in reality, I take his word for it. Lately, though, that feels like an in-my-face reminder of who I'm betting on if I buck Wes's advice and don't take this offer, so I force myself to sit on the stool and face the endless columns.

Unfortunately, that only starts a new loop of intrusive thoughts. *You're in over your head. You've never understood what it would take. You've been running an entire business on vibes and a vision from a drunk girl at a party.*

Fuck. I really miss her.

I really need to let this go.

And I have no idea how to even begin to do that.

I pop in my AirPods and put on the focus playlist I found online, but the train's pretty much off the rails by this point. Thoughts of Noel are like fingers at the back of my neck, drawing my attention away from any task I attempt.

My phone vibrates on the counter, and I grab for it, practically overjoyed at the distraction. I swipe my thumb across my phone screen to open a text from Greg. He's rounding people up to watch the Bruins at The Coppersmith. Em's already there, and the yeses and nos chime in from the rest of the guys. I quickly send a thumbs up emoji and grab my car keys.

It's a short drive across the bridge, and the guys have saved me a seat at our usual table in front of the television. I slide in between Em and Trev, already feeling better. Like I've emerged from the Noel-cave I've been in and into the sunlight.

"How's the recovery going?" Derek asks me when I pass on

a pint from the pitcher he's holding. "Any idea when you'll be back at hockey?"

"I'll make the end of the season."

Greg winces. "You must be bored out of your mind."

I know he feels like shit about breaking my ribs, so I try to summon a smile. "It's fine. A little rest never killed anyone."

Em snorts into her pint glass.

"What?"

"Is that what you're doing at the boat launch the other night with Noel? Resting? I bet there were a few other cars down there filled with people *resting*."

"Actually we were on the lighthouse side, and since I'm not seventeen, it wasn't fucking like that."

So much for getting my mind off of it.

Trev shakes his head. "Only Jamie Bishop could pick up a woman while sporting a black eye."

I ball up a napkin and toss it at him left-handed. Chase uses his goalie reflexes to bat it away before it hits a woman at the table behind him. Trev should talk. I'm pretty sure he was missing a front tooth when he met his wife Julia. He used to have a reputation for being borderline insane on the ice. Now he designs banking software. Also, my eye is nearly back to normal except for some yellowing around the cut.

"Nah," Chase says. "Women love a mysterious facial wound. He's probably doing better than ever."

"I didn't pick her up," I say with a little too much venom in my voice. It gets their attention. Though, now that I have it, the panic sets in. I *really* don't want to talk about this. The first time I mention a woman to these guys in years, and it's after I've already fucked it up.

I've backed myself into a corner, though. Trev rolls his hand to tell me to spit it out, and I clear my throat. "You remember the party a few years ago, with the fortune teller?"

"Not exactly something you forget, J." Chase chuckles but I'm not sure if it's with me or at me.

I tug at the collar of my hoodie. "Anyway, well, she's back in town and I..."

I what? *I guilted her into hanging out with me and now I'm dreaming about her mouth? I tried to kiss her and she ran away? I need her to tell me the future of my business, but now the only future I care about is whether I'm going to get to see her again?*

Fuck, what if I don't get to see her again?

A high-pitched squeal distracts me from the cold sweat creeping up my spine, and for a blessed second everyone's attention turns away from me. The women at the table beside ours are greeting two others who just arrived: A tall brunette in knee-high boots and a very familiar blonde who I last spoke to when she was declining to pick me up at the ER.

I tip my head back and groan at the ceiling. *Really?*

Em leans in, dropping her voice. "Is that—?"

"Yeah. It is." There's something almost cosmically on the nose about Kelly's timing, bursting into my line of sight while I'm trying to forget how stupidly hooked on Noel I am.

She spots me immediately, shuffling around chairs until she's beside mine. "Jamie?"

I tip my chin politely even though I'd rather have pretended not to see her. "Hey, Kel."

"Oh my God. What the hell happened to your face?"

I guess she forgot all about the other night when I called her from the hospital. "Hockey," I remind her.

"Oh." Her eyes slide over my chest then back up, her lip between her teeth. "Well, how's the rest of you?"

Then she drops herself into my lap, grabs my face with her manicure pressing painfully into the bruise she just comment-ed on, and kisses me.

One of my stepfathers used to talk about bell ring moments, where all of a sudden something becomes so clear to you that you can't believe what an absolute dumbass you were before that instant. As quickly as the very public proposition is out of her mouth, the first emotion Kelly has ever elicited from me hits me square in the chest. I'm pissed.

"What the fuck, Kel?" I stand up, dumping her back onto her high heels.

"What's wrong?" She looks genuinely confused which is even more embarrassing.

"We're not... This isn't." I lower my voice to a harsh whisper. "The last time we talked, you left me at the fucking ER."

"Jamie, come on." She tucks her hair behind her ear nervously. "We were never '*ride home from the hospital*' friends."

I glance at Em and the guys, the tips of my ears burning at the way they're watching me with various curious expressions. They know as well as I do that my reaction here isn't typical. I'm not even sure I have a right to it since it's exactly what I told Greg that night—*it's not that kind of relationship*—but for some reason it still feels like a slap of heat across my cheeks.

This would be easy, falling back into Kelly. I'd have to dust off my pride a little at the fact that she could totally ditch me when I needed her and I'd still be there with open arms, or an open invitation to my bed, but I could do it. It would hurt a hell of a lot less than the memory of Noel running away from me.

But it could also never feel as good as Noel taking care of me on my couch. Her hands in my hair on the fire escape. *Goddamn it.*

"That's a general human compassion kind of thing, Kel." I step around her, pulling out my wallet to toss some cash on the table for my share of the food that hasn't even come out yet. Greg can take it home to his kids. "I'm going to head out."

"Jamie," Em calls, catching up to me in the parking lot.

With my knee the way it is, I can't outrun her, so I reluctantly pull to a stop. "What?"

"That was shitty of her," she says, tipping her head in the general direction of the bar, and I know she heard Kelly say the thing about us not being "ride home from the hospital" friends.

Jesus, this day sucks. The last *three* days have sucked.

"Yeah. It was shitty," I say. An early fall drizzle has cropped up while we were inside, and I tip my face to the sky, imagining it washing away the last hour of my life. Unfortunately, when I open my eyes again, I'm still in this parking lot.

"What's going on here?" Em asks, staring at the side of my face.

"I think I'm having a moment."

"Should I call an ambulance?"

I shake my head. "No cure."

Em nods, tucking her hands in her coat pockets. "Is this about your psychic girlfriend?"

"Please stop."

"Come on, Jamie." She waves a hand at me. "I'm not wrong about that lovesick look on your face. You obviously like her."

I give my best derisive snort. *Of course* I like her. She's beautiful, and funny, and so fucking sweet I could get a cavity just looking at her. She's timid in a way that makes me want to wrap my arms around her and protect her from the world like goddamn Captain America, and when I'm not playing out superhero fantasies in my head, I'm thinking about taking her clothes off.

"Liking her isn't the problem," I say.

"Enlighten me then."

I mean to tell Em I don't want it, or I'm not looking for the complication. All my standard lines that I feed Greg and the guys on a regular basis, but instead what comes tumbling out of my mouth is, "I have no business with a woman like Noel. I'll just fuck it up."

I may have already, I just don't know how.

I admit I don't see it coming when Em's response is to drive her fist into my bicep. Hard.

"The fuck?"

"Why would you say that?"

"I'm injured, you demon."

"I barely touched you. What is your *problem*?"

I rub at the numbness in my arm. "I'm trying to be realistic."

"No, Jamie, you're being a coward. You're playing down on purpose so you don't fail. You've been doing it since we were kids, and it's starting to get real old."

I gape at her like a fish gulping air. "Taking that bartender's therapy license a little far, aren't you?" Em and I are close but typically we keep it pretty light. It's not like her to deliver advice that doesn't come cloaked in a joke.

From the look on her face, though, I'm *not* getting off with a joke. "Since you mentioned it, why are you behind the bar every night? You own the damn place."

"I like bartending. How did we get here?"

"Because it's the same damn thing. You feel comfortable bartending. And you're comfortable with the Kellys of the world because you think they can't hurt you." She flicks my shoulder. "How'd that work out, huh?"

"From one commitment-phobe to another?" I snap. "Not so great." I'm being a dick, but this conversation is grating on me, and I know her too. She's been dating Cara Andrews exclusively since this summer, and she still won't admit she doesn't want to see anyone else.

"First of all, this is my speech, so screw you. And second, you're not afraid of commitment, Jamie. That's never been your issue. You're afraid of being the guy no one will commit *to*."

Em can tell by the way I flinch that she's made a direct hit, and her expression softens. "Sorry, but it's true."

I drag a hand over my mouth, my ribs aching less from the break and more from the beating muscle behind them that's been bruised for the last two years. I fucking hate that Em knows me this well, but it's like Noel said: You can't hide from family. I guess that includes friends who have known all the previous versions of you.

I have a list of those versions of me I'd rather forget, but the one that involved a ring and a humiliation that makes Kelly's seem like a minor slight, that one won't go the hell away.

Em leans back on her heels in a way that feels like the laying down of a sword. Probably because she knows I'm about to go down a hole that's tougher than any shit she could give me.

Becca and I didn't just break up, we imploded, and the wreckage is still stuck in my skin like shrapnel. Even after two years, I struggle to hide the way it gets to me when she comes up in conversation. Of course, like the rest of my bad decisions, she's still hanging around this zip code, so it happens from time to time.

Now, the memory comes without my permission. Becca's face the night I asked her about what Noel told me. Her shocked expression layered over a pitying one.

"*How did you know?*" That's what she said. Not "*It's not true.*" Not "*Let me explain.*" But "*How did you figure it out?*"

And to be fair, I *hadn't* figured it out. Noel told me. What I thought Becca and I were doing was so far from what was actually happening. I had a ring, and she had a better option. I felt like I'd been dropped back in school, confused and struggling to keep up with what everyone else understood. Praying no one could tell. If Noel hadn't seen it, who knows how long it would have continued, me stupidly unaware that I was the butt of the joke.

But she did tell me. I returned the ring, turned down the job, and two weeks after that, I got the money like Noel said I would. It was the proof I needed of what was for me and what wasn't, and I've kept my heart stored safely at Fortune ever since.

And that worked out just fine until now. Until Noel showed up again, and all the defense mechanisms I've spent the last two years honing crumbled with one wide-eyed, blushing smile. I feel like I've been in one of those highway trances where you look around and find yourself home without re-membering making the decisions that got you there. Here I am, obsessing over Noel, without ever deciding to let myself get here.

"Look," Em says when I've been silent long enough that the rain is starting to soak us both. "I get it. If you don't try, you can't fail, right?"

I let out a tired laugh. "That's one benefit."

"But you also can't move up. Be better. Grow. All I'm saying is this fear you've been hiding behind lately, it isn't you. Stop counting yourself out before you even play. You're too good for that shit."

I nod, but a bigger realization is settling onto my shoulders, heavy and painful, and demanding my attention. The real problem is that it's *Noel* who's too good for that shit. She's too good for me to pretend this is still some business arrangement when it's become so much more than that. And she's too good for me to just let this go the way I did with Becca, without even trying to figure out what went wrong.

Em's right. If I want a chance at keeping Noel around, I'm going to have to tap into that part of me who used to not be so afraid to take a risk.

"Are you gonna charge me for this?" I ask Em to break a little of this tension.

She shakes her head and sighs like I am insufferable. "I hate that you made me compliment you just then."

"Had one at the ready though, didn't you?"

"Whatever. You still leaving?"

I nod. For the first time since she's been out here busting my balls, Em smiles. "You going to call your girl?"

"Yeah. Yeah, I'm gonna call her."

Eighteen

Noel

"**D**O YOU THINK ROSÉ or white goes better with Doritos?" Kate asks, holding up a bottle in each hand.

It's Friday night, and we're sitting on the floor in front of the fireplace, eating junk food and wearing the onesie pajamas that we bought each other for Christmas last year. As one does when your fate takes a hard left.

I point listlessly to the pink bottle, and she unscrews it, pouring me a cup. "So, you do know sleepover rules apply at any age, right? If something happened with Mr. Destiny, you're required to tell me the whole truth."

My eyes slip closed, and Jamie's mouth at my neck flashes behind my eyelids. A memory this time, the past instead of the future, but it brings the same unsteady feeling.

"You're not actually sleeping over." I gulp my wine and top it off.

She shrugs. "I'm too old to sleep on the floor."

"You don't want to sleep without Colin.

"Whatever. The sleeping part doesn't matter. We have the rest." She hands me an elastic and brush so I can get to work putting a fishtail braid in her hair. She already did mine. Space buns. I hate her.

"Turn around," I tell her, gathering her hair.

She shuffles to the side, and I settle behind her, working out my words while Pixie climbs my back, trying to eat the bunny ears on the hood of my pajamas. I scoop her up and redeposit her on the couch. The truth is, I didn't need to be reminded that I'm bound by code to spill my guts. Extreme circumstances call for extreme opinions, and that's Kate's specialty.

"I don't think we should call him that anymore," I say, running the brush through the ponytail I'm making.

"What?"

"Mr. Destiny."

"You never thought we should call him that, and you called the guy I was dating freshman year Trench Coat, so you don't get a say."

"He wore a trench coat!"

"Exactly, these nicknames don't come out of nowhere. This one stays."

I heave a sigh. "I have to tell you something."

Kate's head whips around, ruining the braid. "What?"

I know what she's expecting, and I can't bear to look at her face when I disappoint her, so I turn her shoulders away and start again on her hair. "Do you remember I told you that night about the tattoo on Jamie's back?" A crack threatens my voice, and I pause to repeat what I've been telling myself for the last three days: *I shouldn't feel this way. I shouldn't be so... devastated. I barely know him.*

Kate nods. "The quote you couldn't read."

"Yes, that one." The words bunch like cotton inside my

mouth. I don't want to speak it, give it more credence. But I also can't keep it trapped inside my brain, rattling around with the memories, turning them sour. "Well, I saw it again, in person, and it's... different."

"What do you mean it's different?" she asks around her cup of wine.

"I mean it's not the same. Like at all. Not even close. The words I saw are just gone and instead it's a drawing of a wave."

She looks at me over her shoulder, her forehead creased. "Maybe he had the other one removed."

"Doubtful, but even if he did, why wouldn't I have seen the new one? Wherever the vision took place, I haven't been there yet." I picture the fireplace, the snowy mountains I saw. "It wasn't here at the cottage and it wasn't at his place. If it hasn't happened yet, I should have seen the one he has now. And there's another thing—a scar on his right hand." Faced with this new development, I realize I didn't give that little clue due diligence. "It wasn't there when I..." I wave a hand near my head. "He said he got it after we met but also after he opened the brewery that he claims he only has because of me. Day of, actually. How can that be? If it all worked out like I said, then I should have seen it."

Kate shrugs like I haven't just debunked this whole thing. "I mean, it can't be an exact science."

"Can it not?" Kate knows even less about this than I do, and I only know that Nana believed in it, and everyone thought she'd lost her mental faculties well before she actually had. "What's the point if it can be wrong? Why not just use your horoscope or a fortune cookie to see the future? You'll have an equal chance of being correct and it won't come with a heaping side of terror."

"Okay, well maybe it was right back then but it changed. Maybe *you* changed it by running away that night. Like the

Butterfly Effect or whatever."

"I didn't run away. I went home because I had to."

"And you didn't come back for two years." She waves a hand in front of her like a game show host revealing a prize. "So it's a little different. It could be that making a conscious decision to ignore a huge gift from the universe had an effect on when and how the vision came true. I mean, what if you hadn't left that night and you two had been in love this whole time? Maybe if you had been here, he would have picked the other tattoo." Her eyes go wide, and she breathes out a little, "Woah. This shit is seriously wild."

I deflate with a gust of air. The way she's casually explaining the possible rules of this with a straight face is another layer on the crazy cake. If we can change the future, then how can someone see the future in a vision? And how are we ever supposed to make a decision again knowing the outcome could affect literally everything else? I have a hard enough time making myself click the alternate route on my GPS because I'm terrified there's a Mac truck barreling my way if I choose to veer off course. Then of course there's the opposite scenario, where I was supposed to take the shortcut and doom myself because I stay.

"Orrr," I say. "It could be a very big warning that none of this is real." When I say it out loud, my stomach sinks like a stone. I absently drop Kate's half done braid.

This is why I never let myself believe in Nana's readings. Getting my heart set on something that could blow up in my face was something I'd already learned not to do. I didn't need to seek out more opportunities to get my hopes up.

Kate reaches back to tie the braid I've left dangling, then shifts so we're shoulder to shoulder. "Do you honestly believe that? After everything?"

"I don't know. I don't know if it matters at this point. You just said I could have changed the whole thing by leaving that night. What if I changed something else?" *Something I already had my heart set on.*

My body sags. That's the thing of it, right? The thing that had me running away from him on the beach, my hands clutched over my heart as if I could keep it safe from the reckless path I started down. If one thing has changed, then it's possible that whatever I saw between Jamie and me has too.

I've had three glimpses of what I took to be the future, and so far only a couple of minor details have been right. I started to tell myself that, despite the dwindling evidence, it wasn't reckless to believe in it because I *wanted* it to be true.

And I should have known better. That's the trouble with letting yourself want things. It has the dangerous side effect of making you forget all the reasons it won't work. You pack your kid up and take her on a road trip to chase a man you had one night with. Or you hop in a van you bought on Facebook Marketplace for three-hundred-dollars and probably some weed, drive to California, and end up with completely foreseeable engine trouble because you never thought past the wanting part.

I mean, what if I did let myself fall for Jamie's adventures and carefree smile and careless hair? Then what? This is a short stay, a sabbatical to find what I need to fix my life back in Connecticut. What am I even doing?

It's not that it didn't occur to me that I was exploring this connection with Jamie here, a place I'm only staying temporarily. I just truly didn't have much faith in it at first. And then I was caught up in it. Believing that the little things I like so much about him were messages from the universe. But there were never any directions past this feeling in my belly. Never any safety net like Colin suggested. In the real world, where magic doesn't exist, it was never going to work. I was never going to have him.

"I tried to listen to the universe, Kate, but I'm not going to drive myself to the bottom of a lake because the signs say there's something there. This tattoo thing is a warning that I need to do what I came here to do and go home." My voice cracks on the last word, and something sharp spears my chest.

Shit.

Kate grabs my hand and squeezes. "You wanna know what I think, Noel?"

I sigh. "I'm not sure."

"Well, too bad. I think you've been so busy looking for cosmic signs, that you're missing the ones right in front of you. You're disappointed, babe. When you came here, even that was hard to muster. That has to tell you something."

I consider that, that maybe the way I miss him *is* the sign and I'm ignoring it.

But it's also entirely possible that you can find a sign for anything you want to be true if you're gullible enough.

The fact is, whether magic is real or not, I have no proof I can count on it to be on my side.

"I am disappointed," I tell Kate. "I'm disappointed in myself. This has been too much from the start. I'm still me, just three hours north."

She stares at me for a longer than a comfortable amount of time, then nods. "Okay."

"Okay?"

"Yup. Whatever you say, Noel." Kate gets to her feet and heads down the hall. "It's your life."

"Where are you going?" I call from my spot on the floor. "Since when has it ever been 'Whatever you say, Noel?'"

"Did you get rid of Nana's stuff under here?" she asks, voice muffled, and I shake my head, picturing her on her knees, pawing through the plastic containers beneath the sink.

"Are you serious right now?"

"What? You seemed like you wanted to drop it, so I'm dropping it, and like I said, sleepover rules apply. Bingo!" She comes back holding a small storage cube and a quilted glass bottle with a bubble sprayer, spritzing her wrists. "It smells like her."

I swallow down a lump. "Are you trying to make me cry, because it's not going to take a lot."

"Of course not. Unless you're willing to admit you want to cry and then we can dissect that."

I shake my head, and she plops down beside me. I reach for the bottle, spraying my cleavage while Kate dives into the makeup. It's been over a decade since we've touched this stuff. The gaudy lipsticks probably expired a decade before that, and neither of us would be caught dead in this color eyeshadow palette as adults. Kate pulls out a glittery blue and waves it like a taunt.

"Fine," I tell her. "Do your worst."

She laughs evilly, but I'm grateful for the distraction when she presses her fingers to my eyelid, holding it closed. I want to sink into the comfort of this memory even if it takes me a whole package of makeup wipes to clean my face at the end of the night.

I picture us doing this as kids, Nana puttering around the kitchen, mixing Shirley Temples and making us popcorn, pretending not to eavesdrop. I always assumed that was how she got the information she needed for the "visions" she'd have later when Kate would beg her to get out the candles. Obviously, I'm remembering it differently now.

"I saw your paintings," Kate says. The soft brush touches my lashline and I try not to think about Staph infections.

"They're not what I need to be working on."

I feel her shrug even though my eyes are closed. "I think you need to be working on whatever makes you happy. You know, I was afraid you wouldn't settle in here. That you would live out of your suitcase the whole three months."

I wince at the way I've been avoiding Nana's room. Her door is still closed, and I've taken to giving it a wide berth every time I pass it, like it might fly open on its own and force me to look.

"I didn't bring enough clothes for that," I reply.

Kate leans back to look, then gestures for me to close my other eye. "Noel, I don't think this is the end that you think it is. Even if you changed something with Jamie, even if you *didn't* see your future, don't be disappointed in yourself for believing in something for a little while. *You* three hours north was always different from *you* at home. That's why I wanted you to come here to figure out your shit."

I squeeze my lids shut again. I'm going to be a blue, glittery mess if I let these tears come. If I let any of it—

There's a loud pounding on the door, and we both jump. "Who's coming here?" Kate asks.

"It's probably Colin missing you."

She snorts. "I invited him. He said thanks, but no thanks."

I scoop my wine from the coffee table and head to the door, unlocking the deadbolt and swinging it open.

It is not Colin, and despite knowing very few people in this city, I could still name a handful of them I would expect to see standing on my porch before Jamie.

"Hi." My voice is barely more than air.

He runs a hand over the back of his head and tips back on his heels. "Hey, Noe."

It's self-preservation, I think, the way my brain forgets just how handsome he is until he's standing in front of me. He's hatless, wearing the green hoodie that I love. The one that makes his eyes change from the color of cream soda to the bottom of a river when the sun shines through.

And I'm dressed like a rabbit with blue eyelids. Oh my God.

The fact that he only gives this a fraction of an eyebrow raise hits me low in my belly. There's no smart remark, no flirting—just a twitch of his jaw. A nervous dart of his eyes over my shoulder. Longing tugs me like a lasso to the center of my chest.

"What are you doing here?"

"I hope it's okay. I did actually call first but—"

"You called me?" I'm absolutely wrecked that I didn't see it, which is maybe one of those non-cosmic signs right in front of me. I pat the pockets of this ridiculous outfit but my phone is somewhere else. Probably under the coffee table or behind a wine box on the counter. "I didn't see it, I was—"

"Having a one-person costume party?" The corner of his mouth twitches.

I huff out a laugh. "Um, there are two of us, actually."

I turn to see Kate staring wide-eyed over the back of the couch. "Holy shit, it's you."

Jamie watches helplessly as she crosses the room and pushes his chest with her index finger like she expects it to go straight through. "I wasn't prepared."

At least she looks as ridiculous as I do with her lopsided braid and dog pajamas.

"Kate, right?" Jamie asks.

"Good memory. You look *exactly* the same."

He doesn't, though. His hair is different. And the scruff on his face. But she wasn't paying as close attention as I was that night.

Kate stares at him for a few more beats, then turns to me wide-eyed. The room gets a good ten degrees warmer. Finally, she claps her hands once like a gavel. "I'm going to go."

"Oh, you don't have to…" I say half-heartedly. I love her, but suddenly I really want her to go.

"I do." She darts to the bathroom and comes back with a pack of makeup wipes, shoving a few in my hand. I swipe the damp cloth over my blue eyelids while she buzzes around the room gathering her things.

And then she's gone.

"Here, come in." The rain that started as a drizzle earlier this evening has turned into a downpour. A raindrop falls from the zipper of Jamie's hoodie as he steps through the threshold, toeing off his sneakers.

"This place is identical to my stepdad's," he says, looking around.

"Is it?" I like that for some reason, that he might know his way around.

"It's a good thing the door was locked the night I passed out on your porch." He nods toward the door to Nana's room, still closed. "I would have headed straight for your bed."

I laugh because his flirting is back and I'm so relieved by it, but it's also an awkward reminder that he wouldn't have headed to my bed because I'm sleeping in the loft like a child.

I push that down and gesture to where he's holding a small paper bag in the crook of his arm. "What's that?"

"Oh, I brought you this." He seems nervous, color blooming on his neck as he reaches into the bag. It's a grocery store kalanchoe with the most gorgeous peach flowers, and I think my heart might flutter right out of my chest. "To paint," he says. "You said you were done with the hops."

"I am." I take it from him and clutch it to my chest.

"None of the real floral shops were open, or—"

"I love it, Jamie."

He nods once. "Good. I'm sorry I interrupted your night with Kate."

"It's fine. Really." I set the plant on the counter and touch my thumb to a tiny leaf. It's a double flower variety, so each bloom has about twenty petals in a tight little cluster. I can't wait to sketch it. "Um. How was your day?"

"It was..." He laughs. "Not great."

My face falls. "Do you want to talk about it?"

"I *really* don't."

"Oh. Okay." I suppose I don't deserve his bad days after the way I left things. He starts to say something else, but I interrupt him. "I'm just going to—" I gesture to the bunny onesie "—go put literally anything else on." God, *why?*

"You don't have to," he says. "I mean... it looks cute. You look cute." He scratches the back of his neck.

"Thank you. But I definitely have to." Tail firmly between my legs, I run upstairs and strip out of the onesie and into a pair of shorts and a tank. The hoodie I stole from him is draped over the chair in the corner, but it probably wouldn't be appropriate to put it on now. Instead, I grab a long sleeve T-shirt, quickly tugging my hair out of the buns.

And then I sink to the bed and breathe through my hands. I'm not sure how I'm supposed to proceed here. If there's some puzzle involved in this, some secret code I'm supposed to figure out, I can't imagine why the universe thought I was the girl for the job. It took being slapped in the brain by a psychic vision multiple times before I even dared to believe it.

Everything seemed to fall into place before I saw that tattoo, and I just don't know what to make of this new development after everything else. The magic things that came true and the real way we are after such a short time. If this thing is taking requests, I could really use some clarity, an easy explanation that turns this back into a sure thing. But instead, seeing him like this, unsure and tentative, it makes the whole magic thing seem even more like a dream.

I'm past being impolite, hiding up here, so I head back downstairs and find Jamie crouched down low, letting Pixie attack his hand.

"Hey."

"I didn't know you had a cat." He scoops Pix up, and all of the soft parts inside my heart collectively swoon.

"That's Pixie." Pix rubs her face on his chin. "She does this with everyone."

"Aw, lie to me, would you?"

I laugh. "Sorry. She's sort of a flirt, but I'm sure this is genuine."

"She's beautiful." He teases her with the string on his hoodie, and she grabs it with her claw. "Look at those big gold eyes just like your momma."

"Are you talking to my cat in a baby voice?"

"Um, that's the only way to talk to a cat, Noel. Otherwise they don't understand. Oh my God. Have you been talking to her in a regular voice this whole time?"

I laugh harder, my heart aching with the way it stretches. "What was I thinking?"

"How long have you had her? She looks like a kitten."

"She's three. Nana adopted her when she was already sick. It was kind of a given that Pixie would outlive her, so she's always been a little bit mine. Sometimes I think she knew I would need her."

The vulnerability I've let slip has his eyes back on me, and my cheeks warm again.

"Um, do you want a beer? I actually have some of yours."

A grin explodes across his face. "No. Thank you. You go ahead, though. Please. Make my fantasies come true."

I smile at his joke, but it's wobbly. I don't know what to do with flirty Jamie after how we left things. After not speaking to him for three days.

A little liquid courage will be a start. I pull out his fall ale and pop the cap, taking a big gulp. There's a tension here, an awkwardness that's all me, and unless I want to explain to him that I thought we were destined for each other, and now, because of his choice in body ink, I'm not so sure, I need to start acting normal. If there is a normal in a situation like this.

"Listen, Jamie—"

"Can we sit down?" He sets Pix on the floor and looks toward my couch.

"Yeah, of course." He follows me into the living room, where I notice too late the burning candle on the coffee table that I swear wasn't an intentional ode to this thing between us.

He seems to notice this too, and he gives me a shy, *well, this is awkward* smile before taking the seat beside me.

"I want to say something."

"Okay." Inside my chest, my heart can't decide what to do, sink like a stone at his serious expression, or do more of that berserk thing from the fire escape. I really wish I could tell the future right now. *My God, the irony.*

"This is really important to me," he says, then clears his throat. "This deal we made, asking you to try to see some cosmic tip. I wouldn't have asked you if it wasn't."

"I know."

"But I realized something the other night on the beach. Before that really, if I would have let myself admit it. I realized that if it were a choice between never getting another glimpse of the future, or getting one and having that be the end of this, of my excuse to see you all the time. Well, I wouldn't... I wouldn't want that." He pulls in a shaky breath. "I missed you so much the last few days, Noe. More than I—"

"More than makes sense," I say, finishing his confession with my own.

"Yeah."

"Me too." My heart firmly chooses the berserk thing, pounding against my breastbone. But I know you can't always trust your heart with these things. Missing. Wanting. These are things that get you in trouble. Missing him doesn't change the fact that holes in this magic make the two of us as end game so much less likely. He doesn't know that part. He doesn't know most of it, the most important parts.

And he's here anyway.

Everything that's happened so far flips through my brain like a photo album. I saw us in bed together somewhere I can't name, with his body different than it is now by a fraction. I saw us on the porch just on the other side of this wall, touching in a way I'm sure I've never touched anyone else. Absorbing his kiss like it was my birthright.

I didn't see us three stories up on a fire escape, me following him like I was possessed by the spirit of someone braver than me. I didn't see us running into the ocean in October in my underwear, touching him with that same bravery. And then freaking out.

How does this thing, whatever it is, decide which movie to play in my brain? And how does this fit? Him sitting here now, confessing that I'm not imagining what's brewing between us, even if what I saw was flawed.

I wish, not for the first time, that I'd asked Nana about this when I had the chance instead of pretending that night on the roof never happened. Looking back, she must have been some kind of professional. She seemed to be able to control it, wield it. We'd ask silly questions, and she'd give us silly answers that maybe weren't that silly after all. But it didn't come out of nowhere and shock the hell out of her.

Or maybe she just didn't tell me that part. It's entirely possible she saw more than what she shared with two pre-teen girls. By the time I was old enough that she might have trusted me with the details, we'd stopped asking. I didn't believe in it. Which leaves me shit out of luck now when I need to know more.

"You really believe all of this, don't you? Like with your whole heart."

He doesn't hesitate. "I do."

My skin bursts with goosebumps at that firm conviction, and with it something reckless and new stirs inside of me.

Kate's right. I am disappointed. I wanted this thing to be my safety net like Colin said. I wanted to feel safe to reach for something without the constant fear that I'd miss it and fall on my face. And I'm tired of this spin in my head, trying to decipher signs and tiny glimpses. I'm tired of feeling more lost than found when I think of how Jamie and I got here. If the universe wants to tell me something, it needs to spit it out.

And maybe it will if I ask.

I don't think everyone who looks into a candle and asks a question will get an answer, but I do know, one time I did.

"We should try it again," I say. "The candle."

Confusion passes over his face, then his eyes go wide. "Noel, no. That's not why I said—"

"I know it's not." So far these visions have seemed to come at random times, but I don't know if I can *make* it happen, if I can ask my own questions the way I did with Nana. Being friends and seeing what happens hasn't been working, so now all I have left is to experiment for both of us.

No matter what's up ahead, Kate said. *You're going to have to move to find it.*

Jamie's still looking at me carefully. "I want to," I tell him. "Really."

He shifts so we're knee to knee. His arm is wrapped around his ribcage, and he looks nervous. It takes me a moment to realize I'm not. I feel safe here, just the two of us, figuring it out together.

"Do you need the cup of water?" he asks.

"Um, I don't think so," I say, figuring it out as I go. "The candle actually didn't seem to play a part the last few times. Let's just... here." Taking a deep breath through my nose, I square his body to mine, sliding my palms to the gentle curve of his pectoral muscles beneath his sweatshirt.

Jamie stiffens at my touch, and I try to ignore it, focus my attention on the hollow of his throat. There's a small freckle there that looks like it jumped the constellation that I know is just beneath his collar bones. I feel unsteady and woozy alright, but it's not the least bit supernatural.

"This is so weird," he breathes. It's half a laugh but his face isn't smiling.

"Totally weird."

With that, I let my eyes close and try to pick up some vibration from the universe, some message in the ether, but I realize quickly I have no idea what I'm looking for. If I can make it happen, will it be stronger than when it surprises me? Will it be a picture again? Or will I feel some sort of burst of emotion the way I felt it when I saw Becca and some other man breaking Jamie's heart? Am I going to pass out? Throw up? Cry? Anxiety spreads like cotton in my lungs, making it hard to breathe.

What if I can't do it? What if I can? What if he doesn't like what I see?

"Hey." Jamie must sense my spiral because I feel his fingers cup my cheek, and it's so tender. So sweet. "No pressure," he whispers.

"No pressure." Blowing a slow breath toward the ceiling, I force my mind to settle on the feel of his skin on mine, the steady beat of his heart beneath my palm. The heat of his body. I imagine a string tied around us, cinching tighter. I let myself imagine it, another glimpse of the future coming to me. I imagine it working but...

Nothing.

My frustration is a wild horse, snorting and pawing at the dirt. There has to be some trick to this I haven't figured out yet. Something I'm missing.

"It's okay," he says, but suddenly it's not.

"Hold on." I study him with my lip between my teeth. He's still bundled up in these layers, damp from the rain. The opposite of his near nakedness on the beach. Maybe I need more contact. "Here," I say, reaching for the zip on his hoodie, dragging it the rest of the way down. "Take this off."

He shrugs it off his shoulders, revealing a threadbare T-shirt. It's heather red, and I notice with affection that it looks truly gorgeous against his fair skin, followed by the odd feeling that I've had that thought before.

My skin tingles with awareness that my mind races to place, but then he turns to lay the hoodie on the arm of my couch, his muscles flexing beneath the cotton tee, and it's like someone has reached inside my skull and flicked my brain. *His T-shirt.*

I press my fingers to the logo on his chest. Crackled white writing that reads: *Peak's Island Summerfest.* "Oh my God."

"What?"

"Where did you get this shirt?" I ask, taking a handful in my fist.

He looks down at it and smirks. "I'll give you one guess."

I've seen Jamie almost daily since I've been here, and I've

only seen this shirt once. In the vision I had at Fortune.

Gripping his shoulders, I gently turn him away from me. The moment seems to slow, the outside edges curling in like I'm entering a tunnel. I drag my thumb along the shoulder seam to where the stitching has given way, leaving a small hole. I knew it would be there, and I clap my hand over my mouth, trying to control my breathing.

"Noe, what's wrong?"

"We're not on my porch," I say stupidly. But maybe that part is still to come. It has to be, right? I know what Jamie told me about the first vision coming true—what happened with Becca, and how he got the money to open his bar like I predicted. But I haven't seen one materialize for myself. Not until now.

This is the proof. It has to be. I asked for it, and I got it.

"Do you want to be on your porch?" he asks slowly, looking one odd exclamation away from calling a doctor.

"Yes," I say. Then, "No."

"What's happening?" His eyes are wide, chest rising and falling quicker now.

"I have absolutely no idea," I say honestly, but I can't keep my hands off of him any longer. I reach for his face, my fingers trembling. "Jamie, I..."

"Christ, come here." He tugs my wrist and I scramble onto his lap. My knees spread out wide to straddle his thighs, palms pressed flat to his chest. The scent of the rain on his skin surrounds me until I'm huffing it, my body drinking him in like liquor. When our eyes lock, I can practically feel my pupils dilate, like every part of me is stretching to take in as much of him as possible.

Jamie's hands settle on my thighs, fingers flexing but staying put. "Noel," he whispers. It's a warning, but it's also desperate, like fingers pressed into the edge of a cliff. "Tell me what we're doing, baby."

My eyes snap back to his, and I laugh outright.

He's calling me baby. I absolutely do not hate it when he says it.

Jamie has never called me that in this realm. *Gorgeous. Sweetheart. Noe.* Never baby.

But he did in the vision at his bar.

My breath has all but evaporated from my lungs, and I wrap my hand around the back of his neck tugging until his mouth is on mine. Jamie doesn't hesitate, cupping my face and kissing me back with a groan of relief. "Fuck, I was afraid you wouldn't want to do this anymore."

I answer with the quietest little moan, and he swallows it with another press, longer this time.

The kiss is sweet, almost chaste at first. *At first.*

He pulls away for the span of one glance, a quick dart of his eyes to mine to make sure I'm still with him, and then his mouth is back, hot and immediately searching. Our lips part at the same time, and when our tongues touch, Jamie makes a noise in the back of his throat of tortured restraint. It's like a magic wand tapping my forehead, lighting up every nerve in my body.

I saw this. I knew this. I was wholly unprepared for this.

Within minutes of our lips meeting for the first time, we're full-on making out on my couch, hands sliding and gripping each other's clothes. We kiss like we haven't seen each other in ages, like we're star-crossed lovers, reunited after dimensions apart. I run my fingers through his hair, shivering at the silky feel of it. Jamie's hands skim up and down my sides like he can't decide where to stop.

"Is this okay?" he rasps.

"It's perfect. So okay." I'm glad he seems to have some semblance of control here, because I've been reduced to pure instinct—to warm my skin with his skin, to press myself against him until pleasure rips up my spine.

My hips roll, and my head falls back with a gasp.

"Yes," he says. "Do that." He leans into the couch, watching, his lip curled in satisfaction.

I roll again, letting a little "Ah" escape, and it's like it snaps something in him, a damn breaking. He brings his mouth to my throat, baring his teeth the way he did in the water. And just like then, it makes me feral. My hands slide beneath his shirt, and his breath catches so hard, I feel his skin jump beneath my fingers, an electric current between us, crackling.

"Take this off." I tug at the hem of his shirt until he pulls it over his head.

I frown at the lingering bruise on his side, but his mouth is back on mine, eating it up, turning it back into a smile. I feel his reaction to each new boundary passed—the hot exhale of a curse word when he pushes my shirt up my belly. A flex of his hips when his thumb finds my breast. He pulls away, suddenly serious. I'm growing wilder by the second. I need more. I need closer. God, I want to claw my way inside of him.

"This is..." He trails off, and all I can say is, "I know." Because I do. This is magic.

I wonder briefly if I should tell him now that I knew this would happen, that I've been waiting for it, but when his fingers notch into my shorts, words far simpler than that desert my brain.

"Can I see?"

I nod, breathless, and he chuckles patiently.

"Tell me, baby, cause I don't wanna just look."

"Call me that again."

He takes my chin in his hand, eyes hooded. "Let me look at you, baby."

"Yes. Look." I raise my arms over my head, and he takes off

my shirt, leaving the tank beneath it.

"Fucking beautiful," he says, before tugging the ribbed fabric down, exposing me, dipping to put his mouth on me. He sucks until my hips lift off of the couch, desperately seeking. "I think that halo's coming off, Noe."

"Ha. Still think I'm an angel, huh?"

"I think you're a very good girl."

Maybe I was, but he's gasoline to what was barely a crackling ember of spirit inside of me these last few months. I feel alive. Like every one of my nerve endings is at attention.

This has to mean something, right? This overflowing feeling in my chest, this frantic need. It has to be a sign that it's okay to look past one little glitch in the magic.

Please?

"Anything," he whispers, and I realize I've said it out loud, a plea to the universe to make good on its promise. "I will give you anything you want, Noel."

There's only one thing in the world that I want right now. "Let's go upstairs."

Nineteen

M
Y BACK KNOCKS AGAINST the railing at the top of the loft, then the dresser. Jamie laughs against my breast. "I'd tell you to be careful, but that's your line."

"I don't want to be careful."

I want wildness, abandon. I want rough hands and filthy words. I'm halfway to mauling him, but he straightens, taking my face in his hands to slow our frantic kissing to small pecks along my cheekbone, my jaw, my neck.

"What are you thinking?" he asks, and God it's impossible to have any coherent thoughts at all with his body against mine, shirtless, jeans bent out of shape in the front, and so low on his hips I can see exactly how far that trail of hair on his belly extends.

"I'm wondering what this will be like between us," I say honestly. This connection, this unexplainable string. I feel it pull tighter with every new place he touches me. A sailor's knot, cinching. I want to know how it will manifest when there's nothing left between us. I want to know how much more I'll feel when he's inside of me.

"It will be good," he says, mouth moving against my skin. "It will be so good."

I shiver from this drafty house and from the anticipation. Whatever else it will be, I've already seen how good it is. "What about you?" I ask, suddenly breathless. "What are you thinking?"

He pulls away and his smile pings up on one side. Mischief. "I'm thinking about the multiple times you told me not to touch you."

A laugh bursts free, and I push at his shoulder. "Yes, I've clearly lifted that ban."

"Good. Let's keep touching."

"Let's." I run my fingers down his stomach, cup him over his pants, and the deep groan he makes causes something in my chest to jump. This boldness is unfamiliar to me, but there's no reason to pretend, to be tentative. He watches me unbutton and unzip, then slide my hand inside. He's warm and pulsing in my palm, and I run my thumb over the wet tip of him.

"So hot," he says. "Fuck. You feel so good."

"So do you." His hips buck before he can get a hold of himself, and the heat of him, the gentle tug of his fingers in my hair while he tries not to thrust into my hand, it sets me on fire.

"Okay, okay," he says, laughing. He gently tips my chin and I pull my hand free. "Too soon. I'm going to come in my pants."

"Take them off, then."

Together, we shove them over his hips, along with his boxers. His cock springs free between us, and like a scandalized virgin, I gasp.

"Hey," he whispers. "Do we need to slow down?"

I shake my head furiously. "No. I'm not... I'm just excited."

He groans at that, taking himself in his fist, stroking once, then he lets go and walks me backward toward the bed. My childhood bed. I suppose this should feel weird but instead it feels exactly right to be here with him.

The backs of my legs hit the mattress, and Jamie gently presses my shoulder, seating me on the edge. My entire world has shrunk to the expanse of skin in front of me. I'm obsessed with his flat stomach, the soft hair on his chest. His never ending torso that seems from this angle to stretch to the sky.

And then he drops to his knees and my view changes: the top of his head, dark hair, wild from my fingers. He parts my thighs, not bothering to take off my shorts, just pushing the loose fabric to the side, and I feel his breath there, then his open mouth, chin, and nose all pressed against my most sensitive parts. I'm practically begging for his tongue but instead he takes a deep breath in.

"God damn." He pauses to catch his breath, eyes locked between my legs. "This is, like, highest tier fantasy shit."

I chuckle nervously. "You didn't fantasize about me."

His smile curls and his fingers dip inside of me. I gasp at the ceiling.

And then they're gone.

Wide-eyed and a little annoyed, I look down to see Jamie run his tongue over his fore and middle fingers, licking like an ice cream cone. "Let's make a deal," he says. "I promise not to lie to you, and you promise to believe me when I say I've woken up more than once with my hand wrapped around my cock because I was dreaming of tasting you."

Heat rushes down my spine and I whimper a tiny, nearly imperceptible, "When?"

This timeline feels crucial. I have to know when these dominoes fell into place. This thing is a constant moving puzzle. I don't understand it. I'm not sure if I'm supposed to.

Jamie's laugh drips with guilt. "If I told you since that night on the roof, I'd be kind of an asshole, right? Considering I was there with someone else. A long time, either way, now let me."

He dives back in, hungry and desperate bursts before he gains control and slows the stroke of his tongue to precise, measured movements that blur my vision. My body turns to a puddle of liquid and bones. All I'm capable of in this moment is taking, and I do, rocking my hips, holding the back of his head.

"Fuck, Noe. I could eat this pretty little pussy for every meal."

"Such a dirty mouth." I laugh at the ceiling. "I knew it would be."

His fingers tighten on my hip at that. "So I'm not the only one who's played this out in my head?"

"Definitely not." I'm the only one who's *seen* it, though. "Come here." I tug his hair until he looks up at me. "I want to look at you."

He moves us to the center of the bed, gazing down at me with hooded eyes. His hair is a disaster, one lock laying across his forehead, the rest sticking up every which way.

It's the same, I think with a full-body shudder. It's *exactly* the same as I saw it.

"Tell me you have a condom," I say.

"In my wallet." His thumb presses my lip. "Are you sure?"

I nod. I'm already squirming, hips lifting toward air, wanting him back with a need I'm not accustomed to.

Thankfully, he's quick, gone and back in seconds, stalking toward me with all of that long-legged swagger. The mattress presses on either side of me, shifting with his movement as he covers himself.

He dips his head, covering my nipple with his soft lips while his fingers brush between my legs, testing, lining us up, and then he's there, pushing forward. We pull in matching breaths, and my eyes flutter closed at the slow, tight fit, the way he takes deep, steadying breaths, and when he hits at the hilt, it's like something that had been spinning around us clicks into place. Like time stops altogether.

He looks down at me wide-eyed and I know he feels it too, the slowing down. I feel my blood drain and fill back up with liquid affection as we lie there eyes-locked, letting it wash over us.

"Fuck, this is intense," he says, reading my mind.

"For me too." His hand wraps around my wrist on the pillow as he starts to move, slowly at first until he finds a perfect rhythm that makes my head tip back and my vision blur. Inside my chest, a balloon of emotion expands painfully against my ribs. I pull his mouth to mine, clutching him closer, and it's with a hazy, back-of-my-brain realization that I *know* it's never been like this before. Pleasure and affection braided so tightly together that I can't decipher where one ends and the other begins.

Even if I'd never seen this play out in a premonition, I'd know by the feeling in my chest how important he is.

And I probably would have run from it.

Now, I roll my hips up to meet him. He pulls my thigh over his waist and I arch into him, putting pressure in a place so perfect that I can't help but I cry out. My nails dig into his skin, and he hisses.

"Sorry," I breathe.

"Don't be. Look at you," he says, propped on his hand, his other hand holding me at the waist while he watches. His hips are a careful, even rhythm, and the way I grip the sheet and grind against him looks jerky and uncontrolled in comparison. Who knew this would be the place where our roles reversed?

I cry out again on the next stroke. It's too much. I can't hold back. My hands are frantic between us, running over his skin, threading through the light hair on his chest.

"I wondered what it would take to get you like this," he says. "Wild."

"It's you."

His stroke slips ever so slightly and his eyes go soft. "Yeah?"

"You get me like this. You're the only one."

His grip on me tightens and his hips pump harder. "Look at me, Noe. It's so fucking good when you look at me."

My heavy eyes drag up to his, and he's right. I hold his gaze as my free hand slips between us, touching myself. Another thing I've never dared to do with anyone else, and he's encouraging me, whispering *yes,* and cursing with his lip between his teeth, while heat builds at the base of my spine.

Jamie hikes my leg up higher, and the wooden headboard slams against the wall. I squeak in surprise, and he laughs.

It's that. Not where his hips pin my fingers in the perfect spot, not the drag of him against that valley of nerves inside me—it's that sound I've come to love so much, that beautiful smile that sends heat rushing down my legs and arches my back.

I go taut with a cry, then boneless, my mind full of exploding stars, my body full of him and the pulses of pleasure he's coaxing from me. With his name on my lips, something cracks so wide open that I don't think I'll ever be able to close it again.

He's right behind me, dropping his weight, and burying his face in my neck with a muffled groan of release.

We lie there like that, Jamie's chest rising and falling against mine, heavy but even, as I shiver with aftershock beneath him. His arm is bent, fingers tangled with mine. "That was..." He doesn't finish his sentence, trailing off into a full-body shiver that I translate perfectly.

"Me too." I've barely come down but I'm immediately warm

again. "Jamie?"

He lifts his head to look at me, eyes sex-drunk and lazy, mouth smiling. "Yeah, baby?"

"Let's do it again."

Twenty

Noel

I WAKE TO THE glorious sight of Jamie Bishop sprawled out on my pink floral sheets, his face in the mattress, his pillow propped under his ribs.

A stomach sleeper...

Bed head that could win a contest...

It wasn't here that I saw us that night on the roof, but I knew these things before I even opened my eyes.

He's sleeping hard and peaceful, and I stare at the ceiling, thinking about the start of all this. Our eyes meeting on that roof. How scared I was when he showed back up on my porch. His suggestion that we see what happens. And now, knowing him in the most intimate way.

God, last night was so intense and new, even I find it hard to believe it could mean anything other than the two of us were meant to do that.

I've never experienced that kind of intimacy. There were moments when I wondered if we'd swapped souls and Jamie's blood was running through my veins. I feel him now in the more physical places—the soreness in my legs from the stretch of wrapping them around him, the scratch of his stubble all over my chin. I'll be wearing him for days.

As if to remind me that contemplating the universe is hard work, my stomach growls audibly. I'd love to stay here and watch him sleep all day, but this is Jamie's schedule—staying up late, sleeping all morning. Mine is accustomed to meals at regular intervals. And coffee.

I lift his fingers one by one from my hip and slip out of bed, creeping down the stairs to the living room to search for the shirt he was wearing last night. I find it on the floor beside the couch and pull it over my head on my way to make a cup of coffee before settling at the kitchen table with my sketch pad.

I've just started to sketch a pointed, veined leaf when I hear the stairs creak, his bare feet on the wood. I tip my head back and smile, waiting for his touch.

"Morning." His hand slides up my neck and into my hair as he leans around to kiss me over my shoulder. His eyes are sleepy, right lid heavier. It's just a tad more pronounced right now, my favorite little quirk. It occurs to me that if someone else were to notice this about him, it would be here, first thing in the morning when he's not yet fully awake. That thought whips a slice of possessiveness straight across my chest, so strong I nearly flinch from it.

"Did I wake you up?"

"No. You're very stealthy. I rolled over to the cold sheet before I realized you were gone." He spins my stool so it's facing him and kisses me again. He has to bend nearly in half, and I think of the way I disappeared beneath him last night. How every inch of my skin was pressed to his and he had more to spare.

"Did you sleep okay? You must have been so uncomfortable." I'd woken up more than once feeling awful for the way I was pressed against his ribs. I tried to adjust but I was trapped, and he was so still. So deeply out.

"I wasn't actually," he says. "I was... cozy. Were you?"

"Very cozy."

His mouth moves to my neck before he pulls away to look at the paper spread out over the kitchen table. "These are yours?"

"Mmhmm. The hops are in there somewhere."

He lifts the loose leaf paintings and thumbs through. "Holy shit, they're gorgeous."

"You sound surprised."

"No, I'm just not much of an art scholar. My only experience with watercolors is from kindergarten."

I snort. "Well, then I'm really glad you're impressed."

"I am. I had no idea they could look like this. I like this one."

He holds up a beach rose I did the other day because I was missing them. "Me too."

"What are you drawing now?"

"Poinsettias. I think I'm going to take your advice. I like doing invitations, custom cards. So I'm doing them."

"*My* advice?"

"Yes. Why do you look so surprised?"

He reaches behind me and runs a finger over the paper, studying what's barely a draft at this point. Just the bones. "It blows me away that all of that talent is just floating around in here." He lifts my hands, kissing my knuckles.

"You think my hands are talented, huh?"

His smirk turns mischievous. "Can't say enough about them, actually."

We kiss again, and my body flushes from my head to my toes, waves of anticipation and need pulsing in my blood. I wonder if it will always be like this. If this connection that sparks between us will continue to manifest physically.

He pulls away, his hand still cupping my cheek. The flock of birds on his forearm catches my eye and I turn to press my lips there. "Where did you get this done?"

"Hay Needles," he says. "On Congress Street."

"It's gorgeous."

"You're gorgeous."

"Did you get them all there?" I ask, wondering about the wave, then the lyrics I saw that never materialized.

"Nah, I'm not attached to any artist in particular. Maybe I'll have you draw my next one."

"Really?"

"Sure, gorgeous. Mark me yours." I laugh, and his hands fall to the hem of the T-shirt I stole, dragging it up my belly. He catches his lip between his teeth, sucking in a breath when he gets to my bare breasts. "Take this off."

"No." I cross my arms, clutching the cotton. "I want to wear it."

He chuckles. "Why? It's been on the floor all night."

"I just do."

"Fine. I can work around it." His hands slip beneath it instead, which is a perfectly enjoyable compromise. Then he sinks to his knees and stretches the tee over his head.

My laugh turns into a gasp of pleasure when his teeth graze my navel, his hot breath trapped against me. "I want to bury myself in you. Stay there all day."

I latch my hands into that bed head. "That sounds like a very enjoyable day."

"But..." He kisses my hip.

"But?"

"I have to work."

"Booo," I whine, and he laughs against my skin, then frees himself.

"Baby, if I'd known I was going to wake up here when I did the schedule, trust me, I wouldn't have been on it."

"Are you sure you're up to it?"

"I need to get back to full time soon. We're about to be busy once the cold settles in and people don't want to drink on decks anymore. But I have the lunch shift. I'll be done by five. There's a thing down on Thompson's Point tonight. I want to take you." I glance at the bruise still lingering on his ribs, and he catches me. "It's low key, I promise. Just music, food trucks. Beer. You can sleep in my bed after?"

"Whose beer?" I ask.

His face lights. "Mine."

"Well, I suppose you have to be there then."

"It would be the professional thing to do." He dips his mouth to my ear. "But just so we're clear, I want you there for purely non-professional reasons."

"Okay," I tell him, my heart glowing. "I'll go with you."

Twenty-One

Jamie

I T'S DUSK WHEN I slide my card into the parking kiosk in a dirt lot at the edge of the point. Noel fidgets beside me, her fingers in her skirt. It's pink and gauzy and covered in flowers, short enough that my eyes keep landing on the hem. Her sweater is pink too. She looks like cotton candy, sweet and delicate. It brings back the memory of how *indelicate* I was with her after she agreed to come here with me tonight, when we'd fallen back into her bed for another couple of hours until I was forced to either leave or be late.

I've never desired to stay horizontal for so long before. Normally restlessness gets the better of me and I need to get up, move. But there were too many places I still needed to touch her, too many words bubbling out of us. We talked about the house, the brewery, what we want to do downtown before the snow flies. Stupid stories from when we were kids.

I told her how Greg's family had a slip off of the East End, and it was a miracle none of us ever drowned falling off the rowboat we used to get out there after dark. She told me how she used to take the ferry to Peaks with her Nana to go to the same festival as the T-shirt I had on yesterday. We figured out we were definitely there at the same time, and my mind had taken that coincidence and run with the what-ifs. Of course, she was a pre-teen there with her grandmother and I was sneaking beer in my backpack with my delinquent friends, so they were just fantasies.

If there's any magic in all of this, it's that this beautiful, perfect woman found some reason to wake up beside me.

With that thought in my head, I grab her hand and lead us down the walking path leading to the outdoor venue. The air's more crisp the closer we get to the water, scented with smoke from the food trucks, and cold dirt. It feels like walking over a bridge toward fall.

I try not to think of it as the season before she's supposed to leave.

It feels like the two of us have grabbed hands and taken a huge leap, only to find we've landed on ground that's not entirely solid. My feelings for her are as solid as concrete, but this part I have no control over.

"Have you been here before?" I ask her, holding her hand a little tighter.

"Nope."

"They do this every week. The organizers came to me a couple months ago wanting to partner. It's one of the last of these before they shut down for the season. I think you'll like it."

"You've been right every time you've said that so far," she says, beaming at me.

After a bend in the path, the huge stage comes into view. They get big acts here in the summers, but tonight an obviously local four-piece folk band is setting up on the ground in front of it. We curve around the stage onto the open grass, lined on the right with a temporary beer garden, a row of food trucks on the left, and surrounded on three sides by the Fore River.

"What first?" I ask, pressing my lips to the back of her hand. "Food or drink?"

"Food. It smells amazing."

We order a couple of sandwiches at the gourmet grilled cheese truck, and I hand the guy my card, but when he gives me the slip in return, I immediately realize my mistake. It's old school and doesn't have the suggested tip amount on the bottom. Heat rushes up my neck as I try to work out the correct percent of the total, but I can practically feel the entire line watching me. Including Noel.

I'm not going to embarrass myself by pulling up the calculator on my phone, so I grab my wallet back out of my pocket instead, handing him a twenty.

The kid's face lights up. "Thanks, dude."

I give him a cocky nod like I'm some high roller not a guy who gets tripped up by simple math.

"That was generous," Noel says when we step to the side to wait for our food.

"I'm a bartender. I tip well." My palms are sweaty so I shove them in my pockets instead of holding her hand again.

"I thought you were the owner of a very successful craft brewery."

"That's my side gig." I wink at her but she's giving me that vaguely psychic look, and I don't think I've pulled anything over.

I'll have to explain myself eventually. She'll see the pen marks on my hand when I need to keep track of beers during a busy shift. Or she'll come with me to watch a game at Coppersmith's, and she'll realize I don't know who's winning even when the score's showing.

"Jameson Bishop." I'm still trying to work out how to tell her when they call my name from the other window. I pick up the sandwiches, gesturing to a picnic table at the edge of the water.

"Your name's Jameson?" She smoothes her skirt beneath her legs to sit, and I hand her a box.

"Yup. Like the whiskey. But no one calls me that unless I'm in trouble."

"Ohh. I'll remember that." Her eyes flash with a mischief I haven't seen from her, and my heart does a tug-o-war with my dick to decide which one likes it more. It's a draw. She's perfect. I want to make an absolute mess of her.

I manage to tamp that down, though, because I also want to take her out tonight. We talk in between bites, her feet crossed at the ankles and tucked between mine beneath the table, trailing off when the band starts and it's too hard to hear each other. We're headed to the beer tap when I see Em at the edge of a blanket near the band, hand to her eyes to block the setting sun. I do a double-take when I notice Cara sprawled out on the ground beside her. Interesting.

I turn to Noel. "Em's here. Do you mind if we say hi?"

"Of course not."

We cross the lawn, waving when Em sees us. "Hey. I didn't know you were coming tonight." I say hi to Cara and give Em a cocky smirk that says, *"and look who you brought."*

She ignores me, though, instead turning to Noel. "I know you."

Noel slants nervous eyes at me, until Em says, "From the launch last month."

"Right. I'm—"

"Noel," Em says. "Like Christmas."

She laughs. "Yes."

I introduce Cara who's staring at me with a too-wide grin. I know instantly she and Em have been talking about me. Before Wes's dad, my mom was married to this guy who had two daughters, both younger than me and obnoxiously interested in everything I did. This is like that.

Cara stands to give me a side hug. Her huge mass of cinnamon-colored curls sticks to my stubble, and I make a show of pushing it down before hugging her back.

"You and Jamie went to school together, right?" Noel asks Em, and it's fucking adorable the way she seems nervous. Like she's trying for something she doesn't know she already has.

I slide my hand into hers. "We met at intramural soccer when we were freshman at SMCC."

Em nods. "He sucks at soccer, by the way. He's too tall to run right."

Noel tips her head to look up at me like she's doing the math on that. "First of all," I say, glaring at Em. "I only played soccer to keep in shape for hockey. It was a commitment to get this good."

"Please remember you're talking to the woman whose porch you bled all over after a hockey game." Noel pats my cheek playfully, then lets her thumb trace the last of the bruise around my eye.

"I took a bad hit because I'm such a fierce competitor," I say, leaning into her palm. "I like to mix it up on the ice. It's dangerous."

Em snorts. "You're a big, dangerous teddy bear, Jamie."

"That's right. I heard you got your brain jostled," Cara says. "Em said you're defying all of your doctor's orders and being a general idiot about it."

Noel's eyes go wide like she can't decide whether to laugh or press for a specific list of my defiances. "Noel's been taking care of me," I say.

They're both looking at Noel now.

"Are you a nurse?" Cara asks.

"I am not. And he hasn't listened to me once."

A connection fires in my brain. "Actually, Noel's an artist, Cara."

Cara lights up at that like I thought she might.

The two of us are in a networking group together which is how she and Em met. People often underestimate Cara because she wears bright, bohemian clothes and as a former theater kid, has a tendency to break into song. She's sharp, though, and extremely ambitious. And she's been talking non-stop about a project she wants to begin by year's end.

"What kind of art?" she asks Noel.

"I'm a graphic designer."

"She's a painter."

Noel flicks a look at me, half chastising, half curious. "Mostly watercolor, but not exclusively."

"Botanicals," I add, repeating Noe's fancy word for plants.

Cara presses her hands together. "Well, that's some fucking serendipity."

I nudge Noel. "Are you taking any commissions?"

"Why? Do you want me to paint your portrait?"

Em barks a laugh. "Oh, I like this one."

Me too, I think. *Me fucking too*. "Now that you mention it. Cara, what do you think? My face could sell a lot of coffee."

"Before the black eye, maybe."

"Ouch."

Cara turns to Noel. "You know the old fish shacks on outer Commercial Street?"

"I do."

"I turned them into a coffee and breakfast stand—The Cara Bean. This summer was our first season, and it was amazing. It's the perfect location to grab commuters from the bridge on their way in and out of town. I've been looking for someone to design a mural for the sides of the shacks while we're off season."

"Oh." Understanding breaks on Noel's face. "What kind of mural?"

"Realistic. Naturey... is that a word? But, like, also fun." Cara nods her head like she's figuring it out as she goes. "Something uniquely Portland. That's all I have so far, which is exactly why I need a designer. I'd be thrilled to talk with you if you're interested."

I'm standing on the edge of a cliff waiting for Noel's answer. It's not entirely selfish, this would be a great thing for her, but also, a job is a very practical reason for her to stick around longer. There's nothing Noel loves more than being practical.

Her eyes dart to mine as if she's heard my thoughts—I'm not convinced she can't—then she turns to Cara. "I'm not sure how long I'll be here. I'm staying at my grandmother's house."

"Long enough to design it, though," I say. "Right?"

She chews her lip, and I bump her with my shoulder. "Well, yes. I mean I could design it from anywhere."

"But you said you've always had more inspiration here."

Cara grabs her purse from the blanket and digs her card out, handing it to Noel. She punches me lightly in the bicep. "Jamie Bishop, you little match maker. Noel, please text me, will you?"

"Yes, of course. Thank you." Noel slips the business card into her purse, hiding her grin between her teeth. I don't miss it, though, and I'm clinging to it hard.

Twenty-Two

Noel

"**D**O YOU REALLY THINK I can do it?" Jamie and I are standing in line for another drink alone after leaving Em and Cara to their date. The card she gave me is practically buzzing in my cross-body purse at my hip.

He looks down at me with an amused smile while his fingers flirt with the hem of my sweater. "Why wouldn't you be able to, Noe?"

I bite my lip. "I've done murals before in school. But this is a bigger job than anything I've done. More complex."

"I bet the last one you did in school was bigger than the one you did before that."

"*Yesss.*"

"That's how it works, right? Opportunities keep getting bigger the more of them we take." The line moves forward, and his hand presses to my back, moving me with it. "I think you should stay here and paint your flowers."

"Move to the beach and become an artist? That's a little

pie in the sky, don't you think?" I laugh a little, but really I'm asking. Of course I know what he'll say. He's bold even when he has no reason to be. What I used to call reckless. Not anymore.

"You're already an artist, so I don't see why it would be." The cashier waves him over, holding out my rum hot cocoa and Jamie's bottled water. "We're going to keep talking about this," he says, letting his hand trail over my hip as he passes me.

He's been touching me all night, his hand on my thigh as we drove here, then firmly clasped in mine when we walked up to Em and Cara. There's no tentativeness anymore, no wondering if fate is going to take a hard left. It's arrived.

"So tell me what scares you about it?"

My eyes snap to his, sure I accidentally said that out loud, until I realize he's picking up our previous conversation. He hands me my cocoa and I flip the lid, blowing on it a few times before taking a sip. It takes me that long to articulate it. "I think I'm worried I'll like it too much."

He snorts. "So the worst case scenario is you accept the job and end up happier than you were before?"

That I fall in love with something I can't keep? Yes. That is the worst case scenario.

I look up from my cocoa to find Jamie's eyes on mine, his full attention on whatever I'm about to say. His face slips so easily from amused to intense, and it has this funny way of pulling me with him, straight into confessions I usually hold a lot closer to my chest. "I think..." I say carefully. "I think I'm still learning how to want things. When I was growing up, everything was ruled by the things my mother wanted. I just got used to going with the flow, being happy with whatever was left."

His nose scrunches and his lip curls up. It's an expression

somewhere between confusion and distaste. "What's she like? Your mom."

I blow out a breath. "She's... difficult to explain. If you met her, you'd probably love her."

"Why's that?" he asks in a tone that sounds more like "I doubt it."

I chew my lip, considering how to describe a lifetime with Elena Kasey. "Have you ever shown up to a party late, and found everyone around you is already having the time of their lives while you're still sober? And you get the immediate feeling you need to keep your wits about you because some-one—*someone*—needs to be responsible. But you're also so tired because you need a break too, and why should it be you all the time?

"That's what life with my mother is like. She's always having the time of her life, and ever since I was a kid, I've been mak-ing sure she has a glass of water or a ride home. Metaphori-cally, I mean. It's usually a lot more expensive than an Uber."

"Sounds like you were a very good kid," he says, taking my hand and starting toward the water edge.

I sigh and tip my head back. "That's what she always said. She used to brag that her life didn't have to change much when I was born. She used to tell everyone what an easy kid I was, how even as a baby, I never cried. I think it was the other way around, though. I was easy because I had to be."

"Why?"

"It's just, she had me young, and she had a lot left to do, so we did it together. I guess there's really only ever been space for one of us."

Jamie nods, slowly pulling to a stop when we're at the edge of the point. He wraps his arms around me, settling my back against his warm chest, and I sink into the comfort of it. "Maybe it works out for her this time," he says quietly. "The van thing, and you get to have your turn."

I soften my response with a laugh. "It literally never works out. Somehow she got in her head that the world is an oyster full of endless pearls. And when she realizes the particular one she's chasing is plastic, she comes back."

"Maybe it doesn't work out for her then. But maybe it works out for you in the in-between. I know it's hard to break dynamics like that, ones that were set when we were kids. Trust me, I'm pretty sure my brother still sees me as a delinquent teenager no matter how successful Fortune is. But your mom's not here right now to take up that space, Noe. You're holding it for her assuming she'll need it back. I'm not saying that's not a good assumption, just that right now, while it's empty, you can fill it with whatever you want. If she comes back, well, you do what you have to do, but you do it from where *you* are."

I let that advice wash over me, mix with the affection I have for the person giving it. Here, in Maine, has always been my space. That's why I loved it here. A few months of in-between that I got to fill with what I wanted. That part hasn't changed, I realize. I've been avoiding it for two years because I was afraid it wouldn't be that for me anymore without Nana, but as soon as I came back, I found it waiting for me.

I found *him* waiting for me.

"Huh."

"What?"

"Nothing, it's just... that was really wise."

Jamie laughs awkwardly, and I tip my head to see his cheeks pink. "I don't know about that."

"No. It was. What you said about how your brother sees you. Why do you think that?"

He blows out a breath. "When I was younger, I had a really hard time in school. I wasn't on meds yet. Adderall."

"You have ADHD?"

"And dyscalculia."

"What is it?"

"It's like dyslexia but with numbers. I try to store a number in my head to, like, track how many beers I've poured of each kind, or keep score in a game, but they just..." He makes a fluttering motion by his temple. "Disappear."

"That's why you donate money to the children's learning center," I say, remembering the sign from his launch.

He shrugs. "I was in college when I got diagnosed. It would have been helpful to have something like that when I was younger."

I look up at him, eyes wide. "*College?*"

"A professor of mine saw me writing numbers on my hand. It was an applied math class, so it was pretty mortifying. Turned out he had the same issue. Hooked me up with a counselor, and I took some tests. I got a prescription and a pamphlet."

"Brewing," I say. "It's calculus though, isn't it?"

He smirks. "I don't do that in my head, Noel." I push his shoulder with mine. "I've never had a problem with advanced math like that anyway. Quiz me on times tables though, and I'd better either have my phone out or a third grader nearby to cheat off of."

He laughs, and I notice the small shake in it, the way his dimple only flashes instead of stays.

"You're embarrassed by it," I say, and *wow*, Noel. Way to stumble upon a wound and dig.

"I'm not," he says firmly. Then, "Not the way I used to be. I'm more... eternally frustrated by it. When I was a kid, it was worse. My mom used to hide my homework from Wes's dad, stuff it in her purse on the way home from school. *She* was embarrassed by it."

Something flares in my chest, a protective urge. Jamie's face inspires all sorts of adult thoughts, but it's easy to imagine him as a kid when I look at his eyes. They spark and smile even when he's frowning. His wild streak intimidates me sometimes, but right now he's reminding me that Peter Pan was actually just a lost boy.

"Anyway, I made it harder than it had to be. In all of my teenage wisdom I chose to deal with it by fucking up harder at life than at school. I was so afraid people would think I was stupid, I let them think I was trouble instead. Turns out that was a harder reputation to shake."

"Small city," I say quietly.

"Right. One night... " He hesitates before blowing out a breath. "I was at a party meeting Wes of all people. I only just walked in when it got busted up by the cops. I hadn't had a chance to get myself into trouble yet, so it was mostly just a hassle, until they started pulling kids aside, checking IDs. Anyone underage, like me, they started giving those tests, you know? To see if you've been drinking. Walk a straight line, all that. I did what the cop said. Then he asked me to count backwards from twenty, and fuck, he might as well have asked me to perform brain surgery. I couldn't do it."

"What happened?"

"He took me in. Cuffed and everything. I did the breathalyzer test at the station and cleared myself, but I still had to sit in a cell and wait for Wes's dad to come get me."

"Shit."

"It was humiliating, getting hauled in like that." He swallows roughly, then as if on instinct, he puts on a smile meant to lessen the weight of that admission. It's only half of his regular one, though, and my heart throbs with an ache so deep, I feel it in my toes.

I'm suddenly filled with rage at that waitress for the dirty looks, and his mother for hiding him instead of helping, and anyone else who added to this humiliation. It's something I've always struggled with, admitting the things I long for instead of locking them up like a secret. I'm wondering now, looking at Jamie's half smile and moody eyes, if maybe admitting them is the only way to get them. If Jamie Bishop longs for someone to be on his team, I'll nominate myself for captain.

"Anyway," he says. "Now that I've told you my most embarrassing moment, wanna make out again?"

I snort and let him have this change of subject. "Funny, I thought your most embarrassing moment was when you passed out on my porch in a puddle of blood."

He tickles my waist, and I giggle a little too loudly. It makes an embarrassing echo on the glassy water in front of us. Jamie's delighted by this. "Actually, that was my best moment."

"How on earth was that your best moment?"

The grin on his face loosens to something softer, a little sappy. "Because it brought me back to you."

If I needed any more evidence that I'm following my own fate to a tee, it comes the following weekend when Jamie and I go out with Kate and Colin.

"He is smoking hot, Noel," Kate says. "Those tattoos, that scruffy face. *Gah*. He wears a T-shirt very well, too."

We're sitting upstairs at a vaguely-Irish bar with views of the water and walls painted a moody blue. In the room beside us, a band plays a cover of "Southern Cross."

I roll my eyes and let her have this objectification because it's all true and this is the double date of Kate's dreams. She's waited years to actually like someone I'm dating, and Jamie has spent the night thoroughly charming them both. Not that I expected any less. I've yet to meet someone who doesn't love Jamie Bishop. Besides Fran.

"Eyes to yourself, Katherine, or I'll tell Colin." He and Jamie have gone to the bar to get another round.

Kate cackles and takes a sip of her cocktail. "So tell me how it works."

"How sex works? Kate, I've known you way too long."

She dips her fingertips in her drink and flicks gin at me. "I mean how the psychic thing works. Can you, like, read his thoughts while you're doing it?"

My cheeks flame and I glance at the bar again to make sure Colin and Jamie are still out of earshot.

"Dad's not listening. Spill."

"Ask me a serious question and I will."

"Are you in love? Is he? You'd be able to tell, right?" Kate clicks her tongue and presses her hand to her heart. "Your face is practically glowing."

"Oh my God. I highly doubt a few orgasms have changed my complexion."

"You underestimate what stress can do to your pores. But seriously, how do you feel?"

I take a deep breath and let it out slowly to keep from gushing. It doesn't work. "I feel... wild. Desperate. Like I can't get enough of him."

Kate's eyes bulge, and I cover my red cheeks with my hands. "God, this wasn't supposed to happen." Not this fast. Not this... intensely.

"Seems to me," Kate says, "this is exactly what was supposed to happen."

She's right, of course. According to everything we've seen so far, it *was* supposed to. I've gone from looking for holes in the magic, to letting it wash over me, bring me back to life. And this new perspective has opened up a whole new box of possibilities.

"I have to ask you something," I say.

Kate leans over the table, somehow instinctively knowing this is secret-worthy.

"Remember the vision I had at the bar?"

"The one with his tongue in your mouth? Yeah."

"The one where we were on Nana's porch. It was summer."

She wrinkles her nose. "Okay?"

It seems like a small detail, but it's been swelling in the back of my brain since the other night when I met Cara. And this new perspective is asking: What if it's connected? Me and him and me and here. *Me and Cara's mural.*

"Kate, if I convince Vi to give me this job, I won't be here past Christmas. Even if I don't get it, come May, I need to have tenants here. I haven't been back here in the summer in years because I can't afford to."

Kate tilts her head. "You think that was the point of the vision? That you should stay longer?"

"I don't know. Except for the one about Jamie's career, they've all just been the two of us *together.*"

I've been searching this thing for rules, some sort of pattern. I thought it was the touching at first, but Jamie and I touch *a lot* now. All of this time, all of this closeness, and nothing. And I couldn't *make* it happen when I tried.

But they do have something in common. Every time I've had one, it's been when I tried to walk away from him.

That's exactly what I was doing when I first saw us up on that roof. The very first thought I had about him before I even lit that candle was: Not for me. I chew my bottom lip, playing it back. I saw Becca. I saw the money. But I didn't see me and Jamie until I tried to run away from him.

At the beach that night, his hands were all over me and nothing, until I bolted from the water. That night at Fortune, I was running away too. Because he scared me, the way he wanted to dive into this thing instead of cower. Then, I thought he was reckless, foolish.

Now...

I glance at Jamie across the room, then back to Kate. "I just started thinking maybe there's more to it than just, you know, the horny part."

We already know Jamie's career is tied up in whatever is making me see these visions. What if mine is too? What if I have proof that I could have this? What if I already *saw* myself having it: Kissing Jamie in the rain in the summer. Here.

I wouldn't have met Cara if I wasn't with Jamie. And I wouldn't have been there with him—holding his hand, meeting his friends—if I hadn't seen it. If the visions hadn't set us on this road.

"Do you think that's crazy?" I ask Kate.

She gives me a look that says *what about this isn't?*

"Colin said he thinks this thing is trying to tell you something. If he's right, maybe this is it. Kiss Jamie. Don't leave. Boom. Universe Achievement unlocked."

I laugh, but Kate's face is oddly serious. "What?"

"It's just... It was always this easy, Noel." She waves a hand, gesturing to the whole of this transformation I've been through in the last weeks, from matte and colorless to filled to the brim. "You just had to let yourself want it."

This hits me with a quick pang of longing for time lost, but just as quickly I decide to allow myself some grace for this too. I may have needed a kick in the butt from some unknown power, but I'm here now, letting my heart lead me by the wrist.

The guys come back with their beers, and I slide over, letting Jamie in beside me. His arm wraps around my shoulder, his lips finding the top of my head, and once Kate has him engrossed in a conversation, I quietly pull my phone from my

purse and send Cara a text.
Noel: I'd love to talk to you more about your project.

Twenty-Three

Jamie

"**J**AMIE, FOCUS." WES SNAPS his fingers in front of my face, and I jerk out of the trance I've been in for the last few minutes. It's his own fault. He put like seven spreadsheets in front of me and my brain instantly scrambled them all.

I'm running on about six hours of sleep total this weekend between Noel and a couple of shifts at the bar. This morning, I woke up to her in my bed, the blanket slipped down her body, showing me everything from her dark hair spilled over her shoulders to those sexy dimples above her ass. My body was spent and wrung out, and I still couldn't decide if I wanted to slip back under for another few hours, or climb over her, wake her with my mouth, and go again. I chose the latter.

"Yeah, looks good, man." I shove the spreadsheets away, hoping he can't tell I have no idea what I'm agreeing to.

Wes scoops the papers into a stack, tapping them on his desk. "Fine. Agenda item two: NEBev. I hope you took some time on your vacation to think about it."

I snort. "By vacation, do you mean my doctor-ordered time off?"

"Seems to me, if you can work behind the bar again, you can take a meeting with their guys. This isn't the kind of decision you make at game time."

I close my eyes and rub at my temples. If he actually thinks I've been avoiding thinking about this decision all together, he has less faith in me than I thought.

There was a time when Wes and I had more to say to each other than just this tug-o-war, and if I'm honest, I miss it. The first summer I moved into his dad's house was tense and awkward—two fourteen-year-old boys whose parents decided we were brothers one day—and I don't know if it was the arrogance of that age or that we'd both been through it before, but eventually these lines formed. Wes and me on one side, our parents' chaos on the other. It was a chance to forge our own stability, something that might last even if our new family didn't.

And it did last. Wes and I have never had much in common on the surface, but he's the only person from the revolving door that was my childhood who kept me after he wasn't required to. Part of me wonders if I should agree with him about this just to get a little of that back. But a stronger part of me wishes it was him who felt that way.

"It's only October, Wes." I pick up a pen and spin it between my fingers, feeling agitated and like I need to move. "Lay off."

"I'd love to lay off, but *I don't wanna* is not a business strategy. You're acting like a child avoiding his homework."

"Does that make you the teacher? Because I don't take assignments from you." I feel myself resorting to cockiness, and I also feel the way it misses like a boxer catching air with his fist.

"No, you just take all your business advice from me so you

can sip beer and pour it."

My teeth grind together. "We each get paid to do what we do."

"Sure, until we don't. It's called job security, Jameson, and it's important to those of us who think beyond tomorrow. That's what this offer gets us. That's what you're missing with your stubborn refusal to take it seriously."

Security. You'd think growing up the way I did, bouncing from house to house, a new step family every few years, security would be a white whale, but I just can't make myself see it that way. Instead, that security he's talking about feels like an accusation that I'm in over my head and need to be bailed out.

"I am taking it seriously, Wes. That's why I sounded so serious when I told you I needed more time."

"I know this success isn't something you were prepared for, Jameson, but it's time to be greedy because there's no guarantee it will last."

"Tell that to Sam Adams."

"When we have Sam Adams money, I'll stop telling it to you."

"Is there a third item on this agenda, because I do have to get out to the bar."

"Actually, there is. I talked to Ronnie today," he says, and I know immediately where this is going. Damn this tiny little city. "Had to square up for the hops delivery. He said you brought Noel to the farm."

"And?"

"And you promised she had nothing to do with this, then you bring her to a business meeting."

I laugh for real this time. "Come on. It was my day off. I go there all the time."

"I told you we're not making decisions based on this bullshit fantasy anymore. Fucking hell. Do you even understand the amount of money at stake right now?"

"I know exactly what's at stake. Look, Noel and I aren't your concern, and neither is what I do at the farm, or our suppliers. It's all in my purview."

"I know you, Jamie." He crosses his arms over his chest. "You were eventually going to listen to me like you always do. But now you're digging in even harder, and only one thing has changed."

Actually, a lot of things have changed. And yeah, I wanted Noel's help at the start of this, but it's complicated now. I meant what I said to her that night on her couch, and the last thing I want is for her to wonder if that's what I'm thinking about when I'm with her now. It's not. But that's also none of Wes's business.

Wes takes my lack of response as agreement, and I let him have it. "Don't forget you have Sugarloaf next weekend for their Fall Fest," he says as I push out of the chair. "Thousands of people will come through. Make sure you're prepared."

I perk up slightly at the reminder. I love these kinds of events, getting to hand out my beer to people and nerd out about hops and spices with them. It beats ties and sales calls any day. Sure as fuck beats these spreadsheets. I knock my fist on his desk and head for the bar. "It's handled."

"Do you want anything to drink?" Noel calls up to me from her kitchen.

"I'm good. Just come to bed." I'm lying on her bed, still in a towel from the post-work shower I convinced her to share with me.

She crests the stairs, her hair pulled up haphazardly, wearing another one of my shirts, and the entire contents of my chest cavity turns to liquid. She's the most beautiful thing I've ever seen.

"It's so cold," she says, dancing on her toes.

"Come here and get warm." She throws a knee over my waist, seating herself in my lap. I immediately run my hands up her bare thighs, groaning as my fingers disappear beneath the hem of her shirt. I may not have whatever gift Noel has. I can't *see* the future, but here I feel it settle over me like warm water. Nights downtown. Lazy mornings with her fingers in my hair.

I picture the winter that's nipping at us, keeping each other warm like this. Waking up with her head on my chest, her leg slung over my waist. Holding her hand under the table at dinner.

I don't picture her leaving to go back to Connecticut at the end of the year. I don't even let myself think about it.

"Hey. Where'd you go?" Noel leans forward, slowly pressing her mouth to mine, and I realize I've been in my head for more than a polite amount of time.

"Sorry. I'm here." At the taste of her, I'm sucked right back into the moment. Her hair falls around us, blocking the light from the lamp on her nightstand, and I deepen the kiss. Her lips are pink and bee-stung from my stubble but I can't make myself stop. "Do you want to come to a thing with me next weekend?"

"Do I have to dress up?"

I snort. "Weird lead off question, but yes, actually. It requires a short dress. Preferably cleavage-bearing."

She shakes her head. "Fresh."

"I have to go to Sugarloaf Mountain for a festival. I thought maybe we could stay at the hotel. You could paint while I work if you wanted. The mountain has good views and—"

She presses her fingers to my lips. "Yes."

"Yeah?"

"Of course I'll go."

"Good." I let out the breath I was holding and sit up to kiss her again. And promptly smack the top of my head on the slanted ceiling. "Shit," I hiss, falling back onto the pillow. "That's the third time I've done that."

Noel claps a hand over her mouth. "Are you okay?"

"I don't know. Better come check."

She frowns. "You're too big for my bed."

"I'll just stay horizontal. Come sit."

She quirks an eyebrow, a smile hinting at her lips. "I am sitting."

"On my face, baby." I give her hips a tug, and her hand slaps the angled ceiling above my head to keep from tipping over. She giggles but it turns to a moan when I press a kiss between her legs. Soft. Sweet, in case she's sore from before.

"I thought we were going to bed," she says. "I've been tricked."

"Do you want me to stop?" I pop my thumb in my mouth, then press it against her, making a slow circle. Her eyes roll back.

"Don't you dare," she says, then quieter, "I'm meeting Cara tomorrow morning. About her mural."

Pride for her distracts me and I stop moving. "Yeah? Are you excited?"

"I don't know. I haven't really let myself think about it yet."

"Why does that not surprise me."

"What doesn't surprise you?"

"That you have this amazing opportunity but you're putting your excitement on ice." I lift my head and press my tongue flat against her. "Noe. This is awesome. *Feel* it."

She mutters a curse under her breath. "Do you always give advice with your head between a woman's legs?"

"I don't always do anything." I swat her ass lightly, then soothe it with a squeeze. "Admit you're excited."

She squirms above me, an inch from riding my face, but I hold her just shy of the pressure she wants, that I'm dying to give her.

"It's just..."

I nudge her with my nose, and she hisses.

"I don't like to get excited about stuff until—Ah."

I crane my neck, letting her feel my breath on her skin, but nothing else. "Noel."

She whines, then laughs. "Okay, fine. It is pretty amazing."

"It's fucking awesome. Will you come by the bar after you're done?"

"Stop teasing me and I'll do whatever you want."

I press up and suck hard.

"Okay. Yes. Yes."

"That's my girl. Now spread your legs and let me kiss you good night."

Twenty-Four

Noel

CARA BEAN COFFEE IS a bright and colorful row of converted fishing shacks on the working end of the waterfront. I arrive as the sun is rising over the water, painting it a beautiful sherbet behind the rusty white fishing boats. Jamie's words—*feel it, Noe*—warm me from the inside as I park in the dirt lot and head to the door.

I *am* excited for this. This is the kind of work I dreamed of doing when I applied to art school. But everyone's a dreamer in school. *I'll be a painter, or a writer, or change the world at the helm of a non-profit*, say like ninety percent of undergrads. Then you graduate and the real world hands you your first bill, your mother moves into your condo, your family gets sick, and suddenly all of that seems like a fairytale.

Working as an artist full-time is something I hadn't even considered before I met Jamie. But he's inspiring, supportive in a way I haven't really experienced. Not that Kate and Colin haven't supported me in my work, but their advice has always been more of a careful nudging, like leading a spooked horse. Jamie's never cared about being careful. He grabbed my hand and started running the minute we met.

Cara steps from the middle of the three buildings, meeting me on the small deck overlooking the water. "I'm so excited you're here," she says, hugging me like we're old friends. "I swear meeting you the other night just seems like serendipity."

I try to keep my laugh from sounding unhinged. I want to scream: *You have no idea*! as I follow her inside. She's laid open a notebook of inspiration photos on the roughhewn counter-height bar and we pull up stools.

"I've thoroughly scoured your Instagram," she tells me. "And I really think our ideas are going to work so well together."

"I think so too."

Portland is full of murals like the one she wants. It seems every building has donated a piece of its brick and stone facade to color—painted lighthouses and boats and abstracts. As a kid obsessed with art, it felt like some special heaven made just for me. Getting to design one myself, leave my mark on the city I love so much? It's as serendipitous to me as it is to Cara.

"So," Cara says. "Tell me all of your thoughts."

I pull out my tablet full of sketches I put together. "Well, you could probably see from my socials that flowers are sort of a specialty of mine." She nods along as I pull up my last line of floral invitations on Etsy, admittedly old now but suddenly my most relevant portfolio. "I think that works especially well with the organic slant to your brand. Maybe some honeysuckle like this." I point to the rendering on my screen. "Chamomile blooms aren't the most decorative but I could sprinkle them amongst some of the other natural elements that are in your teas."

This idea came from seeing Jamie's hops plants in a new light, how pretty the plain flowers look inked onto his bicep. "I can pull the colors here," I wave a hand at the stools we're seated on, a mixture of nautical blues and greens, "for the abstract behind the blooms."

When I'm finished flipping through the digital sketches, Cara's face is beaming. "I love it."

"You do?"

"So much!"

I bite back the full watt of my grin to maintain some professionalism, but inside I'm bursting. "I think it will be quirky like you wanted, but really push your brand from behind the design."

"It's brilliant. Really, Noel. I guess the only question is what you said the other night, that you're only here temporarily. *Sooo*, after it's designed..." She gives me that gap-toothed smile that takes years off her face in the same way Jaime's dimples do. "Are you going to stick around and paint it?"

I know this *is* the question, and it's met with a somersault sensation inside my chest, a knee-jerk: *This can't be real.*

Though, who would have thought any of the rest of it could be real? This serendipity, this fate. So much has changed since I showed up here afraid of the emptiness I thought I'd find being here without Nana. It's been filled with so many other things that I was missing—painting like I used to, more time with Kate. And things I didn't even know I was missing, like Jamie and everything he comes with, including this opportunity. I could barely stand for him to leave my bed this morning. How can I walk away from him now? If I trust the visions, I know he's where I'm supposed to be. And he's here.

He showed me how to want things, and the visions showed me that all of these things are tied together. Everything I want is in this place.

Kiss Jamie. Don't leave. Boom. Universe Achievement un-locked.

It has to be the point of all of this. I think I'm supposed to stay.

"Yes," I tell Cara. "I want to do the whole thing."

"Then you're hired!" She stands and wraps her arms around my shoulders. I brace myself for the panic to come, the *oh my God, what did I just do* dropping in my stomach. But it doesn't. I'm not sure it won't when I have to actually make this call to Vi, but for now, excitement rushes up my body. I hug Cara back and it spills out of me in giddy laughter.

It kind of feels like I can't lose.

Twenty-Five

Jamie

B Y MID DAY, I'M antsy behind the bar. I know Cara's going to fall in love with Noe's work. It's a perfect match for Cara Bean, the florals and bright colors. But I don't know if Noel will accept it. If she'll stay. I'm trying not to get my hopes up high enough for the fall to be devastating.

I deliver an order to the end of the bar just as Wes emerges from his office. I forgot he was still here. He doesn't usually stay this late, though I haven't been here in a while, so maybe that changed without me noticing.

I glance at the door for the hundredth time. If he sticks around much longer, worlds are going to collide.

"Can I get one?" he asks.

"Sure." I pull a glass. I don't need to ask what he wants. He only drinks our original ale. Sometimes I think his faith in me only went as far as a one hit wonder.

I slide it to him, and he takes a long pull.

It's terrible timing and perfect timing when the front door

swings open, and Noel walks in, both hands clutched around her messenger bag strap across her front.

Finally. I know this is about to bite me in the ass with Wes here, but I don't care. I'm so happy to see her.

I leave Wes, stepping around the bar to meet her at the wait station, pulling her flush against me. "Hey, gorgeous." My voice sounds tight, caught in my throat.

"Hi." Her hands slide over my shoulders, and she pushes to her toes, kissing me softly. My blood heats instantly. It's such a small thing, a kiss hello, fingers at the back of your neck, but when you haven't had it in so long, it's dizzying.

When she pulls away, she bounces a little. Her lip is tightly between her teeth, eyes wide. She's excited. It has to be good news.

"How'd it go?"

"It was so good, Jamie."

I press a thumb to her chin, my heart in my throat. "Does that smile mean you said yes?"

"Yes. I said yes."

My breath rushes out in a gust, and I wrap her in a tight hug, lifting her onto her toes.

"I think we're going to work so well together," she says into my shoulder, and I'm listening, I really am, but my whole body is vibrating with relief. I want to punch the air. I want to carry her right up those stairs, drop her in my bed, and show her how desperate I was for this answer.

She gives a little squeak when I squeeze her too hard, and I set her back down with a kiss that I have to force myself to to end.

"Sorry. Fuck. Tell me everything."

"Cara's giving me, like, complete creative control. I haven't been this excited about a project since college. Thank you so much for introducing us. For setting this up."

I laugh. "I'm not taking any credit, Noel."

"But you should! It's no different than my *intervention*." She whispers that last part, and I instinctually glance behind me at Wes. Of course he's watching me. Us.

"Well, I think it calls for a celebration, either way," I say. "I'm off in an hour. I'll take you out."

"Cara asked if we had plans tonight. She said maybe we could all go out, her and Em."

I can tell she's excited about this too, and I jump at the chance to tuck her deeper into my life. "Will you sleep in my bed afterward?"

"Yes," she says, bouncing on her toes. "Yes. Yes. Yes."

This fucking girl. "Then it's a date. Sit here," I say, heading back behind the bar. "I have to work, but I want to look at you while I do it."

She settles on a stool, slipping off her coat and pulling the elastic band out of her hair. Her smile is enormous, and I can't take my eyes off of it.

Which is probably why I didn't notice Wes until he moved closer, leaning his arms over the back of the stool beside Noel.

"Aren't you going to introduce me to your girlfriend, Jamie?" Wes says, and my teeth grind together. If he ruins this good mood for her, I swear to God...

"Noe, this is my brother Wes. Wes, Noel Kasey."

"Oh, hi! It's so good to meet you!" Noel puts her hand out, smiling. She doesn't know he's being a dick. Why would she? She didn't grow up with his mood swings and there really shouldn't be any reason for tension. But there are landmines everywhere in this conversation, buried way before she got here.

Wes leans forward, clasping her hand, shaking it. "Ah, the famous Noel."

"I don't know about that." Her smile fades, and she shoots

a nervous glance at me.

I warn him with a look, but he ignores it. "Well," he says. "You're practically his other business partner, right? Or advisor, I suppose. As an obviously interested party, I have to ask: Did Jamie ever mention how he failed his attempt at a business major? He had to do a fifth year to even graduate. It must be important to your process to have all the information, right? So he surely wouldn't leave anything out."

"Enough," I snap, and Noel gapes at me.

Wes takes the last sip of his beer and pushes the glass at me with a smug smile.

Damn it. I rarely let him get to me, and I know he considers it a win that he made me break character just then. "It's been a pleasure, Noel," he says, slipping on his jacket. Turning to me, he lowers his voice. "There's a reason you didn't try to run this place yourself. You'd be wise to remember that."

Twenty-Six

"WHY DID HE SAY that to you?" I have to nearly shout this because Jamie is power walking ahead of me, long legs eating up the cobblestone street. We're almost to the restaurant where we're supposed to meet Em and Cara and I don't want to let this go until afterward.

Jamie seems to realize I can't keep up and finally slows. "It's the price of doing business with Wes, Noe. It's fine."

"It was awful." As the captain of Team Jamie Bishop, Wes is now squarely on my shit list.

"His moods are factored into my salary." His cheek hitches up in his Jamie Smile but I know how well he wields that charm, and I'm not falling for it. I tug him to the edge of the sidewalk, and he follows reluctantly. I can tell he's bracing for something. What, I don't know, but there's a *please don't* in the slump of his shoulders.

"Jamie." I press in close and take his face in my hands, scratching at the stubble that's starting to become a beard.

It's a testament to the rightness between us when his body loosens like an untied knot. "It's an old dynamic," he says quietly. "Like I said."

Except he didn't. Not more than that simple platitude. I know all about Jamie taking a chance after my reading, turning down the job, getting the investment, but I don't know how Wes fits in. "What he said, about you not doing it without him. Why didn't you? Why factor in his moods at all? You could just take your idea and run with it."

He pulls away, huffing a laugh. The edges of it are sharp. "What?"

"You heard what he said. Brewing beer is one thing, Noe. Turning it into a business takes a certain skill that I don't have."

"Says who? Wes?" I don't know who I am to talk here. I've made plenty of excuses for not doing the things that scared me, but I'm trying to be different, and he's the one who inspired me to do that. It's a shock to see Jamie Bishop unsure of himself. He's a risk taker, a dreamer. This knee-jerk diffidence doesn't compute. "Not everyone who runs a business has a degree in it, Jamie."

"Sure, but most of them can understand a profit and loss statement, read a spreadsheet." He blows out a resigned breath. "Look, Noe, it's not just about the..." He gestures to his head, then shakes it. "I have bad instincts, okay? That gut feeling that guides people? Mine doesn't work."

I'm incredulous to the point of petulance on his behalf. "Give me an example."

"When I was sixteen, I saved up enough money to get a car. I found a used Jeep Wrangler, soft top. I wanted it." An expression similar to lust flashes on his face. "I don't know, call it hyperfixation or emotional attachment to an idea, but I had to have it. So I did. Lemon would be a nice way to describe that thing."

"It's a car," I say. "You were a kid."

"I wasn't a kid when I went to that party and ended up with a misdemeanor on my record. I wasn't a kid when I... *Becca.*" We both still at her name for different reasons. My reason tastes a lot like jealousy. "The point is I get these ideas... these obsessions, and my brain conflates how badly I want it with an assurance that it will all work out. I can't tell the difference."

I swallow, my neck prickling. "And I removed that variable. With the vision."

"Exactly. Becca, she was hard against me taking that chance, but I really felt like this time was different, that I wasn't going to get this wrong. Except I always feel like that. Then, you told me I was right this time. There were at least two people who thought this was a good idea. And that was enough."

Okay, I tell myself, working out this history. It's fine because I *did* know he was right. It's not dangerous for him to feel that way now given all we've seen.

"And Wes?"

"Look, everything happened really fast after that night on the roof. I'd just lost a six-year relationship, I was unemployed with a dream in one hand and seed money in the other, and I knew it for what it was. A once in a lifetime opportunity. The way things unfolded, I needed to make decisions right away. I needed a business plan to go to the bank with. I needed profit projections. Just the online loan application was overwhelming. I panicked. I realized that even though I knew it was the right path, there would be decisions to make daily that could sink me, so my first business decision was to take it out of my own hands."

He looks away sharply, red washing over his cheekbones. That night at the point, he wasn't embarrassed, but *this* is something else. That was history. This is now. This is the future.

It's starting to fall together, the way he has it in his head that the whole of his success is just some fluke, why he's leaning so hard on another vision before he makes this decision. People have been telling him what he can't do his whole life through one message or another. That night on the roof, I told him he could.

"Do you regret it? Going into business with him?"

He thinks for a moment. "Yes and no. I don't think I'd be here without Wes. He carries a lot of it. But I'm not sure we're headed to the same place. The whole thing is going through some growing pains, I guess."

"Because you disagree about selling?"

"Maybe he's right. Maybe I don't take his advice and I give up a fuck ton of money just to run it into the ground on my own. Or maybe I make the right call about not selling, and the growing pains break into something better. Maybe he leaves altogether. I haven't exactly made any big calls on my own before."

Because I told him what to do.

"I'm not risk averse, Noel. I've taken a lot of them in my life, but the stakes are higher now. I have employees, business partnerships with people who I used to work for and who took a chance on me because of it. I have community initiatives I've worked my ass off to develop. My reputation. I know what it feels like now to be thought of as a success instead of a failure, and I don't want to lose that feeling." His eyes meet mine with a seriousness that rarely shows itself. "What happened on that roof was magic, Noe. You know that, right?"

I nod, but I'm a little uncomfortable with it suddenly. I want to tack an asterisk onto my agreement. *Yes, it's magic, but so are you.*

What if my psychic assist only backed up his fear that he couldn't do it alone? I'm worried maybe knowing the future wasn't as helpful as he thinks. And I wonder what it will mean if it happens again. If I see what he wants me to. Especially now that I know about the tiny hiccups, that there are pieces that are right, but not exact.

But on the other hand, we're together. Happy. Just like the vision showed me. If I'm looking for signs that are right in front of me, that's the biggest of them all—the way my life has changed for the better since I followed the visions. And they're his signs too. They always have been.

"I think," I tell him, smoothing my palms over his chest. "That growing pains are just that. Growth."

Jamie smiles softly at me, fingers sliding into my hair. He tilts my head, kissing me in a way that's meant to end this conversation. "I don't want to talk about this when we're supposed to be celebrating you," he says. "Let's go back to that."

"Okay."

I tuck my hands around his waist, dipping under his jacket, beneath the hem of his shirt, and he jumps. "Jesus, your hands are cold."

"Sorry." I press them higher on his back, teasing, and he shivers.

"We have to get you some warmer clothes." He dips to run his nose along my jaw, whispering in my ear. "Because you're staying here."

My stomach somersaults at hearing it out loud, this very new decision. I don't even know the details yet, but I know it will work out. We'll figure it out together. "Mmhmm," I say. "I'm staying."

His real smile is back when he plucks the hat from his head—a Fortune beanie he just added to his merch line—and pulls it over my ears. I decide right then I'm keeping it along with the hoodies and the T-shirt I've acquired. "Does it look good?" I ask, tipping my shoulder and doing a little pose.

"Too good. Let's ditch Em and Cara and go home. I want to see you in only that hat."

He grabs me around the waist, pretending to drag me in the direction we came, and I laugh. "Stop. You promised to take me out."

"I promised we'd celebrate. There's more than one way to do that." He sets me back on my feet and his expression turns soft. Something tingles in the back of my brain, like déjà vu. This scene. The affection on his face. The people bustling around us. It all feels familiar.

I reach up to touch my head and recognition locks into place. It's the hat he was wearing in the vision I had at the beach. A navy blue beanie. It's on my head now, but it's the same one. And the dark scruff that's been filling in on his face over the last few weeks, it was there too. I saw it.

The rest of the vision unfurls in front of me like a Choose Your Own Adventure game. It's cold. We're on a cobblestone street lit by lamp light. "Ha!"

"What is it?" He laughs.

I don't wait for him to corner me the way I saw. I press myself up against the wall, and tug him by the front of his jacket, grinning as he slaps a hand against the brick wall above my head. Just like I knew he would.

People turn to look, just like I saw.

And then he's there, fitting his knee between my legs, kissing me in that way I remember felt like a confession. And now I know what he's telling me with his mouth on mine and his hand in my hair. Things that have come true between us in the few short weeks since I saw it. I know everything that's going to happen. I feel it before he even touches me, that bruising grip on my thigh as he draws it over his waist, and inside, I'm a swirling ball of lust and magic.

Twenty-Seven

Jamie

I'M A COASTAL CITY guy down to my bones, but there's something about mountain air that's as good as a drug. October hovers around ten degrees colder in Carrabassett Valley than it does in Portland, and the fall leaves are far more brilliant for it. Our tent is an eight-by-eight easy-up with three taps—the blonde, the orange, and the IPA—and huge coolers of cans for the fall ale. A vinyl banner with my logo is strung up behind us. I take a quick glance down the row of beverage vendors and do a mental fist pump. Ours is the longest by far. I've been talking hops and swiping mobile pay for four hours straight, and I've missed this *exhausted from work instead of pain* feeling.

Noel's off with Cara, enjoying the festival, and Em elbows me in my barely-healed ribs. "Hey. This is good," she says, a rare serious smile on her face.

I lift my hat and wipe my forehead. "It's better than good," I say. "We're killing it."

She laughs. "Damn, I missed this Jamie."

I raise an eyebrow. "Which Jamie is that?"

"Confident Jamie. Different from Cocky Jamie, by the way. Cocky Jamie gets on my nerves."

I make a face. "Weird. You never said anything."

She laughs at my joke and greets a gray-haired couple. Collecting their green paper drink tickets, she pours them two pints before turning back to me. "It feels like the old days. When you first started and you were just happy to be doing your thing. And it's pretty clear you're disgustingly happy now," she says.

"Happiness *is* really gross."

Em snorts. "She's very sweet to you. I'm glad you finally figured out you deserve that." Em tips her head to the bustle in front of us. "And this. Because you do."

Sometimes, I think all of the women I know are a little psychic, otherwise I'm not sure how Em knew that's exactly what I've been tossing over since that argument with Wes, and my conversation with Noel after it.

The fact is, Noel and I are very new. New enough that if she'd started to question her choices after Wes's not-so-subtle reminder of my liability, I wouldn't have had reason to be surprised. But she didn't. She'd given me the benefit of the doubt. Easily. She'd assumed that my biggest insecurities are unfounded. That I'm capable of something I've always assumed everyone knew I wasn't.

"I've been thinking more about NEBev," I tell Em when there's a small lull in the line.

She looks over at me with a cocked eyebrow. I've been candid with her about this offer and the issues it's causing between Wes and me. It's wildly unprofessional since she works for both of us, but she has a vested interest. She deserves to know that the brand that she's given the last two years to could evolve into something different than what she signed up for when I poached her from Java Jolt.

"Is Wes wrong about you asking Noel for help? I'm not judging, I'm just asking."

"He wasn't at first." I'm interrupted by a customer and have to pour a couple of pints before turning back to Em. "Would you work for me, if it was just me?"

I brace myself to be let down easy, but her laugh surprises me the same way Noel's reaction did. "Jamie, I've never been Wes's biggest fan."

"I mean, I get why you wouldn't invite him to a party, but he knows what he's doing. He's good at it."

She shrugs. "So are you. A hundred people can do what Wes does, J. As far as I'm concerned, you're the talent. Where you go, the rest works out."

I greet another customer, feeling my blood start to buzz. This is my wheelhouse—working the crowd, describing how different ingredients work together, toting our community initiatives. I've always been good at this part. Always loved it. And maybe that's more important to our success than I thought.

Noel and Cara duck under our tent, each holding a cup of something clear and carbonated, and definitely poured at someone else's tent. "Cheating on me?" I joke, nodding at Noel's cup while I hand off the one I'm pouring.

"Another beer will never touch my lips, Jamie." She presses up to kiss my cheek, but I turn at the last second and steal her mouth instead. It's not exactly work appropriate when I slide my tongue over hers, but I'm the boss, right?

"That's not beer," I say at the taste of fruit on her mouth. "It's hard seltzer."

Em and I exchange twin looks of disgust, and Cara taps the brim of Em's hat. "Don't be a beer snob, babe."

Noel runs her fingers over my back as she takes the stool I haven't had two seconds to sit on yet. "Hey, were you able to check in?" Our luggage is still in the truck since we had to be here before breakfast.

Noel shakes her head. "They said the room won't be ready until four."

Exhausted as I am, I'm not disappointed. When she agreed to come here with me, I called to change my reservation from business economy to a mountain view room. Having her check in alone wouldn't have the same effect as walking in together and seeing her face. I want her to know that it matters to me to be good to her. That I'm successful and serious.

The crowd thins for a brief hiatus, and I step between her knees, dipping to press a long kiss to her forehead. When I pull away, she blinks up at me with wide eyes, her mouth pushed into a pout like she can feel the weight of my thoughts.

"Hi," she says again, just for me.

"Hi." I press my nose into her neck, huffing the scent of the lodge that's baked into her hair—fire and cocoa.

She pushes the brim of my hat up and scratches her nails through my hair. "Why are you rubbing on me like a cat?"

"I'm trying to get pet."

I feel her giggle against my cheek. "Fresh."

I take her cup and sniff it, making a face. "Dump this out and drink my beer."

"So jealous."

"Can't help it." I slide my other hand down to the hem of her sweater and tug. "This too. Wear my brand. Let me put my mark on you."

Her lashes flutter into a playful eye roll. "Whatever you want, love."

Love. The word is a swift dropping in my chest, a whooshing sound in my ears like something flying by that I want to catch. Which is entirely different than the last time I felt it, when I was cutting any thought of loving someone out of me.

"Well?" She tilts her head, and I realize I'm staring.

"Right." I pull away, reaching beneath the merch table to pull one of our hoodies from a box.

She takes it and slips it over her head, pulling her ponytail free. "There you go," she says. "All yours."

I *really* like the way that sounds.

Twenty-Eight

Noel

I'VE COME TO ADMIT that Jamie is full of good ideas but asking me to tag along on this trip might be my favorite. Cara and I spend the whole day outside, breathing mountain air and accumulating enough samples of beer and seltzer to leave my cheeks red and my body warm.

At seven, the beer garden closes, and Jamie packs up for the night. We make up an excuse, flimsy and barely worth the lie, and ditch Em and Cara, practically running to our hotel room to be alone.

"Come here," Jamie says, his hand snaking around my stomach while I try to open the door.

"Stop." I giggle and bat at him. My brain is static, swirling with need, and unable to complete rudimentary tasks. Anyone walking by will think we're breaking in with the way my fingers fumble. "Let's get behind this closed door, please."

Finally, the card beeps and I push through, leaving him there with a promising kiss. I close myself in the bathroom to freshen up, and while I splash my cheeks with water, I hear Jamie opening drawers and see the light flip on. I hear the sound of the television booting up, snippets of sitcoms and sportscasters before it lands on soft music. My reflection grins back at me.

His casual romance is so damn sexy. I've thought so since he plucked a hops flower from the vine and rubbed it on my pulse point like an expensive perfume. I could tell from the quick look I got on the way to the bathroom that this room isn't a business trip room. There were flowers on the end table, and behind me in the en-suite is a jetted tub.

Matching fluffy white robes hang on the back door. I strip out of my clothes and wrap myself in one, then pad barefoot back to him. Jamie's eyes flare with the same anticipation I feel in my belly, and I think of what I confessed to Kate. *I can't get enough of him.*

"Cute," he says, lifting the tie on the robe. His eyes have gone hazy, skipping over me like a rock on water, and his tongue swipes his bottom lip before he pulls it between his teeth. I want it between mine. "Gimme two minutes to shower, and I'll be back to take that off."

He disappears into the bathroom, and I drop onto the bed, sliding my legs over the duvet to build some warmth while I check out more of the room.

It's fancy like I thought. Huge bay window, TV over the fireplace. I reach for the remote to adjust the volume, and a blip of recognition freezes my hand before my brain catches up with it.

The fireplace.

A blanket of pebbles covers my skin as I climb off the bed and cross the room, pressing a hand to the faux stone veneer. Jamie only turned on the bedside lamp, and the switch for the overhead is on the wall by the mantel. I flip it, turning over my shoulder toward an overstuffed chair in the opposite corner. Sure enough, the art hung behind it makes my breath catch.

My hand flies to my mouth. I might be getting used to these pieces of the future coming true, but *this* is a huge one. The bed I was just lying on—bright white comforter, heavy wooden headboard, navy blue blanket folded at the bottom—It's *the* bed. I found it.

The memory pours down my spine, making my hair stand on end. This is where we were. Jamie and I. This is the room from the vision. His T-shirt, the cobblestone street, now this. These visions are like Tetris pieces falling into place, complete with music and explosions, and a weird sense of accomplishment. I remember Kate's words—Universe Achievement unlocked—and stifle a giggle. "This is insane."

"Do you like it?" Jamie steps out of the bathroom in just his boxers as I'm peeking through the heavy curtains, marveling at the view I knew I'd see. The mountains, snow only at their tips.

I turn to him with my fingers pressed to my lips. "What?"

"Do you like the room?"

"Yes." I step into his arms, pressing myself into hot, bare skin. "I like it very much. Have you been here before?"

"Nope," he says. "First time."

My blood rushes so quickly, I'm lightheaded, and when I speak again there's an emotion in my voice that I can't hide. "Thank you for taking me here."

"You're welcome, baby." His brow furrows, a hint of worry at how serious I sound, until I catch his chin between my fingers, and stretch to kiss his mouth, another *thank you,* and an *I can't believe this is real,* and something so much more whispered in the silence of my lips lingering on his.

When I pull away, his expression has shifted from sweetness to raw hunger, an eyebrow arched in challenge to see if

I'll match it. I step backward, my fingers trailing between my breasts, down to the plush tie on the robe. It's barely a tug to get it to fall open, hanging loose and oversized off of my shoulders. Cool air washes over my front, followed by a trail of heat where Jamie's watching me. His lips are parted, eyes as dark as the starless sky outside of this fated hotel room.

"Get on the bed, Noe."

"You have a bossy side." I laugh. "I think I like it."

"I have some other things in mind that you might like." His grin hitches up on one side, playful and cocky, and then his arm sweeps around my waist and my feet leave the ground entirely. I'm dropped onto the mattress with a bounce and a girlish laugh that quickly turns breathless when I'm pushed to my back by his big, looming body.

"Have I mentioned how much I like ending my day with you?"

I stretch my arms above my head like a cat. "Me too. Sleeping alone makes me sad now."

"Same. I like you tucked against me." He kisses my collarbone, my shoulder. "I want to keep you warm." His knee notches between my thighs, and his lips suck at my neck. "I like how you keep me still."

I laugh lightly. He's a terrible sleeper. I've taken to draping myself over his chest like a human weighted blanket. "A perfect fit?"

"Yeah." Jamie pulls back, a lock of wet hair flopped onto his forehead and a mischievous grin on his lips.

"What is that look?"

"I can't decide if I want to worship you or do dirty things to you."

Excitement pops in my blood like fireworks. "You can do whatever you want. Have whatever you want."

Because I want it too, and I think... I think the universe just told me it's mine.

Jamie groans, burying his face in my neck. His hands haven't stopped moving over my skin, making a circuit of my ribs, my hips, my thighs. "Noel, fuck. I..."

"Whatever you want," I whisper.

I feel the moment he decides, even before he takes it. Before he rolls off of me, seating himself at the edge of the bed and scooping me into his lap. This is how we were when his mouth first touched mine, the way I saw us on the porch. Another perfect fit. It lessens our height difference, lets me stare directly into those cream soda eyes and lose myself while our tongues touch, and teeth press into my bottom lip. This place, this latest layer in our story peeled away is an accelerant to the fire in me that lights so easily for him. A fire that, before I came here, I wasn't sure I possessed.

Jamie pushes the robe from my shoulders, and it drops to the floor behind me. His hands finally settle on my ass, tucking me as tightly to him as possible. "I've been waiting for this all day," he says, rocking his hips slowly until my head falls back in pleasure.

"Me too."

"I've been half hard for hours, thinking about it. So unprofessional."

I snort. "Good thing I like you better wild."

He likes that, lids lowering in satisfaction as he slides a hand between us, curling his fingers inside me. My hips tilt toward his palm, and I cuff his wrist, holding it there while I work myself against him. I'm greedy and indulgent, running my other hand over his tight abs, dipping into his boxers and notching my knuckle into the V cut of his waist.

"Look at you, grinding all over my hand like that. I think that halo's broken for good, baby."

My laugh is pulled tight, cut off by the building of pleasure between my legs. I *am* grinding all over his hand and I don't care because his fingers are heaven, slow and patient and determined. I push up higher, giving him room to go deeper, and I break so quickly, so violently that I'm dizzy from it. I fall into his chest, dissolving into a pile of bones and stardust as he falls backward onto the mattress and takes me with him.

"That's exactly what I wanted," he says, looking as orgasm drunk as I am. "God, I love watching you come." A blush spreads over already burning skin when I feel him pressed into my stomach because that feeling is entirely mutual, and it's what I want next.

I wrap my hand around him, and we both hiss, and then he's rolling over me. I adjust my grip, and he pushes into my fist, thrusting, taking, eyes glossy and half-lidded.

He leans in, pressing his forehead to mine. "From that first night, Noe," he says against my mouth. "I think I... I always hoped that you and I were part of the deal."

I nod frantically, shivering with what he's said. "Me too." I had proof we were and I still had to make myself believe it. Jamie's unbridled hope is exactly what makes him so beautiful to me.

I release him, and he palms the back of my thigh, putting me exactly where he needs me. Then with one rough thrust, he's pushing inside, taking what I said he could have. It's hard and fast, and not at all romantic the way I'd half assumed a moment captured in a life-changing vision might be. It's perfect, and I think that's just it. The visions didn't need to show me something I could already imagine for myself. They needed to show me something I didn't even know existed.

I think of that night on the roof, the clench of my thighs when our eyes met. My surprise at it. The jealous stab when Becca had claimed him from a moment I'd stupidly thought was ours. Except it wasn't stupid because look at us now, here.

I tuck my chin to my chest, watching the way his hips grind against me. Long, indulgent strokes wringing out every last bit of pleasure.

Jamie's next breath is a muttered curse, and we're so close. So close that when I find his eyes again, I see myself reflected in his irises, like we've melted completely into each other. Like every past moment we've lived has been for this future.

I wake before Jamie. He's shirtless beside me, and as usual, flopped onto his belly, cheeks red from sleeping in this too-warm embrace we're sharing. His arm is the most delicious dead weight over my hip and the sun is streaming through the window at our feet.

I'm even laying the same way I saw myself, cheek in the pillow, half turned toward him. It's eerie and undeniable, and one thing's for sure: I have to tell him about the visions. This train is going too fast for me to hold on by myself.

He stirs behind me, the heat of his yawn fanning over my shoulder. I have to force myself not to burst out in hysterics when his hand sweeps my hair aside, running over my shoulder and down under the blanket, just like I knew he would.

The rest is a surprise, though, because this is where the vision ended.

"Hey," he whispers in my ear. "Fancy meeting you here."

I'm swept by a full-body shiver because—*gah*—I know he's being cute, being *Jamie* but what a thing to say.

I turn in his arms, tipping my chin to see his sleepy eyes. "Did you forget you packed me?"

He grins. "Definitely not. I don't think I'll go anywhere without you from now on. You're my favorite thing."

I swoon inwardly. He's so casually declarative.

He stretches an arm over his head, still grinning. "Hope you slept okay. I'm fidgety in an unfamiliar bed."

"I didn't feel a thing," I lie, and he pinches my side. "Hey, Jamie?"

"Mmm."

"What you said about the night we met. Did you mean that? You... felt something that night?"

He makes a face and pushes his hair back. "You must think I'm an asshole."

I scrunch my nose. "What? Why?"

"I was there with Becca. I would never have acted on it, I just... you were so beautiful. It seemed almost... important." He laughs, bewildered, and champagne bubbles rise in my blood.

"I don't think you're an asshole. I think you're probably better than most to feel guilty over it even now, after... everything. But I also think I knew that about you from that first night. That's why I told you what I saw, why I didn't just run away. I could just tell you were good."

He tilts his head, watching me with an expression that says there are things he knows about me too. That he can feel something coming. "I'm glad you did tell me," he says carefully.

"It's just..." I pause to press a kiss to the freckle beneath his collarbone, smoothing the hair on his chest. The words feel too big for my mouth after all of this time, but I have to tell him. I want to. This is a secret I want to be in on together. "There was something else."

We're so close I feel the tiny stiffening in his spine. His hips tilt a fraction of an inch away. "Something else in the vision?"

I nod, my lip between my teeth.

"What?"

"This."

Jamie props himself on his elbow, looking down at me.

"This... what?"

"This us. I saw you and me *here*, Jamie. This hotel room." I sit up and tug the sheet over my naked chest, feeling suddenly exposed. I doubt it after everything else, but there's still the tiniest possibility he'll think I'm crazy. "I recognized the room when we got here last night. That's why I asked if you'd been here before."

He sits all the way up too, staring at me with an unreadable expression, maybe the first I *haven't* been able to read. The champagne bubbles fizz faster, close to bursting. "Say something, please."

"Are you serious?"

"Yes."

"You didn't tell me," he says, running a hand over his mouth.

For a true believer like Jamie, he doesn't look happy or impressed like I thought he would. I start to wonder if it was a mistake, confessing this. "Are you mad?"

"No." He shakes off his expression and slides his hand up my neck and into my hair. Then drops it just as quickly. "I'm not mad."

"You're something."

"I'm just—You knew this whole time?"

"I wasn't sure. Some things changed and—"

"What do you mean? What things?"

My mouth snaps shut. I'm suddenly hesitant to list them out. It doesn't matter because there are more things that came true than things that changed, but I don't want to give voice to the different ones. Not with the way he's looking at me. There's still a big question that Jamie wants an answer to and there's no use in casting doubt on his hope for that by picking this apart. We're here. It happened. It's happening.

"It was just a few details," I say lamely. "Are you okay?"

"I'm... letting it sink in." His voice is off. The knot in my stomach pulls tighter.

"I didn't tell you because I wanted to see if it would happen on its own. And it did!"

"Well... not entirely on its own," he says, his face pinched in confusion. "Because you knew."

I bite my lip again. "Right."

He pulls away from me and runs a hand through his hair. Cold trickles down my spine at that nervous tic. He's anxious, and I don't know why. I was entirely unprepared for this reaction.

"Jamie," I say quietly. "You've wanted me to have another vision since we met. Now you don't like the idea of it?"

"It just feels different. Being about me and you. I don't know..."

I cross my arms over my chest, feeling awkward and unsteady. "Last night, you said you hoped you and I were part of the deal."

"I know, it's just—" He stops, shakes his head. "You're right. I don't care how it happened."

"Me neither," I say, quick to reassure, to fix this. "Everything's happening exactly how it was supposed to, right?"

"Right." He swallows again, punctuating his agreement with a nod.

But I can't shake the feeling that I'm trying to convince him of something he was sure of before now.

Twenty-Nine

Jamie

I T WAS ME AND *you. Here.*

I tip my head back beneath the shower in this apparent-ly fated hotel and let the hot water pound my face. I'm freaking out about what Noel just told me, and I can't decide if it's the good kind of freak out or the bad kind.

Part of me wants to hold onto it the way I did when she told me about the money, about opening my business. The way I did when she told me about Becca, and I avoided marrying someone who clearly didn't love me because of it.

On the other hand, it's hard not to hear something else in that confession: Noel's only mine because she saw it in the vision.

I open the tiny soap packet and scrub my skin, trying to metaphorically wash away this train of thought. It's an old habit, like Em said—counting myself out of the equa-tion—and I want to keep from going down that hole right now. Noel's been sleeping in my bed or me in hers since our first night together. I'm not misinterpreting this thing between us.

She knows me. She chose this right along with me.

But I also know her; how careful she is. I can still picture her running away on that beach. Would she have chosen any of this if she didn't have the vision behind her? Would she have even agreed to see me again after I passed out on her porch? Or kissed me on her couch that night? All of a sudden, it feels wholly unlikely that the two of us end up together without it.

And why didn't she say anything? Maybe she's just been going along with it, hoping I'd grow on her.

The thought makes my stomach clench and I shove it away. *She did not say any of that, Bishop.*

Fuck. My pep talks were never very effective.

The bathroom door clicks open, and I hear Noel make that tiny squeak she makes when she's cold. "I'm coming in," she yelps, right before the curtain slides and she steps over the tub edge, arms around her chest, dancing on her tiptoes. I pull her under the water and spin so she's getting most of it.

When she's wet her hair, she looks up at me with her lip between her teeth. "Hi."

"Hi, Noe." I lean down to kiss her so I don't have to force a smile. My hands squeeze at her like she's an apparition about to disappear. *Jesus. Quit acting weird.*

Now I'm self-conscious, and I reach for the shampoo, squirt some in my palm.

"Are you sure you're okay?"

"Of course," I say, but I wouldn't believe me either with the way my voice has gone all raspy.

Noel rests her cheek on my chest, fingers smoothing over my sides while I work shampoo into her long hair. I try to let myself enjoy the warmth of her skin beneath my fingers, the way she burrows in, gives herself over to me. I close my eyes and tell myself to feel it, but they pop right back open. "It's just… what if you have one about someone else?"

She looks up through the water, brow furrowed. "A vision?"

"Whatever it is."

"Now it's 'whatever it is?'" There's hurt in her voice that's worse than anything so far, but something's telling me to loosen my grip on this. "Jamie. I think the point is that I won't."

"Right." I clear my throat and step back while she rinses the suds I've made in her hair. I've never been good at saying the right thing when I start to feel like this. Like I'm on the outside of something. Like I was misunderstanding a thing that everyone got but me.

This feels like one of those moments. I can't shake the feeling that I earned this with about as much effort as I earned everything else I have. Good fortune. A lucky break I stumbled on. Absolutely nothing to do with me.

But if I'm already down in the count, I can't risk her re-thinking this entire thing because I'm being weird. I need to figure out a way to accept what she told me, because this is exactly where I want to be.

She squeezes water from her ponytail, and I cup her elbow. "Come here." She does, and I press her bottom lip with my thumb, my other hand slipping around her waist. "When you saw us," I whisper. "What were we doing?"

"We were in bed." Pink flushes up her neck, and I press my mouth to it and slide my knee between her legs.

"Was I touching you?"

"I couldn't see your hands. After they slipped beneath the sheet."

"I know I was. There's no way I could keep my hands off you." I'm impossibly hard for being pissed off and confused about two minutes ago, but I need to feel instead of think. To slip into instinct.

Noel tilts her chin, kissing a drop of water from my jaw,

and I notch us closer, my arm contracting around her waist to bring her to her toes. I can feel her melting into what I'm starting here, molding like clay beneath my hands, and it soothes my anxiety. I just need to see her react to me, to us together. Something I can't misinterpret.

Her bottom lip is pushed out and swollen from how long we kissed last night, sleeping, then waking to her fingers on my stomach. Her leg wrapped around my waist. That was all real.

Now, I scoop my hands beneath her thighs, pressing her back to the shower wall while we kiss so I can make it real again.

"I haven't ruined it?" she asks, as I fumble between us, centering myself between her legs. "It isn't weird now?"

"No, baby. It isn't weird." I slide in slow, my head falling back at the warmth of her. "It's fate."

I just have to trust it's still on my side.

Thirty

Noel

T HE NEXT FEW WEEKS are a blur of soaking up the dying light at the cottage and spending late nights in Jamie's bed when he gets off work. He hired someone to take a few of his bar shifts, but his schedule at the brewery has ramped up while he gets a new ale ready for a winter release. Most of our time together now comes after dark.

Some nights I sit on a stool at Fortune and watch Jamie work. Some nights I stay in and sketch or watch a movie with Pixie. Jamie lets himself in after I've fallen asleep, stripping off his work clothes and curling his body around mine until we inevitably forget that sleep is necessary and stay up touching and talking in a way that feels more intimate than sex. Though, there's a lot of that too. I think I've had more sex in the fall of this year than in all my years combined.

For whatever reason, I opened something in Jamie with my confession at the hotel, and I've come to realize this is part of how he sews it back up. Whenever my mind tries to linger on his weird reaction, I force myself to remember that I spent two years telling myself that Jamie Bishop didn't exist just so I didn't have to confront the implications of fate on a potential relationship. Even after the universe dropped him on my porch again, I poked a hundred holes in the idea of us, before finally holding this up to the light of what I know to be true—that whoever is in charge of these things got the two of us very right.

The rest of my life is like a garden in the spring, a new bud appearing with each sunrise. It's safe to say my sabbatical has officially ended. I've been working on the designs for Cara's mural, more inspired than I've felt in months, maybe years. I see Kate and Colin for dinner once a week. And I've been hanging out with Cara outside of work too.

Last weekend, we met for drinks downtown when Jamie and Em were both working at Fortune. Cara ordered a Corona, begging me not to snitch, and I'd dutifully ordered Jamie's fall ale because I truly love it and because I swore beverage loyalty. I know he was mostly kidding, but I like the way his face lights up when I drink his beer. I like any time that sweet, handsome grin is aimed at me.

And I like the idea that a friendship with Cara is part of this package delivered straight from the universe. She's full of stories I don't think I'd otherwise get to hear, things she heard from Em. When she told me the details of the skylight story Jamie mentioned at the beach, we'd laughed so hard we'd nearly sprayed beer out of our noses, and then she'd grabbed my wrist on the table, a sudden sappy look on her face. "I just love you two together. Becca, she was... " She'd paused, seeming to choose those words carefully. "Well, she was hard on him."

"You knew her?" I'd asked, equally careful.

"Mmhmm. Weirdly, I knew her before I knew Jamie. From

rec camp when we were, like, twelve. And then, you know, from around."

"Small city."

"Very. It's not a judgment on her. Or him. Just… them together."

I nodded along, pretending not to be wildly jealous at the reminder that there even *was* a them together. Part of my problem is that I've been living in the past in a sense. Like Jamie said, settling for old dynamics with my mother. Avoiding Nana's house because being there alone wouldn't be the same as it used to be, and it might hurt. But Jamie and I have been about the future since we met, and I don't like thinking about him and Becca.

So I'd smiled, and sipped my beer, and said, "That's because he's supposed to be mine."

On Fridays, Jamie has at least a twelve hour shift on the brewery floor. Today, he's been gone since before dawn, and I plan to use the forced separation to work on my watercolors again. The other night while I sat at the bar waiting for him to finish his shift, I'd doodled a few designs for holiday cards that, if I really buckle down, I could have ready by Thanksgiving. I *want* to have them ready.

I pop my headphones in my ears and grab the jar candle Jamie and I used weeks ago to try to read his future. They've been part of my regular painting routine now that I'm not blocked often enough to need brain breaks. But when I light the wick, it sparks, then fizzles, and a plume of black smoke signals that it's just about empty.

"Shoot." I chew on the end of my pencil. I don't want to

mess with my system now when I've been on such a roll, but the drug stores aren't even open yet to buy a crappy Halloween candle to replace it.

A lightbulb pops on in my brain, and I remember the box of votives Nana kept on hand for snowstorms—shoved at the top of her closet—and I hop off of the stool and head toward her room. It's probably because I'm engrossed in the upbeat playlist I've made myself, eager to work while Jamie's gone so we can play when he gets back, or maybe my mind is too filled with these new ideas that I'm not paying attention, but it isn't until my fingers wrap around the knob on her bedroom door that it hits me what I've done.

It's silly the way I freeze, debating whether to push it all the way open or slam it shut.

It's silly, too, the way my throat swells.

And yet, I can't bring myself to move.

It's Kate's voice I hear in my head first, because it always is: *Are you really going to take a job here, move your life to this house, and continue to just never set foot in this room?*

But it's Jamie who I hear next. I think of what he said about me holding space for Mom instead of filling it. I'm holding this literal space open too, afraid that if I embrace what this room is now instead of what it was, I'll lose something forever.

I've been living here without her for weeks now, though, and I haven't lost anything. I still feel her here. I think of her, and I don't cry, I smile. And it hasn't once felt like losing what it was. It feels like gaining the color I was missing when I arrived here. It feels like storing something precious in a box for safe keeping, and getting to live inside the box with it.

I thought the memories would hurt too much, but instead they've been like light switches flicking on in the darkness that I was wallowing in, leading the way out.

I feel things every day now. I feel optimistic about my work.

I feel like I have friends here, more than just Kate and Colin. I feel joy when I wake up early with Jamie's arms tightly around my stomach. I feel the tingling of the winter on the horizon, knowing I'll be cozy and taken care of. And I feel like I'm ready to have all of this place.

I've made some big decisions over the last month, but when I turn the knob, this tiny step feels like the biggest.

The tiny step turned out to be not so tiny. I'm starfished on the living room floor, exhausted and catching a cat nap, when I hear Jamie's car pull into the gravel drive, then his footsteps on the front porch. I bolt upright to meet him at the door. I'm so excited to see him, to show him how I spent my day. I got the candles from the top of Nana's closet, but I didn't work on my watercolors.

I open the door before he can, and grab him by the front of his jacket, kissing him hello. When I pull away, my smile feels too big for my face.

"Hello to you too," he says, laughing.

"I want to show you something." I pull him through the door, left up the stairs to the loft. Of course he plays along, letting himself be manhandled, smiling amusedly. When I get to the top, I pause. "I did a thing."

"What sort of thing?"

"A big thing." I step around the railing, and he crests the landing behind me.

And his jaw drops. "Wow."

"I know."

He steps past me, catching my hand on the way, and heads to the new desk sitting in the middle of the space. I spent two hours putting it together, setting up a permanent place for my laptop and sketch pads, which he briefly thumbs before turning his attention to the wall behind it. The upper shelf is lined with Mason jars filled with brushes and some with flowers I bought at Trader Joes.

"These are yours?" He turns toward the floral watercolors I framed and hung in the corner. I have a pile of floor pillows in front of the window so I can sketch there.

I nod. "All the paintings I've made designs from."

"They're beautiful."

The easel that's been in my trunk since I got here is set up in the opposite corner, a stool from the kitchen in front of it, a paper lantern hung above it. Pixie is curled beneath it.

I think back to the day I toured my condo in Connecticut. I'd envisioned the second bedroom to look something like this eventually. But then Mom lost her job, and a month later, her apartment, and she moved in. I went back to working at the kitchen table.

This is even better, and it was mine the whole time.

"Where's your bed?" Jamie asks.

"Oh, uh, it's in the garage." That was probably not my best decision, to do that by myself. I'd basically propped the mattress on its side and tobogganed it from the top of the stairs, hoping for the best. "The one downstairs is bigger."

His eyes snap to mine. "You…"

"I did. Come see." Jamie follows me back down the stairs, to the door that's been closed since I arrived. It's closed now too, and I lean my back against it, biting my lip, stalling for effect.

Jamie pokes my stomach, and I kick it open with a little, "Tada."

After I finished moving my clothes to Nana's dresser, I went to Target and bought a new pot for the kalanchoe Jamie bought me. It's on the window ledge, getting the correct amount of sun. I got rid of the guest basket and Maine guide books on the bookcase, and gave it a coat of paint. Finally, I dragged my biggest purchase in from the car, a gorgeous floral print rug, and fit it in the middle of the room.

Then I sat on it criss-cross and cried hard and ugly. But I wasn't sad the way I thought I would be when I finally opened this room up and saw for myself how empty it was. I was relieved that I suddenly knew exactly how to fill it up. I was emotional in a good way. And I was really proud of myself for the way I let myself feel every ounce of it.

It doesn't feel wrong anymore, to be here without her. It feels like stepping into the future. I have the visions to thank for that.

And Jamie. I turn to him, watching as he drags a finger over the bookcase, then sits on the bed. "You kept hitting your head," I remind him. "Upstairs."

"Noel..." As usual, he doesn't want to take credit but I'm giving it.

I sit down beside him. "Jamie, you and I don't fit in the loft, and you and I are so much of this place. What it is now instead of what it was."

He closes his eyes, pressing a long kiss to my forehead, and I can feel the way this settles something in him. "I would have helped you do all of this," he whispers.

"I know. But I needed to do it alone." It was a long overdue conversation between Nana and me. Not a goodbye so much as... showing her that I'm okay. "Besides, I'm not done. I still need a chair for that corner. You know, to throw clothes on."

He nods firmly. "Right."

I gesture to the window. "I want to put more plants here. Oh, maybe an indoor tree!"

He laughs, and those dimples are carved in so deep, I want

to press my finger there, let them swallow me.

"What do you think?" My teeth dig into my lip. I know what he's going to say but I need to feel it—the full force Jamie Bishop effect.

And he must know that because he pounces, pulling me into a bear hug and burying his face in my hair. "I think it's about damn time."

I think he's right, as usual, and so Monday morning, I wait until Jamie leaves for his weekly sales meeting with Wes, then I roll to the still-warm spot he's left in my bed to make a call I've been practicing all weekend.

After a brief hold, the receptionist transfers me to Vi.

I don't expect her to be shocked. Afterall, it was her who told me to decide if Ned's job was something I wanted. I guess in a way, she saw the future too.

"I won't lose you completely, then?" she asks after I've broken the news.

"No." Even with Cara's job, I'm not nearly ready to support myself full time, and Brickstone has helped me make a name for myself even if it's in an adjacent field. Staying freelance will allow me to pick my projects, work toward my own goals alongside Vi's. Of course, I'll also still pay for my health insurance, but I'm figuring that out. "I'm going to move here, though," I tell her.

"Well, it's a good thing you work remotely."

"You were right, Vi. This was a gift, and you have no idea how much I appreciate it."

We hang up, and I feel settled and filled to the brim with what comes next, and I feel the same contentment in my bones when I call a real estate agent in Connecticut next, and we discuss the logistics of listing my condo.

Take a leap, Noel. All signs point to the universe catching you.

I haven't had any more visions since that night at the beach, but enough of them have come true that I'm not just leaping into this new life, I'm swan diving.

Thirty-One

Noel

THE FOLLOWING THURSDAY, JAMIE takes the day off, and we spend the entirety of it in my new bedroom. An early snow shower flutters outside, and his breath is soft and even on my chest.

What started as him helping me hang some new artwork on the walls turned into trading orgasms for most of the afternoon. Every project we do—the shelves he helped me build for my plants, the curtains we hung in the loft—ends this way, but I'm happy to indulge it.

I run my fingers through his hair when his weight begins to press into me, and his breathing starts to slow. "You have to get ready for hockey soon." Now that his ribs are healed, he's back to playing every week, and I usually go with him.

"I just decided to quit hockey, actually," he mumbles into the side of my breast. "My job too. Everything but you."

"Mmm. Two starving artists."

He lifts his head and grins, eyes brighter than I expected for how close to sleep he just was. "I've been eating well lately, haven't I?"

I gasp playfully. "Fresh. And in my grandmother's house."

"It's your house, baby."

I smile at the ceiling. My house.

"I'm getting an award," Jamie says later as we drive out to the ice rink. It's a full moon, and all of the hard surfaces downtown shimmer with light hitting frost. Like magic.

I turn in my seat to see his quiet little smile. "What award?"

"For my fall ale. Best in Industry."

"Jamie! That's amazing."

He touches the brim of his hat, cheeks coloring. "Thanks."

"Will there be a ceremony?"

"I think so. A dinner reception."

I nod, mentally picking out an outfit and planning some sort of private celebration for afterward. I'm so grateful for this win for him. There's been a noticeable anxiety coiling in his muscles the closer we get to the end of the year. Except for the small detail of not being able to get a hold of my mother again to tell her the news about the condo, everything seems to be falling into place for me, but Jamie still has a decision to make before we know what his career future looks like, and the magic hasn't been cooperating. I don't know what to make of its sudden disappearance.

When he pulls into the parking lot at the ice arena, I stop him before he can open the door, climbing over the console to sit in his lap and take his face in my hands. "You're brilliant and inspired and loyal. You deserve it all."

He looks at me with open affection, drawing me closer by

my hips. "I love you, Noe. Tell me you love me back and I'll already have it all."

I pull in a surprised breath, and he swallows.

"I've wanted to say that to you for a while." His hand on my chin trembles so slightly that I'd have missed it if I wasn't so in tune with his touch. He's nervous, and wow—for once, I'm not.

I feel like a child tucked safely in my bed, warm and ready to dream. I've phrased it a hundred safer ways over the last few weeks. I adore him. I admire him. I miss him. I *want* him. But no. That's not even close.

"I love you back," I say.

Jamie's eyes have always been his softest feature but right now they're nearly liquid. Pools of honey staring back at me with overt longing. He pulls me flush against him by the lapels of my winter coat, and kisses me deeply.

After the game, most of Jamie's hockey team comes back to Fortune, filling in the row of booths by the back window. Em tips her head to the ceiling, looking like she's praying for patience.

"Do you have a reservation for a party this size, sir?" She glares at Jamie when we break off from the rest of the group and meet her at the bar.

Jamie flashes his dimples. "No, but if you pour everyone a round, I'll get you in on the pizza I'm ordering."

"Deal."

"I'll order it," I tell him, pressing my palm to his cheek and catching the edge of that smile with my thumb. It's easier for me to work out how much to feed all of these men, plus me and Em. And if he's drinking, he didn't take his meds. He's likely to forget he said this, leaving us all starved.

"Use my app." He hands me his phone and kisses my jaw. "Thank you," he whispers.

"I'll be over in a minute." I linger at the bar while I pull up the menu to his saved pizza place.

Em pours my beer before she gets started on the guys' order. "Are you going for sainthood hanging with these idiots all night?"

"Fun fact: I was canonized as a child." I scan the bar. "Where's Cara tonight?"

"She's catering a dinner for the mayor."

"*What?* That's amazing."

"Right?" Em's grin goes soft. I admit Em's a lot harder to read than Cara or Jamie. Comparatively, she's a brick wall, which I've always found intimidating no matter how kind she is to me, but sometimes... Sometimes she's clear as day.

"Good for her," I say.

"She said you've got the designs nailed down for the mural."

I nod. "We have to finalize the color choices and then we can scale it. Decide on placement." Spanning three buildings with one design was a challenge but it's been an exciting one. I've even switched places with Jamie a few nights, working until the morning hours, being cajoled to bed. He's been my biggest supporter. I want to be that for him too, but what he wants is a vision, and I can't seem to give him that.

I turn over my shoulder to look at him because I already miss his face, but instead I see Wes, hovering at the end of the bar, hands in the pockets of his dress slacks. He catches me watching and his eyes narrow. My skin prickles. "I don't think he likes me."

Em follows my gaze to the table. "Who?"

"Wes. He's always looking at me like I'm the villain in a

mystery and he's the only one who's figured me out."

I'm not his biggest fan either, after our one and only meeting. What he said was cruel. I don't like how he plucks Jamie's insecurities in a way that only family can do.

"Don't tell Jamie that," Em says. "They don't need another reason to fight." She tilts her head. "Or hell, go ahead. Wes has it coming."

I want to ask her more about this but her eyes flick over my shoulder just before Jamie's hand snakes around my waist, dipping under my shirt. "What are you doing over here?"

"Talking to Em." I stretch to kiss the swoony look on his face. For some men, alcohol is like a switch that turns them aggressive and competitive. Others turn philosophical to the point of pompousness. But Jamie is happy, adorable, and affectionate. It's very clear to me why he got away with his youthful mischief for so long.

"When are you coming back?" he asks.

"After I pee. Save me a seat."

He pats his thighs, indicating that's where I'll be sitting. Then he leans into my ear. "And later it's right here." He makes a crude gesture with his tongue.

"Oh my God." Giggling, I press my palm to his face and push him away. My cheeks are on fire when I slide off of the stool and send him back to his friends.

I turn the corner, fanning my face, and nearly smack into a powder blue dress shirt. My gaze climbs the buttons until I get to a tan neck and black stubble. Wes.

I have to fight the instinct to turn and run in the other direction. Instead, I straighten my shoulders. "Hi, Wes," I say.

"Noel." He looks like he's as confused on how to play this as I am. I'm hoping that means he knows he was a raging jerk the last time I saw him and he's feeling bad about it.

Glancing over my shoulder, he asks, "How are things with

my brother?"

"Your brother is amazing. You must be proud of him for the award he's getting."

"Of course. Jamie is exceptionally good at what he does."

I set my hands on my hips and tip my chin, pretending to be bold. "Best in the industry, actually."

"Exactly the kind of thing that makes his brand highly sought after," he fires back. He watches me for a beat before licking his lips and leaning casually against the wall. "Did you know Jamie and I have a sixty-forty split?"

I did know this but I'm unsure where he's going with it, so I deflect. "That's not really my business."

His grin at that makes my skin pebble. "Except when you're giving him business advice."

"I'm not..." I trail off because if Wes knows Jamie is hoping for another vision, then I'll be caught lying. If he doesn't, then there's a reason for it.

"What that split means," he continues, "is I can spend the last few years getting all his ducks in a row so to speak, and then he can do something foolish, and I'll be stuck dealing with forty percent of the fallout."

The nervous feeling of having bit off more than I can chew starts to swirl in my belly but I push it down. I don't like the implication—that Jamie is someone who needs to be managed. I cross my arms and glance toward the exit. "I'm on his side, Wes."

He arches a dark brow at me. "You think it's me against him?"

I shrug, pretending that answer doesn't shake me a little.

"We're not on opposite sides here, Noel." He seems to get frustrated at this, huffing a breath. "Look, something you need to understand about Jamie is that he thinks he has something to prove to the world, and when he's being smart, it's a good motivator. But when he's not being smart, it makes him bull-headed. You're not doing him any favors by coddling this part of him."

"Coddling?"

"Jamie thinks you're the reason he has all of this." He vaguely gestures to the main bar. "That's why he's clinging so hard to it. It's bullshit."

I flinch at the venom in that last word, and he shakes his head. By the slight curl of his lip, I can tell he senses he's getting to me.

"You're his out from the pressure of making a tough call. Don't you see that? I mean, for Christ's sake, I have an MBA, Noel. Jamie has a BA in communications that took him five years to get and, oh, a magic girlfriend. He's in over his head, and he brought me on to explain these things to him."

What started as a tiny flicker of anger in my chest roars up. What an absolutely shitty thing to say. "He has his own ideas, Wes. This whole thing was his idea." My shoulders are pushed back, chin tipped, but I can hear the shake in my voice. "Maybe if you didn't always expect him to fail, you might be able to see how much he's succeeding."

"Maybe, Noel, if you didn't think he was destined to have this, you'd see how unlikely it is."

I feel a little bit like I've been knocked in the head when I make my way back to the table where Jamie and his friends sit, talking and laughing. My ankle wobbles as I take a seat on his knee, and he catches me around the waist, pulling me snug. His lips find the spot beneath my ear, a warm smile pressed against my skin that would normally have me curling into him for more, but I'm distracted, battling a buzz of discontent. *I'm his out. The visions are his out.*

I haven't had to analyze this magic in a long while. Not since the hotel. I've just been enjoying the benefits of it, the me and Jamie part, but that conversation was a reminder of what's still left unsettled.

Ever since that night Jamie confessed why he partnered with Wes in the first place, I've been worried that maybe he's giving the magic more credit than he's giving himself. Maybe that's the same thing as what Wes said. *Coddling that stubborn part of him.*

But Jamie doesn't just *think* this is fate. He knows it is. We know it is. The things I saw came true—Fortune, me and him—and he has every right to bet on this even if I never have another one.

Except the little pieces that are different. The ones he doesn't know about.

"Noe?"

"Hmm?" Jamie's said something to me that I missed because I'm staring at his hand wrapped around the pint glass. The scar on the back of it seems to stare back at me.

"Do you like it?" He nods at the beer in my hand, his winter ale. He's launching it tomorrow.

I shake away my train of thought and smile at him. "I love it."

Jamie's friend Greg smiles at us over his pint with a look I recognize. There's no denying the meaning behind it. It's the look I gave Kate the first summer I met Colin. It's the "*my friend is happy, so I am too*" smile.

My stomach cinches again. I wonder what Greg would think about Wes's way of looking at this. If my part caused more harm than good.

Jamie's relaxed, his palm flat on my stomach, head tipped

back in the booth. If he has any inkling his brother is on the warpath tonight, he's hiding it well. Maybe Wes has turned his sights completely on me.

After the last customers cash out, leaving just our little group, Em turns off the sign and joins us. She takes the seat next to Greg, across from me, and as if she's tapped into some Girl Code instinct, she lifts an eyebrow in a silent *Everything okay?* gesture.

I nod back with a forced smile because what's bothering me isn't exactly something I can have a quick chat in the bathroom about. Maybe I shouldn't be talking about it at all.

I lean my head back and whisper in Jamie's ear. "I think I'm going to go to bed." I'm suddenly exhausted to my core, the beer pulling my eyelids down like a dumbwaiter.

"Okay." Jamie looks at his full beer, then up at me. "I'll just finish this."

"No, stay," I tell him, cupping his face.

He glances at the back door that leads to his loft. "You'll sleep here, though?"

I nod. I'd already planned on sleeping here tonight.

"Are you sure?"

"Mmhmm."

"Okay, I'll only be a little while."

It feels like minutes, but it must be hours later when my eyes snap open at the sound of the front door opening. The quick flash of middle of the night fear melts away when I recognize the sound of Jamie's palm on the wall, then his sneakers hitting the floor. I turn to watch him pad across the room on bare feet, the rest of his clothes peeled off and dropped like breadcrumbs in the glow of the nightlight in the kitchen.

"Hi," I whisper, my voice scratchy with sleep. I roll to my side and lift the blankets.

Jamie slides in, gathering me in his arms. "Hi, baby. Sorry, I didn't mean to wake you up."

"What time is it?"

He presses his mouth to my hair. "One."

"You stayed late."

"Is that okay?"

"Of course." I nuzzle into his neck and breathe him in. "Just missing you. You know watching you play always gets me hot and bothered."

He hums quietly, thumb stroking up and down my spine. "I played hard for you tonight," he says. "I'm sore everywhere."

I shake my head, laughing at his wildly transparent attempt at convincing me to put my hands all over him. He knows I'm powerless to let him hurt, and he's always so grateful for touch. "Come here."

He shifts lower, swapping our heights so he can bury his face in my chest. "I love you," he whispers into my cleavage while I knead where his shoulder meets his neck, and my heart fills like a balloon. He's beautiful in this low light. The shadow in the grooves of his muscles makes them look like they've been sketched. His dark hair flopped onto his forehead like ink on canvas. It's no hardship, soothing Jamie's body.

"I love you too," I tell him, tasting those words again. Savoring them. I press my face to the crown of his head. "Even when you smell like a brewery."

He laughs with a surprised jerk of his chin, dimple winking at me like I'd hoped. Then he hooks my leg with his and rubs his chest over me.

"Stop!" I giggle. "I showered. I smell like lavender and

chamomile."

"You *did* smell like lavender and chamomile," he says. I laugh and squirm, but he doesn't let go. "Now you smell like beer and lavender."

I go boneless with a half giggle, half sigh of defeat. "Fine. I still love you."

"Noe?"

"Mmm?"

His hands are already pulling my shorts down my legs, and I arch to meet him. "Will you love me with your body?"

He settles in the cradle of my hips, pulling a *yes* from deep within my chest. I can't imagine a time I would turn him down. Like stars in the same constellation, we're made to be together, side by side.

When we finish, it's nearly dawn, the dark outside at its heaviest, just before it tips toward light. Jamie and I have done some sort of body swap, though, because while he's beside me, stock still except for the repetitive brush of his thumb over his sternum, I'm restless and too hot. I hate that Wes's words have made it through sleep and sex, and still sit here, muscling between us. Flopping onto my stomach, I kick a leg out, and Jamie lifts his head to look at me.

"Come here." He hooks my waist with his arm and pulls me under his weight. "Why are you fidgeting? It's like sleeping next to me."

I laugh softly and roll again so we're face to face. Wrapping my arms around him, I let my fingers dance over the tattoo on his shoulder. Tracing it from memory.

"I think you like that one the best," he says, eyes closed.

"You're always touching it."

I swallow. "What made you get it?"

He shrugs lazily. "I wanted something that would cover my whole shoulder. I wanted blue ink. I like the beach."

I don't expect the mild disappointment that settles in. I'm not sure what I wanted out of bringing this up now, but if there was some grand story behind why it's different, then maybe I'd glean some lesson about this whole thing.

But it seems like it was a whim. Not exactly careless, but a decision that didn't require any thought. Just *poof.* Different.

I push him onto his back and prop myself on my elbows above him. "Have you decided what you'll do about your offer? From NEBev. It's almost the end of the year."

"Uh—" I know he wasn't expecting to talk business right now and his brain is slow to change lanes. "I guess I'm maintaining my avoidance strategy for now?" It's a question. He has no plan. He's waiting just like Wes thinks. My shoulders fall.

"But have you been thinking about it? What you want."

"Of course. That's all I think about, besides you." He gives my butt a light slap, and it echoes in the dark. He's distracting. Deflecting.

I sigh. "I haven't had a vision about your career since that first night, Jamie."

"I know." He's quiet for a minute. "You still could, though. I mean, we don't know."

"Right." I pull my lip between my teeth. "And if I do have one about the offer, that's how you'll make your decision?"

"Why are we pillow-talking about corporate acquisitions, Noel?"

"I was just thinking that's how all of this started, and it's sort of still hanging over us."

"I think it started when I managed to pitch a semi with two broken ribs and a concussion." His grin is mischief. Unserious.

"God, that tank top you had on when you threatened me with your shoe."

"Jamie."

He seems to catch on that I'm not joking, and he tightens his grip, pressing a kiss to my hair. "Noel, I told you that first night, there's no pressure."

Right. And I didn't believe it then either. I turn my chin, but he guides it back. "This offer is hanging over *me*. I love the way you take care of me, baby, but I don't want you losing sleep over this."

"I just don't want to disappoint you if I can't do it." *Or be your out if I can*. My voice catches and I bury my nose in his neck. God, Wes is a dick for putting this in my head. Everything was perfect a few hours ago. Jamie and I have come so far from our supernatural start, but maybe there are still consequences left to discover, more layers to peel away, more questions. It was naive of me to think following the universe would stop being confusing.

I look up to see Jamie's face has fallen, dimples disappearing into a serious expression that's so rare, it jolts me. He presses his thumb to my bottom lip. "You believe in me, don't you, Noel?"

"Yes, of *course*."

"Then I don't need anything else." He strokes my hair until my head falls to his chest. "Besides, even if you don't have another vision, we still have the first one, from the roof. If that's all I have to go on, it seems to have worked out pretty well."

I'm quiet for a moment, considering this and all of the what ifs we still don't have answers for. An idea comes to me. "Roll over."

He does, burying his face in the pillow while I stretch to the nightstand where he keeps a pen and paper. I uncap the pen with my teeth, and Jamie stiffens when the cold tip touches his skin. "What're you doing?"

"Drawing your next tattoo."

His head lifts from the pillow, peering over his shoulder. "What is it?"

"Wouldn't you like to know," I say, sketching between his shoulder blades.

"It feels like a flower."

I pinch his side. "You're no fun!"

"I'm sorry," he says, laughing. "I'll stop guessing."

"It's an iris." I draw the beard of it, then swoop a line down his spine for the stem. "Flowers have different meanings. This one means wisdom to make hard choices." Another swoop. "In case I don't have another vision to help you."

He's face down in the pillow, but I see the corner of his mouth curl. "So damn sweet."

Thirty-Two

Noel

I WAKE THE SAME way I fell asleep, beneath the right side of Jamie's body, his bed head tickling my cheek. The light coming through the window is tinted bright white, like maybe it snowed a bit while we slept. Just the thought of it makes me shiver, and I nuzzle into his body heat, but I don't fall back to sleep fast enough, and my brain makes the quick walk from snow to winter to the end of the year. Wes and his accusations. Fate and its layers, upon layers, upon layers.

"I can feel you thinking," Jamie mumbles.

I grin at the scratch in his usually honeyed voice. The late night still has its claws in him. "Only about coffee," I lie. "Nothing philosophical."

Jamie lifts his head, peering at me through one eye, nose scrunched guiltily.

"What?"

"You finished the bag last weekend. I forgot to grab you more." He rolls to the edge of the bed and stretches his arms over his head. The iris is still perfectly intact on his skin. "I'll walk to the store."

"Wait." I can feel the beer from last night making my body swell. "I'll go too. I want the exercise."

We pull on clothes and sneakers, and Jamie lets me borrow another Fortune hoodie, bringing my collection to four. The air is a cold slap when we head out toward downtown. The closest place with halfway decent coffee is a local bakery, and Jamie heads for the counter while I bee-line to the carafes.

I'm pouring too-hot French vanilla roast into my to-go cup when I hear a voice over my shoulder. "I know you."

"Sorry?" I turn and smile brightly at a smallish blonde dressed in a bright green pea-coat and jeans. Her hair is pulled back and she has pearls in her ears. She's not smiling back.

"You're the girl from the roof."

Oh, God. Becca. I didn't recognize her. Why didn't I recognize her?

I open my mouth and close it again, unsure how to make casual conversation with Jamie's ex, and by the looks of it, she isn't interested in niceties. Her brows are drawn down, her mouth tight. She looks older now, which obviously makes sense; it's been two years. I'm stunned and on top of that, growing hot with worry. As uncomfortable as this little re-union is for me, Jamie *really* isn't going to like it.

"Holy shit. Is that a Fortune sweatshirt?" Becca shakes her head like I'm some bad dream she's trying to forget.

I tug nervously on the strings of the hoodie, two sizes too big for me and quite obviously not mine. "It's... uh..." I think about lying. Is it possible to get away with her not knowing

I'm here with Jamie? I know how this looks. Maybe I can text him and tell him I'll meet him outside.

But before I make the decision, Jamie's boyish laugh echoes through the bakery. She recognizes it as well as I do, and her eyes track to where he's chatting with the man behind the donut counter. She blinks at him, then turns to me with her nose scrunched. I feel the exact moment she puts it together.

"No way. You're here *with* him?" She laughs bitterly. "Well, isn't that interesting."

I swallow, wishing I could say it's not, but the fact is she has no idea just how interesting it is, me and him—us.

Her eyes narrow and what I thought might be genuine hurt morphs into indignation. "I'd love to know how you ended up with Jamie after that night. I mean, I've seen him around of course. I haven't seen you."

"It's new." My voice sounds like a string about to snap.

She crosses her arms across her chest and looks me up and down. "Quite the long game."

"Sorry?"

"The show you put on that night? It was just to steal him? God, couldn't you just get his number from one of the boys? Shoot your shot like anyone else?" I swear her fingers tremble when she tucks a stray hair behind her ear. She's shaken. Angry.

This reaction doesn't mesh with the villain I've made her out to be in my head all of these years and my skin starts to tingle with an incoming storm.

"I wasn't shooting my... I wouldn't... You were cheating on him," I say with more confidence than I feel, because this part of the vision? It's never been any of my business. Certainly not enough so that I can throw it back in her face here.

Becca and Jamie's relationship is something I don't like to think about for obvious reasons. I'm a bystander, a particularly intimate one, but standing by nonetheless.

Becca shakes her head like she can't believe my gall either, bringing up her past crimes. "Wow. Well, that's one way to spin it." She leans in closer. "I wasn't *doing* anything," she hisses. "I didn't... I didn't go through with it."

Something heavy drops inside of my chest. "I don't understand."

She huffs a laugh. "Good to know you did your due diligence before messing with my whole life. Why couldn't you just leave us alone?" She looks at him again and laughs. "Well, I guess I know now."

Possessiveness scratches inside of me when she refers to herself and Jamie as "us." It's not a feeling I have a lot of experience with, but I try to hold onto it because underneath it is a thick and thorny fear.

I want to fire back, tell her that he's *mine*, actually. I saw it. But instead, my breath starts to skip and go unsteady because I get the distinct feeling there's something I'm missing here.

"What do you mean you didn't go through with it?"

"I mean I didn't cheat on Jamie the way you lied and said I did."

"You would have," I blurt. Or else I wouldn't have seen it. That has to be it. She didn't get the chance for that fate to play out because I saw it in the candle first. "If I didn't tell Jamie, you would have gone through with it."

Except I don't know that for sure, do I? What if it was like the tattoo? Or the scar? What if she really would have changed course if I'd left it alone?

"How on earth would you know what I would or wouldn't do? I met Jamie when I was just out of high school." She flicks her eyes toward him again and this time I can't bear to follow because something is unraveling, and I can't seem to grasp the end of it to pull it tight again. "Jamie, he's impulsive, he always has been. He doesn't think things through."

I feel that scratchy instinct to defend him like I felt with Wes, but Becca has just put her foot on that same perspective, giving it more weight.

You're not doing him any favors by coddling that part of him.

Wes must have loved Becca.

"He was talking about getting married and in the same breath talking about quitting his job and brewing beer for a living," she continues. "And then I started grad school, and I met someone else. He just seemed to have his head on, you know? Nothing happened. I mean, it wasn't physical." Her fist tightens around her coffee until I'm afraid the cap will pop off. "God, this is *so* none of your business. I wouldn't be telling you any of this if he'd just listen. If I'd gotten to explain, maybe we could have worked it out." Her voice cracks. "When you love someone the way he and I loved each other, you work things out."

This feels so much like a shove that I actually take a step back. I feel a sensation in my chest like seams tearing. The fabric that holds us and everything I've found here together, coming undone.

This can't be right.

Your girlfriend, she's sleeping with someone else. That's what I told him, and I was wrong.

I think I'm going to be sick. I think maybe Becca can tell and she's glad for it. She hates me that much. Who can blame her? She had him, and now she doesn't. Because of me.

My brain fills with nasty images. It's not from anywhere supernatural, just my own vivid and cruel imagination. Jamie and Becca together. Happy. I picture his smile—the one I love the best—pressed to hers, and I physically recoil. Then I see Becca heartbroken, sobbing, because of a foolish, reckless woman at a party.

A hand lands on my waist, bringing my mind back to this awful interaction, and Jamie's voice, soft and surprised, comes from somewhere above my head. "Becca?"

Becca looks at Jamie, then back at me. "Are you going to tell him now that we're all standing here again? Because he's refused to speak to me for two years."

"Tell me what?"

"I know who she is, Jamie."

"Good memory." He sniffs. He's playing this off, but I see him. He's confused and guarded. His jaw is so tight, I want to reach up and massage it. I also want to leave. Now.

"You two should talk." I put my hand on his chest, then think better of it and pull back.

I turn to go but Jamie cuffs my wrist, his eyes pleading. "Noe, wait."

Despite every nerve in my body begging me to flee this conflict, my heels sink back onto the floor.

"She lied to you," Becca says, jabbing a finger in my direction.

"I didn't."

"Oh my God. Will you please tell the truth?"

Jamie laughs but it's not his usual laugh. There's no warmth. No childlike joy. I think of the expression "If looks could kill" because there's a dagger in the one he's giving her now. "And what is the truth in your mind, Bec? Because I thought it was you sleeping with someone else when I had a damn *engagement* ring on hold."

"That's what she lied about!"

Jamie shakes his head, and I manage to pry my wrist free from where he's still clutching it.

Becca doesn't notice. She's not looking at me. "If you'd have listened to me, you would know that."

I picture his face that night, add it to what I know about him now. He was blindsided. He felt stupid. Of course he wouldn't have listened.

My palms sweat, and each breath I take feels like it's being dragged over a washboard. Maybe it's the jagged pieces of my heart. I need to get away from this so I can think.

"I'm going," I say. It's a tiny thing, my voice. Shaky and weak, but they both swing their gazes toward me. Panic is rising in my throat along with bile. "I need some air. Jamie, I'll see you... after."

For someone who's been known to see the future, I sure spend an awful lot of time wishing I could go back. Back to before Wes made me question the benevolence of this magic. Back to Jamie's bed before I decided to come to this stupid bakery. But no matter how much I wish, I can't find a way. There's been a lot of magic in our lives, me and Jamie, more than most people get, but time travel isn't our particular brand.

It was no more than five minutes before he came looking for me, but it was long enough for more to be said between them. More confusion cleared up for him and stirred up for me. I didn't ask. I *couldn't*.

Now, he trails a few steps behind me, hands in his pockets, eyes on the cobblestones while we head down the street back to his place. Questions fire at me from all sides in the silence: Would he still have left her if he had all these details? Would he have gone all in on the rest of it if he'd known there were holes in this?

When we get to the landing, I wait, arms wrapped around myself while Jamie opens the door, holding it for me. The heat of his apartment feels less cozy today, more oppressive. He still hasn't spoken. I don't know if he's giving me the space I demanded when I ran out of there or rethinking every interaction we've ever had, but wondering is killing me. "Jamie, I—"

"I just need a minute, Noe."

I freeze, the blood draining from my face. *The latter, I guess.*

He rounds the kitchen island, putting it between us like a shield, gripping the edge with white knuckles. "What were the other differences?"

"What?"

"You said a few things were different from what you saw, right? But you never told me what."

My jaw tightens with panic. I didn't tell him because I didn't want to think about it. But the chickens have come home to roost. They always do. "Your tattoo," I whisper.

"My..." he lifts his arm, looking at the hops wreath wrapping his bicep.

"Not that one. The one on your back."

His forehead creases. "Okay. How?"

"It wasn't a wave. It was words. I don't know what it said."

"So you know it was different but you don't know what it was before?"

"It was a little... blurry? And it was partly covered by the sheet."

"The sheet?"

"I saw it when I saw us. We were in bed. At the hotel." I don't know why I'm blushing after everything we've done, but

I burn from my cheekbones to my ears.

"Okay," he says. "Is that it?"

"The scar on your hand," I say miserably. "It wasn't there."

He glances at it, then shoves his hand in his hair. "These are tiny things, Noe."

"Yeah. They were. Until now."

I try to pull that night back into my head, search for any other signs that I was wrong, but the memory seems to come at me from another angle. Something that's been hidden in the bushes, stepping into the light.

All I can see looking back at it now is how badly I wanted him. The minute I saw him. After everything that's happened, I can be honest with myself about that. I'd felt it, a quick pulse of desire that flipped my heart and shot heat between my legs. The kind of whole-body impulse that I never give in to.

Whenever I've felt that kind of want, I've shoved it down with both hands. But not that night. I let myself look. Think about it. Imagine it.

What if that's all it took to manifest this thing? What if *that's* all it was that put those pictures in my head? A selfish disregard for anything but my own wants.

I knew I should walk away, but I didn't. Just like when I found him on my porch and decided to bring him to the ER myself.

Wait.

My eyes snap to him. "You told me it was true. That's what you said at the hospital. Didn't you even ask her?"

Guilt flashes in his wince. "She said there was someone else. That was enough. I left and I blocked her number."

"After six years? Why wouldn't you at least hear her side, Jamie?"

"The rest of it came true. What was I supposed to think?"

"Oh my God." That's what he said at the hospital. *I couldn't ignore that one when the rest was so spot on.* The back of my neck is damp with sweat, and I strip his hoodie off and find my jacket on the back of the couch. "I should go. You have to get ready for the launch."

It was last season's launch when I agreed to see him again. I'm not sure what kind of sign that is. I can't read them anymore. Or maybe I never could.

"It's nine-thirty in the morning, Noel. We have hours. Stay." He looks nervous, pulling his hands from his pockets to grip his hair.

"I have to feed Pixie."

"I'll go with you then," he says. "Hang out at your place until I have to be here." He's on my heels as I buzz around gathering my things. His fingers grab for my hip, but I twirl out of reach.

"Noel, *please*. Look, let's just... forget it happened. It doesn't matter."

"Of *course* it matters," I cry. I didn't think it was possible, but he's just made this infinitely worse. Tell me it was all a dream, tell me she's just angry and lashing out, but don't tell me I messed with his entire life, and it doesn't matter.

"And stop doing that, Jamie. Stop pretending everything's going to be fine because you want it to be. We've made a lot of big decisions based on that night, and I was wrong. And you're hoping to use the same flawed magic to help you with the next one."

He links his fingers behind his head, pacing. "Okay, well, what if we just tried it again? Maybe we haven't been trying hard enough to make it happen. Just one more time to clear it all up."

His words echo in my brain like the ringing after an explosion. He cannot think that is a good idea. "*That's* your solution? Dive deeper into this?"

"It's better than you running away."

God, I'm so tired of that accusation. Maybe that's what you do with something like this. When some force you don't understand hijacks your life. Maybe running away was always the right call. Hasn't anyone considered *that?*

"Come on, Noel." He reaches for my wrist, and I let him take it.

"I can't force it. That's the one thing—the *only* thing—we know about this."

"I know, baby, but we could try, right?"

"Jamie." I huff his name on a sigh. What is it about him that ruins my logic and instinct? "You don't even own a candle."

"You said the candle didn't matter." He draws me against his chest, circling me with his arms. "Just stand here with me. We'll focus. Try."

I nod, but I don't curl into him the way I would have before. Instead, his body pressed to mine makes my heart race in a different way. A bad way. A warning way. It suddenly feels really dangerous, playing with this force that I don't understand and has the power to wreak havoc.

What if I see exactly what he wants me to and he makes another huge financial decision because of it, only to find some hole later?

And what if I get some confirmation that other things I saw that night aren't true, that the thing I have my heart set on isn't as sure as I thought it was?

What if I see Jamie and me again, and like his tattoo, it's changed?

The blood seeps from my face. Jamie's not the only one who's been making huge decisions because one domino fell that night on the roof. My condo is about to have a For Sale sign in front of it. I turned down guaranteed income with Vi for a dream. All because I thought it was tied up in the same vision that gave me him. *You don't make major life decisions on a freaking candle.* Isn't that exactly what I told him?

I press a hand to my chest, and it's covered in sweat. The tattoo, the scar—those were little holes in the magic, hints that this could all change and I ignored them because I wanted to. I wanted him. But this isn't a little hole. This one is a gaping wound. I can't chance it.

"I don't want to do this," I say, pulling out of his grip. "Jamie, this is too important to play around with. Even if I see something, it could be wrong."

"Noel..."

"No. We don't know what we're doing. It was foolish to make decisions this way. What if this whole thing was bullshit from the start?"

Jamie's face falls, and I hear what I've said. My stomach plummets.

"I didn't mean—"

"Shit." He takes a step back, knocking into the counter. "I just realized you're talking about us."

"No." I say. "No, I'm not."

"That's what you said: Big decisions, flawed magic. All of it's bullshit."

"I just meant it's all tied up, Jamie."

His jaw works like he's trying out words before speaking them. "I don't understand why it matters, Noel. Sure, some details were off, but it still happened. Me and you, we still happened. That's what you wanted to see, right? When you were testing me all that time?"

The spiral I'm in halts on a dime and I blink up at him. "You think I was testing you?"

He licks his lips and looks away. "Weren't you? Isn't that why you didn't tell me what you saw?"

"*No.*" An ache pulses through my chest, and I press my hands to my temples.

"You said you wanted to see if it would happen on its own."

"It wasn't a test. Or maybe it was, but not of you. Of the visions."

"It's the same thing, Noe."

"It's not."

"That night at the beach," he says. "That's when you saw my tattoo. You freaked out. That's why, right?"

My jaw clamps shut. I can't lie to him, and the truth to that question won't help here. Besides, I can see him working out on his own. His brow is drawn, eyes bouncing around my face.

He tips his head. "But why did you change your mind?"

"Jamie."

"Why did you agree to see me again that night at the bar? Why did you put your condo up for sale? Decide to stay here with me?"

"It doesn't matt—" I bite off the end of that sentence. I'm a hypocrite. How can one piece matter and not the rest?

"*Why*, Noel?"

"Because I saw us! There at the cottage. In the summer. I thought I was supposed to stay."

His eyes are desperate. I can practically see his heart banging around in his chest. "Would you have stayed without it?"

"I don't know," I whisper.

His whole body sags, and it's like a knife twisting in my gut to see all that buoyant hope that fuels him deflate before my eyes. I'm torn between wanting to fix it, to patch him back up, and taking it as the sign that it probably is. He's supposed to be the believer here and he doesn't have any left either.

"Everything between us," he says. "It's just been a calculated risk for you."

"I didn't say that, Jamie. I'm just confused."

"I'm in love with you. Not the idea that I'm somehow supposed to be with you—*You*. There's nothing confusing about that for me. You can't say the same. I'm sorry, but that hurts no matter how you put it."

"That's... you're making it seem simple, and it's not." I press my palms into my eyes, frustrated at the way this is spinning out of my grip. "God, I wish I'd never looked into that stupid candle. Why couldn't we have just met like normal people? Out at some bar somewhere."

"Come on," he says, and the coldness of it snaps my head up. "You think we'd be standing here if you didn't look into that candle? I'm not exactly your type, Noel."

"That is *not* true."

"Maybe I passed your test, but I wouldn't have even had the opportunity to take it without that vision, so I'm sorry you wish you never had it, but I can't say the same."

"Jamie. That's not... I'm not..." The hurt on his face makes me desperate. I step to him, curl my fingers in his shirt. "You said yourself you wouldn't have taken the risk on your business if you hadn't seen the future. If you thought you might lose. You just asked me to do it again so you can decide what to do next! You did the exact same thing. You're doing it now."

"That's not even remotely the same, Noel."

"Of course it is! We were both scared. Of holding onto something that could be taken away. Of loving—" my voice cracks and I clear my throat. "Of loving something that would hurt if we lost it. You made me feel a lot of things really quickly. You have to understand how overwhelming that was."

"It was overwhelming for me too! Believe it or not, you're the first woman I've been with who could see my future, let alone tell me we were destined to end up together. But you know what that looked like to me, Noel? It looked rare, and special. Something you don't let pass you by even if it leaves you with more questions than answers. Even if you're scared."

His name is a hoarse whisper from my throat, but he's

already turned away from me. He walks to the door and grabs a hat and his keys from the hook on the wall. "I'm going downstairs. Stay or don't. Whatever you think you're supposed to do."

Thirty-Three

Noel

T HE BREAKDOWN COMES IN the car on the way home. Tears that seem like they're being pumped from a never-ending well. I bat at them intermittently as I replay the moment when the surest thing in my life spiraled out of control.

As I cross the bridge out of town, I file back through every reading Nana ever gave me or Kate for a sign that I've missed a vital step in being able to interpret them. But there's no rhyme or reason. Some came true, sure, but they were never as concrete and life changing as Jamie. Nothing that was enough to make a believer out of me. Not until him. So why throw this wrench in now? Why did this *thing* put on such a spectacular show just to convince me to follow it, only to pull the rug out after I got attached?

I huff a watery laugh at my windshield. Attached sounds so trite. So shallow. Attached was the crush I allowed myself to have on Jamie in the beginning, before I tumbled into this deep, cavernous love. Now I'm attached to him in the way my limbs are attached to my body.

This wasn't the deal. Sure, I ignored some things, but I followed the signs I understood. I did what I thought I was supposed to do, and now the entire thing has been reframed. The visions may or may not be fatally flawed, and I may have altered more than one future on the advice of a hallucination. My heart trotted after this idea that he was somehow promised to me, chasing after *fate* like a puppy into traffic. But the heart, big dumb muscle that it is, doesn't have eyes or ears or any other faculties to allow it to sense danger. The heart just wants to feel and feel, until it's finally felt the cut that stops it.

This feels like that cut. I took a man who believed in magic and love, who taught *me* to believe, and proved him wrong.

The sun set at the beach around five, but even in the dark, Kate finds me easily. I guess Jamie's little mischief spot wasn't as desolate as I thought that night. It's a good thing because when I drove here—maybe hoping to lick my wounds, maybe secretly hoping to find him here doing the same—I didn't think about how I was going to get home. Given the amount of wine I've already drank, it won't be in my car.

Kate pulls her coat tight around her as she hurries across the sand toward me. Beyond her, I see Colin in the parking lot, standing in a long coat and scarf, leaning on his car.

"I feel like maybe you downplayed the emergency of this situation," she says, taking in the vignette of heartache I've made on this sand. "What are you doing?"

"I'm drinking wine on the beach," I say. I reach for my phone, which is playing Patsy Cline's "Walking After Midnight" at an unreasonable volume, and hold it up as if Kate wasn't already made aware of that part when she pulled up. Luckily, it's freezing out here, so there's no one to be disturbed by the soundtrack to my patheticness.

Kate steps to the edge of the blanket I brought. She's looking at me like I'm a wounded animal she's stumbled upon. It's not that far off.

"I think Jamie and I broke up."

"*What?* No. No. No," she says, plopping down in the sand beside me. "What happened?"

"We had a fight. I think it was a big one."

"About what?"

I tell her about what Becca said, how it threw everything into a tailspin. "He asked me to try it again, to read him. How can he ask me for that? How can he trust any of it anymore? I almost did it before I smartened up, Kate! God, it's like I just follow him anywhere he leads. I get stupid around him. Since that very first night."

"Welcome to love, babe." When I don't laugh, she sighs and leans back on her hands. "It's not stupid to trust him, Noel. He obviously trusts you."

"Well, that's a mistake. Look what I've done so far. I told him lies about his girlfriend and charted his whole life on a different course." And then I took him for myself. A fist squeezes my heart. I thought he was mine and I swan dived into him, thinking he was destined to catch me. Instead I took him down with me. And Becca.

"It wasn't a lie," Kate says. "And it led him to you. I'd say that's a pretty good course."

"But I stole him."

"No way, Noel. I mean, you didn't see or speak to him for two years! I practically had to force you to go on your first date with him."

"It wasn't a date." I sniffle.

"See? You wouldn't even go on a date with him." She grabs my hand. "I know this feels like a huge deal, babe, and I totally don't blame you for needing to talk it out but think about it. Jamie's a good guy, right? Sweet, successful, handsome. A catch, some might say?"

I nod, lip between my teeth.

"So Becca screwed up. She's mad at herself, and she took it out on you. It's human nature, Noel. We want to blame other people for our biggest mistakes. If Jamie wanted to give her another chance, he had plenty of time."

Which is half the problem. He wasted that time believing in magic. Just like me, he thought he knew the ending. He thought he was making the right choice because I told him he was. But it turns out it was a roulette game from the start. Maybe the visions come true, maybe they don't. Maybe he's mine, maybe he isn't. What's the damn point in any of it?

"He said it didn't matter—the differences—and I know I told myself the same weeks ago, but that was when it was small stuff. This is huge. Saying it doesn't matter is crazy."

"Maybe it *doesn't* matter to him." She shifts onto her knees and pushes my hair off of my face. "Jamie's not a pawn in your vision, Noel. Have you considered that maybe he's seen enough, even without the supernatural assistance, and he knows what he wants?"

Oh, I've considered it. That's always been the difference between me and Jamie. He jumps with his eyes closed and his fingers crossed. But I'm not like him. I've never been like him, and isn't the way it's all blowing up now proof that living like that only gets you hurt? This morning, he looked at me like I crushed his heart in my fist because that's what love does. It always leaves you worse than you found it. I thought I had a way around it, I thought this magic wouldn't hurt us, but I was so wrong.

"Maybe all this wanting is the craziest of all of it," I say miserably. I fall flat on my back and at the same moment, the music stops. Turning my head with some effort, I see the battery in my phone is dead. Tragic. "You didn't see his face, Kate. I'm not sure he knows what he wants anymore anyway. Somewhere along the way, I changed our destiny, or I misunderstood it, because this hurts too much to be the plan all along."

Kate scoots backward to avoid the splash of the creeping tide, closing in on my blanket. "Well... if you think you changed it, Noel. Change it back."

Another piece of my heart wilts at her advice. If there's one thing that's proven true so far, it's that I can't control this. That's what makes it so dangerous.

Colin drives me home because he's as good of a soul as they come. Head pressed against the glass of the back seat window, my thoughts narrow from the infinite implications of the universe toying with me to the persistent ache inside of my chest that's been building since this morning. I miss Jamie so much. My favorite person. My best friend. All of the colors that have filled in over the last few months are gray again.

Part of me wants to ask Colin to bring me to Fortune, but I'm a mess, and a little drunk, and I think maybe seeing me would just confuse him tonight when he needs to focus on work. I should probably take Wes's advice and stay far away from any of his business endeavors from now on.

The car swings into the gravel driveway, and the headlights splash on a vehicle parked in the driveway. For one hopeful beat, my droopy heart sits up inside my chest, thinking it could be Jamie, even though I know he'd be cutting it too close coming here before the launch.

It's not a little gray sports car or a truck with Fortune's logo painted on the side, anyway. It's a car I don't recognize with Pennsylvania plates, which means it's either a rental or a complete stranger.

Kate turns over her shoulder with her eyebrows raised, and I shake my head. Colin wordlessly cuts the engine. All three of us pile out of his car just as the front door to the cottage opens, and there, standing on my doorstep, is the most timely reminder of how strong the force of chaos is in this world. My mother's here.

Mom steps out onto the porch holding a squirming Pixie in one arm, waving wildly with the other. I'd forgotten she had a key, not that I expected her back today anyway. I wonder if she went to Connecticut first. If she saw the For Sale sign.

Oh, God. It's not just Jamie. There's an army of consequences lining up for me to face. More chickens coming home to roost. I'd made that decision knowing full well Mom would show up eventually asking for her room back. And she'd be out of luck because I wouldn't be able to bail her out.

Well, here she is. And here I am, without any of the assurance I pictured myself having when I broke the news to her: *Your steadfast daughter has been wildly reckless, Mom.*

"Elena." Kate pastes on a smile to greet my mother, but her hand clutches the back of my coat protectively. I manage to wipe at my eyes and attempt to huff enough salt air to get rid of my leftover sniffles before Mom comes trotting down the steps to throw her free arm around me.

"Surprise!" she says, rocking me back and forth on the gravel driveway.

I free Pixie from her arms, snuggling her to my chest, and poke my head around Mom's shoulder. "Is Dennis with you?" I ask, trying to sound completely at ease with the idea of a strange man following my mother here to be my new roommate too. Kate and Colin exchange a look that I read as *we're not leaving if he is.*

"Oh," Mom says. "Well, no. That didn't work out." She waves a hand at her hair and I realize with a start that it's about ten shades lighter than when she left. "Break up blonde," she explains, and I notice a wobble in her chin.

"Are you okay?"

"No, honey." She touches my cheek in one of those quick maternal gestures that slips in every once in a while. "But you always know how to fix me up."

"Well, let's go inside," I say, slipping my hand into hers. "It's cold." And just like the tide overtaking the patch of sand I was trying to wallow on, my mother's problems wash over mine.

Thirty-Four

Noel

I PROMISED KATE AND Colin I'd be fine, and my phone is still void of any messages from Jamie, so it's just Mom and me tonight.

"She might be your monkey, but this doesn't have to be your circus," Kate said as she hugged me goodbye. I appreciated the reminder, but dealing with Mom's life imploding is actually a lot more familiar and easier to deal with than the storm happening inside of my own heart.

It takes me a half hour to change the sheets in Nana's room for Mom and make a space in the loft again for me. I drag a sleeping bag in from the garage, and fold up my easel to make room on the floor. God knows how long she's planning to camp here.

If she'd shown up yesterday, I would have just gone, taken Pixie and run to Jamie's place. To him, to the comfort and safety of being in his orbit. But it's not yesterday. It's today. And it looks nothing like I thought.

I set us up with some tea and we sprawl out over Nana's old plaid couch with the fireplace roaring at our feet. The chill of the beach has settled into my bones, so I'm decked out in flannel pajama pants and, embarrassingly, wrapped in one of Jamie's zip-up hoodies.

Since Mom showed up with only what would fit in her backpack, completely unprepared for the temperature change from West coast to East, she's in one of Nana's long cardigans. She looks like a child playing dress up.

"So then he said he needs more room to breathe than the van." She dabs the corner of her eye with her sleeve. "I pointed out the window to the literal desert we were parked in and said 'you've got acres of room, you foolish man! Go wander the sand for a bit.' I don't know, Noel. Some people just don't know what they want from one minute to the next."

I nod absently, unable to even respond to that ridiculous judgment coming from her. She's been bouncing from one thing to another her whole life. Men, jobs, adventures. I keep that thought to myself as usual.

Instead, I reach across the cushion and squeeze her wrist, offering her the box of tissues on my end table. She takes one and in the same motion reaches for Pixie, scooping her from my lap to hers. A little squeak of protest escapes me, but she doesn't notice. She goes on about California, about Dennis and how his adult kids weren't supportive of his decision to sell his house to do the whole van thing with my mother either, and I hate the bitterness creeping into the back of my throat. I hate it but I can't seem to fight it off this time. I should be a good daughter, a sympathetic ear. I'm trying to be whatever she needed from me when she came here. But I can't be the port right now when my heart is a swirling storm.

It hits me like a rogue wave, that I've never even been a mess before. I found the emotion I'd been looking for here, found it in droves. Only for it to end in my first ever emotional breakdown on the beach. For a panicked moment, I think I'll actually burst from the ache. This is what wanting does to you. This is why I've never wanted to be like her.

My breath starts to stutter, and my eyes spill over like two raging rivers. "I actually can't do this right now," I blurt.

Mom pulls back a bit, blinking at the interruption, and I follow my first real foot-putting down moment with a broken sob that shakes my shoulders.

"Honey, are you okay?"

I shake my head, batting at the tears streaming from my eyes. "No. I'm not," I tell her. "My heart is broken, and I can't stuff down my feelings to make room for yours anymore. These ones are too big."

Mom's eyes are saucers. "Heartbroken? Honey, over what?"

Despite myself, I laugh, utterly vindicated at her question. She doesn't even know Jamie exists. She doesn't know his name. His face. That dimple that knocked the wind out of me. How his eyes are just the tiniest bit asymmetrical, and a color that I've tried for hours to recreate with paint or chalk or pencils before I realized I wasn't talented enough. How he always sleeps on his stomach. How everyone, *everyone* loves him but he loved *me*. Even when all I ever gave him was hesitation.

All these things have happened to me since I last saw my mother and she doesn't know because she didn't think to ask. She touches down when she needs my help, never the other way around.

Such an easy kid. Barely ever cries.

I think I saved all those tears for this moment right now. With a half sob, half groan of frustration, I move to stand, to leave this conversation for what it is—shallow, one-sided at best, certainly not any help toward putting my heart back in my chest—but she must see it on my face, this despair, because she catches my wrist and tugs me back to the couch. "Tell me," she says.

"I fell in love. Real love, and I hurt him. I made him think he wasn't good enough, but really he was too good. I want him too much, and I'm scared of it."

"You've always been full of nerves," she says with a pious shake of her head.

I choke on more tears. She's right. I *have* always been full of nerves. Terrified to want or to love, because her kind of love is chaotic and untrustworthy and scary, and it's the only example I've ever had. Until now.

Loving Jamie is like a hug after a bad dream. A cup of tea after a white-knuckle drive in the snow. He's my wild streak and my calm place. One minute he's the wind and the next he's the sturdy ground, and I don't know if I ever could have seen that coming even with a glimpse of the future.

Mom points her teacup at me. "You know, Noel, your Nana used to say 'Life is one part fate, two parts figure it out.'"

I run a hand under my nose. "What does that mean?"

"It means humans have a knack for screwing up a good thing. God knows I do. You know she knew about you before I did. Saw it in a candle. I was only twenty years old," she says, like I'm not acutely aware of the youth I stole from her. How she ended up taking mine in return by leaning on me the way she did.

"But before that, I had these plans to go to Europe when I graduated high school. I wanted to study art like you. Well, first I was going to backpack through the countryside, but then I was going to get serious. I had the money too." She waves a hand. "It was the nineties. Everyone had money then."

I've heard this story a hundred times, and I nearly give up again, dump my tea and head to bed just so I can have some peace to wallow in, but she keeps going.

"Anyway, I hadn't even told your grandmother about this plan, and then one day, she was reading my candle wax and she saw the whole thing. Wine and paintings and French men." She winks. "And you know what I did? I picked your father. Stupid me, I guess."

I flinch at the careless reminder. My whole existence is a result of that "stupid" decision, but I don't have any more pain to dedicate to her, so instead I go back a step. "I never heard Nana say that, the thing about fate only being part of it."

She shrugs. "Well, maybe she didn't think you'd want to hear it. You were always her biggest skeptic."

I sniffle scoff. Those were the days. I wish I could go back to being a skeptic, forget all of these glimpses and half-clues as to what's in store. I think of the belief draining out of Jamie's eyes and it's like pouring lemon juice on a cut. I finally did believe in magic, and it betrayed me.

Except... maybe what Mom's saying is it didn't.

Two parts figure it out.

After I saw Jamie's tattoo, I asked Kate what the point of seeing the future was if I could change it, but what if that's the *whole* point? Or at least two parts of it.

I've had signs that it could change this whole time. Jamie's tattoo, the scar. I ignored them. I feared them because I thought they challenged the magic. But maybe they weren't evidence that the visions were wrong. Maybe they were little bits of accountability. Proof that our choices matter too.

That's what I told Jamie when he first shocked me with his story about getting the money for his business. He still had to know what to do with it. That's what I've been hoping he'd figure out about himself and his ability to run his business, that it's more about him than he thinks. But I've ignored the way that could also apply to me, to us.

I sit up a little straighter, and Pixie stretches her front paws, trotting back to me.

Mom's saying Nana saw her having a whole other life, but she chose something else. She made choices and the future changed. Sure, I saw Jamie and me together, but even after he showed up on my porch, I could have refused to see him again like I did the first time. I could have said no to Cara despite the vision, left when I was supposed to and taken Ned's job. I could have never come here at all.

Every time I tried to turn away from Jamie, the universe lodged him back into my brain, showing me a new version of us—the first vision on the roof, his bar when I tried to walk away, then that night on the beach when I *ran* away. But the moment I went all in, the visions stopped.

What if the lesson isn't that Jamie and I are a destiny that I got a glimpse into? What if it's to show me what I *could* have if I stop talking myself out of the things I want and into something safer. If I stop telling myself that loving anything enough that it could wreck me is akin to madness.

When I thought I was following fate, I let myself love harder than I ever have, let Jamie love me back because I thought I couldn't fail, but he's not a pawn in my future. He's been choosing this all along too. He believed in fate but he also figured it out. He's always been braver than me that way.

I close my eyes and picture him—pushing through the things that he struggles with, terrified he's going to make a mistake but going after what he wants anyway. Handing me his heart with so much trust in his eyes—and there's a sudden quiet in my brain, like dipping my head under water and losing the ambient noise. Only one message floats around in there now. It's not a vision, but a peaceful realization.

I haven't lost the future I could have with him or this house or this new life. I'm just at the figure it out part.

"This is new," is all Mom says while I clutch Pixie to my chest and cry so hard I'm snotty and sweaty in this oversized sweatshirt.

"It is," I choke out.

A moment passes with Mom just staring at me like I'm some sort of bug under a microscope. Then she nods resolutely. "My little hot mess," she says. "I like it."

I give her an incredulous sniffle-laugh. Only her.

Then I wipe a hand under my nose and push my shoulders back, chin tipped. "Good," I say. "Because I put the condo up for sale and I'm moving here. The spare room is only available for visits."

Thirty-Five

Jamie

I WAKE UP TO my phone buzzing beside my head.

Em: Plan on buying me lunch after we play. I'll be there in five.

With a groan, I drag myself out of bed. At some point during the launch last night, she took my phone and added a calendar event to shoot hoops at the rec today, claiming I look like shit and exercise might help. I know she's babysitting me more than seeking out my company, but I suppose it's better than drowning in self-pity for another day.

I shove my phone in the pocket of my pajama pants just as she knocks. "Thanks for dressing up," she says when I open it.

"I just need a minute."

She follows me inside, and I can feel her silent judgment at the mess. My dress shirt from the launch is on the kitchen island. A pizza box and a six pack of empty bottles litter my living room.

I do a quick brush and swish of mouthwash and throw on shorts and a dirty shirt. I'm going to get sweaty again anyway.

Em drives, and I plug my phone into her dash and scroll my music. Five minutes in, her fist hits my bicep. "Cut the shit."

"Sorry." She can't stand when I let a song play for a few beats, then change it. My brain feels like a rubber ball tossed into an empty room, and I can't focus on anything beyond the basics of feeding myself. Sleeping. Working.

Wes spent the night reminding me that a winter ale launch means the end of the year. Time running out. Not only has my hope for a psychic tip imploded, but it's a lot harder not to acquiesce to his advice fresh off my latest misread with Noel.

I shut the radio off altogether, suddenly hungover, or car sick, or love sick.

Em pulls to a stop light and stares at me. "Are you going to tell me what the hell is going on?"

It was *not* lost on her that Noel wasn't there last night celebrating the launch with me. I hid behind the busy night, then left early with an excuse that I'm not on the hourly schedule, so my shift was over when I said it was.

The first time I embraced the boss role Em's been pushing me toward, and I used it to be a dick.

By the time I got to my apartment, I'd spiraled into a full-on panic wondering if this was more than just a fight with Noel. If she might disappear completely the way she did two years ago. The thought made me feel like there was a vacuum hose attached to my lungs, sucking all of my air.

I toss my phone in the cupholder and tip my head back against the headrest. "I think I fucked it up."

Em blows out a breath. "Jameson, I'm usually the first one to jump on you for being an idiot when it comes to women, and I don't know the whole story, but I don't get the feeling you did this by yourself." I turn my head to look at her but she's staring thoughtfully out the windshield. "Let me guess. Something scared her?"

I press my palms into my eyes. "Yeah, that's kind of her thing."

"It's yours too."

I'd take that punch if I thought I deserved it, but I handed Noel my whole beating heart. Even after the hotel when I started to get that *playing with fire* feeling, I pushed through it.

"I went all in with her, Em. Even scared, I was doing the hard thing. But once again, I was the only one. Christ, what is it about me that makes loving me so damn conditional?"

Em turns to me, her eyes wide. *"Jamie."*

"No, don't pity me, just tell me what it is because I've been trying to get it for a long fucking time, and I can't figure it out."

"You're asking the wrong question, J. If someone thinks that about you, then they're not for you. But tell me why on earth you think Noel is one of those people, because as an outside observer, that is not what I see."

But that's a big chunk of it, isn't it? What's missing to the outside observer. The thing Noel kept even from me.

"Noel and I were part of the vision she had that night on the roof," I confess. "She *saw* us the same way she saw everything else. She told me on our trip to the mountain."

This stuns Em silent like I thought it might, but not for long. "And you didn't like that."

I huff a laugh. I more than didn't like it. It pressed on a bruise I didn't even know was still there, but I stuffed it way down deep because the thought of losing her was way worse than a stupid blow to my ego.

But the thing about shoving stuff down and never dealing with it, is it becomes like a smear across your vision. Like someone has taken their thumb and pressed a blurry spot in the center of your sunglasses, or dragged their dirty palm down your windshield. Your whole world becomes filtered through this thing that's between you and whatever you're looking at. I couldn't see us the same way after that.

I was an imposter. A fraud who got here by some stroke of luck. Just like my career.

I rub at my chest where it feels tight with anxiety. "It turns out the vision was wrong anyway. Becca didn't even cheat on me."

"Hold up. Becca *what?*" Em puts her blinker on, her eyes darting between me and the road. "The baggage from that is, like, half of your personality."

I roll my eyes. "Well, it was wrong. Apparently a few of them have been wrong, but Noel failed to mention that until we ran into Becca and it all came out. Everything I thought happened, didn't. Our whole break up was over a misunderstanding."

"Jesus. So are you two... talking again?"

I look at her, incredulous. "I don't want Becca back."

"Jamie. This is hard to keep up with."

"I don't want Becca. Whether she went through with it or not, what we had wasn't what I thought. I just want to quit getting shit so wrong all the time. Do you know what that's like, to never be able to trust your head?"

"You're not a head guy, Jamie. You're a gut guy. And if Noel's the opposite, maybe that's why you two work so well. Yin and yang and all that."

"Yeah well, she doesn't see it that way. She said she wouldn't have even stayed here if it wasn't for that vision."

Em's face softens. "If she thinks that, she's lying to herself. People do that when they're scared. You tell yourself you need Wes because you're scared to fuck up what you have. So she told herself she needed whatever calling this fate gave to her. I personally don't think either one deserves the credit you're giving out." Em turns into the long driveway to the rec center, slowing for some kids crossing the road on bikes. "I mean, seriously, Jamie. If you can't see the way that girl looks at you, I don't know how to help you."

"Not to sound cocky, Em, but a lot of women look at me."

"Sure," she says, pulling into a parking spot and cutting the engine. "They look at you—" she pushes her finger into my cheek before I can dodge her. "Noel looks. At. You." This time her finger lands directly in the center of my chest, and I swear I feel it sink right through the bone and scrape against my heart. I have to turn away.

"Look, this is all way out of my wheelhouse—psychic visions, destiny, and all that—but I do know that ever since I've known you, you've been fixated on some future version of yourself that you're still trying to achieve, and the whole time, there's been a you right now who's pretty fucking great. If Noel says she loves that you, I think you should believe her because I would bet it was a big deal for her to say it. I bet she was scared as hell."

The weight of that bears down on me at once, and I picture Noel that night I passed out on her porch, rightfully terrified. I knew she was scared that night at Fortune too, when I begged her to be a psychic conduit for me even after she admitted she was here dealing with some heavy stuff of her own. I haven't really considered how scary the rest of it is, though. The enormity of what I asked of her. Carrying the fact that she and I might be destined all by herself.

I still think she should have told me, but I can see why she didn't. Why it was easier to navigate that part without adding my expectations to it. I've put a lot of pressure on her even after promising I wouldn't. And worst of all, I didn't even protect her when she started to crumble from it. Instead, I was immediately defensive.

Maybe I haven't been the brave one after all.

"I'm a selfish asshole," I admit with a gust of air.

Em snorts. "Hardly. You just got your feelings hurt, Jamie, and it's okay to say when something hurts. This whole situation seems like it touched a nerve for both of you, and I'm actually kind of proud of you right now for not pretending it didn't. I think you've leveled up a little bit."

I laugh quietly, but I'm thinking of what Noel said about growing pains being a sign of growth, and praying that's what this ache in my chest turns out to be. Em's right about me being caught up in the future, wanting that future *me* I envisioned to come to fruition, but maybe part of that growth is realizing that it's the unknown where you find the greatest possibility. God knows teenage me wouldn't have been able to look into a crystal ball and see my life today. And I can't see tomorrow, but I can see that everything I accused Noel of—following fate instead of my gut, worrying about what might be instead of what is—I've been right there going along with it.

The next morning, I head to the brewery as soon as the sun is up, my head spinning with ideas and a new resolve to focus on the present. There are things I've been kicking around for months, waiting to bring up with Wes. Waiting on the right time or the right mood. Waiting to ask permission to do what I want with my own damn company.

I'm here before everyone except for the cleaning crew. Wes's office is at the taproom, but I kept mine here when we opened that location. The bar is distracting, and some days my brain can't overcome that, but I also like being around the art of it. Listening to the machines chug, the guys on the floor working and laughing. The smell reminds me of my garage brewing days. I never felt over my head then.

By noon, I've filled the white board on my wall with lists, things that have been caught in the wind for months. I write them in columns, give them dates, and color code them by priority. Then I check off the things I can do right now, before I even talk to Wes.

I decide to officially make Em the general manager of the taproom and extract myself from the bar schedule. I want to put my effort into bigger things than pouring beer. I didn't run it by Wes because I don't have to. That's our arrangement, and I'm going to start handling my own side of this.

But I also know this part isn't a big risk. There's not a lot of trouble I can get into moving people around. I save the big jump for the afternoon.

Wes lives on the West End of the city in a brownstone that his dad bought him as a college graduation present. Every time I come here, which admittedly isn't often, it reminds me how deep-seated these differences between us are. Our motivations. What drives us. I just hope this conversation will show me they're close enough to still work.

I parallel park in front of his door and jog up the moss-covered steps. He answers on the first knock. "I've been calling you all morning."

"I've been at the brewery. I wanted to watch today's malt churn."

His expression is blank, and I wonder how it is that I'm just now realizing the machines there are as foreign to him as his spreadsheets are to me. I have done a lot of waking up today.

"Why are you here?" he asks.

I push past him, heading to the kitchen. I grab a bottle of our IPA out of his fridge, prying it against his wall mounted opener. "I've been thinking about the offer."

"It's about time."

I blow out a breath. "We have a good thing going here, Wes."

He leans a hip on the granite island. "Of course we do. Corporations like NEBev don't buy failing businesses, Jameson."

I shrug. "They're not going to buy this one either. My answer's no."

"Jesus Christ, Jamie." He pinches the bridge of his nose like I'm exasperating him. "You can't be serious. You've been talking about making something of yourself since I've known you. Being bought out by a major corporation is the epitome of success. I put it on a silver platter for you. What the hell are you thinking?"

"I'm thinking it's not my version of success." I sink against the wall, running a hand over my face. "Look, Wes, you're right about the fact that I came into this with a chip on my shoulder. And maybe making the news for being sought out by a corporation like this would have been the gold star I've been trying to earn for the last, I don't know, twenty years. It's just, I think maybe I've moved past wanting to prove something to everyone. At least not at the expense of my own dreams. It's kind of time I grew out of the whole *fuck you, world* thing, you know?"

He lets out a surprise laugh. "This just some epiphany you had overnight?"

I wish. If I had, maybe I wouldn't have twisted everything up with Noel. "I guess I just realized that proving myself to everyone is worth less than finding the person you don't have to do that with."

Someone who believes in my ability to figure it out on my own. I don't think I need to know the future anymore, as long as she's in it. If I fucked anything up in all of this, it was not realizing that sooner.

"One can only assume you're talking about your psychic girlfriend."

"Stop," I say. "That's the end of that shit too. And, yeah, I'm talking about Noel, but I wish I was talking about you too."

His eyes flash with surprise and he nods once. "Look, I know I can be an asshole—"

"You told Noel I almost failed out of college."

He throws a hand in the air. "And look what came of it! You got proof she's not like Becca or any of the others since her."

"*Wes*. Jesus, man."

"Okay, that was wrong. I know that." He scrapes his palms over his face, blowing out a breath. "So what happens if we keep growing, and you realize you're not cut out for this?"

I stutter at the question I've been asking myself pitched out loud. "You think I'm not?"

"I don't know, but it's a valid question if you want me to fall in line."

"I'm not asking you to fall in line. I'm asking you to be my business partner."

"Convince me then."

"Convince you?"

He crosses his arms. "You're disorganized. You're soft-hearted. You refuse to make the tough calls. Tell me why I shouldn't walk away."

I haven't forgotten there's still the possibility this is where our partnership ends instead of strengthens, but hearing him admit it takes a little wind out of the cocky sail I blew in here on. But I meant what I said about not being in this to prove myself. Acting on defensiveness and hurt feelings isn't how I want to move forward.

"Because you're the opposite of all those things, Wes, and that's why it works. Surrounding yourself with the people who can do what you can't, who can help you, that's not a weakness. It's smart business. And I'm also creative. I'm a good salesman because people trust me. And I'm a damn good brewer. I can do this without you, Wes. I'm not sure you can say the same. If we're going to keep working together, I won't keep treating this like a favor you're doing me."

He stares me down, that jaw twitch I'm so used to on full display.

"Well?"

"You forgot cocky. And fucking petulant."

I shrug. "I'm a work in progress."

"It wasn't an insult."

I laugh, shaking my head. "Christ."

"All right. You want to bet on you, Jamie. Let's bet on you."

"You really told Wes to fuck off?" Em's stacking pint glasses when I get to the bar.

I spin my key ring around my finger. "I told him I made my decision. And the answer's no."

She puts her fist out, and I bump it. "That's some boss behavior, Jameson."

"I am actually the boss."

She presses a hand to her heart and pretends to wipe a tear. "So. Next topic. Have you talked to Noel yet?"

I haven't. I'm ready now, though, and an idea came to me on my way here. Something Noel said before she left my apartment. Something I can't seem to get out of my head.

"Actually, I was hoping you would text her for me."

Em growls in frustration, chucking a bar rag at me. "Jesus, Jamie. You're really going to choose this part to punk out on?"

"Wait," I say. "I'm not punking out. I promise. I have an idea."

I explain my plan to Em, and this time I don't let myself consider any other fate besides this working.

Thirty-Six

Noel

MY MOTHER LEFT ON a bus early this morning. One night of Mom duty, and she was off on the next adventure. She said something about a friend she knew in Vermont and a longing for some mountains after all of that flat desert.

But it doesn't matter where or why she's going because she's going to be fine. I saw it in the way she was so unfazed by the breakdown that seemed so dangerous to me. I saw it in the way she referred to my deep-seated fear of love as me being "full of nerves." Maybe you can't truly have one without the other—true happiness without the risk of being gutted by it, and maybe what I've called recklessness all these years was her understanding that better than I did.

Either way, she's not my circus anymore. Maybe she was never even my monkey. She could have been a better mom. That's not negotiable. But we're both adults now, and it's time I start taking my responsibility for our dynamic. Taking back my space.

Last night when I finally fell into bed, exhausted and shocked that I'd just received some helpful advice from her of all people, I'd ached to call Jamie, hear his voice. Tell him all of the things I'd figured out about this magic.

But he was celebrating his launch event, an achievement that I'm not sure I have a right to be a part of until I fix this. Was I destined to screw it up and not be there with him or is this one of those opportunities I missed out on because I didn't take what was right in front of me? I don't think it matters. The result was the same. Me missing him.

The buzzing of my phone makes me jump and my pinky smudges the petals of the orchid I'm painting. I quickly dab it with a wet cloth, swiping open my screen with my free hand. I know I just promised to be the one to reach out and grab fate, but I can't help but hope it's Jamie doing it first.

It's not, and the last thing I expect to see on a Sunday afternoon is Em's name on my caller ID. I pick up the remote and silence the music I'd been using for company, half hoping it will stop ringing before I make a decision on whether or not to answer. I can't fathom why she would want to talk to me right now. Sure, we were friends for a little while, but I didn't expect to get to keep her if Jamie and I aren't right, and I'm still working out how to fix us.

"Hi, Em," I answer with my heart in my throat.

"Christmas," she says. It's cheery, if not a little strained by circumstance. "Are you free tonight? There's a band I want to see downtown and Cara's busy."

"Oh. You didn't want to ask Jamie?"

"One of us should be at Fortune," she says. This feels like a non-answer, but I suppose she doesn't owe me an explanation for where Jamie will be tonight.

There's a part of me that's hesitant to see Em before I see him, like I'm betraying him by spending time with his friends when I don't know if he'll accept my apology, but then I have to laugh at yet another opportunity landing in my lap. Almost like fate is looking at my little declaration and saying: *prove it.*

I want Em too. And Cara. And the house. I want this whole place and everything in it. Everything I thought was my destiny and I now know is my opportunity.

And this can be my practice yes before the big one.

"I want this," I say, and then I realize that we're talking about a few drinks and I'm being really weird about it. "I mean, I'm free. I'd love to."

Em chuckles. "Nice. Meet me at Asylum at eight."

"Okay. Hey, Em?"

"Yeah?"

"Thank you."

There's a beat of silence where neither of us know how to respond to what I've said. Finally, she says in a soft voice I haven't heard from her before, "Everything's gonna be okay, Christmas."

She hangs up, and in what seems to be my new default, I burst into tears.

I walk into Asylum a few minutes before eight. The space is dark as soon as you get past the front door, blue lights lining the walkway to the stage area where the band Em wanted to see is setting up. There are a lot of people here and I didn't make an exact plan about where to meet her, so I decide to hang at the bar in hopes she'll head here first.

"What can I get you?" a guy in a T-shirt and black velvet vest behind the bar asks me.

I see one of Jamie's beers on tap and a *whomp, whomp, whomp* noise sounds in my head. I'm such a sad sack.

"Fortune draft, please." I hand him my card, and he takes it with a nod. A minute later there's a pint glass perched on the edge in front of me. I take a deep pull of it to settle my nerves. I came here knowing I want this—to keep my friendship with Em—but I know it's contingent on making things right with Jamie. This is a visitor's pass. I'm definitely not a member here until I've earned it.

My eyes are on my phone when I feel the humidity build, a small crowd of people filling in the space to my left. I slide down to get out of the way and accidentally bump into a solid torso on the other side of me.

"Sorry," I say, tearing my eyes away from my texts. "I didn't— Jamie?" I blink up at him, and my heart launches into my throat. The light from the bar glows behind him like a halo, and I have the thought that maybe I manifested him by my constant looping Jamie Thoughts. Things like that don't sound so crazy anymore.

But then he smiles, and I know he's really standing here by the way his dimple strikes me square in the chest. "What're you—"

"Shh." He presses a finger to my lips, and I freeze. "Hi."

I swallow. "Hi."

He sticks his hand out and I stare at it, then him, then back to his hand.

He waits patiently until I reach out and shake it. *What is he doing?*

"I saw you from across the room and I think you have the prettiest eyes I've ever seen. I'm Jamie."

The band launches into a song and people swell around us, muscling for a better view. I blink at him, confused.

Jamie leans down, letting his lips brush my ear. I feel the

contact like a beam of sunshine after a storm. "What's your name?"

"Noel," I say shakily, suddenly remembering what I told him. *I wish we'd just met like normal people. Out at some bar somewhere...* My heart batters my chest.

He grins. "What do you do, Noel?"

Tears gather in the corner of my eyes when I think about how I answered this months ago. Now, I say, "I'm an artist. I have my own business."

"Me too. A brewery downtown." He steps closer. "Have you been here before?"

I shake my head, the back of my nose burning. When I can't make myself speak, he nods, giving me a shaky grin. "It's a cool place. You'll like it."

"Yeah... Jamie—"

"Tell me something else."

I tip my head, trying to make sense of this opportunity so I can grab onto it. I don't know what to say to fix all of the ways this went wrong. I'm terrified the chance will slip through my fingers while I'm stuttering. But when our eyes meet, I recognize the fear in his too. And the way he's doing it anyway, clinging to hope that I'm not going to break his heart. I know that look, and I know exactly what he needs to hear.

"I'm afraid a lot of the time," I say. "But I don't want to be anymore."

Emotion washes over his face but he keeps going with this game like he knows that me choosing him in this pretend do-over is as important to me as it is him. Jamie needs someone to bet on him; I need to place that bet. I've seen what the other option has to offer. Numbness and a life that looks good on paper, safe, but void of any joy—and I don't want it.

"Well," he says. "I know we don't know each other yet, Noel, but if you're scared to take a leap, I'll go first, and I'll catch you at the bottom, baby. Always." His voice wobbles. "I can be that for you."

"No." I shake my head. It's my turn. "I want to be that for *you.*"

He blinks at me, clearly caught off guard by the way I've taken the reins of this apology.

"When I came back here, I was terrified there was something inherently wrong with me because I couldn't feel anything. I wasn't happy when good things happened, I wasn't sad when bad things happened, I was just... numb, muted. And then you came along, and I was afraid because I felt too much. You're like a sponge that soaks up life, Jamie. You're fearless and a big dreamer, and you have *so* much to love. Being with you is like spinning in a Tilt-a-Whirl. I can turn the steering wheel or try to throw my weight into one side to slow the damn thing, but momentum always takes it. And for the first time in my life, I let it because I thought I saw the happy ending I was destined to get at the end.

"But the thing is, I was still just along for the ride. I think that's the point of all of this..." I wave my hand around my head. "...magic. Fate isn't going to hand me this life risk free, but the risk is worth it because the reward could be so good if I dare to choose it. Just like the vision didn't give you your career, Jamie. You still had to choose to put your heart on the line and go for it. And you can change your mind any time and give it away if that's what you want. And I can change *my* mind any time. I can choose to get off the ride because I'm scared, and if I do, this thing between us that brings me so much happiness will just not happen.

"And I think what Becca said freaked me out so much because I hadn't realized that yet, the part that we're both responsible for. You were right. I wouldn't have chosen you if I didn't have that vision."

His face falls, but I curl my fists in his shirt and tug him closer. "It's not because of who you are, Jamie. It was never because of that. If I'm being honest, I wanted you the minute I saw you. It's because of who I am. Or who I was. I was afraid to let my feet leave the ground, to get swept up by something and lose control. I didn't want to get hurt, so I surrounded myself with things that wouldn't leave a mark when they disappeared. I know now that I was numb because I wasn't choosing anything worth caring about, and I care about you so much. I love you so much."

"I love you too, Noe," he whispers. "So much."

"I wouldn't have chosen you without the vision, and it would have been the greatest mistake of my life."

He takes my cheeks in his hands and I realize with the swipe of his thumbs that I'm crying. His eyes shine under the bar light.

"I want you. I choose you. And I promise, the next time I'm scared, I'll run to you instead of away from you. I don't think I could love you more, Jamie. But I can love you braver if you'll let me."

I wasn't exaggerating when I said Jamie is like a sponge sucking up life, but when he squeezes his eyes shut and breathes through his nose, I think this is the moment where he overflows.

We're attracting attention from the rest of the people now, making a scene. I'm my mother's hot mess, and I don't care. I can't not touch him anymore. I launch myself into his chest and cry all over his shirt.

Jamie presses his mouth to the top of my head, breathing through my hair. "I want that too, Noel. All of it. And for what it's worth, you scare the hell out of me too."

Despite myself, I laugh.

"But I love you. We'll figure it out together, right?"

"Yes." I peel myself out from under his chin and push to my toes, kissing him with each, "Yes. Yes. Yes." I knew he would, but when he parts his lips and kisses me back, I finally go warm with relief. Jamie's hands go to my waist, lifting me for a better fit, and it's familiar and safe, and the nerves disappear. He's choosing me back and I already know I can trust him.

"I said no, by the way," he says against my mouth, and I pull away just enough to see him. "To NEBev. To Wes. I'm not selling Fortune."

My breath rushes out and I sink against him.

He laughs. "Relieved?"

I want to admit that I've been hoping and praying he would say this, but instead I play it cool. This has always been his decision even if he kept trying to give other people a say. Even me. Especially me. "Are *you* relieved?"

"Yeah. I am."

"Then I am too."

"Can I take you out on a date?" he asks, valiantly trying to keep up this game in between the kissing and touching. "I'm getting an award in a few days. There's a dinner."

I wipe my hand under my nose and sniff. "Sounds impressive."

"I'm kind of a big deal around here," he says. He gives me the Jamie Smile, complete with a wink. My legs turn to jelly. "Hope that doesn't scare you off."

I laugh, delighted. "I would love to go to dinner with you."

He rolls his hips against my stomach mischievously, but it's the look on his face that melts me—relief, love. "Fuck, I missed you, Noe."

"You just met me."

He laughs and squeezes me tighter. "I think I've been missing you my whole life."

Six Months Later

Noel

J AMIE SAID ONCE THAT opportunities get bigger the more of them you take, and it turns out so do the nerves. Big, dinosaur-sized butterflies nest in my stomach as I stare out the kitchen window. The peony stalks in Nana's—*my*—garden are six inches high, and a trio of chickadees hop around the grass in front of them searching for worms. It's spring, and today is the mural unveiling at Cara Bean. I have to present my first professional commission to the world, or at least the city, and there's been a slight tremble in my fingers since I woke up before the sun did.

I hear the bedroom door open, then the wood floors creak as Jamie steps into the kitchen behind me. He hasn't slept at his apartment since we crashed there after going out on New Year's Eve. He's becoming a little bit of a homebody, actually.

"You have to get ready soon," he says.

"I know."

His lips sweep my cheek on his way to the fridge for an

energy drink. He's still in pajama pants and bare feet, bed head raging. He's clearly in no hurry, but that's because I have to leave before he does.

I stretch my arms over my head and gaze at the new tattoo on his back. The iris I drew months ago centered between his shoulder blades. He had me recreate it on paper, and he got it permanently done a few weeks ago.

"What time will you be there?" I ask, chewing my lip. I've kept my promise to be braver over the past few months. I'm already contracted for another mural job. It's at the second Fortune location that Jamie and Wes are opening this fall in Kennebunkport, so I had a bit of a leg up in the process, but I've also been doing watercolor tutorials on my website, and I finally gave Vi an official three month notice so I could focus on my Etsy store.

Still, when the nerves do start in, it's him I seek out. Because he's always there. And he always makes it better.

Jamie likes to say our nervous systems are perfect partners. When mine is an anxious mess—like during that call to Vi or the day my mother texted to say she'd lost her passport while in the Philippines—he reaches into his devil-may-care heart and transfuses his calm into my veins.

And when his is fried and unfocused, I lend him my executive functions until he can resurface. Jamie's busier than ever, even though he's only behind the bar in the event of a staff shortage. Getting his second location up and running is *work*. But we have nights, and all winter we've had weekends until the festival season ramps up again. And we take care of each other instinctually, our jagged parts fitting into each other like puzzle pieces.

I've come to believe that is what a soulmate really is.

Now, he steps behind me, kissing my shoulder. "I'll be there before anyone else."

I nod and take a deep breath, transfusion complete. "Okay. I'd better get ready."

The ceremony goes off without a hitch. There's a mimosa bar and Cara made all of the pastries herself. When it's time to cut the oversized ribbon she ordered to wrap around all three buildings, Cara makes a speech. She says it's like I read her mind with my design. Like I saw inside her head and painted her thoughts. I don't actually know if Cara is aware of my brief psychic powers (it hasn't happened again) or if it was a wild coincidence that she chose to phrase it that way, but it felt like the past and the future tying together in a pretty bow.

When it's over, Jamie leads me by the hand to the parking lot. I'm giddy and light on my feet, and I can't stop smiling.

"There were so many people." I tip my head to look up at him, eyes wide, and he smiles back at me. When we get to his truck, he pushes me against the door and kisses me like he's been wanting to do it for hours.

"It's just the beginning, Noe. People are going to see your work all over this city."

I want that. I'm not afraid, I say in my head because my mouth is otherwise occupied.

We pull apart before I'm ready, but we have to be at a restaurant further in town. Jamie drives, and I'm still buzzing when we walk in.

Kate and Colin arrive moments later, Cara and Em a bit after that. Then Wes.

He was at the Cara Bean too, in the back, arms crossed looking entirely pissed off. But I know now that he wasn't. It's literally just his face. It took me a while to come around, but when I decided to look past our first few interactions, I saw Wes for what he *really* was. Shy in a way I could definitely commiserate with. A fellow wallflower who isn't quite sure which space belongs to him. And, more importantly, Jamie's brother who he's happy to have a better relationship with now that they're moving forward as independent business owners.

At the restaurant, we eat and drink, and when the waiter has cleared our plates and brought another round, Jamie's fork clinks against his water glass as he pushes to his feet.

"Let's have a toast." His hand cups my elbow, lifting me out of my seat before I can protest, and I bury my face in his shoulder and groan, hiding the red blooming across my cheeks.

Jamie clears his throat, and I hear Kate whoop before I look up at everyone.

"Well, shit. Now that I've pulled her up here, I'm afraid I'm going to fuck this up." There's a smattering of laughter, and he tugs at his collar before turning his eyes toward me. He's never been able to hide a thing on that beautiful, expressive face, but still, the emotion there tonight catches my breath and whisks it away.

"Noel, I didn't think there was anything in this world as beautiful as you until I saw you with a paintbrush. You're amazingly talented, but you're also patient, giving, and kind. The rest of the world is about to see your magic, but I promise I'll always be your biggest fan."

"I'm yours," I whisper, and he presses his forehead to mine.

We're staring into each other's eyes when Wes shouts, "You have to toast, Jameson."

"Oh. Right." Jamie raises his glass, his mouth popping open, then snapping shut. "To..."

He looks helplessly at Kate.

"To destiny!" she calls out, and glasses clink around us.

Jamie dips his head so his lips are at my ear, and touches his glass to mine. "To bravery, baby."

I forgo the sip of my wine and *cheers* instead with a kiss, tipping to my toes to press my smile to his. His lips part and his tongue slips over mine, deepening the kiss in a way that is entirely inappropriate for a crowd. I eat it up like candy. Let them see me want.

After dessert, people shrug on their coats and linger over goodbyes. The waiter brings back Jamie's credit card slip, and I slide it toward me, filling in the tip for him. He squeezes my thigh under the table in a private thanks, and we head out the door to the street, hand in hand.

"Can we make one more stop before we go home?" he asks.

There's a glint in his eye, and I match it with a raised brow. "Where?"

"You'll see."

The city lights are on, though the sun is still lingering low behind brick buildings and old glass. The cold of early spring sends a shiver through my entire body, and Jamie takes my hand in his, leading me uphill, away from the water. We take a left and walk two more blocks, then head up again, toward Congress St. We pass the museum, and the sidewalks turn from brick to cobblestones. Jamie shifts from holding my hand to holding my elbow so I can balance on them in my heels.

When we get to Monument Square, a light mist rises from the stones around us, making it all feel like a dream world. But it's definitely a real place because I've been here with Jamie once before... but higher.

"What are we—?"

"You'll see."

I look up at the brick buildings, side by side and lining the square. He leads me toward a door at the corner of the most familiar of the triplet buildings. We wait maybe four minutes in the cold before a group of college-age kids pushes out, slipping their coats on as they go. Jamie grabs the door and gives them a nod, as if he's been standing there waiting to greet them. As soon as they stumble off, he tips his head and I reluctantly follow him into the stairwell.

"*Jameson.*" I'm trying to go with it, follow his lead like I have been for months. But he also hasn't taken me on any trespassing adventures since the fire escape.

"Trust me, baby." He gives me the Jamie Smile, and I sigh.

When we reach the top landing, Jamie wraps his knuckles on the metal fire door, and it swings open. There's a kid, maybe nineteen, wearing a Bruins tee and a bored expression standing there. He exchanges a nod with Jamie and lets us pass, then disappears the way we came.

"What on earth..."

My eyes bounce from Jamie's mischief smile to the roof. It's exactly the same, mismatched potted plants, an indoor/outdoor rug, string lights, and when he slips his hand into mine, I feel whatever force was at play that night pulsing in our joined palms, flowing from me to him on a current.

My legs are wobbly as Jamie guides us toward the edge, to the wall where he was sitting that night when I first laid eyes on him, so beautiful and happy and wild. He steps behind me, and when I press my hands to the brick and lean forward, I gasp at the view. My prize for daring to come so close to the edge this time.

I can see the water from here, the glitter of the rising moon and a hundred lights on the glassy surface. The sound on the streets below us rises like steam, mixing through the air.

"Don't look so nervous," he says with his mouth at my neck, and I laugh because I'm sure I do, but it's not a bad nervousness. It's anticipation, excitement. It has nothing to do with a psychic connection or me and Jamie being destined for each other. I know him inside and out and I *know* it's a good thing, whatever we're here for. I know by the flash of his dimples like he can't contain them. The way he keeps only half of the air he needs in his lungs when he's gearing up to say something he's practiced. I'm vindicated in that intimate knowledge of Jamie Bishop when he says, "Let's get married."

Except I have to admit, I didn't know it would be that.

I turn over my shoulder, mouth hanging open, and he catches it with a kiss. When he pulls away, his smile rivals the view.

"I promise this isn't off the cuff. I've thought it through. And if you need time, we can have a long engagement. If you don't need time, we can do it this summer. I want all the things, Noel." He pauses for a thick swallow. "Am I freaking you out?"

"Amazingly, no."

His hand slides over my hip, pulling me flush against him. "Maybe you just knew it was coming. Somehow."

I laugh but the back of my nose burns with emotion. I haven't had a single vision since Jamie and I chose each other, but I didn't need one to know if he asked me this someday, I'd say yes. He made it clear from the beginning that he would jump for me. Jumping with him is a choice that I plan to keep making.

His hand trails up over my neck, sweeping my hair aside to make way for his lips. It's a long press that has my eyes slipping closed and my back arching, and then I feel him sink, his heat sliding down my body, leaving my upper half cold. When I open my eyes again and turn, he's there on one knee.

"Almost forgot this part," he says with a bashful smile and

color on his cheeks. He reaches into the pocket of his coat, and my hands cover my mouth. "I love you, Noe." He flicks the box open with his thumb to reveal a vintage looking diamond ring with filigree flowers on the band. "What do you say? Can we start our destiny now?"

"Yes." I laugh, that same girlish giggle he's gotten from me from the start. I bend and reach for his jacket, tugging until he's back on his feet and arms are around my waist and his lips are in my hair.

"Yeah? You're saying yes?"

"Be crazy together, right?"

"Forever."

Acknowledgements

Five years from my very first book release, and here I am again, trying to find the words for this section entitled Acknowledgements. This book was different for me. Not only because it's in present tense—steep learning curve—but because it was hard.

When I started this manuscript, I knew two things: my first three books were received better than my fourth, but my fourth was where I wanted to go as a writer. So what does one do with that data? Fawn for almost three years, debating whether I really know what I know about this craft and this business. If it's enough to love what you're doing. Write and delete, and write again. Flesh out B stories, then cull them. And generally destroy my own mental health until MY character arc as Romance Author in Crisis finally wrapped.

On draft 3,498 of this manuscript, my agent asked me what I *wanted* to write, and I said without thinking "I want to write about two people who are broken in exactly the right way to fit into each other." And I realized then that I was driving myself crazy over plot points and character wounds, beats and word count, but what this book in particular was about was the theme. And I knew this because I had changed the plot so many times, yet in every iteration, the theme remained. Which was eerily apropos for a book about how much impact our decisions have on our fate.

And so I also think it's apropos to do this acknowledgement section a bit different. Of course, thank you to my CPs and beta readers, friends who talked me down. My agent and editor who read a million drafts of this book. Sophia for her instas, Fiona and Rebecca for their life-giving Google Docs comments, Sarah Jane for my character art. The city of Portland for being an inspiration of its own.

But also to Liam, whose character I cut after being with me for two of these three years. To the real estate agent whose purpose was deleted somewhere in 2022. The snowy drive Jamie made to get to Noel, that no longer made sense but will forever remain headcanon. That original meet cute that I still think was funnier if not appropriate. Two seperate moments in Nana's kitchen that ended up in the "cuts" folder—one that involved a faucet and a nod to the local hardware store, and the other that got reworked in the name of pacing, and remains the only one I'm still not sure should have. To the arcade—I'm sorry there could only be one of those beats and I gave it to the fire escape. To the lightning storm that I've decided (because I am the master of this universe) happens somewhere postscript. And to Jamie and Noel, for all of the things you went through while I decided which way to bring you together. The theme says you lived each one of those alternate timelines, and in each one, you ended up happy. Because you were the two parts fate, and I finally figured it out.

Keep Reading for an excerpt of
Wish Lists & Road Trips
available now in e-book, print, and audio

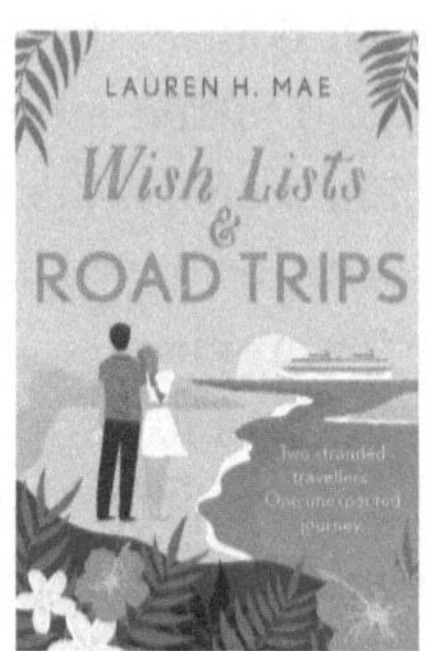

Chapter One
Pura Vida
Nick

"You're going to be late, señor."

My driver leaned against the hood of his cab, chewing casually on a toothpick as he shouted his warning.

I peered over the edge of the wooden zipline platform, surveying the jungle canopy while gripping my flimsy-looking harness. I wasn't nervous about the ride. My brother Alex had been making me do shit like this since we were kids—rickety roller coasters, jumping into the lake from an old, fraying rope swing he'd found at our uncle's camp, the race car driving lessons he'd bought me for my twenty-first birthday. I wasn't exactly fond of near-death experiences, but I was used to them.

What had my blood pumping in my ears and my neck slick with sweat was the fact that I only had one shot to check "zipline over the rainforest" off of Alex's list. I still didn't know how I was going to pull off the most important part.

I'd made it all the way to the top of this tree, though, and I'd paid this local cabbie a hundred U.S. dollars to get me here. I wasn't about to fail.

"I'm going," I hollered to Javier. "Just... give me a minute." I stuck my hand in the cargo pocket of my shorts, turning over the little green tin in my fingers. This marked number eight of ten on Alex's list. Almost done.

My attention bounced from Javier's impatient get the fuck on with it face—translated across dialects by his wide eyes and his watch held above his head—to the three-hundred-foot drop ahead of me. No kid's rides, the letter had said. If I had kids, I wouldn't let them anywhere near this thing.

"Keep it running," I yelled. Javier only scrunched his face

in reply. Our ability to converse was limited to snarky facial expressions.

Luckily, the guy who'd hooked me up to this thing translated my instruction. With an easy segue that my broken ninth-grade Spanish envied, the guide turned back to me and said in perfect English, "Now or never, dude."

Wasn't that the truth. This shit was a one-time deal. A promise—something I was going to complete, then consider myself un-indebted.

I checked the fit of my helmet one more time, then stepped to the ledge where the scent of permanently wet soil wafted around my face. Shit. Okay, maybe I was a little nervous. This wasn't a swing ride over the relatively shallow lake at my uncle's camp.

My stomach started to tighten. Maybe I can just do it from here.

No. I knew Alex. That was the easy way out. I unzipped my pocket and popped the top of the tin just enough so that I could tip it with one hand while hurdling over the treetops.

Now or never.

"Let's go." I nodded to the guide who motioned with his hand to another guy perched carelessly on a tree branch. Tree Guy took a casual glance down the line that didn't look to me to be all that thorough, then made a chopping motion.

The guide behind me slapped my shoulder. "Buena suerte, chico," he said. "Don't forget to get your picture code at the desk before you leave."

"Thanks." There's nothing like an upsell to make you feel a little less like an adventurer.

I ran my fingers through my sweaty, helmet-wrecked hair. I'd somehow managed to look like I was about to birth a toucan in the souvenir picture, so that was great. I clicked on the second digital file I'd received, but that one was just as bad. It really didn't matter what I looked like in the photographic evidence, but it annoyed me just the same.

I opened my texts, typing with one hand while Javier maneuvered the cab around a donkey pulling a cart full of bananas.

I finished number 8. It's getting harder.

I attached the picture and hit send.

Seventeen minutes passed before I got a response. Long enough for my mind to wander away from jungles and cabs that smelled vaguely like weed, and land in the world of job permits, unfinished budgets, winter build schedules... the way my dad had looked nervous and stressed when I told him I'd be away from the family business for two weeks to do this for Alex. My brain had been so far away from that zipline, that when the text had come in, I'd swiped it open carelessly, not even taking a breath to prepare myself.

Willow: It's getting harder for me too. You're amazing, Nick. I love you. XOXO.

The back of my throat tingled and I rubbed at my jaw, staring out the window at the thick green palms and vibrant red and yellow huts whizzing by. This place, Costa Rica, it was like a dream. I could hear Alex in my head, going on about the picturesque scenery, the rich culture. It made sense, him wanting to be here forever, but me, I needed to do this thing and get home.

I typed out a quick "love you too" to Willow and my gut squeezed like a fist, nagging at that little part of my brain that had been conditioned since childhood to think that any little twinge of pain was a death sentence. I could thank my mother for that.

Tossing my phone aside, I unzipped my pocket and pulled out the tin, carefully wrapping it in a bandana and securing it in my backpack between my *Spanish for Beginners* book and three extra pairs of boxers because it was hot as balls in this place.

I did it, I thought. I'd better not miss my boat, asshole. Satisfied, I zipped it up and settled the pack on my lap. Then Javier shouted something I couldn't understand and slammed on the brakes. My face bounced off of the seat in front of me and the cab banked to the right, the front tires landing in a ditch. "What the—?"

"Señor," Javier said. "You're going to be late."

Chapter Two
Watching the Ships That Go Sailing
Brit

Three-fifteen.

When I'd heard the reboarding time for today's port announced over the PA system in my cabin I'd thought: What an absolutely craptastic coincidence.

I dropped onto a wooden bench on the dock and fiddled with the new sleeve of colorful string bracelets wrapping my wrist while my mother aired an updated list of her grievances.

It had grown exponentially this week.

"This whole thing is a humiliating mess, Bridget." Her polished voice lilted through the phone. "It's the last time Cheryl Williams calls me in a favor with her personal florist, I'll tell you that much. My God, I'll have to find someone else for the Christmas party. And of course I ran into the owner of the Luxe. Did you know they couldn't fill the date? Imagine their embarrassment when people saw the ballroom empty on a Saturday night." She paused for a dramatic breath. "Bridget, are you listening?"

I muttered an obedient "of course" into the phone, but I was still stuck on this weird temporal event. Three-fifteen. Three-fifteen.

That number kept coming up over and over. The change from my ten-dollar bill when I'd bought a coffee and pastry at Penn Station before boarding the ship, the number on the cab I'd taken from my hotel. Oh! This was my favorite—the price of the colorful scarf tied in my ponytail. I'd just purchased it at a roadside shop and even with the exchange rate in Costa Rica, I couldn't escape it.

I knew it was a coincidence. A random fluke, or at the very worst, a mental manifestation of my guilt. There was only the slightest of chances that it was the result of a head game the universe was playing with me to remind me of the day I'd disappointed two hundred and fifty people in one fell swoop. A personal record, even for a professional disappointment like myself.

Three-fifteen. March fifteenth. Eight days ago. My wedding day.

At least it was supposed to be.

Just to avoid any bad luck, I'd decided I wasn't going any-where at three-fifteen. After spending the afternoon taking a van tour of the Costa Rican rainforest and shopping artisan tents in the local village, I came back to the dock early. I was entertaining myself by watching bright white fishing boats bob on the crystal-clear turquoise water while I took this call.

"The money we've lost on deposits isn't even the worst of it," my mother continued. "Your father is furious at the way you treated Sean. And his parents! How are we going to look them in the eye? We go to the same club!" Her voice was a familiar melody of faux concern and genuine exasperation. I hated this song.

"I can't help you out of this one, Bridget."

"I'm not asking you for help," I said. "And there's nothing I need to get out of." Because I wrenched myself free, thank you very much. "Sean and I are done. Daddy has to accept it."

"Yes, well that's not his strong suit. Though, leaving a mess certainly seems to be yours. You won't believe the trouble we've gone through to cancel this wedding."

"I'm sorry I caused you extra work." I wasn't. Neither of my parents had done any of that dirty work themselves. They had "people" for those things.

My mother let out a heavy sigh. "We forgave you when you squandered your education to start your silly makeup business, Bridget, but I really thought you'd started down a more responsible path being with Sean. I'm sorry but I can't support this. You're on your own."

She hung up and I nearly laughed even as my eyes stung with tears. When had I ever been anything but?

My 'silly makeup business' was a growing freelance gig and a beauty blog that got ten thousand hits last month. The money I made from paid partnerships helped put me through cosmetology school. Sure, I had to keep a part-time job for now, but I had big plans.

None of that mattered to my parents, though. To them, it would always be a hobby that wasted my potential. Potential for what, I'd never been clear on.

I wiggled the bare ring finger on my left hand. The decidedly un-bridal, pink manicure that I'd given myself for my Instagram series on cruise-ship inspired makeup palettes glinted in the sun. It felt lighter, my finger. Though it was probably in my head. How much could a ring really weigh? Not enough to say, oh, yeah, there's a difference there. It was a symbolic lightness. Free of Sean. Free of the version of me that I'd grown to hate. Free to be whoever I was supposed to become.

Free of a roof over my head.

I pushed that thought aside. It didn't matter that I was technically homeless until the check I was waiting on cleared. I'd been twenty-five for eleven weeks and counting, and after liquidating the last of the stocks and bonds where my grandfather had invested my trust, I was finally getting the first disbursement.

When I got home from this trip, I was going to use that money to buy myself a shelter from this storm. Working out of my car felt like amateur hour. I wanted square footage. I wanted salon chairs and styling cabinets. Mirrors and lighting. A sign on a post out front. Not to mention a place to live that wasn't my parents' house.

I had it all picked out, my new studio-slash-apartment. A place where I could build my own happy ending and set my dreams in motion. Dreams that were mine. Not my father's, not Sean's—mine.

I'd just closed my eyes to draw pictures of those dreams in my head when a guy in a black T-shirt plunked down his backpack, causing a flock of birds to screech and scatter and startle the bejesus out of me.

He dropped onto the bench across from me, pushing the brim of a well-worn baseball cap off his head, and buried his face in his palms. Before he hid it from me, I'd thought that his face looked vaguely familiar, like maybe I'd seen it in passing, but that was silly. I'd been on a boat for a week. Where would I have seen him?

It was a nice face, from what I could see: dark, vacation-style stubble and a strong, square forehead and prominent nose. His profile looked chipped out of the side of a mountain, but the headlong view of his face was softer. His cheeks were round and boyish. It was a surprising contrast.

He rubbed circles into his temples with his thumbs, stretching the sleeve of his T-shirt with each tiny flex of his biceps. I should definitely stop staring, but somehow I'd forgotten all about the gorgeous ocean view surrounding me, and decided there was nothing else worthy of my attention while I waited for this ship. Besides, he couldn't see me.

Until his head popped up like one of those Whack-a-Mole games, and he looked straight at me.

I froze, my mouth hanging open. It wasn't being caught that made my heart do a frog jump in my chest. It was the way his pastel-colored, sea-foam green eyes looked alien against his tan skin and almost black hair. How did he walk around with eyes like that? Buy coffee, ask for directions? Were people constantly awestruck?

For God's sake, Bridget. You were engaged less than a month ago.

But it couldn't hurt to look. Emotionally, Sean and I had been done for a long time. And our relationship certainly hadn't stopped him from looking. Or touching.

I fought off the familiar wave of humiliation and loneliness that came with Sean's memory and went back to stealing looks at Alien Eyes. It wasn't just this guy's face that had my interest piqued. He looked like he was going to be sick. Even from here, I could see he'd sweat through the back of his T-shirt.

I watched him unzip his backpack and dig around. He huffed a sigh and turned to me. "Do you have a pen?"

I blinked at him for an awkward number of seconds before answering. "Um... No. Sorry."

I was wearing a sleeveless white handkerchief dress and lace-up wedge espadrilles. I didn't even have a purse with me. Where would I hide a pen?

He nodded, his eyes shifting away. He seemed like he'd forgotten the pen dilemma altogether. Did he have sunstroke? Why was he acting so weird?

"I'm sure they have one at the ship agent's desk," I said, wanting to keep up the conversation for no other reason than I was half-infatuated with his face.

His shoulders slumped like the space between us and the desk could be measured in miles not feet. "Will you watch my backpack for a minute?"

My burgeoning crush wavered as a robotic-voiced warning from every airport and docking station that I'd been in on this trip played in my head: If someone asks you to hold a bag for them, don't do it. Report it immediately.

He was a little jumpy. His knee bounced furiously, and he was swallowing more than he should. Either he was going to be sick, or he had a couple of kilos of cocaine in that backpack.

I looked around the empty pier. Who was I supposed to report him to, though? The guys pulling in their fishing nets? It seemed dramatic.

His alien eyes took on a very human exhaustion while he waited for my answer.

"Of course," I said, feeling a little naive, not for the first time since I'd started this solo vacation.

He pulled his large frame up and walked stiffly to the desk like he might be in pain. I took note of his stuff, safely where he'd left it, then slipped my phone from my bra and sent my best friend Meri a picture of the ocean to keep from staring at his butt. He had a really nice butt. Like he must spend all of his free time doing squats nice. I blushed just looking at him.

Meri texted back. **Gorgeous. I hope you're enjoying every minute of your Sean-free vacation.**

Guilt kept a smile from blooming at her snarky response. I

couldn't seem to shake it, especially with all of this three-fif-teen nonsense.

Pen in hand, Alien Eyes dropped back into the seat and nodded his thanks. He picked up the clipboard he'd left on the bench and began scribbling. His hand was too big for the pen, I noticed, and he was a lefty. He probably had terrible handwriting.

"Are you filling out a job application?" I asked cheekily.

He raised an eyebrow and I gestured to the clipboard.

"Yeah," he said. "Ship captain."

I snorted a laugh, and he ran a hand over his chin, scratch-ing. "I missed my reboarding time," he said. "By an hour. Apparently, it's a paperwork nightmare."

"You were on a cruise? And they left you here?" My arm hair stood up, my mother's voice whispered in my ear: See, Bridget! Dangerous!

"Yup."

"They didn't wait? Or come looking?"

He huffed a laugh from his nose, his eyes on the clipboard. "It doesn't work like that."

"Wow. That sucks." I was suddenly ecstatic for that obnox-ious three-fifteen reboarding time. Turned out, I was being responsible by showing up this early, not ridiculous. I could admit being responsible hadn't been high on my priority list thus far. At least not as high as working on my tan and proving something to everyone who'd ever known me.

He picked his head up and peered at me, seafoam swirling. "What are you here for?"

"I'm on a cruise too. The ship is coming in an hour." I glanced at the phone I was still using to keep my hands oc-cupied. "Actually, forty-five minutes."

He straightened, turning over his shoulder, and looked out to the water, then back at me. "What do you mean it's coming?"

"Here." I waved a hand at the dock where I'd disembarked this morning for a day of exploring with just my phone, passport, and credit cards tucked in my bra.

He cocked his head, studying me like I was the one being weird. What's this guy's deal?

"It's a cruise ship?" he asked, even though I'd literally just said that it was.

"Uh, yeah."

His thick, black lashes blinked at me and he licked his lips. "They don't leave and come back," he said slowly. "It's a hundred-and fifty-thousand-ton ship, not an Uber."

Heat crept up my neck, but I wasn't sure if it was indignation at his tone or the understanding that was starting to stir in the back of my head. "Well, this one must have," I said with my practiced everything is fine voice. "Because this is where I left it, and where they said to be back."

"And are you the only one on this cruise?"

"No." I followed his eyes around the dock and my heart dropped like a hundred-and fifty-thousand-ton rock. Then my breath started to come out all wiggly and uneven. Oh God.

"Seems there would be more people here if it leaves in forty-five minutes."

Okay, he had a very valid point, but I'd heard them say three-fifteen. I'd had an entire crisis over it.

"What cruise line?" he asked when I'd gone mute.

Now my forehead was starting to sweat. I swallowed a lump. "Festiva."

He shook his head. "Oh, sweetheart."

"They said three-fifteen." My heart thudded against my chest, but my voice sounded oddly calm even to my own ear. Handle it, Bridget. Take a deep breath and handle it. Do not let everyone be right about this.

"They said three-fifteen New York time," he was saying. "That's one-fifteen Costa Rica time. They said that. They even said it in military time. They said it three different ways."

I met his eyes, cursing under my breath. I'd been so distracted by that number that I must have missed the finer details. Suddenly the sound of the ocean lapping the side of the empty pier was amplified, ringing in my ears, screaming: There's no ship here! Look at this big empty hole! Gone!

Shoot. This is sooo bad. As my mother had just reminded me, I had a reputation for making a mess of things and this was a really big one. Which was exactly what they expected when I told them I was taking my honeymoon cruise alone.

"You're just not made for it, Bridget," my father said. "You can't go galivanting around the world because you feel... stifled." He'd whispered that last part as if it was some shameful thing that would bring embarrassment upon our house if anyone had heard.

My bearer of bad news stared at me, obviously thinking the same. "Are you traveling alone?" he asked.

"Yes." Double shoot. Maybe I shouldn't have told him that. My eyes caught on his again. It was distracting, that color. I was trying to work this out and I kept seeing flashes of alien green out of the corner of my eye.

"How can you be traveling alone?"

I scrunched my nose. "You're traveling alone."

"Yeah, but I'm a guy."

"Oh, I see. I didn't realize your dick came with a compass."

He pinched the bridge of his nose the way my father did when the Red Sox were getting creamed. "You don't need a compass. You need a watch." He stood abruptly, yanking the hat he'd stuffed in his pocket and popping it onto his head. "Come with me."

I most certainly would not. "You missed the boat too," I said, crossing my arms over my chest. The gesture felt childish and I imagined my mother's rolling eyes. I dropped them back down to my sides. "Why would I go with you?"

He took a deep breath through his nose, his eyes slipping closed for two beats. When he opened them again, they'd softened. "I'm Nick," he said, holding out his hand.

I blinked at him. This guy was all over the place. He'd just looked like he was going to toss his lunch over the railing, and now he was apparently going to save my day. I didn't need a White Knight.

"Bridget," I said, reluctant even to share as much. I shook his hand, trying not to have a physical reaction to how big it was. "I'll just go talk to the ship agent. That's what you did, right? They helped you?"

"I'll go with you."

I narrowed my eyes, trying to look fierce and capable. "Why?"

"I'm old-fashioned like that." He smiled, full lips pulling back to reveal bright white teeth, like a perfect picket fence except for the left incisor which turned ever-so-slightly inward. I stared at it for a moment before nodding my acceptance. It was ridiculous, but something about that tooth said trustworthy. If they'd all been perfect, I would have marched away.

Get Wish Lists & Road Trips at all major retailers

Lauren H. Mae loves to write characters who fall in love the hard way. She lives in a house full of boys in beautiful Portland, Maine. When she's not writing, you can find her listening to the saddest Taylor Swift songs and letting the Red Sox break her heart.

Visit Lauren H. Mae online at:
www.laurenhmae.com
Instagram and Facebook: @laurenhmaeauthor

www.ingramcontent.com/pod-product-compliance
Lightning Source LLC
Chambersburg PA
CBHW030521190726
48283CB00006B/1718